All Our Shimmering Skies

Trent Dalton is a staff writer for *The Weekend Australian Magazine* and a former assistant editor of *The Courier-Mail*. He's a two-time winner of a Walkley Award for Excellence in Journalism, a three-time winner of a Kennedy Award for Excellence in NSW Journalism and a four-time winner of the national News Awards Feature Journalist of the Year. His first book, *Boy Swallows Universe*, was an international bestseller.

Praise for *All Our Shimmering Skies*

'A work of shimmering originality and energy, with extraordinary characters and a clever, thrilling plot ... unputdownable'
Sydney Morning Herald

'Even better than *Boy Swallows Universe* ... There's a whiff of southern gothic here, with Molly reminding me of Scout Finch from *To Kill A Mockingbird*' *The Australian*

'Tumultuous and ultimately beautiful ... poetic and full of grace'
Herald Sun

'The book is alight with joyous candour, extravagantly beautiful writing and a series of intriguing jungle-set pieces'
Adelaide Advertiser

'A magical realist epic grounded by a vividly evoked sense of place and a cheeky sense of humour' *West Australian*

Praise for *Boy Swallows Universe*

'One of the best Australian novels I've ever read . . . The characters are human and complex, the writing is fast-paced and heartfelt, and every sentence is surprising . . . This book will stay with me for a long time'   *Guardian*

'*Boy Swallows Universe* hypnotizes you with wonder, and then hammers you with heartbreak'   *Washington Post*

'A true Australian masterpiece'   *Marie Claire*

'The best Australian novel I have read in more than a decade . . . The last 100 pages of *Boy Swallows Universe* propel you like an express train to a conclusion that is profound and complex and unashamedly commercial . . . A rollicking ride, rich in philosophy, wit, truth and pathos'

Sydney Morning Herald

'A towering achievement. It is the *Cloudstreet* of the Australian suburban criminal underworld'   *Herald Sun*

'A story in thrall to the potential the world holds for lightness, laughter, beauty, forgiveness, redemption and love'

The Australian

'Filled with beautifully lyric prose . . . the characterization, too, is universally memorable, especially of Eli and August. At one point Eli wonders if he is good. The answer is "yes," every bit as good as this exceptional novel'   *Booklist* (USA)

'Funny, tender and raw . . . It is a remarkably compelling story, but what really makes *Boy Swallows Universe* shine is its use of language. Dalton has invented a kind of clipped, poetic vernacular that colours the entire book . . . there's something distinctly picturesque about Dalton's language that makes it inherently Australian . . . A wonderful, unexpectedly beautiful portrayal of boyhood and destiny'   *Better Reading*

'The book is plotted like a murder mystery, with the requisite twists and turns providing illuminating surprises right to the last page. Scenes are rendered in intimate detail, the characters are as real as your family and the writing is glorious'
Adelaide Advertiser

'Oh my God. Wow. It's just superb. I've always looked out for Trent's work because he has a magic about him: what he sees, how he explains things. He can describe a kitchen table in a way that makes you want to throw your arms around it. After reading *Boy Swallows Universe* I realise that his genius isn't really just about writing so much; it's about hope, and his instinctive and infectious "Yes" to one of the most plaguing questions of the human night: can tenderness survive brutality? This novel confirms Trent Dalton as a genuine treasure of Australian letters'
Annabel Crabb

'As a brilliant journalist, Trent Dalton has always intimately understood how fact is often stranger than fiction. Perhaps it took someone like him to produce a novel so humming with truth. Call it a hunch, but I think he might've just written an Australian classic'   Benjamin Law

'I've finally had a chance to immerse myself in this − a truly incredible book, one where I feel I will miss the characters as if they're real friends. What an achievement'   Leigh Sales

'Stunning. My favourite novel for decades. Left me devastated but looking to the heavens'   Tim Rogers

'An astonishing achievement. Dalton is a breath of fresh air – raw, honest, funny, moving. He has created a novel of the most surprising and addictive nature. Unputdownable'
David Wenham

'I couldn't stop reading from the moment I started, and I still can barely speak for the beauty of it. Trent Dalton has done something very special here, writing with grace, from his own broken heart'   Caroline Overington

'This novel is a raucous, moving, hilarious triumph – a major new voice on the Australian literary scene has arrived'
Nikki Gemmell

'A gothic humdinger, wrapped around a love story, wrapped around a riddle, wrapped around the universe: this is the book that has everything'   Richard Glover

'Enthralling – a moving account of sibling solidarity and the dogged pursuit of love'   Geoffrey Robertson QC

'It's fresh, original, it's dripping with promise. A voyage of wide-eyed wonder'   Radio New Zealand

'*Boy Swallows Universe* is a wonderful surprise: sharp as a drawer full of knives in terms of subject matter; unrepentantly joyous in its child's-eye view of the world; the best literary debut in a month of Sundays'   *The Australian*

ALSO BY TRENT DALTON

Boy Swallows Universe

All Our Shimmering Skies

TRENT DALTON

THE BOROUGH PRESS

The Borough Press
An imprint of HarperCollins*Publishers* Ltd
1 London Bridge Street
London SE1 9GF

www.harpercollins.co.uk

HarperCollins*Publishers*
1st Floor, Watermarque Building, Ringsend Road
Dublin 4, Ireland

First published in Great Britain by HarperCollins*Publishers* 2021
1

First published in Australia in 2020 by HarperCollins*Publishers* Australia Pty Limited

A catalogue record for this book is available from the British Library

HB ISBN: 978-0-00-843837-1
TPB ISBN: 978-0-00-843942-2

Typeset in Bembo Std by Palimpsest Book Production Ltd, Falkirk, Stirlingshire

Printed and bound in the UK by CPI Group (UK) Ltd, Croydon CR0 4YY

MIX
Paper from
responsible sources
FSC C007454
www.fsc.org

This book is produced from independently certified FSC™ paper
to ensure responsible forest management.

For more information visit: www.harpercollins.co.uk/green

For Fiona, Beth and Sylvie

THE FIRST
SKY GIFT

Molly and the Epitaph

A bull ant crawls across a curse. The bull ant's head is blood red and it stops and starts and stops and starts and moves on through a chiselled gravestone letter 'C' and Molly Hook, aged seven, wonders if the bull ant has ever been able to see the whole of the sky given all those magic gravity angles bull ants walk. And if it has no sky to see then she will make a sky for it. The bull ant follows the curved bottom of a 'U' and moves to an 'R' and winds through a twisting 'S' and exits through an 'E'.

Molly is the gravedigger girl. She's heard people in town call her that. Poor little gravedigger girl. Mad little gravedigger girl. She leans on her shovel. It has a wooden handle as long as she is tall, with a wide dirt-stained sheet-steel blade with teeth on its sides for root cutting. Molly has given the shovel a name because she cares for it. She calls the shovel Bert because those side teeth remind her of the decaying and icicle-shaped fangs of Bert Green who runs the Sugar Lane lolly shop on Shepherd Street. Bert the shovel has helped dig twenty-six graves for her so far this year, her first year digging graves with her mother and father and uncle. Bert has killed a black whipsnake for her.

Molly's mother, Violet, says Bert is Molly's second best friend. Molly's mother says her first best friend is the sky. Because the sky is every girl's best friend. There are things the sky will tell a girl about herself that a friend could never tell her. Molly's mother says the sky is watching over Molly for a reason. Every lesson she will ever need to learn about herself is waiting up there in that sky, and all she has to do is look up.

Molly's bare feet are dirt-stained like the shovel face and there are copper-coloured lines of cemetery clay where her elbows and knees bend. Molly, who is right to consider this rambling and rundown and near-dead cemetery her queendom, hops onto a slab of old black stone and kneels down to put a big blue eyeball up close to the crawling bull ant and she wonders if the ant can see the deep dark blues in her eyes and thinks that if the ant can see that kind of blue then maybe it will know what it feels like to see all of the vast blue sky over Darwin.

'Get off the grave, Molly.'

'Sorry, Mum.'

The sky is the colour of 1936 and the sky is the colour of October. Seen from the blue sky above and looking down and looking closer in and closer in, they are mother and daughter standing before a goldminer's grave in the furthermost plot in the furthermost corner from the gravel entrance to Hollow Wood Cemetery. They are older and younger versions of themselves. Molly Hook with curled brown hair, bony and careless. Violet Hook with curled brown hair, bony and troubled. She's holding something behind her back that her daughter is too busy, too Molly, to notice. Violet Hook, the gravedigger mum, always hiding something. Her shaking fingers, her thoughts. The gravedigger mum, burying dead bodies in the dirt and burying secrets alive inside herself. The gravedigger mum, walking upright but buried deep in thinking. She stands at the foot of the old limestone grave, grey stone weathered into black; porous and crumbling and ruined like the people who paid for the cheap graves in this cheap cemetery, and ruined like Aubrey Hook and his younger brother, Horace Hook – Molly's father, Violet's husband – the penniless drunkards who are tall and black-hatted and sweat-faced and rarely home. The black-eyed brothers who inherited this cemetery and who reluctantly keep its crooked and rusted gates open, overseeing cemetery business from the pubs and the gin bars in Darwin town and from a lamp-lit and worn red velvet lounge five miles away in the underground opium brothel beneath Eddie Loong's sprawling workshed on Gardens Road, where he dries and salts the Northern Territory mullet he ships to Hong Kong.

Molly plants her right hand on the grave slab and, because she wants to and because she can, she spins off the gravestone into a series of twirls executed so wildly and so freely that she's struck by a dizzy spell and has to turn her eyes to the sky to find her balance again. And she spots something up there.

'Dolphin swimming,' Molly says, as casually as she would note a mosquito on her elbow. Violet looks up to find Molly's dolphin, which is a cloud nudging up to a thicker cloud that Violet initially sees as an igloo before changing her mind. 'Big fat rat licking its backside,' she says.

Molly nods, howling with laughter.

Violet wears an old white linen dress and her pale skin is red from the Darwin sun, hot from the Darwin heat. She's still clutching something behind her back, hiding this thing from her daughter.

'Stand beside me, Molly,' Violet says.

Molly and Bert the shovel, stout and reliable, take their place beside Violet. Molly looks at the thing Violet seems struck by. A name on a headstone.

'Who was Tom Berry?' Molly asks.

'Tom Berry was a treasure hunter,' Violet says.

'A treasure hunter?' Molly gasps.

'Tom Berry searched every corner of this land for gold,' Violet says.

Molly finds numbers beneath the name on the headstone: 1868–1929.

'Tom Berry was your grandfather, Molly.'

There are so many words beneath those numbers: cramped and busy and too small, filling every available space on the headstone. It's less an epitaph than a warning, or a public service message for the people of Darwin, and Molly struggles to fathom its meaning.

LET IT BE KNOWN I DIED ACCURSED BY A SORCERER. I TOOK RAW GOLD FROM LAND BELONGING TO THE BLACK NAMED LONGCOAT BOB AND I SWEAR, UNDER GOD, HE PUT A CURSE ON ME AND MY KIN FOR THE SIN OF MY GREED. LONGCOAT BOB TURNED OUR TRUE HEARTS TO STONE. I PUT THAT GOLD BACK BUT LONGCOAT BOB DID NOT LIFT HIS CURSE AND I REST HERE DEAD WITH ONE REGRET: THAT I DID NOT KILL LONGCOAT BOB WHEN I HAD THE CHANCE. ALAS, I WILL TAKE MY CHANCE IN HELL.

'What's all the words for, Mum?'

'It's called an epitaph, Molly.'

'What's an epitaph, Mum?'

'It's the story of a life.'

Molly studies the words. She points her finger at a word in the second line.

'A maker of magic,' Violet says.

Molly points at another word.

'Bad magic for someone who might deserve it,' Violet says.

The child's finger on another word.

'Kin,' Violet says. 'It means family, Molly.'

'Fathers?'

'Yes, Molly.'

'Mothers?'

'Yes, Molly.'

'Daughters?'

'Yes, Molly.'

Molly's right forefinger nail scratches at Bert's handle.

'Did Longcoat Bob turn your heart to stone, Mum?'

A long silence. Violet Hook and her shaking hands. A long lock of curled brown hair blowing across her eyes.

'This epitaph is ugly, Molly,' Violet says. 'Your grandfather has tarnished his life story with bluster and vengeful thoughts. An epitaph should be graceful and it should be true. This epitaph is only one of those things. An epitaph should be poetic, Molly.'

Molly turns to her mother. 'Like the writing on Mrs Salmon's grave, Mum?'

HERE LIES PEGGY SALMON
WHO FISHED FOR LOVE AND WINE
THOUGH IT WAS NO FEAST NOR FAMINE
SHE ALWAYS DROPPED A LINE

'Will you promise me something, Molly?'

'Yes.'

'Promise me you will read all of the poetry books on the shelf by the front door.'

'I promise, Mum.'

'Will you promise me something else, Molly?'

'Yes, Mum.'

'Promise me you will make your life graceful, Molly. Promise me you'll make your life grand and beautiful and poetic, and even if it's not poetic you'll write it so it is. You write it, Molly, you understand? Promise me your epitaph won't be ugly like this. And if someone else writes your epitaph, don't make them struggle to write your epitaph. You must live a life so full that your epitaph will write itself, you understand? Will you promise me that, Molly?'

'I promise, Mum.'

Molly wobbles her knees. Molly is restless. Because she wants to and because she can, Molly drops Bert on the dirt and executes a cartwheel beside her grandfather's grave and her yard dress falls down over her face and she's blinded and she can't nail the cartwheel's landing and stumbles and falls into the dirt in a mess of legs and arms.

'Not very graceful, Molly,' Violet says. 'Those poetry books will teach you how to be graceful.'

Molly brushes her floppy hair from her eyes and smiles. Violet directs the gravedigger girl back to her side with a sharply pointed forefinger. Molly picks up Bert the shovel and resumes her place close to her mother's hip.

'Be quiet now,' Violet says.

The stillness of this cemetery, this sun-baked dead collective. Dry season Darwin and every tree in the cemetery wants to burn. Darwin stringybark eucalyptus trees leaning over graves so old their owners can't be identified. Woollybutt trees and their fallen and dead orange-red flowers surrounding each trunk like fire circles, growing in gravelly soil for fifty years and climbing as high as the shops on the Darwin Esplanade. Wild weeds and grasses creeping over memorials to carpenters, farmers, criminals, soldiers and mothers and fathers and brothers and sisters. Kin.

The earth is swallowing up Hollow Wood Cemetery. The dirt below it has eaten the dead and now it chews on the evidence of their living.

Molly breaks the silence. Molly always breaks the silence.

'Is my grandfather down there?' Molly asks.

Violet takes a moment to answer.

'Some of him is down there,' Violet says.

'Where's the rest of him?'

Violet looks up at that blue sky the bull ant hasn't noticed yet.

'Up there.'

Molly flips her head back and takes in the sky, her eyes squinting in the Darwin sun at full height.

'The best of him is up there,' Violet says.

Molly readjusts her footing, shifts her right foot back, never turns away from the sky. There's a single dry season cumulus cloud on the left side of Molly's sky, a fluffy and heaped floating metropolis of warm rising air that looks to Molly like the foam that forms when Bert Green drops a scoop of ice cream into a tall glass of sarsaparilla. Everything to the right of that cloud is blue. Violet Hook follows her daughter's gaze to the sky and she stares up there for almost half a minute, then she turns back to stare at something equally expansive: her daughter's face. Dirt across her left cheek. A blotch of breakfast egg yolk hardened at the left corner of her lips. Molly's eyes always on the sky.

'What is this place, Molly?'

Molly knows the question and she knows the answer. 'This place is hard, Mum.'

'What is rock, Molly?'

Molly knows the question and she knows the answer. 'Rock is hard, Mum.'

'What is your heart, Molly?'

'My heart is hard, Mum.'

'How hard is it?'

'Hard as rock,' Molly says, eyes still on the sky. 'So hard it can't be broken.'

Violet nods, breathes deep. A long silence now. Then four simple words. 'I'm going away, Molly.'

Molly shifts her bare left foot and turns her head to her mother. 'Where ya goin', Mum?' she asks, her right hand driving Bert's blade haphazardly into the dirt. 'You goin' to Katherine again, Mum?'

Violet says nothing.

'You goin' to Timber Creek again, Mum? Can I come, too?'

Violet's eyes turning up to the sky now. Another long silence.

Molly banging her right heel into the dirt, waiting for her Mum to respond.

And Violet seems lost in that sky. Then she closes her eyes and reaches her right arm out to her daughter and Molly watches that hand come all the way across to rest upon her left shoulder. Her mother's fingers are shaking. And Molly can see now that her mother's arms are thinner than she's ever seen them. Her skin, paler.

'Why are your fingers doing that, Mum?'

And Violet opens her eyes and studies her shaking right hand, close up, then hides it once more behind her back. She turns her eyes again to the sky. 'I'm going up there,

Molly,' Violet says. 'I'm going up there to be with your grandfather.'

Molly smiles. Turns her head back to the sky. Eyes alight. 'Can I come, too?'

'No, Molly, you can't come, too.'

And Molly feels thirsty now and her belly turns inside her and the toes of her right foot dig into the red earth beneath her and she makes nervous fists with her hands and the longest nails on her fingers dig so deep into her palms that they dig through the skin. Turn again to the sky. Turn again to Mum.

'I'm not coming back down again, Molly.'

Molly shakes her head. 'Why not?'

'Because I can't stay down here anymore.'

Molly raises her eyes to the sky again. She searches for a town up there. She searches for the house her mum will stay in up there. She searches for streets in the sky and lolly shops and liquor stores. The town beyond the clouds. The town beyond the sky.

'This is the last time you will see me, Molly.'

'Why?'

'Because I'm going away.'

Molly drops her head. Toes digging deeper in the dirt. And she wants to know how her mother pulls this magic trick, how she turns so quickly from the light and into the dark. She's daylight switching straight into night-time, Molly tells herself. Day sky to night sky, with no living done in between. No time in between. No chores. No afternoon tea. Day sky blue with dolphin clouds to a night sky only black.

'What are you feeling inside, Molly?' Violet asks.

'I feel like I want to cry.'

Violet nods her head.

'Then cry, Molly,' Violet says. 'Cry.'

And the gravedigger girl's eyes squint and her body shudders like it wants to vomit and her neck jolts forward and she sobs. Two brief sobs and her eyes have to open wide for a river of tears that turn to tributaries that split through the dry dirt and dust on the girl's face, and these new water lines on Molly's cheeks look to Violet like the creek systems she would see on her father's gold fossicking maps as a girl.

'Keep going,' Violet says. And the girl cries harder and she puts her hands to her face and fluid runs from her nose and saliva drips from her lips and her mother does not touch her. Does not hold her. Does not reach for her.

'Cry, Molly, cry,' Violet says, softly.

The gravedigger girl howls so loud that Violet turns her head, instinctively, towards the cemetery house beyond a cluster of trees, just in case that sound is loud enough to wake her husband from a long daylight liquor sleep.

'Good,' Violet says. 'Good, Molly.'

And Molly cries for a full minute more and then she swallows hard and wipes her eyes with the back of her hand. She grips a fistful of her dress and lowers her face to wipe it clean.

Violet stands in front of her child now, hands still behind her back.

'Are you finished?'

Molly nods, snorting fluid back up through her nose.

'Did you get it all out?'

Molly nods.

'Now look at me, Molly,' Violet says.

Molly looks up at her mother.

'You will never weep for me again,' she says. 'Not a single tear will you shed for me from this moment on. You will never feel sorrow. You will never be afraid. You will feel no pain.

For you are blessed, Molly Hook. Never let a single person tell you any different.'

Molly nods.

'What is this place?'

'It's hard, Mum.'

'What is rock?'

'It's hard, Mum.'

'What is your heart?'

'My heart is hard, Mum.'

'How hard is it?'

'Hard as rock. So hard it can't be broken.'

Violet nods.

'No one can ever break it, Molly,' Violet says. 'Not your father. Not your uncle. Not me.'

Molly nods. She watches her mother look back to the cemetery house. There is fear on her face. There is worry.

Violet turns back to her daughter. 'Now is there anything you want to ask me before I go?'

Molly's head down, staring at the dirt. Staring at a platoon of ants marching towards her grandfather's grave.

'Will I still be able to talk to you?'

'We can talk any time you want to talk,' Violet says. 'All you have to do is look up.'

'But how will I hear you?' the girl asks.

'All you have to do is listen.'

Molly's head stays down.

'No, you can't be doing that,' Violet says. 'You can't be keeping your head down like that, Molly. You must look up. You must always look up.'

Molly looks up. Violet nods, half-smiles.

'Is there anything else you want to ask me?'

Molly scratches her face, twists her left foot in the dirt, something on her mind.

'What is it, Molly?'

Molly's screwed-up face.

'You're gonna miss my birthday,' Molly says.

'I'm gonna miss all of your birthdays, Molly.'

Molly drops her head.

'I won't get any more gifts from anyone,' Molly says.

'You'll still get gifts from me.'

'I will?'

'Of course you will.'

Molly points to the sky.

'But you'll be up there.'

Violet smiles.

'That's where the best gifts come from.'

Violet looks at the sky again.

'The rain, Molly,' Violet says. 'The rainbows. The dolphin clouds. Elephant clouds. Unicorn clouds. The great big bolts of lightning. The sky gifts, Molly. I'll send them all down for you.'

'The sky gifts,' Molly says. She likes those words. 'Just for me?'

'Just for you, Molly. But you have to keep your eyes on the sky. You have to keep looking up.' Violet points at the sky. 'There's one falling now.'

'Where?' Molly gasps, scanning the blue sky.

Violet points to the sky again.

'There,' she says. And Molly squints her eyes and shades her face with her hands to block the glare.

'It's a gift from your grandfather, Molly. It's something he wants you to have.'

Molly bouncing on the spot now. 'What is it? What is it?'

'It's how your grandfather found his treasure,' Violet says, staring at the sky.

'Treasure!' Molly says.

'We all have our own treasure to find, Molly. He wants you to find yours.'

Molly stares harder into the sky, but she can't see the falling sky gift.

'Keep looking up, Molly,' Violet says. 'Just keep your eyes on the sky, Molly. Don't look away or you'll miss it falling.'

Molly stares harder into the sky but she can't see the falling sky gift.

'Keep looking up, Molly,' Violet says. 'Just keep your eyes on the sky, Molly. Don't look away or you'll miss it falling.'

Molly feels her mother move closer to her. Molly feels her mother's arms wrap around her shoulders. She feels her mother's lips against her temple.

'I'm going now, Molly,' Violet says. 'But you must not watch me go. You must keep looking up. You must keep your eyes on the sky.'

And Molly looks at the sky and looks and looks and she wants to turn her eyes away but she listens to her mum, she believes in her mum, she believes her, and she never takes her eyes off that high blue roof and she feels her mum move away from her, hears her mum's sandals crushing leaves and grass shoots behind her, and she wants to look away from the sky and turn her eyes towards those sounds but she listens to her mum because her mum is always right, always true, always graceful.

'You can write your own epitaph now, Molly.' Further away.

'It won't be written for you. You can write it yourself. Just keep your eyes on the sky, Molly.' Further away.

'Keep your eyes on the sky, Molly.' Further away.

'Keep your eyes on the sky, Molly.' Too far away.

Molly keeps her eyes on the sky and she stares up at that sky for so long she tells herself she will only stare at that sky for sixty more seconds and she counts sixty seconds in her head and when she has only five more seconds to count she vows to count another sixty seconds and she does. Ten, nine, eight, seven, six, five, four, three, two, one.

She still can't see the sky gift, so she turns her eyes away from the blue and she sighs, her belly still turning inside, and she whips her head round to where the last sounds of footsteps came from. She looks for her mother. But there are only trees and graves and weeds and mounds of pebbled clay covering the dead, nothing else. And she stares into that still cemetery space waiting for her mother to walk back into it. But she does not.

An image enters the gravedigger girl's mind. A bull ant crawling across a curse. A single word carved in stone. Bad magic for someone who might deserve it. She turns to read her grandfather's epitaph and resting upon the slab of stone by her twig-thin shinbones is a flat, square cardboard gift box. It's wrapped in a ribbon tied in a bow. The colour of the ribbon is the colour of the sky.

Molly leaps on the sky gift and shakes it in her hands. She rips at the ribbon and her belly isn't turning anymore. Her dirt and sweat fingers claw at the sides of the box. At last, an opening, and her fingers rip the thin, cheap cardboard roughly across the bottom edge and something metal – something hard – slides out of the box and into her hands.

She holds it up to the sky. A round metal dish. Solid copper. Old and caked in dirt. She thinks it's a dinner plate at first. Maybe a serving dish for sandwiches. But the dish has raised, sloping sides and a flat base, and it's not much smaller than a car's steering wheel. And Molly's seen one of these before. In the back tray of her Uncle Aubrey's red utility truck, in the old metal box where he keeps his fossicking tools. It's not a plate, she tells herself. It's a pan. A pan for finding gold. A pan for finding treasure. And Molly Hook, aged seven, knows not what to say back to the sky for such generosity, so she looks up to it and says what she can only hope is graceful. 'Thank you.' And in the silence of the cemetery the gravedigger girl waits patiently for the sky to say something back.

Black Rock Frog Rock

The gravedigger girl by the water, four days later. Molly Hook kneeling on the muddy bank of Blackbird Creek, which runs along the eastern edge of Hollow Wood Cemetery. She holds the sky gift. Earth, dirt and silt have turned the copper pan to a dark mud-brown colour. She fills the pan with dry creekbed gravel and duck-waddles without standing into the shallow creek water. With two steady hands, she submerges the pan and the cleaner parts of its edge bounce sunlight off copper and Molly mistakes these magic tricks of the light for early and miraculous strikes of gold.

Gold, Mum, gold. And she turns her head to the sky. Is this you, Mum? Are you doing this? Can you hear me, Mum?

And it makes sense to Molly in this moment when she is so close to her eighth birthday that the god of minerals, that miserable and selfish spirit god of gold, that son of Zeus, Khrysos — whose grave her father and her uncle say they're always pissing on when they're liquored — would grant her a gold strike on this day. This strange day of all strange days, this dark mood of a day when her father, Horace, and her uncle, Aubrey, are over there by the black rock frog rock beneath the sprawling milkwood tree digging a deep dirt hole to rest another human body in for eternity.

She watches them digging. Aubrey Hook is two years older than Horace Hook and half a foot taller. The brothers are aged in their mid-thirties but too much toil and too much Darwin sun have dragged them prematurely into their forties. Both brothers wear wide-brimmed black hats that shadow their hands as they break to open their rectangular and rusting Havelock tobacco tins and roll their smokes, silent as always. The men wear white cotton shirts and black trousers and black work boots covered in dirt. Their spines bend sharply at the top, as if their shoulder blades are pushing their heads over, like they were born disfigured, but it's all because of the shovel work. Digging graves for the dead and all those years they spent digging eventual graves for themselves in the sorry rear end of the Northern Territory gold rush. It takes decades for a spine to assume the dig position, but it catches on eventually, starts curling into a comfortable place, the way Horace and Aubrey will one day curl gratefully into a mud-cake brown-dirt hole just like the one they're digging beside the black rock frog rock.

Aubrey has a moustache but Horace does not. Red kerchiefs round their necks for sweat, white handkerchiefs in their trouser pockets to wipe dirt off their foreheads. Men of bone and skin and work and broken sleep and worry. Men who Molly believes might have been born in dirt. Men who did not come from the place she came from. Men who emerged from the earth they're always digging up. The girl knows if she drove Bert into her father's belly and stomped on the blade shaft with her right boot, she'd find the same red, yellow and brown earths she keeps finding beneath all these old black cemetery gravestones lining Blackbird Creek. She'd find the Darwin kandosols her dad has told her about, those hard Top End soils that hold little water, the sandy and loamy surface soils, inside her own father. Then she'd dig deeper and she'd find no innards in the man, no gut tubes, no organs, no heart, just the verto-sols, the same cracking clays and black soils found beneath the Top End's vast floodplains. She can't picture Uncle Aubrey's insides, thinks he's hollow like the dead, termite-ravaged trees that gave this cemetery its name. All he has inside is shadow.

'Black rock frog rock,' Molly mumbles to herself as she pans.

The black rock frog rock beneath the milkwood tree looks to Molly like the black rock frogs she always sees hopping through Hollow Wood. The frogs remind her of burnt damper. Hopping lumps of burnt bread.

She likes those words. 'Black rock frog rock.' She sounds like a croaking creek frog when she says those words fast. 'Black rock frog rock. Black rock frog rock.' And she laughs.

Molly shakes the pan from side to side, vigorously enough to turn the gravel, gently enough to keep the gravel in the pan. She takes the larger gravel rocks from the pan, washes them clean in the water, discards them. Circular pan movements now, revolutions of gravel and water as dirt and clay dissolve. The gravedigger girl's fingers working lumps of dirt and clay, working smaller rocks to the surface, letting the heavier minerals – the gold, Mum, the gold – settle at the bottom of the pan. The pan goes up and the pan goes down and the dirt spins like the earth spins beneath Molly Hook's dirt-brown bare feet. And she searches for those flashes of gold for forty-five minutes and she never finds them.

But after all the searching, all the sifting, she finds that the sky-gifted pan has been washed clean on both sides. The wet copper shimmers in the Darwin sun and she turns the pan in her hands and she guides a reflecting beam of the sun onto her left palm and she wonders if the beauty of that light on her skin is prettier than any large nugget of gold she could ever find, anyway. Maybe this was the kind of treasure her grandfather hunted across every corner of this land. The treasure of pure golden light.

She's tired now and she lies back on the dry creek bed to rest and she looks up to the wide blue sky and she talks to it. She asks a question of it: 'Why did you give me this?' And the sun blasts whiteness in her eyes and she shields the sun with the perfect circle of the copper pan and she wonders if that's why she received this gift, so she could look up and see only sky. But what she sees when she looks up is cursive. Words. A series of sentences roughly engraved on the underside of the prospector's pan. She reads the words with the same interest with which she reads the epitaphs on the crumbling gravestones of Hollow Wood Cemetery, all those final deep-grief stories yielding clues to the lives of the departed souls, while the mud beneath her right forefinger nail underlines each strange word.

The longer I stand, the shorter I grow,

And the water runs to the silver road

She repeats those words to herself. Repeats them over and over. '"The longer I stand, the shorter I grow, and the water runs to the silver road" . . . "The longer I stand, the shorter I grow, and the water runs to the silver road."'

From the words runs the etched line of what could only be called a map, but it's like no map that Molly Hook has ever seen. She has seen maps of her country. She has seen the dot of Darwin resting like a jewel in a princess's tiara on the left-hand corner of the top of Australia. She has seen the rectangle of the Northern Territory wedged in straight lines between a mapped out and vast Western Australia to its left and the eastern bulge of Queensland to its right. She has stared at all the wondrous names of places she hopes to visit across her Northern Territory when she's done with digging holes for the dead and for her dad. Auld's Ponds. Teatree Well. Eva Downs Station. Waterloo Wells. Each place conjures a vision in her head. Blue ponds where long-legged white storks stand on lily pads the size of Roman shields that float across the noses of sleeping crocodiles. A deep well full of English tea, where fancy men and fancy women in fancy hats fill bone-china cups as they watch lawn games unfold to the sounds of dappled-sunshine violin players. A woman named Eva Downs who looks like that actress Katharine Hepburn and who runs a thriving cattle property with a shotgun in one hand and a martini in the other. That place in the central Australian desert where Napoleon fell back down to earth.

Her father has a prospector's map of Australia from 1914. He keeps it in his work room off the main bedroom that Molly's never supposed to enter. The prospector's map doesn't even have Darwin marked on it. It doesn't even show the whole of the Northern Territory. That map is pink and everywhere outside of what is mapped out as the states of Western Australia, South Australia, Queensland, New South Wales and Victoria is marked simply with the word 'Aborigines'. Depending on the wilting spirit or rabid desperation of the goldminer, these areas marked 'Aborigines' were seen by Horace and Aubrey and their old goldminer friends as either dangerous no-man's-lands or untouched gold-rich money fields ripe for a sharpened pickaxe. But this etched map in her hands is like no map Molly has seen. This is a map from a storybook. This is a map not of towns and cities, rivers and roads. This is a map of wonder and mystery, fortune and glory. And treasure. She remembers what her mother said: 'We all have our own treasure to find.'

A treasure map, Molly tells herself, as her fingernail traces the single etched map line down to a second set of words.

West where the yellow fork man leads

East in the dark when the wood bleeds

She doesn't repeat these words because she can see more words below them and she's too desperate to follow the etched line that travels from north-west to south-east now down the back of the copper pan in a shaky course to another set of words, and a thousand blue butterflies are set free inside her stomach as she runs her short forefinger beneath them.

City of stone 'tween heaven and earth

The place beyond your place of birth

The map line runs on and there are more words to be read on the pan but they are covered in silt. She rushes into the creek water once more and uses her yard dress to wipe the back of the pan completely clean, and she must remember to breathe when she raises her grandfather's sky-gifted treasure map to the blue sky and reads the last collection of words etched into the pan.

Own all you carry, carry all you own

Step inside your—

'Moll yyyyyy!'

Uncle Aubrey is shouting at her from beneath the milkwood tree.

'Get outta that feckin' creek, child!'

The gravedigger girl rushes and splashes out of the water and crawls up the creek edge, grasping at clumps of tall grass to haul herself up and onto the cemetery grounds. Molly can see her uncle standing over the grave he's just dug, leaning on the long shovel he used to dig it. Her father stands next to him, his head down and his black hat in his hands.

'Get over here, child,' Aubrey commands. His long thin arms

and his long thin finger bones are waving her towards him, but she doesn't want to go there.

'May I please stay here, Uncle Aubrey?' Molly calls.

'No,' her uncle says. 'Come here now.'

'I don't want to go over there,' she says.

'Get over here now, child,' Aubrey Hook barks. He's so tall and thin, and his wide-brimmed work hat is black like his eyes and his eyebrows and his gaze. And Molly wants to cry now to show her uncle that she's frightened. Cry, she tells herself. Cry, Molly, cry. Cry and he will understand you. Cry and he will care for you. But she cannot cry in this moment, no matter how hard she forces herself to.

'Dad,' Molly calls.

But her father says nothing. And she knows her father is weaker than her uncle.

'Dad!' Molly calls again.

But her father has gone away in his mind. Gone away, she tells herself, gone away like Horace and Aubrey said her mum had gone away. They said she wandered off into the bush. They said she was lost in the wild and deep country and she couldn't find her way back again. Back to Hollow Wood. Back to Molly.

Horace is frozen in this moment, head down, his hat in his hands.

'You will come here now, child, and you will say goodbye to your mother,' Aubrey demands from the edge of the grave.

Molly grips the sky gift copper pan and hugs it to her chest. I will never be afraid, she tells herself. I will feel no pain. Rock is hard. Can't be broken. She shakes her head. No. 'She's not in there,' Molly calls.

'I beg your pardon?'

'She's not in that hole,' Molly says. She points to the sky. 'She's up there.'

Aubrey is momentarily stunned by his niece's words. He looks at her closely to see where they might have come from, which part of the girl's bent mind. He tilts his head and squints his eyes. Poor little gravedigger girl, he tells himself. Mad little gravedigger girl, he tells himself. Mad like her grandfather, mad like her mother.

'What is that you're holding?' Aubrey barks.

Molly is silent. He takes a few steps closer.

'What is that you're holding, child?'

Three more steps closer and then he stops.

'It's a sky gift,' Molly says, nervously. 'It's my grandfather's pan. He wanted me to have it, so he dropped it from the sky.'

Aubrey studies his niece again and then he removes his black hat and wipes the sweat from his forehead. He breathes and sighs loudly, pulls a hip flask from his pocket, unscrews the cap and takes a long, hard swig. He pockets the flask and runs his dirty right hand across the stubble of his cheeks. And then he marches quickly to his niece, gritting his white wolf teeth, and he digs his wolf claws hard into Molly's right shoulder and pulls her towards the milkwood tree. As he drags her across the cemetery ground, he reaches for the pan in her hands, pulls hard at it.

'Gimme that feckin' pan!' he spits.

'No,' Molly screams. 'No, Uncle Aubrey! It's mine. It was given to me.'

The tall black shadow uncle's hairy black wolf arm wrenches the pan violently from his niece's hands and he tugs Molly Hook towards the milkwood tree and the black rock frog rock, and she digs her feet hard into the dirt to slow their movement but the tall black shadow uncle is too strong. He grips her body like he grips a shovel. Closer and closer to the milkwood tree he hauls her, until she can see the hole in the ground.

'No!' Molly screams. 'Please, Uncle Aubrey. Nooooo.'

A rectangular grave with no headstone. A rectangular dirt prism of air sunk into the earth, with no name and no epitaph. No story of a life. No existence. No goodbye. No luck.

Her father stands at the foot of the grave. Her father can cry, and he's weeping here. Aubrey yanks at the girl's arm and swings her forward to the edge of the grave. 'Say your good-byes,' he roars, furious and volatile.

The girl's feet nearly slip into the grave but stop at the edge where she can't help but look down inside the hole. She's terrified of what she will see, but what she sees is nothing. What she finds is a dig with no end. The hole goes on forever. She could dive into that grave right now and she could fall through the earth for eternity and every muscle in her body wants to do just that. It's a bottomless grave. It's a black void, and this black void proves Molly Hook right and she shouts at her father across the grave. 'I told him, Dad. She's not down there.' She points to the sky. 'She's up there, Dad!'

Her father offers no response to his daughter beyond weeping. Her father has gone away. Gone away like Mum. I will never be afraid, she tells herself. I will feel no pain. I will feel only rage. Then Molly makes fists with her hands and she clenches them so hard that her fingernails draw blood from her palms and she screams. 'She. Is. Not. Down. There!'

Aubrey steps to the side of the grave and talks to his brother calmly. 'Control your child, brother.'

But Horace is blank. Horace only weeps. Molly's banshee screams echo across the cemetery. Loud enough to wake its eternal residents. A scream from the bottom of the endless black void inside her. High and sharp and piercing. 'She. Is. Not. Down. Therrrrrrrrre!'

Aubrey shouts at his brother now. 'Control your child, Horace!'

But Horace Hook has gone away. Horace only weeps. And with every tear her father sheds, the gravedigger girl grows more and more hysterical.

'What are you crying for?' she screams. 'She's not down there. She's not down there. SHE'S NOT DOWN TH—'

And the gravedigger girl is silenced by the back of her uncle's knuckle and bone hand landing flush across her face. Molly Hook falls back hard on the hard cemetery dirt. She wipes her nose and looks at her fingers covered in the same blood that's spread across her face. This place is hard, she tells herself. Rock is hard. My heart is hard as rock, she tells herself. I will never be afraid. I will feel no pain.

Molly looks up at her uncle, who is still holding her grandfather's pan when he turns his back on Molly and looks back down into the grave. Molly stands and wipes her face with her yard dress and she spits half a mouthful of blood on the dirt and then she runs fast at her uncle and she drives her shoulder hard into his back and she pushes against him with her legs. She will send him to hell where he belongs and the quickest route she can see is through that endless black void.

But her uncle doesn't move. His bones are too hard from digging. His bones are too hard from living. 'This is *your* grave!' Molly screams, pushing with all her strength as her bare toes slip in the soil beneath them. 'This is *yoourrr* grave!'

Then she gives up pushing against her uncle and reaches for the pan he holds in his right hand. 'This is mine,' she screams. 'Give it back.' She tugs on the pan and pulls back on it with all her strength and all that is left of her will. 'Give it back.'

Aubrey Hook is still gripping the pan when he turns and smiles at his niece as though he's going to enjoy the thing he's about to do, and the gravedigger girl is still bulldog-clinging to the pan when her uncle swings his right arm with such fury and power that Molly's feet are lifted from the earth and she is thrown through the air and the only thing that stops her wild forward motion is the impact of her left temple meeting the edge of the large black rock frog rock next to the grave. Then she might as well be the one who is falling through that endless void towards hell because everything in her world, even the day sky, has turned to black.

The Seed of a Story

A black flying fox in the predawn pink of a wet season sky. Gravity turns the fruit bat's faeces into a teardrop falling fast to the earth and inside that teardrop is a single seed. Wind pushes the teardrop towards a eucalypt woodland with a vast understorey layer of vibrant green spear grass. The teardrop falls hard and finds its own permanently moist pocket of earth. The sun rises and falls in the sky and rises and falls in the sky and the black flying foxes of the Northern Territory fly east and west with and towards their kin.

Wet seasons turn to dry seasons and turn to wet again, and suns make way for moons and then a tree grows out of a pocket of moist earth where once a fruit bat's seed found a home. It has rough dark-grey bark, stands thirty feet high and has glossy, round leaves that bounce light like the inside of an oyster shell. And from among these leaves, on the morning of 7 December 1941, a small round fruit appears before the world. It is the colour red and it is ribbed all around. It is a red bush apple.

Yukio Miki and the
Black Dragon Sky

His gloved hand reaches for her photograph in the grey blindness of a cloud. 'Nara, make me strong,' he whispers. The photograph is fading, stuck by gum above the circular fuel gauge of Yukio Miki's Mitsubishi A6M 'Zero' long-range fighter. The original photograph was wider: Nara Nui kneeling on the floor beside the right leg of her father, Koga Nui, who was seated on a wooden chair, his right palm resting on his right thigh and his left hand concealed by the long sleeve of his hemp and silk kimono – his winter kimono – patterned with pine trees that Yukio always considered a fair pictorial representation of Koga Nui's existence: towering and bristling and hard to kill with anything but an axe.

Yukio sliced the photograph in half, weeks ago, with his pocket knife pressed against an aircraft carrier mess hall table in Hitokappu Bay, in the Kuril Islands, leaving only Nara to grace the sacred gum space above his fuel gauge. Nara's not looking at the camera in the photograph, and she told Yukio she was looking, in fact, at her nine-year-old niece, Soma, who was walking precariously behind the camera on a pair of empty soup tins tied with rope. It was Soma who was making Nara smile so wide, she said, but Yukio knew the truth, that it was life that gave Nara Nui her smile; it was children and snow and harlequin ducks bobbing along clearwater streams and it was fat fish hanging from her hook and it was a red paper kite stolen by the wind and carried across southern Osaka; it was the air and the sea and the sky that formed that smile. Nara wears her one and only kimono in the photograph, patterned with plum blossoms, winter cousin of *sakūra* – cherry blossom. The plum blossoms always bloomed in time for the cold days when Nara would nestle into the soft cushion of flesh between Yukio's right breast and right shoulder. He would feel her lips moving on his chest as she spoke of their love and their future, and all he saw as he lay with his back on the snow-flaked grass were the gold hearts of hanging white plum blossom flowers against a sky as grey as the cloud he flies through now. It felt, then, like Nara was talking to his chest on purpose and when she whispered 'zutto' – eternally – she really was meaning to say it up so close; she meant to say it directly to his fast-beating heart.

There is a parachute pack stuffed behind his seat. Few Zero pilots carry parachutes. He could slip his on here now in the cloud, he tells himself. The Zero's cockpit can't be jettisoned but it can be opened in flight. He could exit here, slip away unseen by his brothers and feel no shame. The high winds of the Pacific would carry him to a tropical island, carry him to Egypt, to Paris, to London with its big round yellow ticking clock in the night sky. A strong enough updraught could lift him and his parachute up through the clouds, even, through the sky and the stars and into Takamanohara, the Plain of High Heaven.

No, he tells himself. A Zero samurai fights to the death.

Death, he tells himself. Death. The only answer to every question he ever asked about life. The shortest route to heaven. The quickest road to Nara.

*

The shortsword that rattles against metal in the left-side gap between the Zero's pilot seat and cockpit door is called a *wakizashi*. The shortsword's blade is only thirty centimetres long. *Wakizashi* swords were traditionally made for close-quarter fighting or to commit *seppuku*, ritual suicide, but Yukio carries the sword today not for the sharpness of its blade but for the power of the object's story. A gift from father to son. A sword more than two centuries old, passed through the hands of Miki men, all of whom, with the exception of Yukio the fighter pilot, worked in the artisan knife-making workshops of old town Sakai, on the edge of Osaka Bay, at the mouth of Yamato River.

There is an image of a butterfly engraved on the handle end of the sword's blade. The blade was forged in the Miki family workshop in the heart of Sakai, a bustling fishing port and one of Japan's busiest and oldest foreign trading hubs, filled with the sacred air of maritime commerce and tuna blood and the guts of fat red queen crabs. It was in the same modest and small and well-kept laneway knife-making workshop that Yukio's father, Oshiro Miki, passed the *wakizashi* to his first-born son, then aged in his mid-twenties, on the day he left Sakai to join his military brethren in the selective and punishing Imperial Japanese Navy Air Service pilot training programme. Oshiro had told his son the story of the sword's creation many times but on this day of sad departures he felt he needed to tell him again.

'No more stories, father,' Yukio pleaded. He had grown tired of his father's stories. As a boy, Yukio had lived for his father's tales. Tales of how the Miki family had been making blades for six hundred years. Tales of samurai swords forged for great warriors. Tales of how the flames of feudal war were finally extinguished and the need for samurai swords was blown away with the ashes of the dead, and how the Miki family elders then turned their sword-making skills to creating the sharpest fishermen's filleting knives in all of Sakai. Knives forged for cutting the heads off tuna that could still carve through the neck bones of any fisherman foolish enough to doubt the integrity of Miki family steel.

Yukio would sit for hours behind the workshop counter on an upturned wooden wash bucket, polishing and sharpening filleting blades as he watched his father dazzle fishermen with increasingly elaborate tales of each sold knife's mythic creation. Fishermen from the Black Sea and from the Mediterranean and the Pacific and the Atlantic, and from seas as high and cold as the world went, and as wide and warm. They would come to Sakai port to hear Oshiro Miki tell his knife-maker tales. And, every single week, young Yukio was surprised to find that his father had miraculously acquired a new sacred and old blade that he had promised never to part with but might consider selling to one lucky foreign fisherman if he deemed him worthy of the knife's ownership.

'You carry yourself with honour,' Oshiro would say to that week's particularly fortunate customer. 'You have treated my family and me with respect, and for this kindness I will repay you by showing you a most uncommon blade. I will now tell you the story of this blade, but you must never repeat it and you must never speak of where you found this blade.'

What followed was usually a tale of adventure, courage,

sacrifice, tragedy and, always, true love. The blade Yukio's father held in his hands was invariably the sacred object with which the tragic hero of each story managed to overcome a malevolent force – deceitful loved one, old wizard, seductive witch, many-limbed sea monster – standing in the way of true love's triumph. Oshiro would complete these lucrative counter transactions and then turn to his son and whisper about the wonders and importance of story. 'The finest blades are forged not with steel, son,' he would say. 'But with story.' Oshiro Miki knew full well that his customers would speak freely of where they found their precious new blades. He knew his strict requests to keep his hallowed workshop and its treasured stories secret was the very reason Miki family blades were spoken about over tuna nets and chopping boards across the globe.

As Yukio grew into his teens behind the workshop counter, his father taught him how to tell these knife stories to foreign travellers in broken English and broken French and broken Spanish. The stories, he said, could sound even more mystical and significant when told in a few carefully selected English words.

'Love!' Oshiro hollered in perfect English to a wealthy American couple sailing the seven seas, oil money spilling from their pockets. He waved his hands excitedly at the long-married husband and wife. 'I see . . . love!' he declared. And then he explained in broken English that the word 'love' was his favourite word in the entire English language because it was the first word of English he ever learned. How perfect, Oshiro recognised, and how fortunate was he that the first word of English he ever learned was also the language's most profound and sacred and joyous. 'True . . . love,' he said with a smile.

And Yukio watched as the Americans smiled with the newfound knowledge that their shared love, despite whatever feelings they may have harboured to the contrary, was clear and strong enough to cross even the divides of sea and language. Then Yukio's father spoke of how that couple's true love reminded him of a true-love story behind a sacred and expensive *wakizashi* that he just knew would make the perfect souvenir to show their many friends back home in Pennsylvania.

'Was "love" the first word of English my father learned?' Yukio asked his grandfather Saburo Miki, who was an old and quiet and thoughtful man, as they washed dishes that night.

'Ha!' Saburo laughed. 'The first word of English your father learned was "dog". The second word he learned was "fish".'

'Then my father is a liar,' Yukio said.

'Your father is a storyteller,' Saburo said, washing thick brown fish sauce off a dinner plate. 'He tells those stories to fill this plate for you each night. There is a difference between liars and storytellers, Yukio.' The grandfather passed the clean dinner plate to his grandson. 'Some storytellers still make it to heaven.'

*

'Just one more story,' Oshiro Miki said, holding the *wakizashi* in two hands before his son. He prefaced this story as he'd done every other time he told it, by acknowledging its more questionable narrative turns. 'For this story to reach your heart, son, you may need to swallow it down with a sprinkling of salt from the shores of the inland sea,' Oshiro said. 'You should write the facts of this story only on tissue paper. But you should carve its meaning in stone.'

Yukio patiently and respectfully listened, again, as his father spoke of how the shortsword was made in the 1700s by a quietly spoken and diligent knife-maker named Asato Miki, who had discovered that the love of his life, Rina, had left

Sakai in the arms of his younger brother, Uno. All but swallowed up by the dark shadow of grief and betrayal, Asato Miki willed himself to forge the perfect *wakizashi* blade, with which he was determined to cut out his own beating heart and toss it into the furnace that had forged his own murder weapon. For such an impossible act, Asato reasoned, he would need to forge an impossible blade and, in a single, dizzying twenty-four-hour haze of fevered and hate-filled industry, Asato hammered two types of metal together – soft and workable *jigane* iron and hard and deadly *tamahagane* steel – in a furnace so hot he could only work in thirty-minute blasts of furious activity between guzzles of fresh water fetched by his apprentice, which would also serve to cool and harden the blade. Asato felt so strong that day that he came to believe the very breath of Futsunushi – god of swords – had filled his workshop and a dragon's fire had filled his blood. Asato forged the two metals into a single blade so sharp it cut the four legs off the bed he had shared for three years with Rina in four swift strokes.

The tortured ironworker was stunned by a newfound artistry born of pain. He was more stunned, still, to discover that the joy of his newfound gifts had swallowed up the sorrow that had driven him to make the sword in the first place. Asato began demonstrating and advertising his miraculous ironwork skills in sake houses across Sakai by having loose-pocketed drinkers throw objects – apples, oranges, carrots, potatoes, unlucky alehouse kitchen rats – at him, each of which he would slice into two perfect halves with a single swipe of a short but swift sword as thin as a Yamato River ghost.

One day a legendary vagabond assassin known as the 'White Tiger' sailed into the Sakai port, his thick mane of pure white hair braided and hanging almost to his calves. He began asking questions about an impossible blade forged by love and betrayal and loss and hate.

'That sword is not for sale,' Asato told the stranger in his workshop.

'What if I told you the first person I will kill with this blade will be your betrayer, Rina?' the White Tiger asked. 'And what if I told you the second person I will kill with this blade will be your younger brother, Uno?'

Asato was silent for a moment. 'The sword is not for sale,' he said.

The White Tiger reached into a leather pouch slung to a belt around his waist. He raised a closed fist then opened it to reveal a pure white butterfly, which launched into flight from the assassin's soft, open palm.

'Have you heard the story of the gravedigger and the butterfly?' the assassin asked.

'I have not,' said Asato.

*

And so now Oshiro Miki told his story of how the White Tiger told his story of Takahama, who was born into wealth and was highly educated but, despite his good fortune, chose, in the prime of his life, to spend the rest of his days alone, digging graves and tending the headstones of the dead, as caretaker for what was believed to be the most haunted cemetery in all of old Japan. So humble was the caretaker's hut connected to the cemetery grounds that Takahama's wealthy and influential family refused to visit for fear of embarrassment. Years later, when two neighbouring villagers stumbled upon an aged Takahama slowly dying alone on his bed, they called for the cemetery keeper's remaining relatives to visit him at once.

Takahama's long-lost nephew, Hansuke, made it to the old man's bed just in time to witness his final hours of life. As Takahama drew his last laboured breaths, a pure white butterfly flew in through his window and perched itself peacefully on the tip of his nose. The butterfly flapped its wings once, twice, three times. Hansuke shooed the butterfly away, and it flew off and returned and flew off and returned to the tip of the old man's nose. Then Takahama's eyes closed forever and the white butterfly seemed to know this and flew back out the window. Instinctively, Hansuke followed it deep into the haunted cemetery. He ran through grey and black gravestones covered in weed and moss, aisle upon aisle of the never-visited dead. The white butterfly flew left and flew right and then deep into a tunnel of elm trees that ended at a single tomb, where the butterfly rested itself on the only grave in the cemetery without a trace of moss or dirt upon it. Indeed, the grave was as pristine as if the head-stone and tomb had been placed that very day. There was a name on the headstone: 'Akiko'.

Studying the gravestone epitaph, Hansuke began to piece together the story behind his late uncle's decisions. Akiko and Takahama had been betrothed, but Akiko had died the day before their wedding. Since Takahama had already promised to look after his beloved Akiko, every hour of every day, he swore he would continue to do that, even if it meant caring only for her grave.

As he stood pondering this, Hansuke noticed another small white butterfly emerge from the dense forest surrounding the cemetery and flutter towards the one he had followed to the grave, which was still hovering above the headstone. The two white butterflies circled each other for a long moment and then Hansuke edged closer to them, but his movement caused the butterflies to fly away from the headstone and they fluttered up into the sky and never came back down again. The nephew stared at that blue sky above, not with a sense of grief or confusion, but only wonder.

Asato Miki stroked his chin inside his knife-making workshop, absorbing the assassin's tale.

'Well?' the assassin asked.

'Well what?' Asato replied.

'What did you learn from the story?' the assassin asked.

Asato stroked his chin some more, then gave his answer. 'It is a simple tale you tell and there is only one lesson to be learned from it,' he said. 'Transformation. Sometimes they stay with us. And sometimes they wait for us. The lost are not lost. We can change into things. We can transform ourselves. Sometimes for the better . . .'

'Sometimes for the worse,' said the assassin, his eyes turning to the pure white butterfly that was now flapping above his right shoulder. He turned back to Asato. 'I must take your life now,' he said.

'Why?' Asato asked.

'Because you will not share your artistry with me.'

'You haven't given me a chance,' Asato said.

The assassin paused. 'Very well,' he said. 'Show me the full extent of your artistry.'

'How would I do that?' Asato replied.

The assassin turned his eyes to the butterfly. 'Take your sword and slice a wing off this flying white butterfly.'

'That's impossible,' Asato said.

'So is your blade,' the assassin said.

Asato took a deep breath then exhaled slowly. He retrieved his impossible sword from a small locked room off the workshop's furnace area and returned to stand before the butterfly and the assassin. He gripped the sword's handle tight and raised the perfect blade high as the butterfly hovered, as if by will, as if by command, before his eyes. The betrayed sword-maker drew a short breath, tensed his shoulders, fixed his feet to the floor and began to swing his blade – but he immediately pulled out of the swing, and presented the sword to the assassin, handle end first. 'I can't,' he said, shaking his head.

The assassin raised his eyebrows.

'The butterfly's life is already too short,' Asato said.

The assassin lifted the sword to his eyes, laid his forefinger gently on the blade. He turned to face Asato and swung the blade three times. The sound of steel slicing through air was the only evidence of his actions, the blade moving too fast to be visible. Asato heaved a long sigh of relief on realising that he was still breathing.

The White Tiger rested the sword in his open palms then handed it back to its creator. 'You are right, knife-maker,' he said, before turning and exiting the workshop through its rusty-hinged wooden front door.

Asato stood in silence, then rushed to the door, just in time to see the assassin disappearing into the bustling port-village crowd, the pure white butterfly hovering peacefully above his right shoulder.

*

'Well?' Yukio asked.

'Well what?' Oshiro replied.

'What are you trying to tell me, father?' Yukio asked.

'The lost are not lost,' Oshiro Miki said in the silence of the Sakai workshop.

Yukio nodded his head in understanding. 'There is something

I must tell you about sad love stories, father,' he said. 'They are not as enjoyable when they are true.'

Oshiro was silent. Then he nodded sincerely and said, 'The lost are not lost. Sometimes they transform. Sometimes they stay with us.'

And it was with two open palms that Oshiro Miki handed the old fire-forged shortsword to his first-born son, Yukio, before he set off to war.

Yukio received the sword in silence. He walked to the front door of the workshop, then turned to speak to the father he loved.

'And sometimes they wait for us,' he said. Yukio left his father in the workshop and walked out the door in the direction of war.

*

Nara smiling at him now in a winged weapon. Now the deephell machinery sound of Yukio and his airborne brothers, who do and do not fear their death, spread across an attack wave of 183 battle planes in arrow formations: 89 Nakajima B5N bombers carrying 800-kilogram torpedoes and 250-kilogram bombs; 51 Aichi D3A dive bombers, each with a 250-kilogram bomb slung under its fuselage and two 30-kilogram bombs nestled on racks under its wings; and 43 agile Zero fighters flying above it all, closer to the blue sky ceiling, closer to heaven. The vicious snarl of that sound, the growl of it. The wasp of it. The tiger of it. A violent symphony of three-blade propellers slicing air and overworked engines spitting smoke. Red spots on battle wings. All those red rising suns in a morning sky formation.

Yukio's cockpit canopy has a 360-degree view of sky, water

and land. A high green mountain range on Yukio's right side, cloud on his left. It's 7.48 a.m. and he's been flying for one hour and forty minutes. The air fleet banks west and along a turquoise coastline and Yukio reaches quickly for his binoculars. Two glass lenses magnifying the beauty and terror of eight majestic battleships lining the port of Pearl Harbor, on the island of Oahu, Hawaii. There are smaller grey warships anchored around them like mice sleeping beside greyhounds.

Yukio drops his binoculars and his naked eyes find the 'black dragon', an electrifying dark blue flare that's now rising into the light blue sky. They don't know we're coming, Yukio tells himself. The fleet's leader, Captain Mitsuo Fuchida, is speaking loudly and clearly to Yukio and his brothers with that dark blue flare. Speaking without speaking. He's saying only one word. Screaming it through a burning and soaring dragonflare streak. Demanding it. Just one word. *Attack*.

Yukio's left hand reaches for the gunsight fixed between his two 7.7-millimetre machine guns. His right hand reaches for the photograph fixed above his fuel gauge. He folds the top half of the photograph down over the bottom half. He doesn't want her to see this. 'I'm coming, Nara,' he whispers, as his fighter swoops down towards a horizon lit by fire.

The Ways in and Out
of the Maze

Here lies Lisbeth Fleming. Dead at seventy-three, influenza. Buried 1884. Here stands Molly Hook, aged twelve years and nine months, four feet deep in Lisbeth's grave, Bert's blade biting through old dirt that's meeting the sun for the first time in fifty-seven years.

'Water?' Molly asks.

'Break at five feet,' says her father, Horace. 'These old grave-diggers always took shortcuts. They usually called it quits at five and a half.'

A gravestone. A hole in the ground. The girl in the hole, and her father and her uncle, Aubrey, leaning on their shovels above ground, each taking a side of the grave. Around the grave are mountains of dirt and a single pile of rocks beside the rusting mattock that was used to dig them all up.

Molly digs. Molly digs. Molly digs. She wears old brown leather boots, her dig boots, and a pair of brown pants made for boys that Horace found in a Tennant Creek thrift store.

Molly digs, her thin arms, only bone and muscle, filling a

wooden bucket with grave dirt that her father and uncle pull to the surface after every eight shovel loads.

'Dad.'

Horace takes a long drag on his smoke. Exhales.

'Mmmm,' he offers Molly. This is her permission to speak.

Molly digs hard as she talks, heartened by her father's permission to do so. 'I was just thinkin' about how I've dug up six already this week and this will be my seventh and I've been working real hard with the customers as well and I was wondering if you would let me go to the Star with Sam on Saturday night?'

'I can't afford for you to go to no picture theatre, Molly,' Horace says.

'No, no, Sam said he's gonna pay for me,' Molly says.

'Who's Sam?'

'Sam Greenway.'

'The coon boy?'

Just Sam and nothing else, Molly thinks. Her best friend who's not a shovel or a sky.

'Sam's good stock, Dad. He works hard and he's real smart and he's been telling me all there is to know about what it's like growing up out there in the bush, in the real deep country past the Clyde River.'

'And what does Sam tell you about what it's like out there in the deep country?'

Molly stops digging. She turns to her father, up there on the surface, sun shining over his shoulders and onto her face. She puts a palm over her eyes.

'He says it's magical,' Molly says. 'He says there's crocodiles in the creeks as old as dinosaurs and the crocodiles talk to him and he says there's plants out there so big that their vines can suffocate you in your sleep and there's trees with bark so soft you can roll it up and sleep on it under the stars, and the trees talk to you, too. Then there's Ol' Man Rock and he's just a big rock, but he knows the answer to any question you could possibly think to ask him.'

Horace Hook scrapes a cake of mud from the sole of his left boot with a stick. 'I hope he told you, too, about all the criminals who live in shacks and caves out there,' he says. 'Did he tell you about that, Mol'? Murderers on the run from the law, hiding themselves in scrub so thick and dangerous the cops would never dare go after 'em. Thieves and rapists livin' on river rats and peanut bushes. Men sick with pox, women gone brain-mad with syphilis. Kidnappers who'd swap a twelve-year-old girl's virginity for a can of oil. Lunatic child killers who'd cut a girl's heart out and trade it for a fresh orange.'

Molly is silent. Her eyelids blinking.

'No,' she says. 'Sam said nuthin' about that.'

'You go walkin' too far into that deep country, you might never come back,' Horace says. 'So no more bloody walkabouts, Molly, ya hear me?'

'I hear you.'

'Dig, Molly, dig.'

Molly digs. Horace smokes his strong tobacco and enjoys the quiet for a moment. Then Molly breaks the silence. Molly always breaks the silence.

'Sam told me how to eat an echidna, even though I thought it would be impossible to eat an echidna,' she says, dropping another dirt load in the wooden bucket. 'Do ya wanna know how to eat an echidna, Dad?'

Horace sighs, drags on his smoke. 'How do you eat an echidna, Molly?'

'The trick of it is all those spines on top, of course,' she says. 'But Sam says you just cover the spines with a thick layer of clay – you know, like that red ferrosol stuff you told me about – then you whack the echidna on the fire and when it's all cooked you take it out and let it sit, and then you peel back that layer of clay on top and all the spines come off with it and it's like you're peeling back the lid on a can of sardines, except what you have underneath those spines is tastier and oilier than any duck you'd find on a plate in Paris.'

Molly digs, transfers the dirt, counts off the eighth shovel load and lets her uncle heave the wooden bucket to the surface.

'The Star's playin' *The Cowboy and the Lady*, with Gary Cooper,' Molly says. 'You'd like Gary Cooper, Dad. He doesn't talk much in the pictures. He's all quiet and serious, like how you and Uncle Aubrey are.'

Molly looks at her father and, as he always does, her father looks at his older brother, Aubrey. And Uncle Aubrey briefly shakes his head from side to side.

'But I haven't been—'

'Quiet now, Molly,' Aubrey says, his lips unseen beneath his black moustache.

'But—'

'Dig, child, dig,' Aubrey grunts.

Molly digs. One, two, three shovel loads. Four, five, six shovel loads. Bert the shovel clangs against a large rock buried in the grave soil. Molly reaches for a forged steel spud bar leaning against the right-side grave wall. With both hands she drives the spud bar, wedged at the business end, clean into the rock three times and the rock breaks into three smaller pieces that she hacks out with a smaller pickaxe.

More shovelling. Seven shovel loads. Eight shovel loads. Total silence. Horace hauls the bucket up the side of the hole. Molly watches a long black earthworm wriggle along the north wall of the grave. Up, up, up towards the surface. Her eyes go up with the worm and a little further up to settle on a view of Lisbeth Fleming's headstone.

'Who was she?' Molly asks.

'Who was who?' Horace replies.

'Lisbeth Fleming.'

'She wasn't anyone.'

'Everybody's someone,' Molly says. 'Ya reckon she's still got family in town?'

The men say nothing. Aubrey pats the deep lines in his forehead with his handkerchief.

'"Matthew, Iris and George",' Molly says, reading the headstone epitaph. Molly's right boot kicks hard at Bert's blade and the bucket is back to receive another shovel load. She pauses to read more from Lisbeth Fleming's headstone. 'Matthew, Iris and George were her kids,' Molly says. 'I wonder if Iris is Iris Brentnall who worked behind the counter in the saddlery in town.'

Aubrey Hook takes a long swig from a rusting silver hip flask, directs a sharp and perturbed look towards his younger brother across the grave.

'Quiet now, Molly,' Horace says.

Molly digs and Bert's blade tip thumps against wood. Molly bangs the blade twice more. *Thump, thump.*

Aubrey shifts his smoke to the left side of his lips and leans down slowly, bones aching, to grip the mattock resting by the piles of dirt. 'Out,' he says through his near-closed lips.

Molly turns and scrambles up a small wooden ladder resting against the south wall of Lisbeth Fleming's grave. Her father hands her a brown leather water bag. She unscrews the cap and guzzles down the liquid, letting it splash across the soil covering her face and neck.

Aubrey doesn't use the ladder, simply slides down into the

grave, his black boots landing heavily on Lisbeth Fleming's rotting wooden casket. His right boot scrapes away the dirt on the casket top, searching for an entry point. He stomps his boots three times, testing the thickness of the wood. On the third stomp he finds a softer, rotted section. He raises his mattock high with a two-handed grip and drives the mattock down on the casket like he is staking a claim in the earth. Old wood cracking, splintering. Aubrey raises the mattock at the same point, drives it down again.

The shiver along his worn spine is the same shiver of expectation he used to feel in the gold-digging years, a gold shiver. It was the thrill of mining a hole where you could smell the gold and that smell turned into a taste and that taste was blood and metal on a tongue tip. The gold in all those deep rocks was all buried treasure. He and Horace and Violet's father, Tom Berry, and all those Chinamen who followed them down into those holes were all pirates, except they had no treasure maps to work from, only their instinct, only the shivers that ran along their worn spines. That shiver meant success.

Aubrey wedges the mattock between the casket top and its side and pushes hard. Molly, from above ground, watches the casket lid flip up from the dirt like the lid of a jewellery box. But there is no jewel sparkle to be seen inside Lisbeth Fleming's coffin, only bones. The casket's bottom has largely disintegrated. A skull with a mouth full of dirt. Dirt in the eye holes. Dirt in a cracked cheekbone. I will never be afraid, Molly tells herself. I will feel no pain.

Arm bones and hand bones resting upon each other, meeting at the waist of a torso that time and slow earth movement have torn away from Lisbeth's leg bones. There is a book by her waist that Aubrey digs from the earth, prises open with two hands. Pages fused together by decades of damp. 'Bible,' he says, tossing the book to the side of the grave. There is a round tobacco case by Lisbeth's right elbow. Aubrey bangs the case against the mattock, caked dirt falling over his long fingers. He pulls a small pocket knife from his back pants pocket and runs the knife blade along the lid rim. He bangs the case again on the mattock and blows dirt from it that clouds above Lisbeth's skull face. Gripping the lid firmly, he twists it off, drops it in the dirt and tips the case's contents into his left hand. He holds an amethyst and crystal bead necklace to the sun for less than ten seconds then tosses the necklace over his shoulder towards his younger brother, who catches it and lifts it up to the light.

Aubrey kneels down over Lisbeth's waist and lifts her hands up as nonchalantly as he might lift a pile of kindling sticks. There's a pure gold band on Lisbeth's left-hand ring finger. He tries to slip it off, but it's set in place by gathered dirt. Molly watches her Uncle Aubrey wrench the ring finger bone back and forth and back and forth then rip the finger from its socket. He blows on the finger, spits on the finger, makes a cloth of his shirt and rubs the finger like he's polishing his boots. Then Molly watches her Uncle stick the long-dead corpse finger in his mouth, grip the gold band in his teeth like an animal and pull it off. He drops the finger in the dirt and he spits the gold band into his palm. Then he spits on the ring again and polishes it in his shirt before holding it up to the sun.

Even from above ground, Molly and Horace can clearly see the unearthed treasure because there are no earths and no sins and no deaths that can keep the edge of a pure gold band from glowing in the lemon light. Molly observes the way her uncle smiles at it now. His secret smile. The silent affair he has maintained with the glowing. She's studied this bond for some time now.

The gravedigger girl has been reading the poetry books on the shelf by the front door of the cemetery house as her mum told her to do. She's been trying to find bits of her mum inside them, the bits of those books she connected to. All those hardback and dusty books of poems by all those graceful poets like John Keats and Walt Whitman and Edgar Allan Poe and William Butler Yeats and Emily Dickinson, who is Molly's favourite because although she doesn't seem as graceful as the rest, she seems more honest, and not afraid to show when she's mad in the heart and in the head. All that those poets seemed to do all day was study people like her Uncle Aubrey. All those poets seemed to write about were the things you can't see on the outside of people like Uncle Aubrey. They were always writing about emotions like love and hate and envy and regret and rage and they were always using real-life creatures like nightingales and crows and horses to represent those emotions.

Almost a year ago, Molly Hook started scribbling poems of her own with chalky rocks on the backs of random headstones throughout Hollow Wood. She recently wrote a poem with no title about the bond her uncle shares with the glowing. She etched the poem into the back of a nameless gravestone deep in the south-western corner of Hollow Wood. She used all the creatures she sees in the cemetery to represent things inside her uncle that can't be seen from outside. She wrote it out of anger, like all her best poems.

> *The bird said he dug for the bread*
> *The scorpion said he dug for treasure*
> *The worm said he dug for the dead*
> *The snake said he dug for pleasure*

It was a poem about how Molly believed it wasn't the precious metal that her uncle was hoping to find in all these graves, it was the glowing – the brief flash of new light the dug-up gold brought into his world. There was a kind of love in it, she thought. A romance, maybe. Lust, surely. Not the picture-theatre kind, but a darker kind that dwells in shadows and never sleeps. The Edgar Allan Poe kind.

And she has come to believe, lately, that her uncle would do anything for the glowing because the glowing is breathing and eating and drinking and sleeping and fighting and digging. The glowing is all of life and he lives only in the briefest moments when the glowing bounces back into his shadowy eyes. It's a private affair, a solitary lust. She's not supposed to know about it.

He whips his head to the side and catches Molly staring at him. 'Make yourself scarce,' he growls.

*

The gravedigger girl and Bert the shovel standing alone and silent before Tom Berry's grave, with the sun in the middle of the sky. Molly reads her grandfather's epitaph. Her eyes are drawn to the same sentence they're always drawn to.

LONGCOAT BOB TURNED OUR
TRUE HEARTS TO STONE.

Molly places her right hand against her chest. Molly tries to feel her heartbeat because a heart can't beat inside stone. And she can feel the weight of her heart inside her chest, and she could swear her heart grows heavier every year.

Molly has a book of poetry in her left hand. It's the Dickinson book with the hard and faded blank olive-green cover. She has the book open at a poem she likes. It's a poem about the sky and the things that take place above it.

Molly looks up to a clear blue sky today. 'I worked it out,' she says.

And the day sky responds to Molly Hook because it's the graceful thing to do. 'You did?'

'"The longer I stand, the shorter I grow,"' Molly recites.

'You worked it out, Molly?'

'It's a candle,' Molly says.

'A candle!' the day sky says. 'Of course! The longer I stand, the shorter I grow.'

'He's talking about candlelight,' Molly says. 'Tom Berry started out from Candlelight Creek.'

'Candlelight Creek!' the day sky says. 'Of course! So what are you going to do now, Molly?'

Molly says nothing.

'Mmmmm,' says the knowing day sky. 'You gonna go walk-about again?'

Molly says nothing.

Her father would kill her. No more walkabouts. When she was nine years and three months of age, Molly walked deep into the scrub beyond the edge of Hollow Wood Cemetery. She walked off with no water, no food, no shoes. She can't even remember now exactly why she walked off like that, so deep into the wild where the grass was so hard it felt like broken glass beneath her feet. She just kept on walking and she can't recall if the deep country out there was pulling her further in or if this dark and damned cemetery was pushing her further out. Soon she was lost in a pathless mess of towering cypress pines. Horace and Aubrey found her almost two days later, asleep and breathing slowly beneath the shade of a sand palm. Her uncle said she should have been flogged for walking off like that, but her father did not belt her that day because he was so relieved to find his daughter still alive. He thought he'd lost her and he held her to his chest as they padded back out of the deep scrub. He held her tighter that day than he'd ever held her, and Molly remembered there was as much daylight in her father then as there was night-time.

When Molly was eleven years and three months of age, her father woke before dawn one morning by the edge of the Adelaide River, south of Darwin and north of Katherine, to find the camping swag beside his – Molly's swag – empty. He found her deep in the bush beyond the river four hours later, sleeping and breathing slowly in the centre of a low-lying flat cluster of more than a hundred termite mounds, some of them twelve feet tall. Violet Hook had once told Molly that termite mounds like that were meridional and miraculous, built instinc-tively by the white-bodied debris-feeding termites that manage to magnetically align each tall mound in a north–south direc-tion so that the eastern face of each mound is warmed rapidly by the morning sun and the hottest midday sun hits only the thinnest profile of the termite's strange architecture. Molly saw the mounds as perfectly aligned gravestones. Same chalky grey colours. Same colour of stone. The cluster was a cemetery, but a cemetery filled with microcosmic life. Molly saw it as Hollow Wood Cemetery; she saw it as home.

Horace belted Molly that day. There and then, he hit her arse so many times and so hard with his open palm that she could not sit back down in the spot where he'd found her. He did not carry her out of the scrub, but left her to walk back to their campsite alone. 'No more fuckin' walkabouts,' he said, before disappearing back into the thick bush.

No more fuckin' walkabouts.

'Dig, Molly, dig,' the day sky says.

'Why do you say that? Dad always says that. Uncle Aubrey always says that. "Dig, Molly, dig." That's all I ever hear.'

'Dig, Molly, dig,' the day sky says.

'Dig for what?'

'Dig for the answers.'

'But I don't even know the questions.'

'Of course you know the questions, Molly.'

Molly turns her head back to her grandfather's gravestone. She reads more of Tom Berry's last words to the world.

I TOOK RAW GOLD FROM LAND BELONGING TO THE BLACK NAMED LONGCOAT BOB AND I SWEAR, UNDER GOD, HE PUT A CURSE ON ME AND MY KIN FOR THE SIN OF MY GREED.

Molly turns her eyes back up to the sky. 'Why did she leave me down here?'

The day sky says nothing.

'How could she leave me like that? How could she leave me here with them?'

The day sky says nothing. But Molly waits for an answer.

'These are questions for the night sky, Molly.'

Molly shakes her head in disappointment.

'I know why she left. It was Longcoat Bob. It was the curse. Kin means daughters. Kin means granddaughters. Kin means mothers. Kin means fathers. She said I was blessed because she wanted to make me feel better. How could I possibly be blessed, stuck down here with them?' Molly nods her head, sure of her words. 'I know a curse when I see one. I see one every day. A mum would have to be cursed to do what she did.'

'Dig, Molly, dig,' the day sky says.

'Have you seen what they've been doing?'

'Dig, Molly, dig,' the day sky says.

'Robbing dead folks of their most precious belongings.'

'Dig, Molly, dig.'

'She had to be cursed to do what she did and they must be cursed to do what they do. Cursed, just like this whole place. Cursed and damned and dead.'

'Dig, Molly, dig.'

'Dig for what?'

'The book, Molly, the book.'

Molly raises the Dickinson in her hand. She opens the book at the page of the poem she likes about the sky.

'It's called "The Lightning is a Yellow Fork",' she says. 'It's about all the things that are happening up in the sky. She says there's a great big mansion up there and there's a great big dining table inside the mansion and there's all these extraordinary people, all these special people, all sitting around that table and one of those people drops a yellow fork from the table and that yellow fork drops through the sky as lightning.'

Molly stares up at the sky and three blowflies buzz around her face but she doesn't blink an eye.

'A yellow fork, Molly,' the day sky says.

Molly nods. 'Yes, I remember seeing those words on Grandpa's pan, but I can't remember what else it said.'

'Where's the pan, Molly?'

'Uncle Aubrey threw it away,' Molly says.

'It wasn't his to throw away.'

'He said he wrapped it in a rubbish bag with a pig's head and a dozen eggshells.'

'That pan was a gift for you, Molly.'

'A sky gift,' Molly says.

'Sky gifts for the gravedigger girl.'
'Do you have any more?'
'More what?'
'Sky gifts.'
'Always, Molly.'
'How will I find them?'
'Just look up.'

*

Molly lies flat on her back in the dirt clearing beside her grandfather's grave. She stares for ten straight minutes up at the sky, her arms fanned out from her sides. She remembers lying like this with her mother. Mother and daughter, flat on their backs, hand in hand. Molly remembers her mother telling her there was a huge milkwood tree in the backyard of the house she grew up in, a sprawling two-storey cyclone-proof family home for four on the Darwin waterfront. She said that tree had branches like a tarantula raising its front legs, and she and her younger brother, Peter, who was a thoughtful and deep boy just like Molly, would stretch their arms out beneath the shade of the tarantula's legs and look up through those leg cracks to the sky, and they'd pretend the world was upside down and they were actually floating above the milkwood tree and the tree was sprouting from a ground made of blue sky.

'It always amazes me how little time people spend looking up at that sky,' Violet said.

Molly nodded.

'Maybe it's too beautiful,' Violet continued, 'maybe nobody looks up at it anymore because they know they'd want to spend the rest of the day looking at it. I guess we'd never get anything done if we spent all day looking up at the sky.'

'Can something be too beautiful, Mum?'

'Some things, Mol'. Not you. You're just the right amount of it.'

Then Violet gripped her daughter's hand. 'Let's float, Molly,' she said. 'Let's float.' And she smiled and breathed deeply.

'Can you feel it, Molly?' she asked.

'What is it, Mum?'

'The world is turning upside down. Can you feel it?'

And Molly saw clouds shifting across the sky. She saw leaves blowing. She saw movement. 'I can, Mum. I can feel it.'

'We're on top now, Molly! Can you feel it? We're floating. We're on top!'

Molly remembers all of that now and she smiles. She stands and picks up Bert, who's been leaning against her grandfather's headstone. She pads between the rows of the long dead, through avenues of limestone and dirt, back to the cemetery caretaker's house.

The back door to the cemetery house is painted dark green and Molly turns a loose, rusted bronze door knob to enter the downstairs laundry space, where she stops immediately before a curled western brown snake, cooling itself on the laundry's concrete floor. Her friend from town, Sam Greenway, and his family have a word for the western brown snake that Molly can't pronounce correctly, but it's a catch-all word meaning, 'If you come across this deadly snake you would be well advised to change your course and go the long way around.' Molly likes the way Sam's family can say so many things in a single word.

Molly doesn't change course. She wants to drink from the laundry sink tap, and brown snakes can't be gathering beneath the house, so she fixes her eyes on the snake's black head that's resting on the third ring of its own curled brown skin and drops Bert's cutting blade down on the snake's exposed neck so hard and fast that a brief spark flies from the concrete floor as the severed snake head is propelled towards the downstairs toilet running off the laundry.

The snake's headless body wriggles around Bert's blade face as Molly sweeps it and the black head out the laundry door and into the cemetery yard. Molly rewards her efforts by sticking her open mouth under the laundry tap and letting the town water that tastes like rust and dirt flow down her throat and spill over her chin. Then a voice from the front driveway to the house: "'Out damned spot! Out, I say!'"

The words of Shakespeare floating over gravestones, floating over the dead.

"'What need we fear who knows it, when none can call our power to account?'"

The words of a woman, shouting.

"'Yet who would have thought the old man to have had so much blood in him.'"

Molly turns the laundry tap off, the tap grips digging hard into her palm until the tap stops dripping, then scurries out the laundry door and along the rotting grey timber slats of the house's left-side exterior wall. Uncle Aubrey's rusting red utility truck is parked in the long dirt driveway. Standing on the hulking truck's back tray is a slim blonde woman in a striking red polka-dot dress – her uncle's sometime lady friend, Greta Maze.

Truck trays are stages for Greta Maze. Footpaths are stages for Greta Maze. Wet bar tops and soapboxes and bathroom floors and swimming pools are stages for Greta Maze. She stands on the tray with a well-thumbed script in her right hand by her waist, deep into the monologue. "'The thane of Fife had a wife: where is she now? What, will these hands ne'er be clean? No more o' that, my lord, no more o' that: you mar all with this starting.'"

That tight red summer dress with white spots, a fitted waist with cuffs just above the elbows, patch pockets – one for Greta's smokes and matches, another for her hip flask filled with more air than cheap whisky. The sight of that dress makes Molly smile and her smile widens further when she spots Greta's brown and white two-tone, low-heel canvas saddle shoes, the kind Molly would love to dance in one day when she's older and when she's not digging graves anymore. Greta's wild blonde curls all form a great wave that crashes like a force of nature over her left ear. Round brown sunglasses over her eyes, and perfect porcelain skin that will never be tainted by all the exposure it gets to the soft lights of Darwin's beer halls and gin joints and deep Chinatown basement opium dens.

Greta watches Molly approach the truck tray and her heels spring up an inch, her voice becomes louder, her performance more heartfelt, for she now has an audience. She smells her own hands, and her character, her latest grand local theatre role, is repulsed by them. '"Here's the smell of the blood still: all the perfumes of Arabia will not sweeten this little hand. Oh, oh, oh!"'

Greta squeezes her hands together, urgent, dismayed. Crazed.

'"Wash your hands, put on your nightgown; look not so pale."' She paces back and forth along the truck tray. '"To bed, to bed! There's knocking at the gate."'

Greta rushes to the edge of the tray and extends her hand to Molly. 'Come, come, come, come, give me your hand.'

Molly reaches her hand up to Greta, and it's thrilling for her to play a small part in this show. This acting. This art. All the way out here in dead-end Hollow Wood. The actress kneels down and grips the gravedigger girl's fingertips, and the touch of those fingers brings comfort to her character, but that comfort is too brief and too late. And Greta stares into Molly's eyes, breathless and distraught, and Greta removes her sunglasses to study Molly's face, unfiltered, and she weeps in front of her, tears welling in her emerald eyes and falling over the clean, cushioned landscape of her cheeks. And Molly wants to cry with her, but she can't, so she simply stares in wide-mouthed wonder.

'"What's done cannot be undone,"' the actress whimpers, like all hope is lost for her now, and Molly doesn't even know why but she wants to change things for this troubled woman. Then Greta stands and turns away from her audience of one and pads slowly to the other side of the truck tray, the back of her stage, and she drops her head and freezes there in the timeless silence that is broken eventually by Molly's rapturous applause.

'Bravo!' Molly hollers.

Greta turns around to accept her applause, waving to the imaginary audience up in the cheap seats. She puts her sunglasses back on, nods her head twice in thanks, and takes an elaborate bow. Then she reaches for her hip flask. She raises a toast towards Molly then takes a triumphant post-performance guzzle of spirits.

She offers the flask to Molly. 'You fancy a blast?'

'No, thanks,' Molly says.

Greta nods. 'Smart kid,' she says, capping the flask, resting her backside on the tray and leaning her back against the truck's cab.

'I made a meal of that "thane of Fife had a wife" line, didn't I?' Greta says.

'No, not at all,' Molly says, certain of it. 'You were spectacular.'

Greta lights a smoke. 'I was, wasn't I.' She smiles, breathing in then blowing smoke.

'What's it from?' Molly asks.

'The Palmerston Players are doing a two-week run of *Macbeth*,' Greta says. 'That's Lady Macbeth sleepwalking through her castle, rambling all of her black confessions.'

'What's wrong with her?'

'She's mad as a cut snake,' Greta says. 'Her feller's even worse.'

'What's wrong with him?'

'He keeps hearing strange voices in his head, keeps seeing things that aren't really there.'

Molly dwells on this. 'I think I hear voices in my head,' she says.

Greta nods. 'Of course you do, you're mad as a box of frogs.' She winks. 'That's why I like you. Nuts like you and me should always mix together.'

Molly beams a smile. 'I talk to the sky sometimes,' she confesses.

Greta smiles immediately: 'Who doesn't?'

'You talk to the sky, Greta?'

'Sure.'

'Does it ever talk back to you?'

'Sure.' Greta shrugs.

'What's it sound like when it talks back to you?'

'My sky sounds like Humphrey Bogart.'

Molly laughs.

'What's it sound like to you?' Greta says.

Molly looks up to the sky as she ponders this. Turns back to Greta.

'I can't make it out,' Molly says. 'It sounds a bit like me. But me if I was a lot older.'

Greta nods.

'You think it's really the sky talkin' to me?' Molly asks.

'If you're hearin' it, then I guess it's talkin' to ya,' Greta says.

'I sometimes see things out bush that aren't really there,' Molly says, proudly now.

'How wonderful!' Greta says. 'Like what?'

'Like the other week we were way up Rapid Creek and I thought I saw Medusa.'

'Medusa?' Greta echoes. 'Like, scary Greek monster Medusa?'

'Like in Mum's bookshelf up there,' Molly says.

Greta knows the shelf. She's run her fingers along the spines of the dusty old black and brown and olive-green and blue hardbacks that Violet Hook bought mostly from the Collins Bookshop on Knuckey Street, using spare grocery money collected over many weeks. Greta's run her eyes over those titles and admired the woman's taste, wished she had more time to read as much as Violet must have read. Collections of poetry, mostly. Irish poets and English and American poets. *The Song of Brotherhood* by the Australian poet John Le Gay Brereton. She's fond of Victor Daley and his Sydney poems. She's opened his book *Wine and Roses*, and she's smiled at 'The Woman at the Washtub', pictured that poem as her own sad life summary and even her epitaph should her greatest fear come true: to live the rest of her days with Aubrey Hook, trapped forevermore inside the small hot kitchen of the small hot two-bedroom corrugated iron shell of a house he rents in Darwin town and on one sorry, inevitable day be buried in the hard dirt of this godforsaken cemetery.

HERE LIES GRETA MAZE
SHE WAS BORN FOR THE STAGE.
SHE DIED DOING THE DISHES.

'THE WOMAN AT THE WASHTUB, SHE WORKS TILL FALL OF NIGHT; WITH SOAP AND SUDS AND SODA HER HANDS ARE WRINKLED WHITE. HER DIAMONDS ARE THE SPARKLES THE COPPER-FIRE SUPPLIES; HER OPALS ARE THE BUBBLES THAT FROM THE SUDS ARISE . . .'

'Mum had a book on Greek mythology there,' Molly continues. 'And I'd been reading about Medusa and how she turned all them blokes to stone just because they looked at her, and then I'm walking through the mangroves of Rapid Creek and I swear I see Medusa standing in the middle of the scrub up ahead. And she's got all her snakes wriggling from her head and I shoot my head down straightaway because I don't want to be turned to stone but eventually I look up because I can't resist, you know . . .'

'Well, of course, you can't,' Greta says.

'And I look up at her and . . .' Molly says, excited by the telling.

'And did you turn to stone?' Greta asks.

Molly shakes her head, almost disappointed. 'No, because it wasn't Medusa. It was half a trunk from a dead ironwood tree with a shabby hawk's nest sticking out the top.'

Greta drags on her smoke, shakes her head. 'And here I was thinking it was gonna be a Greek monster out in that Darwin scrub.'

Molly shrugs, moves quickly on because she can move quickly on from anything. Beltings. Burns. Bereavement. Burials. Blood.

'What's the spot on the lady's hands?' Molly asks.

'It's blood,' Greta says. 'But it's not really blood. It's guilt. Her and her feller, Macbeth, have done terrible things to get where they've got to, and they're cursed by the past.'

'Cursed?' Molly echoes.

'Yeah, cursed, kid,' Greta says. 'The stains of the past. Ol' Lady Macbeth, she can't wash those stains away.'

Greta drags on her smoke, exhales. 'You ever had any stains you couldn't wash away, Molly?'

'Just cut the neck off a brown snake in the laundry,' she says. 'A bit of blood got on the concrete, but I'll just wash that away with some water, maybe some metho if it don't come out.'

Greta smiles. 'Guess Lady Macbeth could have used a splash of methylated spirits.'

Another drag on her cigarette. Greta studying her script.

'How do you cry like that?' Molly asks.

'What do you mean?'

'How does an actress just cry any time she wants to?'

'That doesn't just happen any time I want it to happen,' Greta says. 'I've got to build up to it. I've got to earn it. I've got to bleed for it, Molly Hook.' Greta points a finger to her temple. 'I'm saying those lines up here,' she says. Then she places a hand on her chest. 'But I'm feeling those lines in here, and all the time I'm feeling those lines I'm also feeling things I've felt before in my life. That's what you gotta do to be true, Molly. You gotta go down deep inside your heart and soul and you gotta find that dark and scary and fragile place you've been to before. You know what I mean. We all have a place like that.'

Molly smiles. 'I wish I could do what you can do.'

Greta shifts the way she's sitting, slides her backside along the tray, leans over the tray edge, taking another puff on her smoke.

'Close your eyes,' she says.

Molly closes her eyes.

'Now keep those peepers shut and go to *your* place, Molly,' Greta says.

'What if I don't like my place?' Molly askes. 'Why would anyone want to go to the place that makes them sad?'

'Because sadness is the truest emotion,' Greta says. 'Happiness isn't to be trusted. It's a bald-faced liar. But the truth of your sadness enriches every other thing inside you, especially your joy. You shouldn't be afraid to go to the place that makes you sad, Molly Hook. The more you go to that dark place inside you, the lighter it gets. You go there enough times, you realise that dark place is actually your sacred place. That place is all of you and the tears you take from that place are just the darkness leaking out, precious drop by precious drop. You following me?'

'No,' Molly says.

'Keep your eyes closed for sixty seconds,' Greta says.

Molly closes her eyes.

'You're standing in darkness,' Greta says.

Ten seconds.

'You don't realise it but you're actually standing inside a large stone cave in total darkness.'

Twenty seconds. Greta studies the girl's face. So trusting. So ready for the experience. So ready to embrace the unknown. She sees parts of herself at twelve. She can't help but smile at the girl because she knows her past and she worries about her future, but the poor little gravedigger girl, mad as a box of frogs, seems to worry about nothing.

'Then you see a line of fire draw a door on a wall of that cave,' Greta says. 'Up, across, down again and back across.'

Thirty seconds.

'Then a circle of fire that is a door knob, and you can touch this fire because it's cool and your hand reaches out to that door knob and you turn that door knob and that door opens outwards and you walk into your sacred place and you see it so close and real that you could reach out and touch the memory of it.'

And then in her mind in this strange and long minute, Molly Hook stands in the dark before an open door and she knows that door is the one to her bedroom just up there in the cemetery house. She hears something beyond the open bedroom door. A thumping sound.

Forty seconds. 'Do you see it, Molly?' Greta asks from the truck tray. 'Do you feel it?'

Molly's eyes still closed. *Thump, thump*. Something banging against a wall in the bedroom down the hall. Mum and Dad's bedroom. Violet and Horace's bedroom. Molly rubs her eyes and walks slowly down the hall, her open palms brushing against the hallway walls. Walking blind but following the sound of the thumping. *Thump, thump*. And she hears something else now. It's the sound of something animal. The sound of the wolf.

Small steps along the hallway and she sees a light to her right and turns to look into the kitchen off the hall. An empty table and a half-drunk bottle of whisky. *Thump, thump*. In front of her is the closed bedroom door at the end of the hall and she reaches her hand out to the door knob and she realises the door isn't fully closed and she can push it open with the gentlest tap of her left hand. And what she sees in that bedroom is a full moon through the bedroom window and the silver light of that floating night sky orb falling on the face of her mother, Violet Hook, lying on her back in her bed, her night-clothes torn from her shoulders. The high, dark brown wooden bedhead banging against the wall. *Thump, thump. Thump, thump*. And there is something animal atop Molly's mother. A thing cloaked in shadow. Crawling and turning like a wolf. And in the moonlight she can see only the creature's hairy arms and claws, its long fingers digging into her mother's ribs. And the moonlit face of Violet Hook turns from the window to the bedroom door and it finds Molly Hook because that face has always found Molly Hook, and Violet Hook begins to weep silently in the moonlight but the weeping doesn't stop the bedhead from banging the wall and the weeping doesn't stop the animal from crawling across her.

Then a voice from the kitchen. And that voice makes no sense to her. '*Molly!*' And the girl turns back to the kitchen light to find her father, Horace, sitting at the kitchen table, his right hand gripping the whisky bottle. Then Molly can't help but turn back towards the moonlight in the bedroom to find the face of the animal that's now raised its head from the shadow. The face of the wolf.

Another five seconds.

'Now open your eyes,' Greta says.

Molly opens her eyes.

'What did you see when you opened the door?' Greta asks.

'Nothing,' Molly says. 'I only saw black.'

'Nothing?' Greta asks, resting her back once more on the tray's rear wall. 'You don't have a single memory that makes you feel sad?'

Molly shakes her head. 'I don't think I can feel sad. I don't think I'm even able to cry.'

'That's ridiculous,' Greta says. 'All kids cry. I cried enough tears as a kid to fill Sydney Harbour.'

'I haven't cried since I was seven,' Molly says.

Greta's face goes blank. She knows what happened to the girl at seven.

'I try sometimes,' Molly says. 'I stare into a mirror and I

think of everything that ever happened to me that should make me cry, but those things never make me cry.'

'What do they make you feel?'

'They make me feel like running.'

Greta studies the girl's face, fascinated. She shakes her head at Molly. 'Well, I guess you're lucky, kid,' she says, returning her eyes to her script. 'Every bastard out there wants to make us girls cry. No such pleasure from our young Molly Hook!'

'My heart is turning . . .' Molly says, softly.

Greta doesn't hear. 'What's that?' she asks.

'Nuthin',' Molly says. She pauses for a moment. 'Greta?'

'Yeah, kid.'

'What do you see when you open the door?'

Greta turns her face to Molly. Weighs up her company, smiles. She comes close to saying something true. She comes close to saying that there is a white room beyond her open door. She comes close to saying that there is a newborn baby girl in that room and that girl is in her arms. But then she closes the door, slams it shut in her mind.

'Naah, sorry hon',' she says. 'Can't give away all my acting secrets.' She looks at the sun. Looks at the sky. Shift the gaze, change the subject. 'Those boys nearly done?' she asks.

'Almost.'

'They make me sick,' Greta says.

'It's not them.'

'It's not?'

'No,' Molly says. 'It's the curse.'

'Oh, of course, I forgot,' Greta says. 'The great curse of Longcoat Bob's lost gold! You still gettin' worked up by all that bush hocus-pocus, Molly Hook?'

'Don't you wonder about all the bad things that have happened to my family?' Molly asks.

'Hate to break it to you, Molly, but bad things sometimes happen around bad people. That's a fact of life. Got nuthin' to do with blackfeller magic.'

'You think I'm a bad person?'

'No, Mol',' Greta says. 'You're not bad. You're not bad at all.'

Greta lies back on the tray now and raises her knees, as though sunbaking. 'That gold wasn't cursed, kid,' she says. 'If I knew where that gold was today I'd be grabbing your mate Bert there and I'd be diggin' for my fortune, safe in the knowledge there are no kinds of magic in this world, black or otherwise. There's only people, Molly. There are good ones and there are bad ones and then there's all of us nuts stuck in the middle.'

Greta's eyes study the script she holds up now to block the full sun from her face. She hasn't noticed, but Molly has, that her summer dress has fallen between her legs, and bruising – scarlet and violet and blue bruising – can be seen on her inner thighs. Finger-shaped bruises. Stains on the skin that won't wash out.

'Do you love Uncle Aubrey?' Molly asks.

Greta takes another shot from the flask, winces on the burn of the spirits.

'Yeah, I love him,' she says. 'But I hate him, too.'

'He's a bad one,' Molly says, matter-of-factly.

Greta pockets the flask. Looks at Molly's face, expressionless.

With the toe of her right boot, Molly traces a circle, a moon, in the gravel driveway beneath her. 'How do you love someone and hate them at the same time?' she asks.

'You'll understand when you find a man of your own.'

'What if I already have found a man of my own?'

Greta turns to Molly, beams a smile. 'Good for you, grave-digger girl! He handsome this boy?'

'Very much so,' Molly says, certain of it. 'He looks like Tyrone Power, except if only Tyrone Power was a blackfeller from out past Mataranka.'

'And what might this boy's name be?'

'His name's Sam, and he's not a boy, he's a man. He's sixteen and he's got a job shooting buffalo with Johnston Traders. He makes good money.'

'Then why are you still here in this shithole cemetery? Why don't you run away with Sam the sixteen-year-old man who makes good money?'

'Dad would never let me leave.'

'Who said you have to ask for his permission?'

Molly's never thought of it that way. Maybe she could just leave. She turns to the front gate of the cemetery house. It's open. It's only thirty or so yards to the front gate. Maybe five more miles into town. Maybe three thousand more miles to Brisbane, Queensland. Maybe ten thousand more miles to Hollywood, California.

Molly grips the side of the tray, swings her body back and forth, bending her knees as she does.

'Why are *you* still here?' Molly asks.

'Huh,' Greta says.

'You should be on stage in London,' Molly says. 'You should be starring in films in Hollywood. Then I could see your name in lights at the Star. "Humphrey Bogart, Vivien Leigh, and introducing . . . the toast of Darwin, Australia . . . Greta Maze".'

Greta smiles. Full lips; a top lip that curls when it feels like it. She likes the thought of those lights. 'Can't,' she says. 'Got too much on my plate, right here.'

Molly's still looking at Greta's thighs, but not just the bruising now. It's the shape of her legs, her femininity, the silver screen in them.

'Greta?'

'Yeah, kid?'

'Is it true that Maze isn't your real last name?'

'It's true.'

'What's your real name?'

'Baumgarten. Greta Waltraud Baumgarten.'

'Why'd you change your name?'

'Nobody wants to see a Kraut name like that up in lights beside "John Wayne".'

'I like Maze,' Molly says.

Greta smiles.

'It makes you seem mysterious, like it's hard to work you out. There are twists and turns all through you.'

Greta nods. 'You can find your way into Greta Maze, but you may never find your way back out,' she says.

Molly smiles. She pictures Greta in silver screen black and white. That perfect face in black and white, emerging from a cloud of Humphrey Bogart's cigarette smoke. Bogie and Baumgarten. Bogie and Maze. Those porcelain pins in black and white. The bruising wouldn't look so harsh in black and white. And the big film studios have make-up artists to cover up that sort of thing. Dottie Drake from the Fannie Bay hair salon told Molly all about the make-up artists in Hollywood, how they could cover up anything, from the bags under Joan Crawford's eyes to Errol Flynn's split lip.

'Do you think I could ever change my name?' Molly asks.

'Of course you could. Anyone can. What's your new name gonna be?'

Molly thinks for a long moment, tilts her head upwards.

'Sky,' she says.

Greta looks up, too.

'I like that,' Greta says. 'You could jazz up that first name, though' – she thinks for a moment – 'give it a splash of Dietrich,' she says.

Molly beams. Gasps the name, whispers it like it's sacred: 'Marlene Sky.'

Greta nods, eyes still up in the sky. 'Well, would you look at that!' she says.

'What?' asks Molly.

'Up there. It's your name up in lights.'

Molly laughs. And they both stare into the sky for a moment, the sky that's so far away from their dark caves and their silly fire-traced doors leading to dark places. Molly looks again at Greta's bruises.

'Greta?' Molly begins.

'Yeah, kid.'

'I heard my dad talking about you to his limestone supplier,' Molly says.

Greta turns to Molly, follows her eyes to the leg bruising. She sits up self-consciously, pulls the dress back over her knees.

'And what did your father say about me?'

'He said you take your clothes off for money in the Edinburgh Arms pub.'

Greta sucks on another cigarette, pulls her sunglasses down over her nose. 'Did anyone ever tell you that you talk too much, Molly Hook?'

'Yeah, everyone,' Molly says.

'I trust your father then told that shocked limestone salesman how those nights I take my clothes off might represent my finest role of all.'

'He didn't say anything about any role you were playing.'

'Of course it's a role I'm playing,' Greta says. 'I'm playing Greta Maze, a thirty-three-year-old actress with too much talent and not enough opportunity who stayed in the arse end of the earth because she thought she loved an older man.'

Greta closes the script, tucks it under her arm and swings her legs over the side of the truck tray, the rubber soles of her laced saddle shoes leaving imprints in the dirt driveway where she lands.

'And what role are you playing today, Molly?' Greta asks. 'Or are you still working on that twelve-year-old gravedigger girl who has convinced herself she's not being raised by monsters?'

Red Tin Thimble

Tapping metal typewriter keys echoing through a house of timber and tin and old wooden stumps. Peeled paint on the walls inside. A hole in the living room wall above a broken and dusty pneumatic pianola, where Molly once watched her Uncle Aubrey drive his younger brother's bloodied head during a mindless and lengthy drinking binge that ended with the brothers shooting nips of paint thinner.

'And have you thought about the inscription on the head-stone?' Molly Hook asks across an old wooden table, her busy twelve-year-old fingers already wiggling above the keys, 'R', 'I' and 'P'.

Mouldy air and sunlight pushing through a faded curtain in the living room where the business is conducted. The Hook family business of burying the dead.

When Horace Hook's in a light mood, Molly sometimes suggests to her father that this cemetery keeper's house feels like a kind of tomb in itself, as dark and dead as the 894 (and always counting) tombs that surround it. She suggests more windows. She suggests more cleaning. She suggests more food to eat. Fewer maggots in the sink. Fewer bloodstains on the kitchen walls. Fewer unwashed forks and dinner plates caked in old gravy. Fewer weevils in the oats in the pantry. Fewer silverfish crawling through Emily Dickinson and William Butler Yeats and Walt Whitman on Violet's bookshelf by the front door. Fewer empty whisky bottles filling the space beneath the kitchen sink. Fewer strips of flypaper hanging from the ceiling, turned black with the stuck dead wings, heads and legs of house flies.

In the two chairs across from Molly's typewriter sit two grieving customers, sixty-eight-year-old Mildred Holland and her twenty-seven-year-old son, Clem Holland. Mildred wears a black cardigan and tightly grips a purse with both hands on her thighs. Her wide-eyed and round-faced son wears white overalls covered in flour. He's come straight from work, the same bakery on Herbert Street where his father, Lloyd Holland, died instantly of heart failure at dawn four days ago. Clem found his father lying amid twelve freshly baked loaves of bread that were sold for half price that same afternoon.

Mildred places her reading glasses on her nose, pulls a rolled piece of paper from her purse, unrolls it and reads from it. 'We wish to have the following words written on the gravestone,' she says. She studies the paper and reads the words out slowly. '"Rest . . . in . . . peace . . . Lloyd".'

Molly taps these words out on the typewriter. 'Good, and what should we write next?' she then asks.

Mildred is puzzled. 'That's all we could think of to say,' she says.

Clem shrugs his shoulders. 'Pretty well says it all, don't ya think?'

Molly nods. 'Would you consider a couple more lines, perhaps, that say something more about the full life he enjoyed before he passed away?' Molly suggests.

'He didn't really enjoy much at all,' Clem says.

'Something about how he cherished his family and friends, perhaps, and how he was cherished in return?' Molly tries again.

Mildred looks at her son, grimly. Looks back at Molly.

'He was mean and sour most of the time,' Mildred says.

Clem turns to his mother. 'When I told people the news, everybody seemed to have the same look on their face.'

'What look was that?' asks Mildred.

'Relief,' Clem says.

'I see,' Molly nods, understandingly. 'If Lloyd had one belief, Mrs Holland, one value that he really lived by, what would you say it was?'

Mildred shrugs. 'He believed in bread,' she says. 'He believed there was something beautiful in creating something that tasted so good out of just, you know, flour and . . . you know . . .' Mildred looks to her son.

Clem nods knowingly. 'Water,' he adds. 'Just flour and water.'

'Flour and water,' Mildred repeats, nodding.

'I see,' Molly says.

Mildred looks around the house. She looks at the closed bedroom doors beyond the hall off the living room. 'Where did you say your father was, again?' Mildred asks.

'He's fallen ill,' Molly says.

Clem smiles. 'Got the brown-bottle flu, has he?'

Molly gives a half-smile. 'Mrs Holland, if you had any thoughts about anything that interested him, then I could perhaps help you craft something that might be a more fitting tribute to your late husband.'

Molly turns to Clem. 'Something his children's children might appreciate half a century from now.'

Molly looks back at Mildred. 'I know I'm only young, but

I've helped many people find the words that are just right for their departed loved one.'

'How old are you, anyway?' Mildred asks.

'I'm thirteen in a month.'

Mildred studies Molly's face, dismayed by the idea of having to think more deeply about her husband. She ponders. She looks at her son, pats a cloud of flour from his shoulder. She shakes her head. 'I guess the only thing that made him happy was a loaf of well-baked bread in the morning.'

Molly nods, swinging the typewriter's carriage-return lever over to start a new line of text. She looks out the only window in the living room, where a slice of blue sky fills half the frame.

'What about this?' she asks. And she speaks the words as she types them. 'Like . . . a . . . falling . . . sun,' she types, 'you . . . closed . . . your . . . eyes.'

Tap, tap, tap. Carriage-return lever. New line of text.

'Like . . . morning . . . bread . . . may . . . your . . . spirit . . . rise.'

Molly looks up at her customers. 'Rest in peace . . . Lloyd,' she says.

And Mildred turns to her son and Clem's eyebrows rise in approval. Mildred beams. 'Well, I quite like that,' she says. She thinks on it some more. '"Like morning bread". Yes, I think Lloyd would like that, too. Yes. Yes. Let's go with that, shall we?'

'Of course, I need to tell you, Mrs Holland,' Molly offers, 'two more lines of engraving on the stone will cost you an additional four shillings, but I find customers don't usually mind paying a little extra when it comes to honouring the departed.'

Mildred turns to her son, Clem. He shrugs, unsure.

'It's only two more lines,' Mildred says, loosening the grip on her purse.

*

A red tin thimble in the centre of the small wooden kitchen table where Molly and her father have breakfast. Horace sweats. He is thin. All limbs and burden. His hair is combed back hard and straight. He stinks of methylated spirits. Alcohol leeching from his armpits and his breath. Beads of sweat above his top lip.

Molly places a white enamel mug of black tea on the table. Her father picks it up with his right hand, which shakes when he lifts the mug to his lips.

'What day is it?' Horace asks.

'Thursday,' Molly says. 'You drank through Monday and Tuesday. Slept through Wednesday.'

'Did I leave you be?'

Molly nods.

'I stayed in my room and read,' she says.

Horace nods now, relieved.

'What are you reading?'

'*The Complete Works of William Shakespeare.*'

Horace nods.

'I think I want to be an actress, like Greta,' Molly says.

'I thought you were going to be a famous poet like Emily Dickens?'

'*Dickinson*, Dad,' Molly says. 'And I'm going to be a famous actress–poet named Marlene Sky.'

Horace nods again, not at all surprised by his daughter's announcement. 'You'll make more money diggin' graves,' he says. 'But I guess you won't get no standing ovation for hiding the dead.' He lifts and looks at his shaking left hand, turns it into a fist.

'What's that stuff you and Uncle Aubrey have been drinkin'?' Molly asks.

'Mind your own business.'

'You're becoming more and more like him, Dad,' Molly says.

'Like who?'

'Like Uncle Aubrey.'

Another shaky sip of tea.

'You look like a shadow,' Molly says. 'Uncle Aubrey is nothing but shadow. You're shadow, too, Dad, but you're light as well.'

Horace says nothing.

'When are you going to stand up to him?' Molly asks. 'He doesn't care about us, Dad. He doesn't care about Greta. He only cares for the gold. The only thing that makes him feel anything is the way that gold glows. I see it, Dad. He's gold sick. He's always been gold sick. He's always talkin' about my grandfather and how gold sick he got, but I reckon Aubrey's as sick right now as a man can be.'

Horace rubs his temples with his fingers, trying to ease the blows of the dropping hammer in his head.

'He thinks that glowing will chase away the shadow,' Molly says, her train of thought burning with new coal now. 'But it won't. It's already too dark.'

Horace rubs his forehead, closes his eyes. There's no telling where a memory will come from; no figuring where and when the sleeping librarian of Horace Hook's memory room is likely to wake with a start and dig into the dusty drawers of lived experience and produce a folder filled with a past-coloured story. Aubrey Hook and Horace Hook throwing rocks at each other's faces. Horace is twelve and his brother is thirteen.

They're pickaxing the face of a goldmine near Tom's Gully along Mount Bundey Creek, far south of Darwin. Their father, Arthur Hook, a seasoned gold prospector, has ridden on horseback to Pine Creek on a supply run. No information in the library on what started it all, only how it ended. Aubrey lands a rock the size of a tennis ball on Horace's right eye. Horace responds with a similar-sized rock that Aubrey does not duck or turn away from but willingly allows to land flush on his mouth, where it dislodges one of his two front teeth. Aubrey searches the dirt floor of the goldmine dugout and grips another rock the size of his metal water canister and throws it at his younger brother, who ducks swiftly out of the way of the deadly projectile. The thrown rock bounces against the chalky mine wall and falls beside Horace's work boots. He picks it up and snap-throws it back. Once more, Aubrey does not duck or turn away or guard his face with his hands. He stands proudly and lets the rock hit his face so hard that it breaks his nose. Blood runs across his chin and down his work shirt. And Aubrey Hook smiles. Red across his teeth. A mouth full of blood. Something in the smile makes Horace turn cold. Something across his brother's face other than blood and rock dust. It's satisfaction.

'Why do you need permission from Aubrey to let me go to the Star with Sam?' Molly asks.

'Be quiet now, Molly,' Horace says.

'I've been watching you both,' Molly says. 'There's something strange about you two. I think that moonshine is sending you both mad. I think you should stop drinkin' for a bit.'

Horace raises his eyebrows. 'Tom Berry's grandkid telling me about madness,' he says. 'I like that.'

'Maybe you've got the curse, too,' Molly says.

'Be quiet now, Molly.'

The girl is silent for a long moment. But then Molly breaks the silence. Molly always breaks the silence.

'I was thinking about Mum the other day,' she says, softly. Horace reacts to that word 'Mum'. He turns his head like he turns his head in pubs when anyone says the name 'Violet' or the word 'wife'.

'I was looking in the mirror of her duchesse,' Molly continues, 'and I was missing her so much. I felt so sad about it, but I couldn't cry. I tried so hard to let some tears out for her because sometimes I feel like maybe she's somewhere where she can see me but I can't see her and if she can see me then I want her to see that I'm crying for her and that way she'll know how much I miss her and how much I hate her for leaving us down here. But then I remembered Longcoat Bob and I knew what was happening.'

'What was happening?' Horace asks.

'The turning,' Molly says. 'The heart doesn't turn to stone right away. It takes time to take hold because the heart is warm and it keeps beating and it keeps fighting against all that cold stone. But, soon enough, it all turns and then you feel nuthin'. All you got inside is cold rock. Like Uncle Aubrey.'

Horace stares at his daughter and he realises how deeply she's lost in a trance of her own thinking. He worries for her. He cares for her. Molly looks at her father.

'And you're turning, too, Dad,' Molly says.

'That's enough now, Molly,' Horace says.

'I can tell, Dad. I can see it happening to you. Kin means husbands, Dad.'

'Let's just have some breakfast.'

'Kin means brothers, Dad. It means uncles and aunties and cousins, everything.'

And Horace slams his fist on the kitchen table.

'Keep goin', Molly,' he barks.

His eyes. That horrifying warning men like Horace give to children like Molly with their eyes, in kitchens like this one. Danger. Do anything but keep going.

So Molly picks up a cutting knife and runs it six times, both sides, along the black leather razor strop hanging from a nail by the gas stove. She cuts three neat slices from a warm slab of six-day-old corned beef and fries them beside two halves of a ripe tomato in a thick black square iron skillet on the stove top.

Horace sips the tea quietly, sits the mug down on the table. His fingers reach for the red tin thimble in the centre of the table. 'You see this thimble?' he asks.

Molly nods at it, turning the tomatoes on the pan.

'This thimble belonged to your mother,' Horace says. 'In the good years . . . when she was clear-headed, I mean, she would sit in the corner over there hand-sewing clothes for you. Pinafores and all that. And I'd be where you are right there. I'd fry up a feed of red emperor I'd caught on the rocks at Frances Bay, and I'd fry some potatoes up with it and we'd boil some muddies, too. And she was happy.'

Horace slips his forefinger into the thimble. Molly plates the corned beef and fried tomato, places the breakfast down for her father. He cuts into the beef, chews it along with the tomato that he's sprinkled with too much salt and pepper.

He rests back in his chair. 'The Japs are comin',' he says.

'Who's comin'?'

'The Japanese. Three hundred and fifty Jap aircraft just blew the arse out of Hawaii. They'll be comin' for us next. These idiots who run this town will take a while to wake up and smell the fiery death fleet heading our way, but you can take it from me, Mol', the war's comin' to Darwin.'

He sips his tea.

'I reckon there's some high-up Jap right now stickin' a big fat red sun marker over Darwin on his map.'

'Why would they wanna come all the way here?'

'They're rat-fucking the Yanks and we're helpin' the Yanks. You've seen all them navy boats in Darwin Harbour. We've got giant fuel tanks fillin' Allied ships. We've got oil tanks and army bases and aerodromes, and all we got protectin' 'em is a few big guns and a couple of barefoot kids with slingshots. Why wouldn't they come to Darwin?'

'So when do we leave?' Molly asks.

Horace places his cup down again on the table. 'We're not going anywhere,' he replies. 'Our ship is about to come in, Molly. War is a goldmine for the gravedigger. Those Japs are comin' and anyone stupid enough to stick around to greet them will be dead within a day.'

'Including us,' Molly says.

'We're not in the firing line. They'll go for the town and the port, mostly. And when the dust settles the Federal War Cabinet will be more than grateful to pay up handsomely to anyone who can give all them sorry bodies a proper burial.'

Horace gets up from the table, ambles into the living room. He returns with a large wooden box filled with bottles of disinfectant and sugar soap and scrubbing brushes. He places the box in the centre of the kitchen.

It's the curse, Molly tells herself. It's the curse that's made him hard. Kin means fathers. Kin means husbands, too. Longcoat Bob turned his good heart to stone.

'I need this place cleaned,' Horace says. 'I need you to dust, wash and disinfect every last corner, every last crack in this godforsaken shithole.'

Horace picks up the red tin thimble, holds it up to Molly.

'I'm goin' in to town and I won't be home until tonight,' he says. 'Before I leave, I'll be hiding this thimble somewhere in the house. To find it, you will need to inspect and clean every nook and cranny. If you have not found the thimble by the time I return, I will know you have not cleaned the house properly and you will be punished. Do you understand?'

Molly nods. It's the curse, she tells herself again. The curse of Longcoat Bob.

'Say it,' he says.

'I understand,' Molly says.

'You understand who?' her father asks, placing the red tin thimble in the pocket of his pants.

'I understand you, Dad.'

And her mind rattles with two words. The turning. The turning. The turning.

*

Cupboard doors opening. Cupboard doors slamming shut. Wipe, scrape, rub, dust. Breathless gravedigger girl on her hands and knees with an old toothbrush scrubbing bloodstains off the hallway floor. 'Out damned spot,' says Lady Macbeth in her mind. 'Out! Out, I say.' But some spots can't be removed.

The girl spreading wax on the floor and rubbing and polishing the old wood. Her kneecaps get so red and sore she ties her father's thick winter socks around her knees to cushion them. She pulls a heavy bucket of water and disinfectant across the living room floor. A cotton mop and a wringer.

It must be here. It must be here. She runs a rag across the dust that blankets the skirting boards of every wall. Breathe. She pulls a wooden step behind her through the house so that she can reach her wire-bone arms up to run the rag across the endless crowning moulds atop every internal wall. Breathe, Molly Hook. Every wardrobe drawer. Every corner of every duchesse, every sideboard, every broom closet. Please be here.

Floors scrubbed, curtains washed. Dig, Molly, dig. It must be here somewhere. Lye dropped down the pipes in the kitchen sink. The kitchen sink and the bathroom washtub scrubbed with a wire brush and scouring powder. She drags three large house rugs down the back staircase and uses the wooden step to help her hang the rugs on the backyard clothesline. She beats the rugs with the rear blade face of Bert the shovel, coughs hard when she swallows decades-old dust. For five straight hours she works. She works through lunch with no break and no food; there isn't even time to stop for a cup of water. She must find the thimble because she feels the curse.

Knobs turning, doors opening, cupboards slamming shut, and now she's opening cupboard doors she's opened thrice before, and now she's dizzy and so tired and she can't keep a single straight thought inside her busy mind. Drawers pulled open frantically and frantically pushed shut. Red tin thimble. Red tin thimble. So small. Nothing to it, really. Just an object that once belonged to her mother, Violet. It means nothing to her and everything to her.

She searches and searches through the sprawling house. Inside cracks and under mats, hands reaching beneath crockery cabinets and finding only the bodies of living and dead spiders. So many cockroaches crawling and so much cockroach shit to pick up in her hands. But she finds no red tin thimble.

The gravedigger girl's heart pounding because she can never seem to find exactly what she's looking for and the curse of Longcoat Bob blows in from the graveyard to mix with the smell of ammonia and bleach and she wonders if it's the ammonia in the bathroom or the methylated spirits in the kitchen or the missing red tin thimble that is making her feel light headed. Her father will come home, he *will* come home, because fathers always come home, sure as the Darwin sun rises each day like the bread in the late Lloyd Holland's bakery. He will come home and she will not have found the thimble and she will be punished and he will not even know the effort she put into finding her mother's red tin thimble. He will not know because he won't be able to see the truth beyond the dark veil of Longcoat Bob's curse that she can feel is so close to her now, and so close to her father because of her, so close it hurts. Her Uncle Aubrey will be with her father when he comes home and they will both be liquored and Uncle Aubrey will be worse than her father because he is all shadow, and he will take on the punishing like he always does because it satisfies him.

She scurries from the bedrooms to the kitchen to the bathroom to the living room to the bedrooms to the kitchen to the bathroom and she spins around on the spot, wondering where her father could have possibly placed that red tin thimble and she finds the locked door to Horace Hook's bedroom where he keeps the buried and unburied treasures of Hollow Wood's ever-trusting dead. And her heart is beating so fast with all the thinking and the work and exhaustion that she can't catch her breath, and she tries to suck more air into her lungs but nothing goes in and she remembers water and she scrambles to the kitchen but then she sees flashes of yellow and purple in her mind's eye and she can't focus on anything and her hands are so cold and the blood seems to rush out of her body and drain like lye into the cracks in the polished wooden floorboards beneath her bare feet and she closes her eyes and sees only a black room and this feels safe so she stops breathing and falls with a thud to the floor of the kitchen of the caretaker's quarters in ruined Hollow Wood Cemetery, where the only people close enough to hear a single sound from Molly Hook, aged twelve years and eleven months, are buried in dirt. And the last thing she sees in the black room of her mind is an audience rising to its feet to give a soaring standing ovation for the gravedigger girl as the side of her skull hits the theatre stage.

'Bravo, Molly!' they scream. 'Bravo!'

*

Seen from the blue sky above and looking down and looking closer in and closer in, she is a brown-haired girl standing in pants made for boys before a dress-shop window on Cavenagh Street, central Darwin. If someone told Molly Hook she had dreamed herself here in this moment, she would believe it because Darwin is a dream at sunset in summer and the dress in the window is the kind of dress Molly wears in her dreams. A teenager's dress and a going-out dress that Molly could wear to a dance or a school graduation or to a Hollywood film premiere on the arm of Gary Cooper, if only she wasn't so busy digging graves in Darwin, Australia. A light blue satin dress the colour of the Darwin sky in summer, resting on the Ward's Boutique shop window mannequin, whose expression-less face says nothing of how wonderful it must be to wear something so beautiful.

It's not long till her birthday. She will soon be able to say she is in her teens. She will soon be old enough to attend the winter dance in Darwin's town hall. She could wear this blue dress to the dance. Perhaps her father will buy it for her, for her birthday. She won't ask how he got the money; she won't ask if it was bought with the gold her uncle bit free from Lisbeth Fleming's dead ring finger. She will wake up on the morning of her birthday and she will open the dress box her father has wrapped for her and she will whisper, 'It's beautiful, Dad.' And he will ask her to try the dress on and she will spin before him and he will smile and she will run into his arms and he will say he's sorry he can't always be like this. And when they embrace, his face won't be unshaven and bristly, he won't smell of spirit and week-old sweat. There will be only colour. Sky blue.

Molly's made her pilgrimage to this untouchable dress twice a week for the past four weeks, but, no matter how many times she wills a different outcome, her pockets are empty when she gets there, and she always turns away empty handed.

She walks barefoot. She dreams and Darwin dreams with her. It refuses to wake up, so the strange daily film-reel dream of the town on the geographical top of Australia during World War II unspools in all its scenes that make no sense. Darwin, which was not made by God but by a theory of evolution. Made by the earth spinning and by 5800 people who lost their footing, slid southwards and northwards on the rocking floors of ships with no anchors, and found the wreckage and flotsam of their lives washed ashore at Port Darwin. Greek and Italian storeowners, Chinese market sellers, Japanese divers, Filipino fishermen, German miners, Afghan cameleers, Thai whores, Malay traders, Javanese labourers, New Guinea labourers, South Sea island labourers press-ganged onto boats and forced to work inside the Darwin dream. A dream that starts in the Timor Sea on a sheet of turquoise coastal water so clear you feel you could dance on its hard glass. A girl like Molly Hook could make slippers out of that sea glass and she could wear them to a Country Women's Association ball with a sky-blue satin shop-window dress.

Those mangroves on the shore would be no place to dance.

The mangroves belong to the bodies of root-wedged dead gangsters and the crocodiles who feast on their sins. But inside that mangrove fringe is a place where humans come to re-invent themselves. A place to change your dream, to change your name, to change your ending. Baumgarten to Maze. Molly to Marlene. Nobody knows anything and everybody keeps it that way. Don't trouble the man in the black hat three stools down along the bloodstained bar of the National Hotel; he's the devil on a day off.

The Darwin sunset is gold then red then purple then black. The town is corrugated-iron fortress homes that fall with a sneeze. Dirt for roads and dirt for air. Cyclone-ravaged for a century. Architectural impermanence. Darwin dreams in sungolds and earth-browns. It dreams in violent rain and wind. 'Nungalinya,' Sam Greenway once told Molly Hook. That's the Dreamtime ancestor in charge of the cyclones and storms that tear the tin skin off town pubs and stores with a single whistle from His lips. Sam said Nungalinya is angry at all the white settlers who keep landing in Port Darwin, keep skipping ashore with their pickaxes and shovels to chip away at Ol' Man Rock. Nungalinya, Sam said, lifts fishing boats from the sea, sucks them into the air and bats them a hundred yards through the wind against shore rocks that smash metal hulls the same way all those white settlers smash the shells of fat-clawed East Point mud crabs.

The Darwin dream has a smell and it smells like the maggots eating all those discarded crab claws. It smells like all the cut ends of vegetables left to rot in Chinatown bins that dingoes and lost dogs tip over after dark. Darwin dreams in drink and sweat. Warm beer and toil. Fat-bellied fist fighters and men who piss in buckets beneath their bar stools. Empty car bodies left abandoned in the streets outside town by empty men who shot themselves dead inside them. It's frontier territory where nothing stays nailed down. America's Wild West all the way down here in Australia's wild north. Some came by boat and some just emerged from the dust; they crawled out of the dirt and dusted off their shoulders and staggered into the Victoria Hotel on Smith Street for three shots of black rum then a glass of water. Darwin dreams in dinner dances and wood-chopping contests and travelling freak show tents where Sydney wolf boys and Melbourne pig girls reel in horror at the ticket-buying Darwin locals staring at them through the glass.

Van Diemen Gulf and Snake Bay to the north. South Alligator River to the east, the Rum Jungle to the south. And beyond it all, the vast ancient wetlands and wilderness of Molly Hook's wild dreams, the prehistoric stone and vine country. The deep country. Suffocating monsoon forests and tidal flats and jagged plateaus and rock formations that tower over the city buildings of the London and New York and Paris in Molly's head.

Giant tree rats just on the outskirts of town. Killer snakes beneath your bed. Killer spiders crawling up your trouser legs. Here are Japanese pearling crews tying down rickety luggers in Darwin Harbour. Here are Christian missionaries instructing Aboriginal servants, whose families once sang on the land where they now dust down church pews. Drunk and wealthy cattlemen and their mistresses skinny-dipping in the volumin-ous water tanks of the abandoned Vestey's meatworks at Bullocky Point. Sunburnt stockmen clocked off and rolling dice in a Mitchell Street gambling hall. There are hardly any cars on the street: most everybody walks or rides bicycles in the Darwin dream.

A fat and drunk man sleeps on the toilet seat of a hot tin earth closet on a corner of Knuckey Street. Molly blocks her nostrils with her forefinger and thumb as she passes. The man's 'long drop' waste will sit for days before being mercifully burned. There's the state school bus that's been parked on Peel Street for the past month, a rusting semitrailer with a long rear tray. On the days when her father bothers to send her to school, Molly and her mates sit beneath a mesh cage, their arse bones bouncing hard on the metal tray at every pothole on the road to Darwin Primary.

Molly ambles barefoot into Chinatown. Half a century ago, the Chinese outnumbered the Europeans here four to one. Horace Hook told his daughter once that the Orientals – the 'Celestials' – called Australia 'The New Gold Mountain', while California was the 'The Old Gold Mountain'. Then the new gold finds got old, too, and half the Chinese left. The other half stayed to keep breaking their backs for five shillings a day building the railway line from Port Darwin to the goldfields of Pine Creek. 'Then when the railway line was finished,' Horace said, 'when there was no more hard labour to be done by the Chinese, the government told 'em they best not lob in here no more.' Horace considered that for a moment. 'Nice bastards, eh.'

Molly nods to an old Chinese woman selling green mangoes from a table at the side of the wide yellow dirt road of Cavenagh Street. She passes a Chinese tailor, a Chinese fruit market, a stonemason's workshop. Four Chinese fishermen walk along-side a thin and hungry brown horse pulling a cart filled with a day's haul of trap-caught fish off Fannie Bay. Another old woman in front of a vegetable market stirs a pot of seafood soup. A Chinese boy by her side wears a white long-sleeved shirt and white pants. His hair is tied by a band in the centre of his scalp and it sprouts from his head the way a bunch of celery rises from dirt. His top button is done up so tight his neck fat spills over his collar. He blows on a red paper wind-mill spinning on the end of a bamboo stick.

Corrugated-iron sheds of blue-grey and rust and Chinese characters on the subtlest signage lining entryways to stores and workshops. Families of fourteen share ramshackle two-storey dwellings made of scavenged materials – old car bonnets and flattened and nailed kerosene tins turned into walls – while the wealthy whites who frequent these markets and stalls live in raised houses where they sip gin on wide, latticed verandas and the air blows against wet kerchiefs around their necks.

Molly sees old Chinese men with hollowed cheeks and white chin hairs finger-shaped so that their beards look like white flames when they blow in the Darwin breeze. One, who has only a bottom row of teeth, rests his backside on a wash bucket as he nails a heel back on to his right black slipper, a smoking pipe gripped in his left fist.

Molly stops briefly outside her favourite store, Fang Cheong Loong's rambling giftware and clothing shop filled with Chinese dolls and red and blue and green cheongsams and camphor-wood boxes carved with the outlines of dragons and emperors and Chinese princesses. She walks past the Crown Bakery and Suns Inc. Tailors to the two-storey, white-walled bloodhouse of Gordon's Don Hotel. She creeps up to the sprawling pub's swinging entry doors and sneaks a look inside, eyes drawn straight to the bar just as two stockmen in shorts fall down arm in arm singing a song about Ireland. They roll into the stool-bound legs of Horace and Aubrey Hook, and it's Molly's uncle who kicks the Irish beer swillers away with a push of his right boot while keeping a firm grip on a foggy glass of brown spirit. Horace Hook, as if by instinct, turns his slow-moving neck and his bloodshot eyes to the swinging entry doors. He's all shadow and he's too dark and drunk to know if it's his only daughter standing beyond those swinging doors or if, in fact, it's the ghost of Lisbeth Fleming and she's come to collect what rightfully belongs to her – Horace Hook's grey-coloured heart and the pitch-black soul of his older brother, Aubrey.

Molly rushes backwards from the swinging doors into bustling Cavenagh Street, bumping into a young Chinese woman carrying a tray of purple plums that nearly spill. 'Sorry,' Molly says. And she runs now because night is here and she needs to go home. She needs to find the red tin thimble. It has to be there. It has to be there. And the few street lights of Cavenagh Street flash on, and Molly runs past A.E. Jolly's store and Cashman's Newsagency and the Bank of New South Wales and the town post office where not a single letter has ever arrived with the name 'Molly Hook' on its envelope. Run, Molly, run. Dig, Molly, dig. Heart pounding. Dirt roads beneath her feet. Speed. Motion. Destiny. But, wait, there's a face she knows on her left. Stop right here on the spot because it's him, it's Tyrone Power in the flesh, by way of Mataranka, south of Katherine, right here on Smith Street, Darwin.

Sam Greenway stands on the footpath beneath the awning of the Star Theatre. He wears a red long-sleeved stockman's shirt and dirt-covered brown pants, and his black broad-brimmed riding hat sits back on his scalp so that his full black mop of hair glows beneath the throbbing awning ceiling bulbs. He's laughing hard and his big wide smile is as bright as the lights that border the partly open-air cinema's roof lining and climb like a string of pearls to a shining ornamental night star rising over Darwin. The same kind of star that drew wise men from the east to Jerusalem, Molly thinks, is now drawing her and Sam Greenway to the silver screen worlds of Ginger Rogers and Fred Astaire and God's other sacred child, Shirley Temple.

The Star's playing 'Darryl F. Zanuck's *Jesse James*' tonight and that title is stretched breathtakingly across the theatre's marquee wall in pistol-shot Wild West lettering. Molly is about to call out to Sam, but she bites her tongue in the darkness of the street because she realises Sam is in the company of two teenaged girls, Aboriginal girls with pretty smiles and long legs, older than Molly, so old that Molly can see how their breasts are filling out their Sunday school dresses. Other Aboriginal families file out of the theatre around them; there are no white families at the pictures tonight.

Of course, those girls see in Sam what Molly sees. They see his spark, his light, his Hollywood charm and they stare at it wide-eyed and dumbfounded, slack-jawed and spellbound by a brief and impromptu cowboy show Sam is giving right there on the footpath.

He fixes his cowboy hat and snarls in the face of an imaginary Wild West lawman. 'Well, Marshall,' he says in his thickest Missouri accent. 'I'm just about done here listenin' to ya rabbit on about my indiscretions and I'm gonna guess your hand don't move half as quick as your mouth.' Sam's right-hand fingers dance above a curved, oversized red and green apple-flavoured candy cane hooked like a pistol over his brown leather work belt. Then his hand moves so fast that Molly sees nothing whatsoever between the candy cane vanishing from Sam's belt and it reappearing, raised in his right hand and firing three shots that explode from his film sound effects lips as his left palm speedcocks an invisible pistol hammer.

When the deed is done and the imaginary lawman lies bleeding in the dirt, Sam triumphantly blows smoke from the candy cane pistol shaft. In a flurry of movement worthy of a circus act, he spins the pistol vertically on his right forefinger, then shifts it into a horizontal spin that lasts a full minute, and those young women he came to the pictures with are so mesmerised by his cowboy skills they can only giggle because their bodies are too frozen by awe to clap their hands. Then, as fast as the pistol was drawn, it is holstered tightly and securely back in Sam's belt. Only now do the girls clap.

Sam tips his hat to his audience with a wink. 'And what brings you fine ladies to a no-good, blood-suckin' town like—' His words are cut short by an imaginary bullet in his back that sends him staggering forward into the arms of his audience. 'It's that feller Bob Ford,' he coughs, imaginary blood spilling from his cowboy lips. 'He done shot me in the back.' Sam falls grandly to the ground, the last beats of a short and tragic cowboy life pulsing out of his shoulders. 'Please . . . ma'am . . .' he whispers up to the taller of the two young women, 'would you grant this sorry outlaw one last kiss before he rides off into hell?' And Molly sees from the darkness of the road that the cowboy's dying wish is granted: the tallest girl kneels over Sam and gently places a kiss upon his lips, a kiss that seems to Molly to last as long as most of the features that show on the Star's big white picture screen. And of course Molly is not the girl to grant that kiss because Molly never dug enough graves to buy the blue satin dress to wear to the pictures and Molly could never look so tall and so beautiful as that lucky, full-busted girl in her Sunday best because Molly's always six feet deep in dirt and dead folks.

Sam closes his eyes for the cowboy's last sleep. The older girls howl with laughter and Molly treads lightly to the scene and stands over her friend Sam, feeling, for the first time in her life, every heavy ounce of the inherited heart that's slowly turning to stone inside her chest.

'Hi, Sam,' she says, softly.

Sam opens his eyes. He beams wide.

'Hi, Mol'!' he hollers. He springs to his feet. 'I didn't know you were comin' out tonight.' He looks her up and down. 'You're gonna need shoes on if you want to catch the next picture. All the whites are coming back for Bogie in *High Sierra*. We just seen *Jesse James*. You woulda loved it. They had that Tyrone feller you like playin' Jesse.'

'Tyrone Power,' Molly says, flatly.

Sam looks her up and down again, deeper this time. 'You all right, Mol'?'

The tall girl wants to go. 'Ya comin', Sam?' she asks. 'We're all swimmin' under the stars at Vesteys.'

Sam smiles. 'I'll catch up later,' he says. 'I wanna stick with me little outlaw mate 'ere for a bit.'

The older girls turn, stroll away along Smith Street.

'I'm not so little,' Molly says, her eyes turned away.

Sam chuckles, nods his head. 'Yeah, I know, Mol'. You're bigger than Bogart in my book!'

He pats her shoulder. 'Wait 'ere for a second,' he says, excited. 'I wanna introduce you to a friend of mine.'

He disappears down a lane off Smith Street. Molly sits in the gutter, rests her elbows on her knees. Horse hooves clop along the dirt road of Smith Street, and Sam moves into the light, bouncing gently on a saddle tied to a handsome dark chestnut horse with white markings on its lower legs like it's wearing long socks.

'This is Danny,' Sam says, a hand rubbing the horse's crest. 'He's a hot-blood colt, Mol'. Real fast. Fit as a bull. Danny and me have been down south huntin' them buffalo through the Rum Jungle. He never stops this feller. Jumps on them beasts like lightnin' strikin'. Bang!'

Sam holds his hand out to Molly. He turns into Jesse James once more. He turns into Tyrone Power.

'Ma'am, would you grant a lonely cowboy the pleasure of your company?' he asks. That impossible smile. Molly Hook cannot hop up onto that horse tonight. Molly Hook needs to get home. But Marlene Sky can take that young man's hand, and Marlene Sky does.

*

The moon and the stars and Molly and Sam and Danny clip-clopping towards the Timor Sea. Molly's arms around Sam's hard flat stomach, her tired head resting on his shoulders. His warm shoulders. The Darwin heat even at night-time making him sweat beneath his riding shirt. The smell of earth and horses and land, and the hope of some alternative road that extends beyond Hollow Wood Cemetery.

Sam revels in Danny's wonder, explains in vivid detail how the horse made him shine in front of his ageing boss, Walt Hale, co-owner of Johnston Traders, one of the region's most seasoned buffalo hunting outfits, which has ties right back to the 1840s, when the Asian buffalo was brought to the rapidly colonised Coburg Peninsula for meat and milk. The multiplying and soon-wild buffalo took a liking to the Northern Territory's vast coastal floodplains, and canny riflemen like Walt's father, Paddy Hale, made a fortune sending buffalo hides overseas and across the country to become industrial-grade leather coverings and belts. The buffalo horns became inlays for gunstocks and fancy handles for knives that international hunters could use to kill more beasts to make more belts and knife handles.

'But it ain't no picnic bringin' a buffalo down,' Sam says. 'They don't just drop like pigeons, Mol'.'

Sam kicks his boot heel hard into Danny's belly and the horse clicks to a trot and then to a gallop. Raised coastal houses pass across Molly's vision in a blur and she holds tighter to Sam's stomach. 'Hyah!' he hollers. And the hot-blood colt speeds along the esplanade towards Darwin Harbour and Sam holds the reins in one hand as he leans over far – too far, Molly says – to his left like a circus rider.

'You gotta get your horse right up close to that chargin' and blusterin' buffalo and you gotta get your rifle tip right against the head,' he shouts. He extends his left arm like it's a rifle in his hand. 'You put that rifle so close you want it touching its cheek. But you need a quick, brave horse to do that for ya, and that's what Danny here is. One hand keeping Danny steady and one hand on the trigger. Bang!'

Danny slows to a walk passing the Lameroo Baths and Lameroo Beach, and Molly wonders if even the horse is stunned into silence by what they see filling the black night waters of Darwin Harbour.

United States Navy warships, moonlit and starlit and spotlit, the reflections of the still harbour waters shimmering against their grey sidings that run on for a hundred yards and more. They are as lengthy to Sam's eye as the dead-grass Australian Rules football fields he bounces around on with his cousins, as wide across the beam as the cricket pitches he mows into the lawn behind the church. Molly tries to count all the ships and she loses track around fifty. Sam's eyes are drawn to an American destroyer. The last time he can recall seeing something so big was when he rode two hundred miles east from Darwin to the Arnhem Land escarpment with his uncle Ernie and they saw Burrunggui Rock lit up by the sunrise. The destroyer is the same shape as that old sandstone rock, but Burrunggui isn't fixed with the guns the destroyer has. Sam counts them: five guns in single mounts. 'Can't see the torpedoes,' he says, wide-eyed.

Patrol boats, auxiliary minesweepers, depot ships, examination vessels, American and Australian troopships carrying men in white shirts Molly can see moving back and forth across decks with the same frenetic pace the moths have when they flap around her reading lamp.

'Dad reckons the Japs are comin' to Darwin,' Molly says.

Sam heels Danny and they move on towards Stokes Hill Wharf.

'Your dad's right, Mol',' Sam says. 'That dirty ol' war's comin' to us now.'

Molly fixes her grip on Sam's stomach.

'Look at all them boats packed in there like sardines,' Sam says. 'They should spread them fellers out. Make 'em harder for those Japs to hit.'

These boats make no sense to Molly in the Darwin dream. These warships make no sense. Purple plums belong in Darwin, Molly tells herself. Cyclones make sense in Darwin. The heat belongs in Darwin, the eternal sweat. Warm beer makes sense here and hand-woven baskets on market stall tables. Fat barramundi belong here and saltwater crocodiles, and the box jellyfish whose sting will make you wish you'd never learned how to swim in Darwin Harbour in the first place – or even kill you outright. Purple plums in the arms of young Chinese women. Purple plums make sense.

'Is this a dream, Sam?' Molly asks, her left cheek pressed against Sam's right shoulder blade. Her eyes look out to the long, curling, wooden-deck wharf running deep into the black harbour, its cast-iron and concrete supports covered in seaweed slime and mollusc shells. Cars and bodies and cranes move around the wharf deck unloading and loading a hulking naval cargo vessel some 120 yards long and 15 yards wide.

'I blacked out in the kitchen today,' Molly says. 'I don't even remember how I got into town. I feel like I just woke up outside Ward's Boutique.'

Danny clops along the beachfront. The gravedigger girl holds Sam tighter.

Danny stops. Sam looks out beyond the wharf. On the horizon, three jagged lines of lightning split the sky, turning it violet.

'The Lightning Man's comin'', Sam says.

Molly knows about the Lightning Man. Sam's grandfather was the one who first told him about the Lightning Man, the spirit god who rides high in the sky on a high-speed vehicle made out of storm clouds. 'Wish I had me one of those to get around on, eh Mol'', Sam said. He told Molly the Lightning Man has powerful ears that know things, that know the weather, and from these ears the Lightning Man shoots rods of electricity down through his storm cloud to the ground. 'But you don't run from the lightning,' Sam said. 'You go to it. Because that Lightning Man's trying to tell you where to find what you need. The Lightning Man comes and then all the good water and food comes with him.'

Another lightning strike in the blackness far beyond the busy wharf.

'I'm leavin' here tomorrow, Molly,' Sam says.

'Where you goin'?' Molly asks.

'I'm going to the lightning, Molly.'

Molly releases her grip around Sam's belly.

'Me family,' he says. 'We're going bush. We're going deep, Mol'.'

'Do you have to go?' Molly asks.

'Big gathering,' Sam says. 'A lot of talkin' needs to be done with the elders about what's comin' with this war and where we all go from 'ere.'

'Where are you all gathering?' Molly asks.

'I can't tell you that, Mol'.'

Molly wraps her arms around Sam again.

'Take me with you,' she says. 'I'll go with you right now. You go ahead and give Danny a big kick in the belly and we can ride away, right now. Tonight. Just go deep into the bush. So deep we never come back.'

Sam turns his head to speak closer to Molly's ears. 'You're not allowed to go where I'm going, Molly.'

Molly closes her eyes. Silent for a full minute. 'Do you care for me, Sam?'

'I care for you a lot, Mol',' Sam says. 'But I'm sixteen and you're twelve and—'

'I'm almost thirteen,' Molly says.

Sam nods, smiling. 'And you're almost thirteen,' he says, breathing deep to finish what he has to say. 'And I don't think it'd be right for me to care for you the way you want me to.'

This heavy stone heart. Cry from it, Molly, cry, she tells herself. But she can't cry, so she opens her eyes again and slides off the horse, walks to a large rock embedded in the sandy banks of the harbour and sits.

'Will Longcoat Bob be there?' she asks.

Sam slips off Danny, too, holds the horse's reins as he talks to Molly's back.

'Nobody knows where he is,' Sam says. 'He's been on a long walk. Longest he's ever been on. Nobody's seen him in almost two years.'

Molly drops her head, traces the circle of the night sky moon in the sand with her right big toe.

'Sam?'

'Yeah, Mol'.'

'Remember I told you about the sky gift.'

'Yeah, Mol'. I remember.'

Molly traces a twisting road running from the sand moon at her feet.

'Remember them words my grandfather etched on the pan?'

'Yeah, the poems,' Sam says.

'Directions,' Molly says, correcting Sam. 'They were directions. But he wrote them for the eyes of poets. Only people livin' poetic lives could understand them. You have to be poetic, Sam. You have to be graceful.'

Sam ties Danny's reins to the post of a rotting fence lining the beachfront.

'Directions, huh,' Sam says.

Molly nods.

'I know where the silver road is,' Molly says.

Sam says nothing.

'It's what you called the glass river,' Molly says. 'It's the same thing. Way beyond the Clyde River. The road you used to walk as a kid.'

Molly looks up at the night sky moon. 'I'm gonna leave this place, too,' she says. 'Everybody else goes away. Why can't I? I'm gonna go find the silver road. And then I'm gonna find Longcoat Bob and then I'm gonna find my own treasure.'

'What's your treasure, Molly?'

'Answers.'

'Answers to what, Mol'?'

'Why he did what he done to my family. How he's gonna undo what he did.'

Sam finds a place on the beach rock beside Molly and he tells her, not for the first time, his deep-gutted full-flesh heart feeling about Longcoat Bob's curse. 'There is no curse, Molly,' he says. 'Longcoat Bob don't work like that. He can't work like that. He's not able. There is only what the land and the sky deems right and wrong.' Sam's said this before, too.

'It wasn't Longcoat Bob who put the dark on your grand-father,' he continues. 'Only the earth can do that. Only that twinkling stuff up there can do that, Mol'. The land and the stars were watching. They both said your grandfather was wrong to do what he done. He took gold from the earth and the earth didn't want that gold took. The earth rebelled, Molly. It turned on your grandfather. You start walking into places you don't belong and it might just turn on you, too.'

Molly dwells on this for a long moment. Then she stands. 'Did you like the film, Sam?'

Sam looks up at Molly. 'Not really, if I'm bein' honest,' he says.

'Why not?'

'You weren't watching it with me.'

Molly smiles. 'Bye, Sam.' She walks away.

'Molly, wait,' Sam calls. But she does not stop. He stands to watch her march into the night, patting Danny the colt's head along the way.

'Bye, Molly Hook,' he whispers, only to himself.

*

Two shadows in the cramped kitchen of the caretaker's house at Hollow Wood Cemetery. The Hook brothers, Horace and Aubrey. White long-sleeved work shirts buttoned to the neck. Black trousers. Both men too drunk to notice they're still wearing their wide-brimmed black hats inside. Molly standing in the doorway to the kitchen. Horace can barely keep his eyes open. He sways in his chair, reaching once, twice, three times for a glass jar with a scratched 'Queen's Olives' label on its side, which is half-filled with a clear spirit that smells to Molly like petrol mixed with a splash of tonic water. Aubrey stares at her through the dark slits of his dead black eyes, his right forefinger circling a small glass of the same spirit. Horace's head finally stays still long enough to see his daughter standing expressionless and mute inside the kitchen. Then a thought reaches his clouded brain. Molly knows it's a dark thought. Horace stands abruptly – too abruptly for his blood and his body and brain to catch up with his legs – and he stumbles to his right and trips on his feet and he falls hard to the ground, his eyebrow hitting the corner of the kitchen stove on the way down. Blood spills immediately from his forehead and he tries to wipe it away but he merely wipes it across his forehead so that he looks to Molly like a war-painted Indian in a Gary Cooper western.

'Dad!' Molly says, kneeling down, hands out to help her father regain his equilibrium. But he doesn't lean on those hands, he only grabs them and reefs them towards his head before scrambling to his feet and reaching for the razor strop that hangs from a nail by the stove. He pushes Molly against the kitchen table and forces her head down hard, knocking his drinking jar off the table and smashing it on the floor. And Aubrey Hook sits perfectly still with his right hand gripped around his glass as he stares into the eyes of his niece while her father flogs her backside and her rear thighs with the razor strop. Up and down and up and down. The movement of the thick leather strop and the pulsing of the kitchen light bulb. Welts upon welts upon welts, blood upon blood. Ten lashes, twelve, fifteen; eighteen in total. And Molly Hook is so truly grateful in this moment for the curse of Longcoat Bob because her stone heart is surely the only thing that is keeping her from crying in front of her dumb-faced, dark-shadow uncle, whose black eyes she refuses to turn away from, no matter how loud that strop whacks, no matter how deep it stings and cuts. Do not look away, Molly. Dig, Molly, dig. Whack and whack and whack and whack. Dig and dig and dig and dig. And Aubrey Hook's lips smile beneath his thick black moustache and he raises a moonshine toast to the gravedigger girl and then he howls with deranged laughter, rejoicing in the music he hears in his head, the music made by leather meeting skin.

Graves at her Command

Sleep, Molly, sleep. Keep the bedroom door shut. Stay right here until they are gone or until they are dead. Her bed is a single mattress on a wooden floor by a duchesse with a small square mirror. Rising damp in the wood walls. It's morning, well past dawn, and Horace and Aubrey Hook still scream and laugh and bellow beyond her bedroom door. She has her mother's copy of *The Complete Works of William Shakespeare*, taken from the living room bookshelf and shaken furiously from the landing to expunge the silverfish wiggling through its fertile pages. A black hardback cover, pages yellowing and brittle. She reads with her belly pressed against the mattress to ease the pressure on her throbbing arse and the whip-welted backs of her thighs, her head leaning over the end of the mattress, her elbows and the open Shakespeare flat on the floor.

The gravedigger girl reads *The Tempest*. It's about the wind and the rain, about the kinds of storms that strike Darwin in the stifling summer when men like Aubrey and Horace Hook turn strange and vengeful like Prospero the sorcerer, who can wield the wind and the rain and who can raise the dead from grim and sorry graveyards. "'Graves at my command have waked their sleepers,'" the girl reads. Sleep, Molly, sleep. *The Tempest* feels like a dream to Molly. One great fevered sea dream. Sleep, Molly, sleep. "'And, like this insubstantial pageant faded, leave not a rack behind,'" the girl reads. "'We are such stuff as dreams are made on, and our little life is rounded with a sleep.'" And she sleeps.

She sleeps for eight hours and her empty stomach wakes her in darkness. She can hear her father and uncle outside now. They are in the front yard working the engine of Aubrey's red utility truck. The motor won't start and the men bark at the car, curse it for not acknowledging their murderous threats. Molly wants to stand, but standing is no longer so easy with the swelling. She pushes herself up with her arms first then bends her knees and that motion puts pressure on her backside and pain shoots through her lower back and into her brain. She opens her bedroom door carefully, slips into the living room on the tips of her toes, the hollers of her long-drunk and stupefied father and uncle still safely at a distance in the yard. She scurries down the house's rear steps to the under-house toilet. Agony now just to pass a small stool. She drops a scoop of sawdust down the long drop.

Back upstairs now and into the kitchen where she opens the icebox and pushes aside a bowl of fried sheep's brains and tomato sauce and fills her hands with three old pork sausages and a block of mould-covered cheese. She opens a small stan-dalone pantry cupboard to find small stacks of mixed canned goods: Spam luncheon meat, Edgell tinned peas and, the only dinner Horace Hook seems to eat these days, Campbell's Condensed Oxtail Soup. Molly takes a can of Spam and a can of peas. She finds a can opener in the cutlery drawer. She fills two empty glass pint milk bottles with water and scurries back to her bedroom, closing the door behind her. Molly drops her food on the mattress and places the bottles on the floor then drags her mirrored duchesse across the room and pushes it against the back of her bedroom door. She lies back down on the mattress on her belly, bites an end off a pork sausage.

For two whole days, barricaded safely behind that bedroom door, she waits out the tempest. And three words keep rattling through her mind like a mantra. Like an enchantment. Like a spell. Like a curse.

Dig, Molly, dig.

*

Dusk. Molly hears the utility truck pulling out of the driveway. Her bedroom door creaks open and the noise of it makes her pause. She waits for signs of life through the house. Nothing. She scans the house, assesses the silent fallout of her father's and uncle's deep dive into white spirit. Lamps on their side on the floor. Chairs on their side. Broken glass in the hallway. She'll be expected to clean this up. She will not clean this up.

She pads into the kitchen. Empty bottles and shattered glasses. A patch of human hair on the floor. Streaks of blood across the walls. Blood and bile vomit in the sink.

Molly fills a cup of water, glugs it down. She sits for a moment at the kitchen table. A beer-stained newspaper on the table covered in bush tobacco and ash. *Northern Standard*. Days old, weeks maybe. It's open at a public notice, an order. Molly dusts off the tobacco, holds the paper up to her eyes.

COMMONWEALTH OF AUSTRALIA
NORTHERN TERRITORY ADMINISTRATION
PROCLAMATION
EVACUATION ORDER

CITIZENS OF DARWIN

The Federal War Cabinet has decided that women and children must be compulsorily evacuated from Darwin as soon as possible, except women required for essential services. Arrangements have been completed and the first party will leave within the next 48 hours. This party will include sick in hospital, expectant mothers, aged and infirm and women with young children. You have all been issued with printed notices advising you what may be taken and this must be strictly adhered to. Personal effects must not exceed 35 lbs. The staff dealing with evacuation is at the Native Affairs Branch in Mitchell Street and will be on duty day and night continuously. The personnel who will make up the first party will be advised during the next few hours and it will be the duty of all citizens to comply at once with the instructions given by responsible authorities.

Remember what your Prime Minister, Mr Curtin, said recently. 'The time has gone by for argument. The instructions of the Federal Government must be carried out.' The Federal Government has made all arrangements for the comfort and welfare of your families in the South. Darwin citizens will greatly assist the war effort by cheerfully carrying out all requests.

There will be hardship and sacrifice, but
the war situation demands these and I am
sure Darwin will set the rest of Australia
a magnificent example to follow.

(Sgd.) C.L.A. ABBOTT,
Administrator of the Northern
Territory.

Molly places the paper back on the table. She pads to her bedroom and slips on her dig boots. Dig, Molly, dig. Dig for your courage. Dig for your soul. Dig for your rage.

Bert the shovel leans against her bedroom wall by a window. Bert's been waiting for this moment and Molly knows it. Molly and Bert walk to Horace Hook's bedroom at the end of the long hallway. His door is locked as always because Molly and Bert are never to enter Horace's bedroom. Molly raises the shovel in two hands the way she might point a spear at a lion and she drives the shovel blade hard and fast into the wood where the lock meets the door. The blade digs in, the old wood splitting and splintering. Molly pulls Bert back and drives him in again and again. Finally he digs in hard and Molly puts all her weight on the end of the shovel and the door cracks and flies open.

Her father's room is dark and smells of sweat and sick and spirits – the liquor kind and maybe the ghost kind too. She slides under her father's bed, grips a large canvas drawstring duffel bag filled with tools, drags it out and dumps its contents on the floor: blunt pickaxes and files, hammers and spades. She takes the duffel bag into the kitchen, fills it with every canned food she can find in the pantry. Canned corned beef, canned corn. One can of Nestlé Sunshine powdered milk.

Molly hurries back to her bedroom, finds her leather water

bag in the corner of her room beside a wide-brimmed yard hat which she stuffs in the duffel bag. Back into the kitchen to fill the water bag then back to her father's bedroom where she digs her shoulder into the side of a chest of drawers. She pushes hard with her legs, her boots slipping on the floorboards but sticking enough to slide the chest of drawers a few feet across the room. Three wooden panels in the newly exposed floor are shorter than those flanking them. Molly kneels down and finds a crack wide enough for her to slip in her right forefinger and pull one panel up. Her left hand removes the other two panels then her right hand reaches into the space not more than one foot deep between the bedroom floorboards and the under-house ceiling. She knows what she's looking for. A black metal box, lidded and locked, not much bigger than the square shortbread biscuit tins lining the shelves at A.E. Jolly's store in town. She does not replace the panels or slide the chest of drawers back where it was. There is no time for that now.

"'While we have time", she says to herself, "'let us do good.'"

The Japs are coming. Time is running out. There is only time enough to be good.

*

Darkness now in Hollow Wood Cemetery. Molly carries a kerosene lamp but she could find her way through this cemetery without a light. She could close her eyes and make it through this death hall, just by running her hands over the shapes of the cemetery headstones.

Martha Sorenson, 1842–1908. Granite stone work. Ridgetop contouring. 'In loving memory of dear mother.' Someone might be alive today who misses Martha Sorenson the way Molly misses her mother.

Teddy Byrne, 1854–1904. Limestone in a bevelled block. 'Sure is dark down here,' Teddy offers on his headstone. Teddy reminds Molly to laugh.

Edwin Harper, 1803–1887, reminds Molly to carry on. 'Edwin Harper. Robbed, stabbed twice in neck, 22 years. Survived sinking of *Fortuna*, 33 years. Met June Mooney, 35 years. Farewelled June, 83 years. Died, 84 years.'

Norman Ballard, 1877–1926. Blue-pearl granite. Gothic top contouring. 'The end and reward of toil is rest.' Molly cannot rest. Not yet. Not until she has opened the black metal box tucked under her left arm.

Bonnie Russell, 1865–1923. Grey limestone. Apex top contouring. An epitaph line that Molly hopes every night in her sleep will turn out to be true: 'Death is only a wall between two gardens.' Molly standing in one garden on one side of that wall, here in the Northern Territory, her garden filled with ironwood trees and fern-leaved grevilleas with orange flowers the colour of fire; her mother, Violet, on the other side of that wall, standing among roses, red and pink roses and nothing else. She's smiling. She's waiting.

So much love inside a cemetery. So much loss, but so much love. It's the one thing Violet appreciated about gravedigging. She called it 'the romance of the cemetery', though Horace never understood what she meant. 'Ain't nuthin' romantic about it,' he said. 'Just holes for dust an' bones.' But Violet saw the poetry in the place. She saw those lines on Cherie Lawrence's grave. 1854–1917. India red granite. A serpentine contour on top:

EVERY DAY AT HALF PAST THREE

A WHISPERED NAME, CHERIE
AND YOU SAIL BACK TO ME
ACROSS THE ETERNAL SEA

A simple line of love for Henry Prendergast, 1866–1909: 'I miss your hand in mine.' The simple reflection on the life of Hazel Collins, 1854–1926: 'Died grateful. Died loved.'

The harrowing epitaphs to children. Violet Hook told Molly that these reminded her to be grateful. 'Love lies below. Hope flies above'; 'We held you for a day. We hold your heart forever.' They reminded Violet of all she stood to lose.

Molly's yellow lamp lights up the darkened cemetery lanes. Her duffel bag hangs on her back with the strap stretching from her left shoulder to her right hip. Bert the shovel rests like a sheathed sword between her shoulder blade and the bag strap. All these gravestones she knows so well. All these life lessons from people in the beyond. Marion Curtis, 1854–1908: 'Loved in life, lamented in death.' Lucille Clifford, 1823–1874: 'While we have time, let us do good.' Molly was raised on these lessons, these headstone messages to God. All that trust in faith.

'Blessed are the pure in heart.'

'Eternity, be thou my refuge.'

'I know that my redeemer liveth.'

'A lonely scene shall thee restore.'

Last words left behind by the dead. Concluding truths after lifetimes endured.

But can she believe them? Can she believe the words of Eunice Milton, 1875–1934: 'Don't grieve, for what we lose comes around in another form'? Because Molly likes that one. She wants to believe in Eunice Milton. She won't grieve the loss of her mother because Violet Hook is still here, in another form. Molly just hasn't found her yet. But she's here. She's come around again.

Now the night sky speaks to her.

'What makes you so sure, Molly?' the night sky asks.

'I can feel her,' she says, because to respond to the night sky like this is to be graceful and poetic.

'Where can you feel her?'

'Everywhere,' Molly says. 'In trees, in flowers, in the rocks, in the dirt.'

Molly rushes on with her lamp. 'Did she come back around in another form?' Molly asks the night sky.

'You've been talking to the day sky again, haven't you?'

'A little bit,' Molly says.

'It's a lie, Molly.'

'What is?'

'The day sky. Be wary of the things it tells you. The day sky is an illusion. It's a trick. You believe it's so blue and so real you can touch it, but the truth is, Molly, the day sky is just more of me. More black. And the black goes on forever.'

'A boundless sea?'

'A black sea with no shore,' the night sky says. 'Never ending or beginning. Never to be trusted.'

In the south-western corner of the cemetery she stops at a gravestone. Molly has found the grave she's been looking for. Thelma Leonard. Upright limestone. Oval top contouring. She places her lamp beside the headstone. She slips off her duffel bag and holds the black tin box in two hands. She runs her fingers over her target connection point, a small hanging padlock at the centre of the tin box. Then, with a fierce swing of her gravedigger girl arms, she smashes the tin box against Thelma Leonard's headstone.

But the box does not break open. There are items in the

box, hard and small, and they rattle and bang against the insides as though Molly's holding a box of lit Chinatown firecrackers. Molly tries again, with another rabid, wild gravedigger girl swing that dents the box but does not break it open.

'What are you doing, Molly?' the night sky asks.

'I'm putting it all back,' she says.

'You don't have time for this, Molly,' the night sky says. 'The pubs are closing in town. They'll be home soon.'

'What makes you so sure?'

'Night skies tell no lies, Molly.'

Molly looks up to the black sky blanket beyond the hanging leaves of the milkwood tree. She looks back down at the black rock frog rock.

'"While we have time, let us do good,"' she says. 'The Japs are comin'. Everybody's gettin' out. Stuart Highway's gonna be full of buses and cars and army troop lorries. They'll be stuck in town for hours.'

'What if they're not in town?' the night sky asks. 'What if they're just at Aubrey's house, sipping moonshine in the old shed?'

The thought of Aubrey fills Molly's arms with warm blood and she tenses her muscles and she bashes the tin against the rock so hard her gritted front teeth feel set to crack. This time the box lid bursts open and flashes of gold and silver spread across the dirt. Jewellery. Necklaces, bracelets, rings. Wedding bands. Engagement rings. Victorian engagement rings. Edwardian engagement rings. Molly takes the lamp and runs it over the ground, her fingers scrabbling for the scattered jewellery and carefully placing it back in the box. More than twenty pieces in total. Diamond. Amethyst. Opal. Pearl. Gold and gold and more of other people's gold, all stolen by her father and uncle and stockpiled in the black tin box until they were ready to take the train to Sydney, where no Darwin loved ones would spot the sacred items in the shop window of a King's Cross pawnbroker.

Here lies Thelma Leonard, 1813–1867: 'Deep peace of the quiet earth to you.' Molly drives Bert into the soil in front of Thelma's stone, her right boot stomping hard on the blade edge. Four quick shovelfuls, not enough time to go deeper. Inside the black box she sifts through the pieces. She remembers Thelma's ring – she remembers them all – a small sapphire in a crystal setting the same square shape as Thelma's gravestone. Molly drops the ring into the hole and fills it in, flattening the dirt with four hard whacks with the back of Bert's blade.

On the eastern edge of Hollow Wood, amid a cluster of flat, square tablet headstones, Molly stops at the grave of Phyllis Quinn, 1865–1914: 'There shall be no darkness. There shall be light and music.' When she reads the epitaphs, Molly hears human voices, as if the grave's owner is talking to her, and maybe that was the intention. Phyllis Quinn's voice is eloquent, a touch of Irish in it. Musical. Phyllis played piano. Phyllis sang Irish lullabies to her children. And there was no darkness in the sunroom of her two-storey Darwin home. There was only light and music. Molly digs her hole, drops the flower brooch inside it, returning it to its rightful owner, the single pearl bud inside the flower buried with a single shovel load. 'I'm sorry, Phyllis,' Molly whispers.

And Molly moves on through the cemetery, corner to corner, grave to grave, returning the objects Aubrey and Horace robbed from the dead. A pink sapphire engagement ring replaced in the grave of Sarah Hill. 'To undreamed shores,' Sarah says on her headstone. Three turquoise balls like blue moons set into a gold ring go back into the grave of Julia Hancock. And Julia's words on her headstone are Molly's reward: 'To live in the hearts of those we love is not to die.' More life lessons. More messages from beyond.

A silver enamel bird pendant for Geraldine Lamb: 'Whither thou goest, I will go.' A ruby and diamond ring for Eva Gordon: 'We come whirling out of the nothingness, scattering stars like dust. The stars made a circle and in the middle we dance.' Crystal pendant earrings for Agnes Herman: 'Because I have loved life, I shall have no sorrow to die.' A black opal ring for Marilyn Prince: 'I know I am deathless. I know this orbit of mine.' Just words on a red granite grave. Lessons.

'"I know I am deathless,"' Molly tells the night sky. '"I know this orbit of mine cannot be swept by the carpenter's compass."'

'Marilyn Prince does not lie,' the night sky says back to her.

'Walt Whitman does not lie,' Molly says. 'Dad said my mum was always talking about that line on Marilyn Prince's head-stone and she asked anyone in town with half a brain what it meant. Someone in a mobile library told her it was by an American called Walt Whitman.'

Molly flattens the dirt with Bert's blade.

'"My foothold is tenon'd and mortis'd in granite,"' she says, reciting more Whitman. '"I laugh at what you call dissolution. And I know the amplitude of time."'

And a voice in darkness adds to those lines. But it's not the night sky. The voice in the darkness is deep and muddled. Drunken.

'"I bequeath myself to the dirt to grow from the grass I love,"' the voice says.

And Molly turns to the voice, raising Bert the shovel to defend herself.

'"If you want me again look for me under your bootsoles."'

Aubrey Hook staggers into Molly's lamplight. The girl draws a sharp, deep breath. Her uncle holds a single-shot .22-calibre rifle in his right hand, rests it on his right shoulder, wobbles it up there dangerously, like it could swing around to Molly any second now.

"'You will hardly know who I am or what I mean,'" Aubrey continues, still reciting Whitman. "'But I shall be good health to you . . . neverthe . . .'" And he struggles to say the words with all the white spirit inside him. He's all shadow. His black hat and his moustache the colour of the shadows passing across the lamplight. "'. . . nevertheless . . . and filter and fibre your blood.'" And Aubrey looks to the night sky. Looks to the stars. He points his rifle upwards, closes one eye to take better aim, then staggers with the effort. "'Failing . . .'" he says, reaching deep into his fogged memory. "'Failing to fetch me . . . at first" . . . "at first" . . . Oh, damn it.' He turns to Molly. 'Do tell me how it ends, Molly,' he says, trying to be tender. 'Your mother used to tell me how it ended. She knew that whole thing almost by heart and there were pages of it. Pages and pages, big words and more big words.'

Molly is silent. Aubrey staggers forward, closer to Molly. He burps, spits, snorts the air. 'Tell me how it ends,' he barks, vicious and frothing, and his intensity makes Molly jump atop Marilyn Prince's grave. She turns her eyes to the headstone then recites: "'Failing to fetch me at first keep encouraged. Missing me one place search another. I stop somewhere waiting for you.'"

Aubrey giggles at this and his giggles erupt into his deranged howl, that sick howl again, something to scare the fruit bats, a laugh so chilling it might bring the black rock frog rock to life, make it hop away south with everybody else who's fleeing Darwin. 'Do you think your mother's somewhere waiting for you, Molly?'

He howls again. 'Maybe she's in the grass,' he says. He looks theatrically beneath his boots. 'Maybe she's under my bootsoles,' he says, inspecting the ground. 'Nope, not there I'm afraid.'

Molly feels cold now, even on a Darwin summer night this still. 'Where's Dad?' she asks.

'Town,' Aubrey says, groggy and brief, and Molly knows her uncle just spoke a lie because her uncle can't lie like the day sky can lie.

'I had to let myself into the house,' Aubrey says. 'Then I saw the strangest thing. Your father's bedroom door was wide open and his drawers were pushed across the floor and damned if our treasured black tin box wasn't missing.'

Molly's eyes fall on the box beside her lamp. Aubrey smiles.

'I thought the house might have been robbed,' Aubrey says. 'Filthy . . .' – searching for the word – 'opportunists . . . Molly. Everybody's evacuating their houses and all through town those evacuated houses are being looted by filthy opportunists making the most of this . . .' – he takes a while longer to find this word – 'precarious . . . situation . . . Darwin has . . . found itself in.'

A wobble. A stagger.

'Imagine that: robbing the homes of people running for their lives from the Japs.'

'Next they'll be robbing from the dead,' Molly says.

Aubrey smiles, waves a knowing forefinger at Molly. Then he relaxes his right arm, lets the rifle down, waves it about. 'I thought I'd better grab Horace's rifle and explore the extent of the burglary,' he says. 'Then, to my surprise, I saw a flicker of light from the kitchen window. Someone was walking through the cemetery. And now, who should I find burying . . . my . . . valuable . . .' – another search for the right word, another stagger – 'tr . . . tr . . . treasure.'

'It doesn't belong to—'

'Be quiet now, child,' Aubrey snaps. 'You talk too much, child. Maybe that's why you talk all that gibberish to the sky. There's nobody left on earth who can stand listening to your drivel.' He moves closer to Molly. He leans down and takes the lamp by its hooped wire handle. His eyes settle on the duffel bag hanging over Molly's shoulder. 'Hand me the bag,' he says.

Molly reluctantly slips the bag from her shoulders, hands it to her uncle who tips the contents onto the ground by his boots. Canned goods and utensils. Water. A thick black book with yellowed pages. Aubrey squats down to examine the book's spine. '*The Complete Works of William Shakespeare*,' he reads.

He stands once more. 'You going somewhere, Molly?' he asks. 'You disappearing into the bush again? You about to get yourself lost in the godless wild again?'

'I'm going to find Longcoat Bob,' Molly replies.

Aubrey laughs, the lamp moving in his hand, sending light to new points of darkness.

'And why . . .' – Aubrey shakes his head, piecing his words together slowly – 'would you . . . seek . . . to find . . . that sssssssnakey sssssssorcerer . . . Longcoat Bob?'

'I'm going to ask him to lift the curse he put on our family,' Molly says, flatly.

Aubrey howls with laughter. 'Of course, of course, the curse,' he says. 'You still believe in curses, Molly?' He nods his head vigorously. He moves closer to her from the shadows. He hisses at her. 'You still believe in sssssssorcery?'

She doesn't look at him. He's Medusa from the shadows.

'Even after everything I've told you about Tom Berry,' he says. Closer still.

'How many times do I have to tell you, child, that some children are born into this world destined to lead lives of pure and unavoidable misery?' He extends a crooked right forefinger and he taps it hard three times on her chest as he says, 'And you are . . .' – tap – 'quite simply . . .' – tap – '. . . one of those children.' Tap.

Aubrey turns and tilts his head to the stars. 'You can't blame Longcoat Bob,' he says, snidely, waving a finger at the sky. 'Blame God. Blame your precious sky. Blame your shimmering stars.' He turns to Molly. He snarls at her. The shadow snarl. 'Blame your mother,' he says. He laughs. Staggers on his feet again.

'I was there, Molly,' he says, his drunk head bobbing on his shoulders.

Molly can't resist Medusa. 'Where?' she asks.

'When your mother gave birth to you,' he says. 'I was there.' His drunk legs move beneath him, but his head returns to the stars. 'I saw the sadness of you arrive from nothingness. One minute your sadness was not in this universe, and the next minute it was.' His hands make a mushroom cloud. 'Pwoof. Like one of those stars arriving up there. You were suddenly . . . here. You arrived, Molly, in all your tragic . . . predestined . . . hardly immaculate . . .' – he turns back to her – 'misery.'

He walks over to her and smiles. He grips her chin, lifts her face to the lamplight.

'It was remarkable how quickly it all unfolded,' Aubrey says. 'The single worst thing that ever happened to us.'

He studies her eyes. 'I do wonder, young Molly,' he says. He laughs to himself and shakes his head. 'If you are so evidently capable of believing in the notion of sorcerers and curses, I do wonder if you are also capable of believing in the notion that the lives of your mother and your father and, indeed, your uncle, only descended into misery the moment you were born. I wonder if you have ever considered the possibility, Molly

Hook, that there *was* a curse given to this family – and that curse was you.'

He keeps hold of her face, stares deep into her eyes. Molly gives nothing away. Her uncle smiles. 'But, alas, still no tears,' he says.

Aubrey staggers backwards four paces then drops himself down on his backside on the hard dirt and grass, rolls himself a smoke.

Molly watches him lick his tobacco papers. I will never be afraid, she tells herself. I will feel no pain. Rock is hard. Can't be broken. 'You ought to believe in Longcoat Bob's curse,' she says. 'Because it has passed to you, Uncle Aubrey. I know this now.'

He does not look up. 'What makes you so sure?'

'Only a cursed man would say those things to a child,' Molly says. 'That curse has got into your heart and turned you black. You're only shadow now, Uncle Aubrey.'

He lights his smoke with a match. 'I won't argue with that,' he murmurs. Then he sucks on his smoke and exhales slowly, the grey smoke floating across the nearby gravestones like the souls of their occupants escaping. 'Now, tell me Molly,' Aubrey asks, waving the smoke away. 'How do you intend to find the elusive Longcoat Bob in all that deep country?'

Molly rests her backside on the soil, tired. 'The sky gift,' she says.

Aubrey smiles. 'Aaaah, but of course, Molly Hook's magical gift that fell from the sky on the day her mother abandoned her like a lame fawn.'

Molly shakes her head in disgust. I will never be afraid. I will feel no pain. 'It was a map leading right to Longcoat Bob's gold and you took it from me and you threw it away because you were so angry and so stupid,' Molly says.

Aubrey stands, moves back closer to his niece.

Molly stares him in the eyes. 'You couldn't see a thing because you were just a shadow,' she says.

Aubrey's menace as he moves. Aubrey's curiosity.

'You couldn't see that you held all the gold you could ever want in your hands,' Molly says. 'He scratched a map on that pan and he wrote directions on it.'

Aubrey nods and he kneels to stare deep into her eyes. 'The man was a lunatic, child.'

Molly shakes her head. She will tell him now. She will show him. She remembers what she read on the bottom of the pan. She remembers the dark place. The banks of Blackbird Creek. '"The longer I stand, the shorter I grow,"' she recites, chin up, knowing and defiant. '"And—'

'"And the water runs to the silver road,"' her uncle says, finishing her sentence.

Molly is stunned, gut-punched by her uncle's knowledge of those words.

Aubrey laughs, shaking his head. 'By the end, Molly, your grandfather was scratching his loopy ramblings on anything he could put a pocket knife to. The scribbles of a broken prospector who had spilled his marbles long ago.'

Molly shakes her head slowly while her uncle nods his.

'The man was brain-sick,' Aubrey says. 'He lost his mind just like his daughter lost hers two decades later and just like his granddaughter is losing hers before my very eyes.'

'But he didn't write them directions for you,' Molly says, forcefully. 'He wrote them for someone who was graceful. Someone who was poetic. That silver road is out past Clyde River and I know how to find it. You'll never know because you're not poetic and you're sure as shit not graceful.'

Molly closes her eyes and braces for the palm across her

face. But it does not come. She opens her eyes again. A puff of Aubrey's smoke. A long pause. Another exhalation into the night air. The thin eyes now of Aubrey Hook. The shadow forming around him. The blackness.

'And how exactly will you find it, Molly?' he asks.

Molly shakes her head. She spits her words more than she speaks them. 'I'll never tell you.'

Aubrey grips his rifle, moves closer to Molly. 'Poor Molly Hook,' he says. 'Mad little gravedigger girl. You think if you find that silver road, then you'll find Longcoat Bob. And what do you think Longcoat Bob's going to tell our little gravedigger girl? Do you think Longcoat Bob's gonna tell the gravedigger girl what happened to her mother to make her so sad? Do you think Longcoat Bob has all the answers? Do you think he'll tell you why she left you behind?'

He holds the lamp to her eyes, so close that the heat of the lamp flame warms the invisible hairs on her cheek. He whispers. 'Is it her you're always talking to up there in the sky?'

His breath smells like turpentine. His lip spit lands on her cheek and chin.

'"Failing to fetch me at first keep encouraged,"' he recites. '"Missing me one place, search another. I stop somewhere waiting for you." Do you think she's waiting for you, Molly? Do you think Longcoat Bob's gonna tell you where she is?'

Aubrey steps back, looks across a lane of headstones. Then he points the rifle at Molly's heart. 'Let me show you exactly where she is.'

*

'Run, Molly, run,' whispers the night sky because the night sky always fears the worst.

Since she was seven years old, she has not spent so long in this corner of the cemetery. She has not spent so long beneath the milkwood tree. She has not been so close to the black rock frog rock.

Aubrey Hook sits on the black rock frog rock. The lamp rests beside his black left boot. He rolls a smoke, his lips still wet from the hip flask nestled in his crotch. The rifle leans on his bent right leg. Molly Hook stands inside a hole in the earth, only one foot deep so far, Bert's blade in the process of going deeper. The gravedigger girl does not respond to the sky.

'Your grandfather was not brain-sick, Molly,' says the night sky, because the night sky never lies. 'You are not losing your mind, Molly. It is, in fact, your uncle who is losing his mind.'

Molly digs, blade into dirt, boot onto blade.

'He's going to leave you here, Molly. He's going to bury you with your mother. Do you hear me, Molly? Do you understand? You are digging your own grave.'

Molly pauses, looks up from the hole at her uncle. The lamp lights only one side of his face. The rest is shadow. A black moustache wet from spirit, strands of brown bush tobacco caught in the nest of hair above his invisible top lip. Molly leans down once more, takes Bert's tall wooden handle. She turns around in the hole so her back is facing her uncle. She digs.

'Why's he doing this?' Molly whispers into the dirt.

'You know exactly why he's doing it.'

'Longcoat Bob's curse,' Molly murmurs, shovelling another load to the surface.

'That sounds like one of those gentle lies the day sky would tell you.'

Molly digs, heaves to the surface a heaped blade of soil the colour of chocolate cake.

'But I know you, Molly. And I know when you know the truth but are too afraid to tell it.'

Molly digs Bert hard into the dirt, rests her aching right arm on the handle for a moment, stares up at the stars sprinkled across the black sky.

'He wants me gone,' Molly says.

'Why?' asks the night sky.

'I make the shadow.'

'Why?' asks the night sky.

'I remind him of her.'

'Who?' asks the night sky.

'Her,' Molly says. 'Mum. I saw the way he looked at her. I saw the things he wanted to do to her. I saw his envy. I saw his lust. The poets all write about it. I saw it in his eyes. I saw it in his shadow.'

Molly returns to her digging. Stop talking to the sky, ignore the night sky, she tells herself. But the sky keeps talking to her.

'You saw a question, Molly?'

'I don't want to ask it,' she says.

'You will feel no pain, Molly. You will never be afraid.'

'I know what the question is.'

'You have always known the question.'

Molly stabs Bert into the dirt and looks up at the night sky.

'What did he do to her?'

The night sky says nothing and that's how Molly knows she asked the right question.

'You can save me,' Molly says.

'How can I possibly save you from up here?' asks the night sky.

'A sky gift,' Molly says.

The night sky says nothing and that's how Molly knows the night sky is thinking.

'Do you remember what I told you?'

'Keep your eyes on the sky,' Molly says.

'Keep your eyes on the sky, Molly Hook.'

*

The night animals of Hollow Wood can see all of this curious scene: the man on the rock and the girl in the hole and the dim lamplight. The fruit bats in the trees. A black-headed python on a cool-air night hunt slipping behind the black rock frog rock, unseen. Two possums bouncing across to a high branch in the milkwood tree, which are startled by the lamplight. A saggy-bottomed wombat lumbering towards the hole suddenly frozen stiff by the sound of Molly's voice.

'Drink break?' she asks, turning to face her uncle.

Aubrey's head is down. He spits a strand of tobacco from his bottom lip.

'No breaks,' he says. 'Dig, Molly, dig.'

Molly digs.

Women and Children First

Evacuations. Daytime preparations. Night-time blackouts. Young men painting Darwin's street lights with dark blue paint. Orderlies from the Cullen Bay civil hospital carrying elderly patients to the waterfront. Women and children first. Nurses to stay and care for the wounded.

Some 530 evacuees squeeze onto the troopship *Zealandia* bound for southern Australia. The ship hasn't been cleaned for months. Minimal toilet and washing facilities. Anyone carrying a suitcase of belongings weighing more than thirty-five pounds – and there are many – has to watch that suitcase being thrown into the sea by guards and their keepsakes, photographs, money, savings, winnings and heirlooms sinking to the sand where the stingrays hide. White Australian families share cabins built for four with as many as twelve. Chinese families are not allowed in cabins at all, but are forced by the guards to spend the long journey south on the open deck.

On shore, a wealthy cattleman in a black suit slams a handful of notes down on the front desk of the office of the State Shipping Company.

'Sorry, Sir, women and children first,' says a flustered young office clerk.

More notes on the counter. 'Just git me on that fuckin' boat.'

Some 187 evacuees sail south from Darwin Harbour on the passenger ship *Montoro*. Some 173 aboard the *Koolama*. A final shipload of seventy-seven women and children on the *Koolinda*. Dazed children on the decks; toddlers confused and frightened by the suffocating rush, gripping doll heads and the sweaty palms of mothers whose husbands remain in town digging sheltering trenches the same way Molly Hook digs graves: blade into soil, boot onto blade, soil into cart.

Two men in singlets smoking by a sandbag filling station. One bloke says to the other bloke that he heard about a bloke who knows a bloke who's handing out cyanide pills. 'If the Japs wanna set up shop 'ere,' he says, 'I'll be stickin' one of those in me pie, thank you very much.'

Dusty and frantic families carrying calico bags full of clothing and food on the long road south. Families near flattened by fast-moving military convoys barrelling north to RAAF airfields, hangars, fuel dump zones, workshops and ammunition stores. Australian Kittyhawk fighters zipping through the sky on test flights. An evacuating mother of three waiting for transport on the side of the Stuart Highway. Her youngest son, eight years of age, holds a suitcase in his right hand. With his left forearm he hugs to his chest a small and plucky Australian terrier with dark brown eyes. In her dress pocket, his mother clutches a National Emergency Services leaflet she found in her letterbox.

Each and every Evacuee will be entitled to take the following articles, as personal belongings:

(a) One small calico bag containing hair and tooth brushes, toilet soap, towel, etc (personal only).

(b) One suitcase or bag containing clothing, and such shall not exceed 35 lbs gross weight.

(c) A maximum of two blankets per person.

(d) Eating and drinking utensils.

(e) One 2 gal. water bag filled for each family.

(f) No Evacuee shall take, or attempt to take, with him or her, any domestic pet, either animal or bird, and any such pets owned by the Evacuees should be destroyed prior to the Evacuation.

The mother gives the boy a look he knew was coming. Grim wartime pragmatism. He hands her the dog and she walks it into the scrub lining the Stuart Highway.

A town of men now. Men who spend their days as clerks and shoe salesmen and taxation officers are rushing through the streets carting the sand that fills the sandbags that will cushion the impact of dreadful things the Japanese plan to drop from the sky. Men who are trawlermen and house painters and fencers and farmers by day are being taught by shipped-in Australian army recruits how to feed ammunition to a Lewis gun, while more seasoned soldiers oil anti-aircraft guns on the oval in the centre of town and another on high ground at Fannie Bay, north of town. Men are loading twenty-eight-pound shells that can soar six-and-a-half miles into the sky. Blazing heat. Soldiers in singlets and shorts, socks and boots. Weary gangs of longshoremen working round the clock, splitting shifts among their full complement of 252 wharfies, unloading shipped armaments – depth charges, TNT and other explosives – from the hulking 6000-ton, 393-foot-long cargo vessel *Neptuna*, moored off Stokes Hill Wharf.

Across town, some families refuse to leave the homes they've worked for because they lack trust. They don't trust the Northern Territory administrators giving the evacuation orders, they don't trust their neighbours, they don't trust the police, and they don't even trust the Japanese to make it all the way down to Darwin.

But dawn comes as it always does and the sky is the colour of 19 February 1942, as it can only be once. In the Tiwi Islands settlement of Nguiu on Bathurst Island, fifty miles north across the sea from Darwin, Father John McGrath carries out his morning duties as head of the Mission of the Sacred Heart. A dry, hot day. Father McGrath says his morning prayers, has his breakfast, moves through the island mission where some three hundred Tiwi Islanders are working in the fields, tending to gardens, and younger missionaries are making their way to the island school. He laughs with the islanders. He believes in humour and the words of Matthew: 'Whatsoever you do to the least of my brethren you do to me.' He has lived with the Tiwi Islanders here since 1927. He speaks their language. Some call him 'The Apostle of the Tiwis'. Others call him John. He will one day be called 'grandfather' by these people and, many years from now, they will bury him in the red earth of this paradise island, with the sons of the island's oldest women taking turns to gently shovel the dug soil back over his resting corpse. 'Nampungi,' they will whisper. Goodbye.

The sound reaches the island first. The vicious snarl of that sound, the growl of it. The wasp of it. The tiger of it. A violent symphony of three-blade propellers slicing air and overworked engines spitting smoke. The Tiwi farmers lower their tools and turn their heads to the blue Pacific sky. Father John McGrath raises his head with them. He believes in things that take place beyond that sky, but he can't quite believe this sight he now sees beneath it.

A great and terrifying swarm of grey and green and silver aircraft in arrow-shaped attack formation, red rising sun circles painted on the undersides of their wings, heading south-east to Australia, but also somewhere more specific and the name of that evolutionary wonder enters the mind of the priest. Darwin, he tells himself. And he runs across the mission yards to an administration room, where he sits himself down at a radio transceiver, call sign Eight SE, linked to a series of communication and navigation aeradio stations scattered across mainland Australia in a network called AWA, Amalgamated Wireless of Australia. He speaks urgently into the transceiver's mouthpiece, sends a message to the AWA Darwin Coastal Station, call sign VID. 'Eight SE to VID,' he says. 'Big flight of planes passed over going south. Very high. Over.'

And a scratchy radio reply is returned from a duty officer in the Darwin Coastal Station. 'Eight SE from VID. Message received. Stand by.'

But Father John McGrath cannot stand by because his heart and his legs are telling him to run, telling him there is already something raining from the high blue sky that is tearing up the red soil of Nguiu settlement, something splitting through timber rooftops and stabbing through walls. Many years from now, around Father John McGrath's grave, the oldest Tiwi women will speak of the priest's bravery and goodness on that morning of 19 February 1942: how he cared for them and led them to shelter, shielding them with his own God-given life. Some will refer to that fire and metal rain as machine-gun fire. Others will simply remember it as war. A whole world war that fell from the sky.

Night Skies Tell no Lies

Her mouth is dry and she longs for the mattress in her bedroom and she longs for the road out of Darwin or the train to Alice Springs or the saddle on Danny the colt who runs like the wind blows. Molly digs slowly. She digs for so long that the sun comes up over Hollow Wood Cemetery and the cemetery stones surrounding Molly and the hole dampen with dew. Soon the hole is deeper than Molly is tall. Aubrey stands at the foot of the grave watching her dig. His flask is empty but what he's drunk in the past twenty-four hours will keep him staggering for a while longer.

During her fifth hour of digging, Bert's blade strikes something hard that Molly mistakes for rock. She drives harder with the shovel and feels an object beneath the dirt break into pieces. Her right hand reaches deep into the soil and emerges into the morning light again carrying a handful of brown dirt and fragments of her mother Violet's shattered shinbone.

Molly reels back against the southern wall of the grave, her eyes now finding a ball of white bone in the dirt, like a wildly struck golf ball just landed a foot from her boots. It's Violet Hook's right kneecap. She turns her head away and her stomach turns with it and she vomits in her mouth but there's no breakfast or lunch in it, only fluid. She spits and she closes her eyes, face tucked in the corner of the hole.

'Please, don't make me do this,' Molly screams.

'Dig, Molly, dig,' says Aubrey Hook, leaning into the grave.

Molly shakes her head. Molly grits her teeth.

'It's you who's mad, Uncle Aubrey,' she says. 'It's you who's lost his mind.'

'Dig, Molly, dig,' Aubrey repeats.

'I know why you're doing this,' she says, not turning to look at her uncle. She breathes hard. Sweat across her forehead, sweat in her eyes. Dirt across her arms and legs. Dirt beneath her fingernails. That circle of bone in the dirt. 'You want to see her again,' she says. 'I want to see her again, too. But not like this. It's not her, Uncle Aubrey.'

The shadow across Aubrey's face. Black as the hat on his head. He closes his eyes and breathes deep. He opens his eyes and raises his rifle to his shoulder, aims the muzzle at Molly's chest. 'Dig, Molly,' he commands.

And then a sound, a wailing sound reaching all the way from Darwin's town centre and through the trees of Hollow Wood Cemetery, between the stone epitaphs of the dead, to the ears of Molly Hook standing deep inside her mother's grave.

An air raid siren ringing out across Darwin. Aubrey looks back over his shoulder, finds the direction of the sound. Molly keeps her eyes on the sky. No more dawn pinks and reds. All blue now.

Aubrey returns his gun barrel to Molly's chest.

'Dig, child, or I'll leave you face down beside her.'

Molly breathes, grips Bert's handle. The air raid siren rings again. Bert's blade is gentle now, more the tool of an archaeologist. No stomping on the blade shaft, just a series of scrapes and gentle digs. She's Howard Carter from the papers and her mother's body is an Egyptian pharaoh sleeping in the dirt. Precious and fragile. But her churning stomach means this is not science. This is not archaeology. This is family. One shovel load, two shovel loads, three shovel loads.

'Deeper,' Aubrey barks.

I will feel no pain, she tells herself. I will feel no pain. I will feel no pain. Dig for your courage, Molly. Dig for your soul.

The day sky says nothing. The gravedigger girl will uncover the bones of her mother alone.

'Deeper,' Aubrey hollers, leaning in to the grave more with each macabre sighting of bone. More leg bones. Arm bones across a waist.

It's not her, she tells herself. It's not her. It's not her. She's not down here. She's not down here. She went up there. She went up there.

The last thin fibres of a dress, earth-eaten and browned by soil, covering a ribcage with three missing ribs. Objects surrounding the skeleton, dirt-caked and heavy. A jewellery box. A pair of dancing shoes. Books. So many books around the skeleton.

'Keep digging, Molly,' Aubrey says.

The shovel goes deeper. More objects. More of Violet Hook's belongings. A porcelain figurine. A teacup. Then Molly's eyes catch the edge of a copper circle. Bert's blade digs around the copper – scrape, scrape, dig, dig – then Molly does the rest by hand, fingers frantically searching for a hold on the copper sky gift she thought was lost, disposed of in a bag of rubbish with a pig's head and a dozen eggshells. She pulls her grand-father's copper pan from the earth, runs her fingers over it, inspects its underside, scratches the dirt off it with her finger-nails.

The words are still there. The directions.

I will never be afraid. Rock is hard. Can't be broken. 'Liar,' she screams. 'You . . . fuckin' . . . animal . . . *liar.*'

'Give me that pan,' Aubrey says from the grave edge.

Molly hugs it close to her chest. 'It's mine,' she says. 'The sky gave it to me.'

Aubrey points the gun barrel at Molly's face. 'And now you're gonna give it to me.'

Molly stays put.

Aubrey cocks the rifle's hammer. 'I won't ask again, Molly.'

Two eyes to two eyes. Blue to black. Light to shadow. Molly tosses the pan to the surface. Aubrey picks up the pan.

'There's no such thing as curses, Molly,' he says, inspecting the words on the back of the pan. 'There's no such thing as sky gifts either.'

He wipes more dirt off the pan, uncovering the third and last set of words Tom Berry engraved. Molly sees a strange light – a brief glowing – shift across her uncle's eyes and she can't tell if it's a reflection from the copper pan or the light of inspiration on his face.

'But make no mistake, Molly, there is such a thing as gold.' Aubrey drops the pan by his boots. 'Keep diggin',' he says.

Molly grips Bert's handle once more. She digs.

'You don't need nuthin' from Longcoat Bob, Molly,' Aubrey says. 'You don't need to find some ol' black witch doctor to give you your answers.'

The shovel blade scraping away more dirt.

'You see this gun, Molly,' Aubrey says. Molly turns her eyes to the gun barrel. 'Here's your answers right here. She took this gun and she got herself lost, too, out there in that deep country. Maybe she went looking for Longcoat Bob, too. We found her four days later. She was lying flat on a rock by Strike-a-Light Creek.'

The shovel blade scraping away dirt.

'I'll never forget her face,' Aubrey says.

Molly turns to her uncle. He's lost in his mind, distant.

'Your mother had a nice face,' he whispers.

He snaps back to the moment. 'Show me her face,' he says, pointing the gun at Molly.

And the gravedigger girl's boots stumble on the uneven soil and she kneels beside the bone frame of her mother, not entirely because she's being ordered to at the end of a gun barrel. There is a space inside the gravedigger girl's mind that wants to see her mother's face. She wants to see the shape of her cheekbones, her jawline. She wants to touch that face. Her soil-covered fingers brush dirt off her mother's skull. Her right thumb strokes a cheekbone. She's dreaming this, she tells herself. She's been dreaming since she was standing outside Ward's Boutique staring at that sky-blue dancing dress. She can do things like this in her dreams, kneel beside her mum like this, touch her bones. She can find beauty in the act. She can make it tender.

Two nasal cavities. She loved this woman, so she can love this bone face. The smooth bone bowl that once carried her left eye now carrying a collection of soil that Molly dusts away as carefully as she dusts off Bert's blade at the end of a long day's digging. The gentle curve of the left-side temporal bone, like an empty rock pool at Butterfly Gorge when there's been no rain.

Dirt falling off that face. But her left hand explores too far – some pieces of archaeology should never be uncovered. Dirt falls away on the upper right side of the skull, from Violet

Hook's frontal bone, her high vertical plate, and there is a hole where the right side of her skull should be. There is no smooth bone bowl around her right eye. There is only dirt.

'How do you do that?' Aubrey asks.

'I have a heart of stone,' Molly asks. 'I will never be afraid. I will feel no pain.'

'There's something wrong with you, child,' Aubrey says.

'I know,' Molly replies.

Molly runs her eyes over her mother's skeleton. It's not her, she tells herself. It's not her. It's not her. She lingers on the chest bones. But it is her. She is here. She is down here, too. There is a thin sheet of worn dress material stuck to her upper chest bones. Her mother's heart once beat beneath that fabric. Molly's hands reach for the material. She will peel it away and she will know the truth. The night sky truth, not the day sky truth. Night skies tell no lies.

But then a voice from the surface. 'Get away from her, Molly.'

Molly swings her head back over her shoulder. Her father, Horace, stands beside his brother at the edge of the grave, five feet above her. He holds a long pickaxe in his right hand. The sight of her father makes Molly snap out of her dream, snap out of her deep-grave fever. She reels back.

'He was gonna shoot me, Dad,' Molly says.

Aubrey howls. A frenzied guffaw. He slaps his knees grandly. He adopts the voice of a twelve-year-old girl. '"He was gonna shoot me, Dad!"' he howls. He staggers to his left, finds his footing at the edge of the grave. Then his face goes dark in an instant. 'Have you seen what your child has done?' he asks, two hands on the rifle handle, balls of saliva gathering on his moustache.

'I've seen what you done to Greta,' Horace says. 'You went

too far this time. She came into town, Aubrey. She told the police. If we survive these Japs, they'll be comin' for ya.'

Horace takes in the scene. His gravedigger daughter. The open grave. His grave older brother. His grave shadow.

'Your wheels 'ave come off the train tracks, brother,' Horace says.

'I'm teaching your child a lesson,' Aubrey shouts.

'You've gone too far, Aubrey,' Horace replies. He stares at his brother while he speaks to his daughter. 'You come up outta there, Molly.'

Molly moves towards him along the uneven surface, stepping on a glass box that breaks beneath her boots. Her father leans down and offers his right arm. Molly grips it with her right hand and is hauled to the surface with Bert the shovel in her left hand, her muddy boots tearing dirt from the grave walls.

'Go back to the house, Molly,' Horace says.

'No,' Molly says.

Horace turns to his daughter. Aubrey laughs.

'I'm never going back inside that house,' she screams. 'It's cursed. This whole graveyard is cursed.'

Molly spots her pan at Aubrey's feet and she rushes for it. Pick it up, Molly, and run for your life. Dig, Molly, dig.

But Aubrey stops Molly in her tracks by swinging the gun barrel towards her chest. 'You gonna attack me, Molly Hook?' Aubrey asks. 'You are brave, aren't you? Braver than my sorry little brother here, that's for certain.' He waves the gun barrel. 'Get over there beside your father.'

Father and daughter standing on the edge of Violet Hook's grave. Aubrey points the rifle at them both, switching frantically between faces. 'I was just trying to give the girl some answers,' he says. 'You know what I mean, little brother? Answers to the girl's questions. Do you have any answers for her, little brother?'

Molly turns to her father, briefly puzzled by these words.

'Let's calm down for a second, Aubrey,' Horace says. 'You need to sleep this one off. Let's go back to the house.'

'No, thanks,' Aubrey says. 'Maybe the girl's right. Maybe this place is cursed. Maybe you two are cursed. Maybe I'd be better off without you both. Maybe you'd be better off in that hole with Violet. Three pretty little faces all in a row.'

Molly watches her uncle's eyes. His eyelids are closing on him involuntarily, his head's rolling. He's tiring.

'I'm so fuckin' sick of diggin' holes with you two,' Aubrey says. His eyelids drop down, open again. 'I think I need to get out of the gravediggin' business, don't you? Get back into the gold-diggin' business.'

Then the sound of engines in the sky. The sound of gas and death and war. The wasp of it. The tiger of it. Molly's senses are sharpest and she looks up to the sky first. Her father looks up next and, lastly, Aubrey turns his eyes to the sky and his face lights up like he's felt the breath of God and his mouth falls open and he laughs. He howls at the impossible sight of a Japanese air fleet moving as one perfect attack arrow across the vivid Darwin blue sky. His drink-skewed vision blurs and the terrible fleet doubles, triples, in number. And he thinks of locusts. He thinks of plague. He thinks of the great ending.

'Insects,' he says. 'Buzzzzzzzzz,' he screams at the locusts. 'Buzzzzzzzzz,' he screams at the sky. And he howls with laughter. He's still smiling when he turns his face back towards Molly Hook and the flat back blade of Bert the shovel smashes into the left side of his face.

More arrows of Japanese aircraft now and Molly rushing for her grandfather's prospector's pan. She scoops it up from the ground and dashes across the graveyard.

'Get under the house,' her father screams.

Aubrey Hook falls to his right, staggers for three paces then finds his footing again on a fourth. Blood runs from the inside of his left ear. His tomato-coloured face. His rage. He shakes his stunned head into action and he brings the rifle to his shoulder and turns towards his fleeing niece.

'Run, Molly, run!' Horace screams as he drives his shoulder high into his older brother's ribcage, now exposed by Aubrey's raised right arm. A rifle shot explodes aimlessly into the sky and Horace and Aubrey roll onto dirt hard, the way shot black buffalo roll onto dirt. And the Hook brothers of Darwin, Australia, twist and turn and wrestle and roll in the soil as 188 green and grey and silver Japanese aircraft soar above them. Some eighty-one Kate horizontal bombers, seventy-one Val dive-bombers and thirty-six Zero fighters in attack formations.

The brothers scratch at each other's eyes and cheeks and they scratch at their shared past. Horace's mouth finds the flesh of his brother's shoulder and he bites deep into it. Aubrey's hands find his brother's Adam's apple and he squeezes hard. Horace's left hand finds Aubrey's left eyeball and his thumb pushes against that white-flesh lychee organ. They are wolves, both, and they want blood, but blood is flying through the sky above them.

'Run, Molly, run!' hollers Horace Hook through his choke-gripped neck.

Molly runs. Past headstones and trees towards the flat yard that leads to the cemetery house. Then a whistle sound, like a boiled kettle whistling, the largest kettle ever boiled, and this impossible kettle is falling through the sky. Now she hears other whistles: five, six in chorus. Giant boiled kettles dropping towards her. The whistle sounds seem to bend, like the very sound is fixed to a curved wire in the air and that wire is arched like a rainbow and that rainbow ends somewhere in Hollow Wood Cemetery. And the whistling gets louder and louder and louder and she knows the falling kettles are getting closer and closer and closer. But she can see the cemetery house now and she will go there even if it's cursed, and she will hide beneath the house and lie flat against the downstairs concrete and wait all this out. Just Molly Hook and the brown snakes cooling their bellies.

Run, Molly, run. Foot after foot. Boot after boot. But the whistling, that terrifying whistling, so loud and so close, it's falling on top of her. A sound is falling on her. A sound that has transformed in the sky into something physical. Now it's so near it makes her fall to the ground and put her head between her legs and her twig-thin arms over her ears and her scalp. And finally the terrifying whistling ends in a violent explosion that rumbles across the earth and rattles Molly Hook's growing bones. Yard dirt rains upon her and she feels like she's sitting beneath a tip truck and a team of town labourers are unloading a tray of council dirt on top of her body, and she knows she must get up and run again because she will suffocate beneath all that flying earth. She stands up and moves forward three steps, but something has wrecked her equilibrium and she falls face-first onto the dirt.

She raises her head once more and tries to focus on something, anything, between the grey smoke and earth debris, and she finds what must be the cursed cemetery house, but it is no longer the house she grew up in. Half of the house is missing, flattened into the dirt. The other half stands exposed, like it has been sliced down its centre and its domestic innards are spilling onto the ground. Molly can see the kitchen stove in broad daylight. She can see her mother's bookshelf, fallen on its side beneath half a tin roof sheltering devastation and destruction, household items – plates, glasses, ornaments – shattered and spread across the yard.

More whistling now. Closer and closer. And Molly watches the earth away to her right explode in fire and dirt, and she runs forward but the earth explodes again up ahead, so she turns and runs and runs and runs back through the smoke and dirt and violence and war. The whistling sounds are all around her still and now she knows they are bombs, war bombs, falling from the sky and thumping into earth, and she barely has time to react to one earth-tearing explosion before she has to react to another, changing her direction with every thunderous eruption.

But then the sounds fade. The whistling is not in the sky anymore. There's only a sharp and thin whistling of a different kind in her ears. A ringing. Run, Molly, run. She can't see her father and uncle. She can't see the scrub in front of her. She can't see the gravestones of Hollow Wood. Run, Molly, run. Foot after foot. Boot after boot. Her heart. Her cursed stone heart somehow beating for her. Pulsing for her. Moving her forward. Run and run and run and then fall.

Molly drops into a hole in the earth. Her feet land hard on uneven ground and her body lands spine-first on uncovered bones. She wipes dirt from her eyes and looks up out of the hole she's fallen into and realises she's in the grave she just opened, a rectangular prism five-and-a-half feet deep in the ground. She turns and finds her mother's hollowed-out face and draws a deep breath, then rolls instinctively off her mother's skeleton. Yet this hole down here feels safe, safer than what's happening up there, so she squeezes her body into the space between her mother's left arm bone and the grave wall. And there she stays. As another bomb drops somewhere on the terrifying land above her, she reaches instinctively for her mother's hand, the thin bones resting on the broken waist bones.

Keep your eyes on the sky, Molly. Keep your eyes on the sky.

And the edges of that grave become a window frame for Molly Hook. Then the smoke drifts away and all that fills the grave window frame now is a rectangle of perfect blue sky and the endless arrows of Japanese warplanes passing across it, dropping their bombs as they go. And time slows now and all that exists in this world is that view from the grave and those bombs look to Molly like bull ants. That's all they are, Molly, bull ants. But that's a day sky lie and the gravedigger girl is scared, so she squeezes her mother's hand.

'Can you feel it, Mum?' she whispers. 'We're on top now, Mum. Can you feel it? We're floating. We're on top!' And seen from the daylight blue sky above and looking down and looking closer in and closer in, through the smoke and the earth debris, they are mother and daughter, flat on their backs and hand in hand, waiting for war to stop falling from the sky.

'We're on top, Mum,' she whispers. 'We're on top, Mum. We're on top, Mum.'

Blood Flowers Blooming

Black ants. From so high up in the sky, through the flat glass canopy window of a top-speeding Zero, all those scrambling soldiers and citizens of Darwin, Australia, look like black ants to Yukio Miki of old town Sakai. Helpless black ants zipping in and out of concrete buildings like the organised-chaos lines of the black carpenter ants he'd stare at as a boy. He would rest his chin on his knee by a pile of firewood near his family's backyard incinerator and watch the lines of carpenter ants butt heads trying to figure out how they were going to make use of such a large plunder of wood. Yukio would run his boyhood fingers along the entry holes to the tunnel networks the ants had chewed inside the fire logs and he'd wonder how creatures so seemingly disordered could create something so smooth and artful. And he would marvel for a full hour at the relentless industry of those carpenter ants and then his heart would hurt when his father, Oshiro, would grip two logs filled with a whole microscopic civilisation of black ants, a whole world built by toil, and toss them so casually into the incinerator. The heat of that stone box. The flames from it. The fire. All that yellow and red.

Everything inside his cockpit is hot and rattling now. Too much noise up here. Greased metal and unprotected mechanical controls: rattling cowl-flap controls, fuel-tank selectors, hydraulic system controls, buzzing electric switchboxes, landing-gear controls. Jammed in hard inside the cramped flying machine, part of the awe-inspiring and awful arrow of thirty-six agile redsun fighters now nose-diving through the air towards central Darwin, Yukio thinks of his late grandfather, Saburo Miki, a strange and thoughtful man, who once told Yukio the riddle of the blood flower. 'The blood flower blooms only when provoked,' Saburo Miki said. 'The blood flower blooms on battlefields.'

All that flame, Yukio tells himself. And he remembers Pearl Harbor. How he kept firing and firing and hoping those American warship cannons would fire back and a direct hit would end it all for him and he would be at peace because he could then stop firing, end it all with his honour intact. All that burning, he tells himself. All that yellow and red turning to black down there. Down there where Darwin is being incinerated. Just like all those Japanese carpenter ants. All that work those people down there put into their little city by the sea, all set alight by Yukio and his brothers. The blood flowers are blooming across Darwin. The pattern of bombs dropped by the Nakajima B5Ns. Bloom. Bloom. Bloom.

Yukio's left hand reaches for the gunsight fixed between his two 7.7-millimetre machine guns. The Zeroes will strafe a series of military installations. The Zeroes will fire at anything in their way and they will shoot those black ants in the back and in the front and in the side, and those black ants will not fire back because they're not ready to.

The low-flying Zeroes on his left and right release their terrifying strafing fire and the machine-gun rounds thump through concrete and dirt and human flesh. But Yukio Miki can't bring himself to pull his trigger. He cannot fire on all those fleeing carpenter ants. And if he cannot fire in this moment, if he cannot serve his brothers as he vowed, then he is a coward and he is an enemy of his brothers and the enemy must be vanquished.

He reaches his right hand out to grip the photograph of Nara. He pulls it from the ball of gum above his fuel gauge and he slides the photograph carefully into the breast pocket of his shirt beneath his puffy flight jacket. And he knows now what he must do, and so he searches through his glass canopy window for a building tall enough to fly directly into at the Zero's top speed of five hundred kilometres per hour, but all the buildings of Darwin have been incinerated. Then he pulls back hard left on his flight stick and the Zero suddenly veers away from the formation in an arcing left turn that makes no sense to his brothers on the wings beside him.

But Yukio needs to fly away from here. He needs to leave the blood flowers blooming. He needs to find the sky again. And then he needs to find a mountain.

The Bone Pillow

Molly wakes. She hears the distant sound of the air raid siren in town. Her head is on its side and her eyes are adjusting to the image of her own left hand resting on the ribcage of her mother's skeleton. Her fingers brush the worn and damp fabric still pressed to her mother's chest bones. She needs to look inside. There are answers inside.

Molly raises her head, rests her weight on her elbow. She stares at the square of fabric and it might as well be a curtain, the kind of curtain one pulls back on theatre stages or side-show alleys to reveal great wonders never before seen. She closes her eyes and her thumb and forefinger grip a corner of the fabric and she gently peels it back, tearing away a layer of clay or mud beneath it. Then the fabric rips and Molly has to peel it back in strips. When she opens her eyes she is staring at the insides of her mother's chest.

Her mother's ribs have a created a kind of home for something. This home is a pocket of air and dirt that has a ceiling of arching rib bones, and there is only one thing inside this home and it is a rock the size and shape of a human heart. A blood-coloured rock like none she has seen before, nestling in a bed of dirt inside her mother's chest. A stone organ.

Molly's left hand digs through the dirt at the base of the ribcage and scoops out handfuls of earth. At first the rock won't move because it's fixed in place by old dirt beneath it, but Molly's fingers claw like a dozer bucket beneath and around it and soon she gets a grip on it and works it back and forth until it breaks free from its dirt casing and the gravedigger girl pulls the blood-coloured rock the shape of a human heart out through the base of her mother's ribcage.

Smooth and crimson. Shaped like a strawberry the size of her father's clenched fist. Heavy in her hand.

Half of the midday sun can be viewed from the bottom of the grave and Molly holds the blood rock up to the sky and whispers one perfect word.

'Mum.'

*

Molly finds her father's left leg beside the backyard thunderbox. She knows the leg is her father's and not her uncle's because the shoe on the leg's attached foot is a brown leather lace-up and Aubrey Hook only ever wears black work boots. The leg lies in the grass like a misplaced theatre prop. Hollow Wood Cemetery is bomb-scarred and ravaged. One half of the cemetery house stands and the rest is rubble, concrete, brick and splintered wood spread across the dirt yard.

For a moment Molly considers picking up the leg. She could slip it into the duffel bag that hangs once again over her shoulder. But then she thinks of where she's heading and she wonders what use she would have all that way out there for her father's bomb-severed but sensibly shoed left leg?

'Who belongs to that?'

Molly looks up to where the voice came from, keeping a firm grip on Bert's handle. Greta. The great Greta Maze, toast of Darwin, all the way from the theatre stage to the blitzed lawns of Hollow Wood Cemetery. A Hollywood starlet. In the flesh, Molly tells herself. Such as that flesh is. Bruises across her arms. A black and swollen left eye. Stitches across her face. Molly tells herself not to ask Greta about her eye, about her face, because she learned the hard way how humiliating it is to answer questions about visible cuts and bruises.

'It's my dad's leg,' Molly says, staring at it.

'You okay, Molly?' Greta asks.

Molly considers this question. She doesn't respond. She turns and pads across the dirt yard, deeper into the cemetery. Greta follows. Greta moves slowly and Molly notices. Greta's insides are hurting when she walks and her right hand clutches the right side of her abdomen.

At the edge of the yard, a one-legged man is sitting in a sprawling oak tree, six feet off the ground. He's wedged in awkwardly, his head pushed down into his lap, between the tree's trunk and three thick branches that thrust skywards in different directions. One of the man's arms is jammed absurdly behind his neck and the other hangs where his left leg used to be. Molly stares curiously at him. Her father, Horace Hook.

'Molly,' Greta says, softly. Not a question. Not a suggestion. Just a name. 'Molly. Talk to me, Molly.'

Molly says nothing. She wanders deeper into the cemetery. In the long aisle formed by two rows of ornately carved headstones and slabs, a human figure crawls along the ground, hauling itself along on its elbows with regular, quiet, brute-effort heaves. Dirt-caked and black, the figure moves like a leech, or like a black grave wraith that has slipped out into the light and now wants to flee back down into the dark.

Molly and Greta reach the feet of the slow-moving carcass and the carcass's owner, Aubrey Hook, senses them walking behind him – the girl, he thinks, the girl with her beloved fucking shovel scraping along the dirt. He drags himself on and on for another twenty long yards before he tires completely and turns his body around and rests his head on the edge of a stone slab inscribed in honour of the departed William Shankland, 1843–1879: 'I will lift up mine eyes unto the hills from whence cometh my help.'

Aubrey's eyes squint in the full sun. His face is black with soil and red with blood. He's reaching deep for breath but he's too tired, too overwhelmed by the scene to catch a satisfactory gulp of Darwin's hot air. He sets his eyes upon Greta and Molly, who stand over him. 'Water,' he gasps.

Molly and Greta simply stare at him. Greta's hand over her belly. The pain inside her. She looks at the man at her feet. The squirming monster. His tattered clothes. The sweat across his face, his arms and legs. The desperate movements of his fingers, patting his own chest. Confused, out of place here by this grave, lost. 'Water,' he says. He coughs hard and the cough turns into a blood vomit that spills over his chin and onto his buttoned shirt.

'Take me to hospital,' he pleads, gargling on his own blood.

Greta leans down to Aubrey. She studies his face. She wonders how her life came to this, how she came to think she was in love with Aubrey Hook. He was charming once. Intelligent. They went to shows together. He showered her with gifts. They met when she was dancing most weeknights. He gave her good tips and then he gave her bad tips. Stick with me. Never leave Darwin. Die with me here in Hollow Wood

Cemetery. Never walk into town and tell the police about the rage places I go and the nights I take you with me.

Greta's hands reach into Aubrey's trouser pockets. He tries to bat her hands away but he's too weak, too spent. Molly sees those hands ferreting through the pockets and then she sees Greta's right hand extracting a set of keys.

'I need a hospital!' Aubrey gargles louder. He spits more vomit from his mouth with a laborious shake of his head. Greta turns and walks away, Molly follows. They head towards the half cemetery house and the one-legged man sitting in the tree, the desperate calls of Aubrey Hook echoing behind them. 'You take me to the hospital now!'

Greta and Molly walk on.

'You are going to hell!'

Greta and Molly walk on.

'I curse the both of you,' Aubrey screams to the sky. 'I curse the both of yooouuuu!'

*

Greta shuffles slowly to the driver's door of Aubrey's red utility truck, still intact and parked in the gravel driveway in front of the bombed cemetery residence. Molly watches her climb awkwardly and painfully into the driver's seat. She closes the door.

'Get in,' Greta says. 'I'll drive you to the hospital.'

'I don't need a hospital,' Molly says through the open window. 'But could you take me to Clyde River?'

'Not going that way,' Greta says.

'All the ways go that way.'

'Not the way I'm going, kid.'

'Wait,' Molly says. 'Where *are* you going?'

'I'm going back to Sydney,' she says, and she starts the truck, gives its rattling engine some heavy revs.

'Wait,' Molly says. 'Let me show you something.' She drops her duffel bag to the ground and reaches in to find the prospector's pan amid the cans of beans and corned beef and the Shakespeare book and the blood-coloured stone the size of her dead father's fist. She passes the pan through the driver's-side window to Greta.

'So,' Greta says, turning it in her hands. 'What am I supposed to do with this?'

Molly points at the pan. 'Look at the back,' she says. 'The words on the back.'

Greta frowns, tries to scan the words on the back of the pan, fails. 'I can't read all those words,' she says. 'They're covered in mud.'

She tosses the pan back to Molly.

'Look, kid, you need to get yourself to hospital,' she says. 'They need to check you for shellshock or somethin'. And once they're done doin' that, you need to get the bloody hell outta Darwin. Them Japs ain't finished with this place.'

Molly holds the pan up. 'They're the directions to Longcoat Bob's gold,' she says. 'My granddad etched them in the copper so he'd never forget them. I can take you there, Greta. Buried treasure. You said if you knew where that treasure was you'd grab Bert right away and you'd dig down for your fortune. Well, you can have it all if you want it. You could be richer than your wildest dreams. You could finally be where you belong. We could go to Hollywood together and you could get your name up in lights and I could change my name and . . . and—'

'I'm sorry, Molly,' Greta says softly.

But Molly pushes on. 'Greta Maze and Marlene Sky,' she

urges. 'You can do it, Greta. You just have to get us to the Clyde River. I'll take care of the rest. You can do it, Greta.'

Greta turns her head away from Molly because she doesn't want the girl to see her crying.

Molly goes on. 'We could go on double dates with Tyrone Power and Gary Cooper,' she says. 'And then we could drive up into the Hollywood Hills and see if we could find Errol Flynn's house and we could ask him to let us in because we're Australians, too.'

Greta wipes her eyes, smiles, turns back to Molly. 'That's a nice film, Mol',' she says. 'I'll be sure to go see it some time.' Then she slams on the accelerator.

'Greta, wait!' Molly hollers. But the truck reverses quickly out through the cemetery gates.

'Wait, Greta!' Molly cries, her sore bones stumbling feebly after the truck. Then she stops and watches the truck speed south on the road out of Darwin. Silence and dust. She drops her head, eyes to the ground, and the ground is covered in domestic debris from the bombed house. This bombed world. And something at Molly's feet steals her attention. She bends down to pick it up. She holds it up to the sky to see it properly, turning it around between her forefinger and thumb. The red tin thimble.

War Skies

The gravedigger girl and a city on fire. A city in a war dream that she can walk through without being noticed because nobody here can see anything but fire.

A portly man sitting in a gutter on Darwin Esplanade, his hands on his knees. His clothes have been blown off and half of the hair on his scalp is missing. He weeps. Empty military tents on the roadside. Homeless dogs and cats sifting through piles of rotting food. Six soldiers sprinting along the street. Soldiers missing arms and legs on stretchers being carried by soldiers with faces covered in black oil. Bandages being wrapped around temples. Shrapnel sticking out of shoulder blades and thighs and chests. Soldiers gone blind. Soldiers gone mad from shellshock, rambling things to the sky that make no sense to Molly. The face of someone senior turning to the gravedigger girl. 'What the fuck are you doing here?' the man barks. 'Someone get this kid outta here, for God's sake.'

Molly runs. On the beach at Doctor's Gully there are men pulling bodies in from the shore. The bodies have drowned in oil. There are bodies still in the water, some floating face down and some face up, and the skin on their arms and faces has burned to a raw red flesh. One man pulls on a soldier's arm in the water and the loose skin on the forearm slides off the bone like a flesh-coloured glove.

The smell of the dead mixing with the smell of exhaust and oil. The smell of cordite and burnt wood and burning buildings. Sailors in small boats lifting desperate swimmers into their vessels. Bodies on the beach shot in the back by warplane machine-gun fire. In the mangroves of Port Darwin two crocodiles feast on the carcasses of drowned American sailors. Terrified in-patients from the evacuated Cullen Bay civil hospital huddle beneath the sheltering cliffs of Cullen Bay. Further along the beachfront is a train, a whole locomotive, upturned by a well-targeted bomb and flipped into the sea. Six railway wagons have sunk into the water with it. A whole war ship, *Neptuna*, a vessel the length of a football field, is turned over on its side in the low tide waters around the wharf, clouds of black smoke rising into the air.

So many sunken ships. USS *Peary*. HMAS *Mavie*. SS *Zealandia*. SS *Mauna Loa*. Oil tankers ablaze. Men still swimming frantically around sinking merchant vessels. The wharf labourers' recreation shed blown to bits. Great sections of the wharf blown away. Soldiers and police and nurses rushing to and from the town's flattened communications centre between The Esplanade and Mitchell Street, which housed the post office, the telephone exchange and cable office. A hole in the ground where the post office once stood; hills of wooden house framing and rubble have been formed by the explosions. A city of fallen masonry. Bodies on the ground covered in tastefully patterned living room house curtains. Another man's body blown into another fork of a tree.

Molly walks on. A.E. Jolly's convenience store has disintegrated, the Bank of New South Wales has been gutted. Sheets of corrugated iron and nails and sheets of fibro are spread across the streets. A naked man gone mad is running through Cavenagh Street shouting Bible verse.

Deeper into suburban streets, homes split in two. Ghost houses with swinging front doors blowing in the wind. More abandoned cats and dogs. Dogs howling mournfully. Two-storey homes built to withstand fierce cyclones flattened by bombs.

An old woman stands dazed by her letterbox, the only thing still standing on her property – her house is a mound of rubble. She speaks in what sounds to Molly like German. She's heavyset and her big arms are raised in confusion and she weeps, she howls, uncontrollably, talking to God or talking to those Japanese warplanes. When she sees Molly, she beckons the gravedigger girl to her. 'Please, please,' the old woman says. She opens her arms out to Molly, suggesting she needs a human embrace, she needs to hold something comforting, she needs to hold the gravedigger girl. Molly approaches her cautiously.

'Did you have family here?' Molly asks.

The woman rambles something loudly through tears in German.

'Why didn't you get out?' Molly asks.

'Please, please,' the old woman says, opening her arms for an embrace. And, reluctantly, Molly moves in close and leans into the woman for a hug. The old woman wraps her arms around Molly's neck and brings the girl's face to her belly. The old woman weeps into Molly's hair, squeezing her tight. And the embrace feels warm to Molly, too, and she wonders if she needed this embrace as much as the old woman.

But then the old woman howls again and grips Molly tighter still, and Molly's face is now being pushed hard into the woman's belly and Molly feels like her head is tucked into a pillow. She motions to pull away but the old woman's heavy arms hold her tight and Molly has to struggle to breathe through her mouth and nose and then she discovers she can't really breathe at all, so she pulls away hard but the old woman simply howls more loudly and presses Molly more firmly against her belly.

'I can't breathe,' Molly says, the words muffled by the woman's stomach. 'Lemme go! I can't breathe.' And Molly is suffocating now.

The old woman can only weep and howl to the heavens. She can't let go. Her grief is too strong and she cannot release this girl and Molly pushes against the old woman but she won't release her, so Molly stomps on the old woman's feet with her dig boots. 'Lemme go!' she yells.

'It's okay,' the old woman replies in a thick German accent, furiously patting Molly's hair. 'I've got you. It's okay.'

And Molly kicks now at the old woman's shin bones. She kicks and kicks and the old woman finally releases her.

'It's okay,' the old woman howls as Molly runs. Run, Molly, run.

*

Looters in the shops. Looters in the houses. Men rushing out of bombed-out hardware stores with tools. Men rushing out of bombed-out homes with rugs and furnishings and bags full of jewellery. Two men lugging a looted piano along Smith Street. Convoys of cars and lorries, civilians and deserting servicemen, rushing south to safety in the distant towns of Katherine and Larrimah and Daly Waters.

Shirtless and brave servicemen staying put to reload mobile anti-aircraft guns.

Chinese restaurant proprietors and Greek café owners at

last convinced of the need to evacuate – they needed to see the actual bombs dropping before they were finally persuaded to leave. Run, Molly, run.

Then stop. A row of town-centre stores with their front windows shattered. Civilians stepping over glass shards to let themselves into locked fashion stores. People walking out of stores, arms filled with three-piece suits. And the sky-blue dancing dress still hanging on the mannequin in the window of Ward's Boutique. Molly presses her face against the glass. She sees herself dancing again, when the earth rights itself and Darwin returns to normal and Sam comes home. She'll be older, then, and Sam will be honoured to walk into a dance hall with her on his arm, wearing a dress like that. Molly watches a woman, a nurse from the hospital, come out of Ward's Boutique carrying two gowns over her right forearm then scurry off up the street. Molly looks at that blue dress again and then slips through the front door of Ward's, her duffel bag over her shoulder, Bert still tucked between the shoulder strap and her spine.

There are no lights on in the boutique because there's no electrical power in town. She walks by racks of gowns and dresses, scans the room. She finds it at the back of the store by the store counter and cash register: the one sky-blue dress left on the rack. She lifts it off by its hanger, holds it up to assess the size. Before trying it on in the changing room, she shuffles through a back door that leads to a bathroom, where she hopes to quench her thirst and wash the dirt and sweat from her face, but she can only manage a few brief sips of rusty water from a tap that then stops running.

In the changing room, she takes off her old boy's pants and soiled work shirt, both heavy with earth and stinking of sweat. She slips into the sky-blue dress and turns to face a full-length mirror fixed to the wall. The dress is too big for her, the hemline hanging well below her knees and the shoulder straps almost sliding off her collar bones. But it works, she tells herself. I'll grow into it, she tells herself. I'll grow.

She straightens her hair. She allows herself half a smile. The sky-blue satin dress of her dreams, something to wear through this nightmare. She walks out of the changing room, leaving her old clothes where they lie. Making her way through the boutique aisles, she hears a deafening siren that's so loud it rattles the shopfront window. She rushes outside to the foot-path.

Soldiers and civilians sprinting in all directions. Nurses holding their hats as they run. Soldiers holding their helmets as they run towards defence posts. 'They're comin' back!' one civilian hollers, tripping over himself as he dashes away from a butcher's shop carrying a ham under each arm. The air raid siren wails again and Molly turns her eyes to the sky. Another squadron of Japanese bombers approaching from the south-west. More bombers, more than twenty of them, attacking from the north-east.

'They're gonna hit the airfield,' a soldier shouts. Then Molly feels as much as she hears the violent pressure-wave of patterned bomb-drops thudding into Darwin earth. Flashes of yellow flame light the horizon and black smoke shrouds the town like a low-hanging cloud from hell. And then a red utility truck screams to a halt at the side of the dirt street, directly in front of Molly.

Greta Maze leans over from the steering wheel and speaks through the open passenger-side window. 'Get in,' she says, a lit cigarette hanging from her lips.

Molly beams wide, slips immediately into the front seat.

Another thundering drum roll of bombs shakes the town

and Greta Maze bounces in her seat. She drags on her smoke nonchalantly and gives her passenger a sideways look, noticing something new about the gravedigger girl. 'Nice dress,' she says, then slams her foot on the accelerator.

THE SECOND
SKY GIFT

The Man Who Hated Gold

Eyes closed. He sleeps flat on his back amid twenty wounded men and women being rushed to Cullen Bay civil hospital in the back of an army transport truck that's been scouring Darwin streets for raid casualties. There's a weight on his chest that makes it hard for him to breathe and this suffocating weight puts thoughts in his head. It's not a dream but it's a memory that comes to him in his sleep. The same memory that always comes to him. Aubrey Hook is fifteen years old and he's being buried alive inside a goldmine and he has the wherewithal to blame his impending death on true love.

Love and hate. Man and woman. Rich and poor. Dirt and gold. His father, Arthur Hook, believed in absolutes and lived in them, too. Arthur Hook loved Bonnie Little absolutely. Childhood sweethearts, they rode horses together. They rode through Howard Springs and Humpty Doo and they rode all the way to Kakadu country and Bonnie Little would let her wild auburn hair spill out from beneath her riding hat and that hair was the colour of the gorge clifftops that she'd stand upon, screaming her name – 'Bonnie Little' – into the ancient echo chamber of a Kakadu chasm. They danced together in

Darwin town hall and they dreamed together of the things they would do once Arthur and his best friend and early goldmining partner, Tom Berry, got lucky in the Pine Creek goldfields.

'You're my lucky strike, Bonnie Little,' Arthur said with wide eyes. 'You're my greatest find.' Because that's what true love is, Arthur thought. True love is a pure gold vein in a dry hillside of dirt and stone. Some will never find that kind of gold seam. Some just don't have the nose for it. But he did. And he loved her absolutely – until the day Bonnie Little fell in love with Arthur's best friend and goldmining partner, Tom Berry.

'Tom?' Arthur gasped. It was New Year's Eve. He and Bonnie were standing in a storeroom off the public bar in the Hotel Darwin.

'Tom Berry?' he gasped again. His best friend. The hapless, hopeless Tom Berry. Clumsy, awkward, bookish, meek, insecure, weak, poet Tom Berry. The friend who begged Arthur to let him accompany him on horseback as he rode into the deep country in search of a gold seam. That schoolteacher type. That literate scholar who possessed, at once, a gold sense as keen as a melon but a worrying gold lust like none Arthur had seen before. He'd nearly got himself killed only two months before, after blasting a hole with too much dynamite. And suddenly, on that New Year's Eve, Arthur wished he had.

'I can't help how I feel, Arthur,' Bonnie said.

Arthur never believed a word of that sentence that fell so slowly from Bonnie's mouth because he was a walking example of how a human can, in fact, help how they truly feel – because he truly felt, every second of every hour of every day after he heard those words, like crushing Tom Berry's skull in two with a large piece of quartz, yet he resisted that profound feeling and just turned away from how he felt. So why couldn't Bonnie Little help how she felt?

From that day on, Arthur Hook could only hate Bonnie Little. And he hated her absolutely. But he hated Tom Berry twice as much as he hated Bonnie and his hate for Tom Berry bled into what later seemed to his fifteen-year-old son, Aubrey, to be a hatred for all of life. Arthur hated the leaves that dropped from trees and gathered on his porch. He hated horses and the sound their hooves made on concrete, and he hated the smell of their droppings as he meandered through hillside paths and range tracks that he took with his young sons, Aubrey and Horace, on gold-prospecting trips through Pine Creek country. He hated the woman he eventually married, June Buttigieg, the only daughter of Stanley Buttigieg, owner-operator of Darwin's fledgling Hollow Wood Cemetery. Poor and sorry June, he told himself, with that lazy left eye that always sat like a fallen mango at the bottom of her eye socket whenever Arthur asked her questions about dinner or weather patterns or what it felt like to carry a child inside her belly. The gravedigger's daughter with the dead left eye. Pull that eye out and bury it six feet deep, he told himself. He hated the way June howled during childbirth and he hated the smell of the black shit that burst from baby Aubrey's backside and over his fatherly fingertips. He hated the tea leaves that built up in the bottom of his teacup and he hated the branches from the backyard oak tree that scratched against his tin roof and he hated the sun that kept on rising and telling him to go to work and he hated the sound of the fiddle players in the Hotel Darwin and he hated the beer that warmed too quickly in his hand and he hated anyone who wished good fortune on Tom Berry because he hated Tom Berry most of all.

Arthur beat his sons. He beat the backs of their ducking heads with his closed fist and each beating made him hate Tom Berry even more because he blamed Tom Berry for stealing the only thing he ever loved and turning him into the kind of man who beats his sons. He beat his sons with rocks and whip handles and sticks and fists and then he watched his sons grow into muscular teenaged boys who beat each other.

'Hate's not such a bad thing,' he told his boys once, swigging whisky under campfire light on a long Pine Creek gold search. 'Never underestimate the power of hate. My hate for Tom Berry is what gets me up in the morning. I hate him so much that it gives me the energy I need to work those mines. I hate him so much I want to steal every piece of gold he'll ever hope to get his hands on. And I will. I'll do it. My hate for Tom Berry's gonna make us rich.' And Arthur Hook drank his whisky and his head turned to his sons, looking through the flames of the campfire. 'What do you boys hate?' he asked.

And Aubrey and Horace turned to each other, both knowing the other's answer but not giving it.

Arthur Hook grew to hate the very gold he was seeking to find. He grew to hate the very mountains that hid the gold he despised. He hated the hills and valleys and ranges that kept their gold secrets from him. In the pubs of Darwin town he would hear whispers of Tom Berry's successes in the goldfields and he would be enraged and he would curse the earth that chose to smile on such a deceitful man as Tom Berry and ignore a decent, hard-working miner such as Arthur.

He drove his pickaxe into those hills and every wild swing was an act of vengeance. Fellow prospectors often questioned his reckless approach. He cut great trenches into the earth but he never took the time to repair the holes he dug, leaving the mountain wounded. Older goldminers would pass his digs and shake their heads. 'That mountain's gonna turn on him one day,' they said, because the older goldminers knew what the blacks knew about the mountain, about the Northern Territory earth. It felt things. Mysterious things. And it rewarded the prospector who felt those things, too, and it punished, they said in campfire whispers, the prospector who ignored those mysteries.

Hate drove Arthur Hook to ride horseback with his sons deep into the scrub beyond Marrakai Crossing, east of fruitful Mount Bundey and the nearby Rustler's Roost goldmine, seeking the long-lost and near-mythical Black Leg Mine. It was named after its owner, Percy 'Black Leg' Gould, a seasoned prospector whose left leg had become wedged under a fallen rock in a trench when he was twenty-two. By the time Percy was found, his leg had turned gangrenous and black, and it had to be cut off and replaced with a wooden peg that he walked on for four more decades before disappearing somewhere in the hills between the Rustler's Roost mine and Mount Ringwood, along the Margaret River. The Black Leg Mine was said to contain great riches just waiting for anyone brave or foolish enough to try to hack through its unstable and unpredictable rocks.

Arthur Hook found what he thought was the Black Leg Mine after he and his sons rode along a precarious cliff-edge track that skirted Dead Bullock Needle, a natural obelisk pointing 150 feet into the sky that wandering and lost cows and sheep have tried and failed to skirt around for centuries, their bones left to rot beside the trunks of tall native trees some hundred yards beneath the cliff-edged needle base. Beyond the needle, along a winding track through thick brush, wide enough for only one horse, Arthur Hook reached the entrance to the mine, a hole in the ground in which stood a long ladder with forty or so rungs. He climbed down with a lamp then followed a tunnel to a rock face crossed by a rich vein of white quartz, and that quartz sent a shiver down Arthur Hook's spine. And he knew that shiver for what it meant. Gold.

He explained to his sons how millions of years ago pockets of liquid had turned solid inside rocks, trapping free-flowing grains and nuggets of gold, and how these gold-bearing quartz veins had waited ever since for the Hook boys to find them and dig them out and make their fortune. 'It's like big ol' bank vaults that are locked up down there,' Arthur Hook said, and he raised his pickaxe, 'and we got the key to the lock.'

And Arthur Hook swung his axe at that underground rock face as if it were the face of Tom Berry himself. He hacked at it, slashed it and smashed it. And for three straight weeks he and his sons worked on that face, Aubrey and Horace lugging buckets of mined ore up the ladder and over to a nearby creek, where they sorted through rocks and panned the most promising dirt, letting lighter materials wash away down the creek and waiting, hoping, for the heavy gold to sparkle at the dirty bottoms of their pans. But the gold never showed itself and a rage grew inside Arthur Hook. 'Where are you?' he screamed. 'Where are you?' And his axe swung and the muscles in his wire skeleton and no-meat body tore and he coughed and spluttered on all the rock dust he was sucking into his lungs.

It was Aubrey who told his father he was working too hard on the rock face, too fast, who told him he wasn't respecting the mountain as he should. That he was too reckless. Too hungry. Too vengeful. That they were moving too fast through the tunnel and they were not propping up the roof of their dig hole with sufficient wooden frames. But his father did not listen, could not listen, because his father was someone else. He was now a man with a yellow light in his eyes, a fire in his eyes, gold in his eyes. He was overcome by the lust for gold. The hatred for gold. The absolutes of it all.

And it was Aubrey who was at the rock face with the ore bucket, standing six safe feet behind his father's flailing rock hammer, when twenty feet of unsupported rock ceiling caved in on father and son. Aubrey saw the tunnel ceiling fall in on his father first and had time enough to turn and kneel down on the ground with his head towards his crotch and his arms over his skull, and brace for the cave-in. Two large boulders wedged a pocket of air around his face, which was pushed hard against the ground, and grey rock dust and debris pressed on his back and for three full minutes he breathed the shortest of breaths while waiting for the oxygen in that small pocket of air to be used up, and in his final moments beneath that terrifying rubble blanket he discovered the only thing in life he cared about.

It was a girl. The image of her entered his mind. She was spinning in a white dress at the school dance that past summer. Violet Berry, the teenaged daughter of Tom and Bonnie Berry. Violet Berry, with the curly brown hair and blue eyes and deep red lipstick. Violet Berry, who he was not supposed to talk to under any circumstances, and that had suited him fine because he always knew she would blind him, make him deaf and dumb, were he to stand too close to those eyes. An angel too precious to say hello to, much less ask to square dance. But now he was so close to death that he had the courage to make a pact with himself. If I survive this cave-in, he thought, I will ask Violet Berry to go riding one Sunday afternoon.

And then he felt a shovel scraping at the rubble mound

above him. He felt a boulder give way and the weight of the cavein release its suffocating pressure on his chest. Then another boulder was removed, and a shovel was frantically digging into the mound, scraping, hauling, shifting the pressure away from Aubrey's body. Soon the dirt around him was loose enough that he could push his right-hand fingers up through it and those fingers found other fingers. His brother's hand. And Horace pulled with all his strength, pulled so hard on his older brother's right arm that Aubrey thought it might come clean away from his shoulder.

Horace pulled and pulled and soon he could see his brother's hair buried in the dirt, coloured grey by the rock dust. Then he saw his face, so grey that it looked like Aubrey had turned to stone beneath that rubble. Finally his brother emerged with the air-sucking gasp of a vampire that had been trapped in a coffin for five hundred years. And Horace fell on his backside beside his coughing and spluttering older brother and the two boys looked at the impenetrable rubble wall before them knowing they both now had to dig for their father, who was lying somewhere beyond it.

But something mysterious kept them from reaching for their shovels and pickaxes. It was a strange and powerful force running through them both, something they knew never to underestimate. It was hate.

*

On the army transport, flat on his back between the human rubble of bloodied bodies, Aubrey Hook wakes with a deep and loud suck on Darwin air. His chest rises then falls back hard on the transport tray. He's punch-drunk and dazed. He looks around him. Men and women. Soldiers mostly. Some have died during the trip. Their eyelids and their mouths still open. Hands on their hearts.

The truck bounces along the uneven streets, motoring fast. Then it brakes and skids to a halt outside Cullen Bay civil hospital. Two shirtless soldiers pull the truck's rear tray guard down and begin hauling the bodies onto hospital stretchers. More soldiers come, reach for the hands and feet of the dead and wounded. Aubrey stands. His head spins but, to his surprise, he can actually walk now and so he staggers to the side of the tray and slides off the back.

'You need to lie back down, mister,' says a young soldier, hauling the dead body of an elderly woman out of the truck.

Aubrey says nothing. He coughs up a mouthful of blood and spits it onto the brown dirt by his boots, then looks down at his soiled shirt, blood-spattered and bomb-torn. He shuffles away from the army transport, his head turned to the hospital entrance where nurses and police officers and soldiers carry too many bodies into the casualty ward. Movement all around him and he moves so slow. One foot after the other. Finding his balance. In his clouded mind, he tries to find purpose. What just happened? Where was he going? What does he need to do now? And he fixes on an image in his head. Molly Hook and Greta Maze standing over him. The brown-haired gravedigger girl and the blonde-haired actress.

There is a temporary medical station under a tarpaulin outside the hospital. A nurse is handing out canvas water bags to soldiers. 'I need two,' Aubrey says softly, his body aching with the effort of speaking. A wooden bucket filled with fruit stands beside the nurse's table. Aubrey reaches for a banana and two large orange and red mangoes. He sits in the gutter of the footpath outside the hospital and glugs down the water, sinks his teeth into the skin of a mango and drives his face hard into its juicy flesh like a rabid dog. Only animal now. Primal. A beast with no past. A beast with only one goal. To find the gravedigger girl and the actress.

An olive-coloured Model A Ford pulls in to the hospital driveway. The driver rushes around to the rear-left passenger door, grabs the hands of a wounded man in a suit, and drags him cumbersomely out of the seat. Aubrey recognises the driver as Frank Roach, one of the business managers at the Bank of New South Wales on Smith Street. Frank Roach pants and strains as he drags the body of his friend along the ground, his arms hooked under the man's armpits.

Roach spots Aubrey watching him from the gutter. 'Well, don't just sit there,' he barks. 'Help me, dammit.'

Aubrey shuffles over wearily, lifts the man's legs and helps place him on a stretcher at the hospital entrance.

'Thank you,' a breathless Roach says to Aubrey, who nods silently. Roach follows two soldiers as they drag the stretchered man into the casualty ward.

Aubrey turns away from the hospital and returns to the fruit and water bags he has left by the gutter. Then he walks casually to the driver's side of Frank Roach's Model A Ford. He starts the car and coughs up another mouthful of blood that he spits out the window. Only animal now. He slams his foot on the accelerator and the wind through the car window refreshes him. But there is something more mysterious than wind keeping him upright, keeping him breathing in one last buried pocket of air. Something dangerous and energising that is fuelling him from the inside. And as the Ford speeds south out of Darwin he knows this mystery force for what it is. He learned long ago not to underestimate its power.

Only animal now. Only hate.

Nine Northern Dingoes

Her face is stained with the stomach blood of the wallaby she ate yesterday. She doesn't bark, she moans, and the sound of that moan tells the younger ones in the pack that she is second in charge behind her partner, the dominant male who walks ahead. Her coat is fire-coloured but the fur on her feet is the colour of snow. She knows a ripple of disharmony has spread through the pack. The dry season was lean and she was forced to kill the newly born pups of another pack mother, as much to maintain her own authority as to allow the spoils of pack kills to spread further. She's been walking through the boggy wetlands for most of the day and she is hungry and tired and wants to go home.

But, ahead, her partner stops behind the screen of a purple turkey bush, so she snorts twice and the rest of the pack instantly freeze behind her. She lightens her step and moves to her partner, stopping when her nose reaches his right hindleg. She is old, but she is younger than him and has better vision and she sees immediately the subject of his gaze. A field of bush apple trees in the distance, the likes of which neither of them has ever seen. The trees are so plentiful and so closely bunched together that the apples on their branches have formed a vast red apple roof that is now sheltering a small herd of wild water buffalo at rest.

She purrs softly to her partner, informing him that she, too, can see the buffalo calf drinking from a small water build-up some distance away from the rest of the herd.

She can twist her neck to face almost directly behind her, and her feet do not even move when she turns to signal to the rest of the pack that it's time to hunt.

Tear Driven

Momentum. No going back, Molly, she tells herself. For the first time in your life you are only moving forward. You might have a copper pan scrawled with directions, but there is only one way to go now. Here to there. Molly to Bob. No going back.

An avenue of creamy pink Northern Territory salmon gums and a red utility truck running between them on a narrow and damp red–dirt road filled with dry holes and full puddles. Beyond the scrub to Molly's left is the rail line running south to Alice Springs. Momentum. Destiny. She feels this. Every moment in her life unfolding precisely as it needed to in order to place the gravedigger girl right here in a fast car beside the actress.

'Faster,' Molly says.

'You wanna drive?' Greta responds, weaving the vehicle through deep potholes in the road. She brakes at a flooded road crossing.

'We can make it across,' Molly says.

'What makes you so sure?' Greta asks.

'Because we're meant to make it across,' she says. 'We've

only just begun. There's no way they'd make us stop so soon when we've only just begun.'

'Who's "they"?'

'Everybody,' Molly says. '*Everything.*'

Greta hits the accelerator and the truck powers into a stretch of floodwater that rises above its old worn rubber tyres and halfway up the front grille. More gas and Greta keeps the steering straight and Molly gives her driver an encouraging pat on the shoulder. 'Almost there,' she says. 'Keep going.'

The car feels like it will stall, but Greta presses harder on the accelerator and the wheels grip the road and the truck lurches back out of the flooded crossing. Molly claps her hands.

'Pass me one of them smokes, will ya?' Greta asks.

Molly taps a cigarette from Greta's pack and lights it for her with two confident strikes of a match. She passes the lit smoke to Greta who sticks it in the left corner of her lips where all cigarettes seem to Molly to belong.

'You need anything else?' Molly asks. 'I got food. Water.'

Greta turns to Molly. Raises her eyebrows. 'We're gonna need more of both, you know,' she says.

'I know,' Molly says. 'I know how to get more of both, too.'

'More tips from your boyfriend, Tyrone Power?'

'He's not my boyfriend,' Molly says.

'He's not? I thought you two were gonna run away together?'

Molly shakes her head. She looks out the window. Two sapphire-blue butterflies are bobbing around a Leichhardt tree with the kind of glossy green leaves Molly could fan her face with in high summer, and yellow and white flowers that look to Molly like peeled oranges sitting on lollypop sticks.

'So when's this turn-off comin'?' Greta asks.

'Soon,' Molly says.

'Read that pan out again, will ya?' Greta asks.

Molly doesn't have to read from the pan. She knows the words by heart. "'The longer I stand, the shorter I grow",' she recites. "'And the water runs to the silver road.'" Then she sniffs. She's got something stuck up her nose, a ball of dried blood, a clump of dirt. Ash, maybe.

'Why did he write all these directions in riddles?' Greta asks, frustrated. 'Why didn't he just say straight up where the bloody gold was?'

'Because those riddles were just for him,' Molly says. She blows her nose into her cupped hand. 'He didn't want anyone else to know what he was talking about. But maybe he wanted my mum to know. And maybe he wanted me to know one day and he knew we'd understand. We'd understand what he was talking about because we look at the world the same way he does. Because we're poetic.'

Molly sticks half a forefinger up her nose.

'You're poetic?' Greta asks.

'Yeah, poetic and graceful, like how my mum taught me to be,' Molly says, not looking at Greta as she pulls a large black ball of snot from her nose and flicks it casually out her window.

Greta shakes her head. 'You sure you know where you're going?'

'Yeah,' Molly says. 'You sure you want to come with me?'

Greta gives a half-smile, eyes fixed on the narrow side road that bends now past a row of honeysuckle trees with showy orange flowers that look to Molly like big fat orange caterpillars who have enjoyed too much plonk, which is why they're crawling aimlessly across the tops of those silvery fern leaves.

'Why did you come back for me?' Molly asks.

'Because you're gonna take me to all that shiny gold,' Greta says. 'And then I'm gonna fly away to Hollywood like you said.'

Molly smiles with her lips closed. 'I think there was something else you came back for,' she says. And the gravedigger
girl turns her head to study Greta's face and she watches her
driver drag hard on her smoke and then she looks past Greta's
perfect profile, past her bruised and swollen left eye and the
line of her forehead and the straight bridge of her nose, to a
line of trees on the right-hand side of the road, and among
those trees she sees movement. Something black and fast. Four
legs. Long black horns. Then something else beside it coming
out of the trees. Charging.

'Watch out!' Molly screams.

And Greta turns her head just in time to see nine large
water buffalo, frightened and reckless, charging at full speed
through the scrub and onto the thin dirt road. Behind them
Molly sees streaks of yellow-orange fur. Two vicious dingoes
pursuing the smallest buffalo in the herd.

One buffalo loses its footing in the uneven roadside and
careens unstoppably into Greta's door, horns crashing into
moving metal. The fierce impact causes Greta to yank the
steering wheel hard left and the truck slides across the slippery
dirt road, then she reefs the wheel right and straightens the
vehicle just as another confused and breathless buffalo charges
across the road in front of her. Greta instantly turns hard right
again, sending the truck flying down the sharp incline at the
side of the road towards a thick cluster of stringybark trees,
then she stamps on the flat metal brake lever and the utility
glides on the wet grass until it crashes hard into the trees,
though thankfully not hard enough to make Molly's forehead
traverse the mere three inches of air required for her head to
make contact with the windscreen.

The buffalo charge on and through the wall of scrub lining
the left side of the road and Greta's neck whips back and forth

and she's so disturbed by what's happened that her fingers remain fixed to the steering wheel.

She drops her head. Breathes deeply.

Then she says, 'Let me get this straight. We just survived an aerial bombing from the Japs, right?'

'That's right,' Molly says.

'Then we set off in search of buried treasure?'

'That's correct.'

'Then we got attacked by a bunch of wild water buffalo?'

'I wouldn't say "attacked",' Molly says. 'But definitely fair to say we were *charged* by about ten water buffalo.'

'What now?' Greta asks.

'Now we walk.'

Molly grips Bert the shovel and grabs the shoulder strap of her duffel bag. She slips out of the truck and closes the door, turns to talk through the open window.

'I'm glad you came back for me, Greta.'

'I wish I could say the same thing, Molly,' Greta says, resting her head in her hands.

'I know why you came back for me, Greta.'

'You do?' Greta replies, rubbing the whiplashed muscles in her neck.

'You were worried about me,' Molly says. And that thought makes the gravedigger girl smile as she walks on down the narrow road.

Greta watches the girl through two cracks that now curve across the windscreen. That strange child. Every last dark thing she's witnessed so far today. And she wonders what mysterious, unstoppable force must be flowing inside that girl to make her do what she is doing up there on that road now.

The gravedigger girl, skipping.

*

An empty dirt road separating bushland walls of banksias with furry yellow flowers that stick out from their branches like hot corncobs spitting butter, and these trees grow beside weeping paperbark shade trees that do their grieving in the open through outbursts of creamy white flowers that look to Molly like Greta Garbo's eyelashes when they flutter in silver screen distress.

'You ever been in deep country?' Molly asks, using Bert the shovel as a walking stick.

'Can't say I have,' Greta says, her eyes on the growing amount of road dirt flicking up on to her canvas saddle shoes.

'You're gonna love it,' Molly says. 'There's so many things you can see there. It's like a different world once you're really inside it. There's magic in there, Greta. You can start to see things the way the animals see things.'

'Sounds like you've been in deep country many times,' Greta says.

'Yeah,' Molly says, marching on. 'In my head I have.'

Brute wandering. Molly knows the secret to a long walk. Never think about the destination. Just think about the air in your lungs, the motion of your arms and legs. There is a rhythm to it, and once you have found it that rhythm can tick-tock through time forever. She loves the great riddle of walking. The more you take the more you leave behind: footsteps. And she looks behind her to see her footsteps stretching as far as she can see along the road that winds back through ironbark borders.

Don't think of the destination. Think of the red-tailed black cockatoo up there in the stringybark, with scarlet panels beneath its tail flaps, like fire is fuelling its take-off. And marvel at the way it flies through the sky. It doesn't fly like falcons and kites fly; instead its wings work hard, like the bird is rowing through the sky, rowing upstream through air.

'Cockatoo,' Molly points.

'Woo hoo,' Greta says, slapping a fat mosquito with an abdomen full of her own blood. 'We any closer to this turn-off?'

'Yep,' Molly says, but her attention is taken by something resting on the branch of a billygoat plum tree. 'Stick insect,' she whispers, approaching the cryptic creature with soft footsteps. The insect is the same straw colour as the branch it rests on. 'This feller has the most beautiful colouring hidden under his wings,' Molly says.

'Listen, kid, are you gonna stop and gaze at every little creature you find among the trees?' Greta replies.

'Just the ones worth gazing at.' Molly beams then moves closer to the insect. 'You ever wonder why things are the way they are, Greta?' she whispers. 'What if this feller was supposed to be right here on this leaf in this very moment? What if he was put here to remind you and me about something.'

'Like what?' Greta asks.

'Like how pretty it all really is,' Molly replies. 'Who decided that gold would be worth so much, anyway? I'd take this feller over a gold pebble any day of the week.'

She blows gently on the stick insect, and the lanky creature raises its head and tail and moves its wings to make a hissing sound and that movement reveals its great treasure, its glorious spoils: a vivid pink at the base of its hind wings, a pink so deep and appealing to Molly that it makes her giggle. 'You're all right, mate,' she says. 'Don't be scared. This is Greta Maze and I'm Molly Hook. We're heading deep into your scrub now because I gotta find Longcoat Bob. But don't worry about us, okay. Greta and me. We're the good people. We're the good guys.'

The insect's head ducks back down and the creature creeps on along the branch.

Molly smiles at Greta then returns to the dirt road. 'Not far now,' she says.

*

A bridge with no guard rails on its sides, stretching twenty feet across the thin freshwater creek running beneath it. The bridge is made of railway sleepers that are permanently wet and rotting. Molly stops in the middle of the bridge and she rests her backside on the edge of a sleeper, letting her legs and her dig boots dangle over the creek. From her duffel bag she pulls her water bag and glugs down four mouthfuls of rusty Darwin tap water, before throwing the bag to Greta, who splashes water across her sweaty face and enjoys a refreshing drink.

'"The longer I stand, the shorter I grow,"' Molly recites. She opens a small tin of pineapple pieces with a rusted can opener, sucks the syrupy juice down first and lifts the wedges of preserved pineapple to her mouth with grubby fingers.

Her eyes follow the flow of the creek, which disappears into a tunnel of foliage, where monsoon vines and scrub and weed have woven together to create a perfect cylinder that snakes off into the blackness. That tunnel, Molly thinks, could be just big enough for the old Ghan train to Adelaide to run through.

'They say you can't see nuthin' in the daylight further up this creek,' she says out loud. 'It gets so dark up there you need a candle to find your way out, even in the daytime.' Molly looks round at Greta. 'That's how it got its name. Candlelight Creek.' She turns back to the tunnel. '"The longer I stand, the shorter I grow,"' Molly repeats.

Greta nods her head, something dawning on her. 'A candle,' she says.

Molly nods. 'Candlelight Creek. The water that leads to the silver road.'

'You plan on walkin' up there?' Greta asks.

'That's the way to the silver road,' Molly says.

Greta feels a cold shiver in her bones. 'It gives me the willies,' she says, looking deep into the tunnel. 'You ever been up there?'

'My dad told me never to walk up Candlelight Creek,' Molly replies.

'Why?'

'He said it's very dangerous.'

'What makes it so dangerous? What's up there?'

'Dunno.'

'Whaddya mean you don't know?'

'Dad never told me.'

'Why not?'

'I was never supposed to go up there so why would he tell me what's up there?'

Molly stands and grips Bert the shovel tight as she slides down a steep mossy embankment connected to the side of the bridge which leads to a path running adjacent to Candlelight Creek.

'Maybe we should respect your father's wishes,' Greta says, standing nervously at the top of the embankment.

'Silver road's the only way to your gold,' Molly says. 'And wherever that gold is, I reckon Longcoat Bob won't be too far from it.'

Greta stares deep into the tunnel of foliage, her bones tingling.

'You got any candles?' she asks.

*

The deep country creaks and moans. Soon the gravedigger girl and the actress are so far up Candlelight Creek they can no longer see where the creek begins or ends. The water is clear, but there's so little light under the archway foliage that the creek looks black and glassy. The thick monsoon vine forest lining the creek narrows and encloses to a kind of natural and suffocating tube of wild growth, only ten feet wide in some parts. Their feet stepping and sliding over moss-covered bank boulders lining the water. The relentless ear scratch of cicadas. The smell of mud and earth and mangrove.

Greta's foot slips on the slimy buttress root of a blush satinash tree and her increasingly damaged saddle shoes land in the shallow left edge of the creek. Gripping the handle end of Bert the shovel, which Molly extends to her, she pulls herself back out.

'Why d'you want to find this Longcoat Bob so bad, anyway?' Greta asks.

Molly pauses to think on this. 'I'm gonna ask him to lift the curse,' she says.

Greta takes a moment to get her breath. 'You know, Molly, there's such a thing as rotten luck and it's a fact of life that it lands on some people more regularly than others.' Another deep breath.

Molly nods. 'I know.'

'Do you think we should talk about what happened to your dad back there?'

Molly turns, looks back up the creek. 'Nah, I don't think we need to talk about that.'

She moves on. Thick jungle now. A closed canopy of palms and ferns and wild weed. Strangler figs germinating in the forks of trees, their aerial roots wrapping round their life-giving hosts and slowly killing them. Vines and climbers merging and turning into suffocating monsters in the dark that seem to whisper to each other. Molly can hear them, talking about the gravedigger girl and all she has seen in her short life and why she's come so deep into Candlelight Creek, and about her troubled father, the good man and the bad man all at once, wedged into the fork of a tree, his leg blown off and resting by a thunderbox. Poor little gravedigger girl.

'Ya reckon Uncle Aubrey is still alive?' Molly asks.

Greta pushing along the creek edge, her hands pulling a spiky fern frond away from her face. 'I fear it's gonna take more than a world war to finish off your uncle.'

'Stop,' Molly says.

'What?'

Molly frozen stiff. 'Stop moving,' she whispers. She stares up along the creek. 'See up there. Eyes in the water.'

Greta leans forward to peer further up the creek. She mistakes it for a log at first. Then two milky white eyes blink in the glassy water.

'Shit,' Greta says.

The eyes disappear beneath the water and then the eyes reappear, breaking the water closer to Molly and Greta on the creek edge.

'Crocodile,' Molly whispers. She can see the creature's body clearly now. Almost twelve feet in length, half of that being its tail. Green-brown scales that shimmer in the water, colours blending like the insides of gemstones; a skin as ancient and earth-born as the old rocks she finds deep beneath Hollow Wood Cemetery. A long snout and a thick jaw and rows of bloodstained, conical teeth — teeth for biting into lizards and bats and rats and wallabies and gravedigger girls who step too far out of Darwin. Then a second pair of milky white eyes emerges behind the lead crocodile and then a third pair of eyes emerges beside the second one.

'You see them?' Greta asks nervously. 'We need to go back, Molly.'

'Wait,' Molly says. 'They're freshies. Freshwater crocs aren't like saltwater crocs. They don't attack like salties. Freshies are more . . .' – she searches for the right word – 'graceful.'

'What are you talking about?' Greta replies. 'Graceful? For fuck's sake, let's go.'

'Sam says he talks to these fellers,' Molly says.

The lead crocodile inflates its body. A warning sign: go back where you came from.

'This is Longcoat Bob doing this,' Molly says. 'He sent these fellers to scare us. He doesn't want us comin' any further.'

'Mol', I'm afraid you're talkin' bullshit now, kid,' Greta says. 'Let's go back.'

'I'm not talkin' bullshit,' Molly says. 'Didn't you wonder why all them water buffalo were charging at us like that? Bob sent them for us, too.'

'They were scared of something and they were running from it,' Greta says. 'That's the natural response, you see, Molly, when you're scared of something, like, oh, I don't know, say, seeing three adult crocodiles halfway up black-arse Candlelight fucking Creek! Let's go now, Molly.'

'I'm not going back,' Molly says. 'That's what Longcoat Bob wants. He wants us to scramble at the first sniff of trouble. Nup. Not me. Sorry, Bob.'

The crocodiles swim closer, their slender bodies snaking stealthily through the water. Molly grips Bert the shovel. Then she talks to the crocodiles. 'My name's Molly Hook and this is Greta Maze,' she says. The three crocodiles pause in the water, all eyes on the humans. 'Greta's a gifted actress who's gonna make it to Hollywood one day. I'm just a girl from Darwin and I've come up here lookin' for Longcoat Bob.' Molly waits for a response from the crocodiles but they say nothing. 'The Japs bombed Darwin all to hell.' She breathes deep, thinks of something else to say. 'They blew my dad to bits. I found him in a tree. That bomb must have lifted him right up off the ground.'

Greta moves closer to Molly now. She rests a hand on the girl's shoulder.

'My dad was all right. He had his problems but he still loved me. He did.' And Molly wants to cry in front of these croc-odiles. And maybe this is what people mean when they talk about crocodile tears: what you shed when you talk to croc-odiles about your dead dad. Cry, Molly, cry. They'll let you pass if you cry for them. Cry, Molly, cry. But she can't. And she tilts her head up to find the sky but there's no sky to be seen this far up Candlelight Creek.

'So I'm gonna go ask Longcoat Bob if he could stop all the bad things that keep happenin' to me,' Molly says. 'And if you fellers could just sit right there and let us pass we'll walk on up this creek and we'll thank you for your grace.'

Molly waits for a response. The crocodiles lie still and Molly nods her head confidently. She fixes the strap on her duffel bag, pulls it tight over her shoulder. She grips Bert the shovel in both hands like a spear and she walks on along the creek edge.

'Follow me, now,' Molly whispers to Greta under her breath. Greta watches Molly walk innocently, almost casually, past the crocodiles and she follows hurriedly in her footsteps. Her eyes can't help but turn to the trio of toothy creatures, who remain deathly still as their eyes − three sets of cold and ghostly and milky eyes with dark coin-slot pupils − follow every last movement of the actress's clumsy course across the slippery ancient rocks that line their creek home.

Greta moves so fast that she eventually overtakes Molly. 'Faster,' Greta says. 'Faster.'

*

Forty more minutes of walking and the creek bends away to the right and Greta can see a patch of grey light at the end of the tunnel. 'C'mon,' she says. 'We're almost out.'

She hurries along the creek bank, her movements more assured now. Greta in a summer satin dress, emerald-coloured, which shimmers when it finally finds the light of a clearing that extends from the end of the suffocating tunnel to a vast freshwater floodplain covered in pink and red lotus lily flowers that stand tall out of submerged rootstocks connected to smooth, green, rounded leaves so wide and flat they look to Molly like circular steps she could walk on to make her way across the deepest wetland pools.

'Look at this place!' Greta screams. The actress starts to run and she breathes the wetland air deep into her lungs and she raises her arms to the sun. To her left is a billabong of vivid water lilies like something from her wildest twilight dreams, perfect suns of gold rising from the centre of each purple flower. To her right is a field of white snowflake lilies, their showy flowers like ostrich feathers made of the desiccated coconut flakes in which she rolls her freshly iced lamingtons on a lazy Sunday afternoon.

'What is this place?' Greta hollers back to Molly.

And Molly screams back to the actress in delight, 'It's Australia.'

They walk on for a few miles, their shoes sloshing through

thick green grass that grows from water that in places reaches up to Molly's kneecaps. It is at least cooling. Greta cups three handfuls and splashes them across her face. At a small build-up of water in a circle of spear grass, Molly kneels down with her grandfather's prospector's pan and washes away the hard cemetery earth that masks the mysterious etchings on its battered underside.

Greta stands at Molly's shoulder, drinking from the water bag. Molly studies the pan. It's smaller than she remembers it being. She runs her fingers over the etched words her grand-father wrote to himself and maybe, just maybe, to his daughter and his daughter's daughter.

T he longer I stand, the shorter I grow
And the water runs to the silver road

Molly's dirt-caked forefinger traces the carefully drawn line that meanders down the circular base, taking occasional lefts and rights, to a second set of words.

West where the yellow fork man leads
East in the dark when the wood bleeds

The line is like a road and the sets of words are like rest stops along that road.

'This pan was a gift to me when I was seven years old,' Molly says. 'My mum called it a sky gift. She said there are gifts that are always falling from the sky. This was one of the gifts that fell from the sky just for me, Greta. I looked up at the sky and when I looked down again my mum had disappeared into the bush and I never saw her again. Then I turned around and this pan was lying at my feet. I reckon she wanted me to have it, but I don't know why she wanted me to have it.'

'Maybe she wanted you to go find that gold for yourself,' Greta says. 'Maybe this pan is your inheritance. She wanted to give you something before . . .' Greta doesn't finish that sentence.

'Before what?' Molly asks.

'Before she had to go away.'

Molly scratches at the pan, soaks it in the water again, scrubs it with her fingers.

'I think she wanted me to find Longcoat Bob,' Molly says.

She soaks the pan again, and a third set of words reveals itself in the afternoon light.

City of stone 'tween heaven and earth

The place beyond your place of birth

Greta kneels down beside Molly for a closer look.

'"The place beyond your place of birth",' Greta considers. She dwells on this for a moment. 'Where was your grandfather born?'

'He was born in Halls Creek, across the border in Western Australia,' Molly says.

'Where were you born?' Greta asks.

'I think I was born in Darwin Hospital like my mum,' Molly says.

'You got any idea what he's on about?'

'Not yet,' Molly replies. 'We haven't gone deep enough yet to find out.'

She soaks the pan again, scrubs at the bottom of the base and holds the pan up to the light once more. Her forefinger runs along more newly revealed words and the mystery of them sends a shiver down her twelve-year-old spine.

Own all you carry, carry all you own

Step inside your heart of stone

'What's that supposed to mean?' Greta asks.

'That's what Longcoat Bob said he was going to do with his curse,' Molly says. 'He said he would turn our true hearts to stone.' Molly thinks of the blood-red rock she's carrying inside her duffel bag.

'But how do you step inside a heart of stone?' Greta asks.

'I don't know,' Molly says. 'Maybe we'll only know when we know. We have to follow the path. One step at a time.'

She traces the map line with her fingernail. 'When we find the silver road we follow this line going down here. And we look for things. I reckon my grandfather saw things like I see things sometimes. Maybe I'll be able to see what he saw when I see those same things.'

Greta raises her eyebrows, takes another swig of water. 'So what do you see now, Molly?'

Molly's eyes follow the thin stretch of what's left of Candlelight Creek, which snakes through the wetlands towards what appear to be, a mile or maybe two in the distance, two towering red sandstone plateaus split by a deep and miraculous canyon.

'The water runs to the silver road,' Molly says. 'We follow the water to that range. The silver road is in there somewhere.'

Then she turns her head to the sun. 'But we'd best get there before dark.' And she keeps staring in the direction of that sun because she can see a flash of silver in the sky beneath it. She puts a palm to the top of her forehead and looks harder at the silver flash.

'A plane,' Molly says.

Greta turns her head to where Molly is looking. The silver plane moves closer. They can hear its engine now, the relentless buzz of its front propeller. Molly can tell how light and agile the plane is by the way it bobs and shudders in air pockets, but otherwise it maintains a steady course that she comes to realise is leading it straight towards them. Greta stands, confused, eyes up to the sky as the plane flies over her head. Then she sees the red circles. The red rising-sun circles of paint on the underside edges of the plane's sparkling metal wings. A Japanese fighter plane. All this way from Japan via Pearl Harbor and the Darwin central business district. All that blue sky and the hornet buzz of the metal fighter cutting through it.

'It's a Jap,' Greta says. 'But what's he doing all the way out here?' The fighter zooms high over Greta's head and banks hard left and circles back around to where it came from and Molly and Greta turn in a circle in the sloshy floodplain grass without taking their eyes off the plane.

'What's he doing?' Molly asks.

'I don't know,' Greta says.

The fighter comes lower this time. It halves its speed and it circles Greta and Molly.

'Should we run for it?' Molly asks.

Greta scans the floodplain. No trees for shelter. There's an ochre-coloured termite mound taller than her, but it must be at least a hundred yards from where she stands in the open wetland. 'We'd be dead already if he wanted to kill us,' she says.

She turns in another circle, following the fighter plane as it orbits the blonde actress in the shimmering emerald dress and the gravedigger girl in the sky-blue dress that she hopes to dance in one day with handsome Sam Greenway the buffalo hunter. The plane circles the girls once more and this time it comes in so close and low that Greta can see directly into the plane's cockpit. The pilot is staring back at her. He leans hard left on his control stick, but his eyes don't care for direction, they appear to care only for the actress whose saddle shoes are waterlogged in the wetland slush.

Greta can see the man clearly now. A hard jawline beneath thick brown aviator goggles. A brown leather flight helmet, fur-lined, with its side flaps covering his ears. Then the engine seems to cut out and the plane appears to be gliding around her and there is no sound, only a metal flight machine floating on the breeze and the machinery of her heart beating fast beneath her chest. The pilot won't stop staring at Greta and now, to Molly's befuddlement, he raises his goggles to his forehead, and his Japanese face looks stunned-mullet puzzled by the actress. The silent plane looks to Molly like a bird, a grey brolga in the low sky with its big black wings outstretched, hovering effortlessly on an invisible wind.

Then the engine rattles back to life and the plane turns and roars back to where it came from, back towards the sun, before circling around once more, but higher now. It soars above Greta and Molly and their eyes turn up to watch it flying towards the two tall red sandstone plateaus.

And Greta and Molly watch the plane fly on its inexplicable course towards red rock and their feet begin to move involuntarily because they are drawn to the image of that silver arrow moving in the sky. But then they stop in their tracks when they see the white mushroom cloud of a parachute with a pilot attached to it falling from the fighter's cockpit. The aircraft flies on as the parachute spirals down towards the floodplain. Beyond the parachuting pilot, the plane nose-dives in a great arc towards the plateaus and it must be moving at two hundred miles an hour or more when it meets a craggy outcrop of red rock and explodes into a brief ball of flame. Molly looks back to the pilot falling from the sky and her feet want to move faster now. These feet have their own instincts and she follows them.

'Wait, Molly!' Greta calls.

'C'mon, Greta!' Molly says, sprinting across the floodplain. 'He wants to meet us.'

'He's a Jap, Molly,' Greta says. 'He's our enemy, Molly! Stop!'

'He's not our enemy,' Molly shouts behind her. 'He's our gift.'

*

Yukio Miki's family shortsword tucked into his belt. His brown leather flight boots making circles in the air as the parachute plummets in a spiral to the ground. He can't see anything on the ground that will help him plan a safe landing. Just long grass. Wetlands. Deep green and black pools of water. Purple flowers. Red flowers. His brown leather boots spin and the world spins with them.

Then he crashes hard and fast into a pool, so hard and fast that his boots touch the marshy bottom. There are reeds and grass spears beneath the surface that he struggles to kick through. He swallows water and pushes his way back up, arms and legs flailing, to the surface, where he assesses the diameter of the small lagoon he has fallen into. One of its banks is only eight or nine metres from him and he attempts to paddle to it, but the billowing canopy of his white silk parachute is sinking into the water and pockets of it are growing heavy and threatening to pull him deep below the surface. His right hand reaches for the chute pack release buckle at his belly, but to open it he must stop the furious dog-paddling that is keeping his head above the water. He voluntarily sinks into the water and with two hands reefs at the buckle, but the heavy weight of the now-sunken chute is pulling on the two metal connectors and jamming them in their sockets. He tugs again but the buckle won't release, and he reaches momentarily for the Miki family blade in his belt, but he needs more air so he pushes back up to the surface and he sees the blue northern Australian sky above him and he looks for the pool edge and then he sees the girl and the woman.

The girl carries a shovel and she smiles and she has brown hair and she wears a sky-blue dress and black boots. And then the woman appears beside her, panting and gathering her breath. That blonde hair that falls to one side over her face. The way she stands in the green dress. He notices there is pink and blue bruising around one of the blonde woman's eyes and then those eyes, those perfect green eyes, find Yukio Miki and they reach into him, deep inside him, and he is immediately frozen by that stare. He has never seen a woman who looks like this and something about her has turned his body to lead, to stone, and he can no longer wave his arms and legs about in the water to keep himself afloat because she has frozen him with that face of hers and he gargles on wetlands water as his dumb blank head sinks gradually below the surface again. And Yukio thinks for a moment how strange it is to die like this and to have that vision – that woman with the green eyes – as the last thing his tired eyes will see on earth. But something about it makes him feel better, makes him feel good and ready now for Takamanohara. It was all worth it. The training. The discipline. The punishment. He will go now, content with that final vision. He will sink into the Plain of High Heaven and the last thing he will hear will be the voice of the Australian girl saying in English, 'Swim, swim.'

His eyes are still open as he sinks down and sunlight breaks through the water and lights the emerald greens in the flood-plain pool and he realises that the water is the same colour as the blonde woman's dress and eyes. And the sinking parachute drags him further and the surface sunlight fades as he descends. It's nice down here, he realises, if he does not fight against the pull of the chute. He could stay here and find peace in the emerald green.

But then through the last beams of sunlight comes a wooden pole, a shovel handle. And Yukio reaches out instinctively for that lifeline as his body sinks deeper, and at first only three fingers of his left hand can grip its end, but that's enough to pull it towards him and get four then five fingers on it, and with those five fingers he hauls himself back up towards the daylight, towards the sky. And the shovel handle keeps lifting him and he rises to the surface to find the girl, that young girl, up to her chest in the water, pulling hard with all her strength, her bony left arm extending the shovel and her right arm gripped, behind her, by the two hands of the blonde woman, who pulls and heaves and pulls and heaves from the grassy bank.

Soon Yukio is close enough to the water's edge to plant a boot on the pool bottom and push hard with his legs while still dragging the buckle-jammed chute behind him. The young girl scrambles to land and she rushes to a canvas duffel bag and finds a small paring knife she has wrapped in an old tea towel. She rushes to Yukio's shoulders and hacks back and forth rapidly at the chute pack's shoulder straps as Yukio leans forward hard at the water's edge.

The straps snap free and the parachute pack sinks into the water followed by the chute canopy and Yukio falls face-first on the soggy ground. He raises his head to give thanks, but he sees the girl with the curled brown hair moving cautiously away from him, her eyes drawn to the pilot's waist. Not to the Miki family sword tucked inside his flight belt, but to the black Japanese army service pistol holstered at his side. She is frightened by the handgun.

Yukio's hand moves instinctively to his waist. He will remove the pistol and holster. He will show the girl he means no harm. But then the shovel blade is suddenly inches from his eyes.

'Don't you dare touch that gun,' says Greta, gripping the shovel in both hands like it's a cricket bat and she's set to knock the Japanese pilot's head over the nearest boundary fence.

Yukio freezes, raises his arms, palms open towards the sky.

'What are you doing this far south?' Greta probes. It's a theatrical performance. Today's role: somebody tougher and harder than Greta Baumgarten ever was. One show only. She knows, deep down, she'll crumble into nervous stuttering any second now.

Yukio speaks a series of Japanese words.

'English?' Greta asks. 'You speak any English?'

Yukio says more Japanese words.

Greta nods at Molly. 'Molly, get that handgun there.'

Molly crawls in close to the pilot. She unbuttons the side holster and removes the pistol with its brown wooden handle and thin black barrel.

'Come up here with me, Molly,' Greta says.

The girl springs to her feet and stands beside the actress.

'Now point that thing at him but, you know, don't shoot 'im,' Greta says.

Molly takes a deep breath and exhales. 'Don't you think that feels a little aggressive, pointing a gun at him?' she asks.

'Him and his mates just blew up half of Darwin, I think we should feel a little aggressive,' Greta says. 'If he moves, shoot him in the legs.'

'I can't be sure I'll do that, Greta,' Molly replies. 'I'll be aiming for his legs but I'll probably get him in the head or somethin' and I don't want to kill any human being, even if his mates did blow up the milk bar on Bennett Street.'

From the ground, Yukio's squinting eyes look up into the sky as he slowly raises his hand and points between Molly and Greta.

'Hikoki,' he says, softly, his finger pointing towards the falling sun. He makes the hand gesture of a plane moving through the sky. 'Hikoki.'

Molly and Greta turn their heads instinctively towards where Yukio is pointing and see nothing but blue sky, and Molly turns back just in time to find Yukio engaging her in a silent wrist bend and then a near-invisible leg sweep that lands her, in the space of half a second, flat on her back and disarmed. Yukio now stands pointing his pistol at Greta.

'How did you do that?' Molly asks, awed and elated. 'That was incredible!'

Yukio points at the shovel in Greta's hands, waves two fingers towards himself as he holds out his free left hand. Greta hands the shovel to the pilot. Yukio passes it straight to Molly. 'Doko ni Iku no,' he says, nodding.

Molly takes the shovel. She remembers to be graceful. 'Thank you,' she says to the fallen pilot.

'You don't have to use your manners around cold-blooded killers, Molly,' spits Greta.

Yukio waves the gun at Molly, directing her to move back beside Greta.

Yukio stands soaking wet in his flight uniform. Goggles on his forehead keeping his dripping fur-lined flight helmet in place. Not a single line on his face. High cheekbones, and cheeks that would be fuller if he ate more. A large deep-brown freckle on his right cheek and two smaller ones above his top lip.

He points at Greta and Molly. 'Doko ni Iku no?' he asks, sharply. He points at them again. Then he gestures a walking motion with his left-hand forefinger and middle finger. 'Aust . . . ralians.' Then another walking finger gesture.

'Where are we going?' Molly offers, courteously.

Yukio nods. Molly nods enthusiastically. She holds up a finger.

'You want to come with us?' Molly asks, her words louder than they would be talking to Greta.

Yukio nods.

'Wait,' she says. 'I need to show you something.' She rushes to her duffel bag, retrieves Tom Berry's copper pan, hands it to Yukio. He's immediately confused by the girl's presentation of the pan.

'You use it to find gold in creeks,' Molly says. 'Look on the back.' She makes a revolution with her finger. 'Turn it over,' she says. And she moves closer to the pilot as he turns the pan over and studies the writing etched on its base. 'We're on a great quest,' Molly says. She runs her finger over the words. Yukio turns his eyes back to Greta, keeps his weapon on her. Molly oblivious to any possible tension in the moment. 'These are directions and clues to buried treasure,' she says, wide-eyed. 'A pile of gold sitting in the ground.' She holds her palms together like she's carrying a large gold nugget. 'Gold!' she says. She points at Greta. 'Greta wants to find that gold because she's convinced no harm can come to her from keeping that gold because she doesn't believe in curses,' Molly says, talking too fast because she's nervous, because she's on her way to find Longcoat Bob. Because she's free. 'All that "hocus-pocus",' she calls it.' Molly smiles.

Confusion across Yukio's face. 'Hocus . . . pocus?' he says, doing his best to repeat the words accurately.

The pilot turns to Greta, who rolls her eyes.

'I don't care about the gold,' Molly continues. 'I just want to find Longcoat Bob. He's the bloke who put a curse on my family because the buried gold was his and my grand-father stole it. But then my grandfather put that gold back because all these terrible things started happening to him and his family members, but even after he put the gold back Longcoat Bob never lifted his curse from my grandfather, Tom, and all those terrible things kept happening.' Molly is making her own realisations as her explanation is unfolding. 'And now . . . and now . . . those terrible things are all happening to me.'

Yukio struggles to make the slightest sense of Molly's words. 'Curse?' he says, repeating an English word vaguely familiar to his ear.

'Yeah, curse,' Molly says.

Yukio makes a walking gesture with his fingers. 'You?' he prompts.

'We're walking to the range,' Molly says, pointing at the two red sandstone plateaus in the distance. 'We're going to find the silver road and then we're going to find Longcoat Bob.'

'Bob,' Yukio says.

'Yeah, Bob,' Molly says.

Yukio waves his handgun towards the sandstone range.

'Aruku,' he says. He waves his gun again.

'Sorry, I don't speak Japanese,' Molly says.

Another walking gesture with his fingers. 'Aruku.'

'Walk?' Molly guesses.

'Walk,' Yukio repeats.

Molly turns to Greta. 'He wants us to walk,' she says happily. Greta shakes her head.

Molly throws her duffel bag over her shoulder. 'You comin' with us?' she asks Yukio, bright and optimistic.

'Aruku,' Yukio says blankly.

Molly marches off through wetland grass up to her thighs. 'I think he's comin' with us,' she shouts to Greta, who runs to catch up with her.

Yukio falls in behind them, his handgun pointing at Greta's back.

'Have you lost your mind?' Greta whispers.

'What?' Molly ponders, innocently.

'He's not coming with us, Molly. You think he parachuted out of his fighter plane and floated all the way down here just so he could take a gentle stroll with us?'

Molly looks back over her right shoulder to see Yukio sloshing through the grass, the handgun still firmly gripped in his right fist. Molly gives him a warm smile, turns back to Greta. 'He's gonna help us, Greta,' she says, never more certain of anything.

'Molly, wake up,' Greta says. 'He's going to walk us into the foothills of that range and he's gonna shoot you between the eyes and he's gonna rape me and if you're lucky, kid, it won't be the other way round.'

'You think he's a bad one?' Molly whispers.

'It doesn't matter what one he is,' Greta says. 'That army came here to kill us, Molly. They've got it in for us and the kinda hate they're carrying is a spell that can't be lifted. You just be ready to pass me that shovel when I give you the sign.'

'Okay,' Molly says.

Yukio watches the blonde-haired woman and the brown-haired girl with the shovel trudge across the soggy floodplain.

'Greta,' whispers Molly.

'Yes,' Greta whispers back.

'What's the sign gonna be?' Molly asks.

'It doesn't matter, Molly, you'll know the sign when you see it.'

Yukio sees the girl raise her right fist and extend her thumb from it.

'What about a thumbs-up?' Molly suggests.

'I was thinking something a little more subtle,' Greta says. 'Just a nod will do. You'll know the nod when you see it. Keep walking.'

They walk for another thirty yards or so through an open field.

'Greta,' Molly whispers.

'Yes, Molly.'

'He can't speak English.'

'So?' Greta replies.

'Maybe the sign could be a secret password that he won't understand?' Molly says.

'Like what?' Greta asks.

'Fat barramundi,' Molly says confidently.

'Fat barramundi?' Greta repeats, dubious. 'Why "fat barramundi"?'

'Was just thinkin' about how much I'd go some fried fish for dinner.'

Greta nods.

'Fat barramundi,' Molly says. 'No way a Jap flyboy would have eaten a fat barramundi before.'

'Okay, Molly,' Greta says. 'The sign is a secret password and the secret password is "fat barramundi".'

Molly nods.

Greta marches on, frustrated by their circumstances, the length of the grass scratching her legs, the humidity of the wetlands, the Japanese serviceman with a pistol walking behind her. Molly walks through the grass with a spring in her step, privately thrilled by the unexpected third-party turn in her quest.

'Greta?' Molly whispers.

'Yes, Molly.'

'Would "Mangrove Jack" work better as a secret password?'

*

Seen from the orange-red sky above and looking down and closer in and closer in, they are three wanderers crossing a vivid floodplain cut by sinuous rivers and wide freshwater channels dotted with lily-fringed waterholes.

The sun low and honeyed. The man in the Japanese military uniform at the back of the group stopping every so often in his tracks to breathe the wild floodplain deep inside him, to take in the vision of all this wild green life. By the edge of a clearwater billabong he pauses briefly to smell a floating vine flower, the kangkong, with its white and pink flowers shaped like trumpets. The intoxicating scent and the depth of the pink colour that deepens and darkens inside the flower's wide throat. It makes him laugh.

'What's he laughing at?' Molly asks.

'He's a nut,' Greta says.

Yukio turns a full circle on his feet, taking in his setting. He raises his palms to the sky, smiling. He wonders for a moment if this very floodplain is Takamanohara, the Plain of High Heaven, and he crossed into it somehow the moment he left his war brethren flying over Darwin. A part of him surely died back there in that bomb-ravaged town, and maybe that was the part of him that broke prematurely through the gates of the afterlife and this, this sweltering, primordial, vine-strewn utopia, is where Nara waits for him.

'Maybe it's the war,' Molly says.

'What do you mean?' Greta asks.

'It messes with their heads,' Molly says. 'I once saw Bluey Scofield acting like this out front of The Vic. He was ravin' about seeing things on the Somme and then he'd smile at a passing pigeon like it was some kind of angel from heaven.'

Across the plain, a troupe of seven dancing brolgas perform a kind of ballet on the grass, and their will to move, their need to share their strange beauty like this, makes Yukio's bottom lip fall. He laughs again. 'Migoto!' he hollers, in their honour. He claps his hands. An ovation.

A pair of masked lapwing birds fly over his head and he nearly falls on his backside trying to maintain his skyward view of their strange bright-yellow caruncles, which cover their faces like they are wearing yellow pilots' helmets and the side flaps are oversized and hanging from the bird's spear-like beak. And he laughs. 'Migotoooohh!'

Further on, Yukio spots an aquatic frog with its legs glued to a floating lily pad, and he plants one foot in the marshy pond to inspect its wide yellow eyes.

'Migoto,' he whispers.

The frog's green and brown skin resembles a perfect leaf that wraps around its body like a tailored suit. Then the frog leaps to a neighbouring lily pad and the fallen pilot nods in thanks, clapping his hands.

Later, by a flowing freshwater channel, closer to the sandstone plateaus, he stops to marvel at a water python speeding across leaf-strewn ground to the safety of a crack-filled rock wall dividing a row of eucalypts. The snake is three metres long and its back is black and brown like the rocks Yukio keeps picking up and holding in his hands, but the snake's belly is the colour of full sun. It looks to Yukio like someone must have painted that colour on the snake – vivid yellow oil paint, still wet – but the headstrong snake leaves no winding yellow trail as it moves towards its shelter.

The Japanese pilot is so mesmerised by this snake that Greta, who stands within arm's reach of the distracted stranger and has noted the pilot has lowered the handgun to his right thigh, sees an opportunity. 'Fat barramundi!' she says.

But Molly misses the secret communication because she is standing beside Yukio Miki with her eyes on the leafy ground, equally captivated by reptile. She smiles at Yukio.

'Fat barramundi!' Greta says, louder this time, and Molly finally hears her. But then she turns her eyes to Greta and discreetly shakes her head. No.

She lifts her eyes to Yukio, smiling. 'Migoto,' she says, nodding her head knowingly. 'Very . . . very . . . migoto.'

And Yukio smiles and Molly spots for the first time the light in the eyes of the pilot, the warmth in his smile, his innocence. That is a silver light, she tells herself. A silver light for the silver road, if not the silver screen.

Greta shakes her head, marches on across the floodplain.

*

Wide spaces between them, walking single file. Greta in front, Molly in the middle, Yukio at the back with his eyes on the woman in the emerald dress. He does not know where the woman is heading and he wonders if she does not know either. The brown-haired girl seems to walk by instinct, as if something deep inside her is pushing her thin bones forward. Her ramblings made no sense, even when she pointed at the copper pan in her bag and seemed so determined to express the deep meaning of the words etched into its base.

Now the girl's feet move faster as the trio near the edge of the severed sandstone range that spreads across the fringe of the floodplain like a fortress for Greek gods.

'We made it to the range!' Molly hollers.

The ground changes from boggy grassland to a series of treelined rocky inclines shaped like giant whale heads leading to one of the towering sandstone escarpments. The rocky outcrops are slippery to walk up and Yukio loses his footing several times and has to cling to clumps of weed sticking out of the old rocks. Wide bowls have been carved out of the rock by water and wind. Strange and unsettling things in the earth that Yukio has not seen before. Inside these perfectly smooth and circular hollows are old animal bones and coals from long-abandoned fires.

Molly spots birds in the tall trees growing in the shadow of the plateau. A red-backed kingfisher. Blue-faced honeyeaters. She stops and waves Yukio over, puts a finger to her mouth. 'Ssshhhh.' She kneels silently and Yukio kneels with her, follows the girl's pointing finger to a rock fig growing in a deep crevice. He squints and finds the subject of the girl's fascination: a perfectly still, crimson finch, so brilliant and so fragile and so red it might as well be made of ruby. And Yukio hears the girl talking English and realises quickly she is not talking to him but to the bird.

'Hello Mr Finch,' she says. 'Have you seen Longcoat Bob anywhere around these parts?'

Yukio smiles. That name again. Bob. Easy enough to say. 'Bob,' he says, nodding.

Molly nods. 'Bob,' she confirms.

And Yukio and Molly stand as the vivid crimson finch flies from the rock fig and shoots deep into the canyon that stretches out before them between the two grand sandstone plateaus divided by a freshwater stream that Molly connects in her head to the channels of the floodplain and, way, way back, to the three crocodile kings of Candlelight Creek. 'This way,' she says.

*

Molly sings. 'Pennies From Heaven'. She sings loud because she wants to hear the echo of her voice climb the canyon walls that are three times the height of the Bank of New South Wales building on Smith Street back in town.

Yukio cups water with his hand and drinks from the thin clear stream meandering through the canyon. Molly and Greta collect dry twigs as kindling for a fire they want to have lit before nightfall.

'Bing Crosby,' Molly explains to Yukio despite his lack of understanding. 'Dottie Drake plays Bing all day in the hair salon. I've always liked "Pennies From Heaven". It's a song about sky gifts. Bing says the clouds are filled with pennies and whenever it rains, the coins fall from the sky. So you shouldn't be afraid of storms because them storms are what shake all the pennies from the clouds, and actually we'd be wise to walk outside with our umbrellas upside down.' Molly has a thought and it stops her in her tracks. 'Do you reckon the hair salon is still there, Greta? I hope Dottie got out before the bombs hit.'

Greta keeps her head down, searching a rock platform now for thicker logs. She moves closer to Molly.

'You reckon anything's left at all back in town?' Molly asks. 'Do ya reckon anyone got—'

'Molly, shut your trap for a second and listen to me,' Greta whispers. 'When the fire starts, you give this feller a nice big can of that corned beef in your bag. We'll get him nice and cosy and the minute he drops off to sleep, we'll grab that gun and run like hell.'

'I don't think he's gonna hurt us, Greta,' Molly says. 'He's a good one. I can see it all over him.' Molly looks over her shoulder to the stream, where Yukio is staring at the water, distant and frozen in his thoughts. 'He's just sad, that's all,' Molly says. 'I think he wants to help us.'

'He's a loop at best, and the worst ain't worth thinkin' about,' Greta says. 'You just stay awake and wait for my signal.'

'"Fat barramundi"?'

'No, Molly, the signal isn't gonna be bloody "fat barramundi". It's gonna be me grabbing you by the arm and silently dragging you away from the strange-fruit Jap flyboy. You follow?'

Molly nods.

'You just be sure to stay awake,' Greta says. 'Got it?'

'Got it,' Molly says.

*

Full stars shimmering in a night sky framed by the canyon walls. A thousand pinholes of silver light breaking through a blanket of black. A frog croaking somewhere wet. Cicadas in the ghost gums, the kind they call the northern double drummer, creating their great wall of sound. A crackling fire on a flat rock by the canyon stream, and on one side of that fire sits Greta Maze with her knees tucked up to her chest and looking through the fire at the Japanese pilot sitting on the other side, who's scooping salty wet beef from a roughly cut open tin. And soundtracking all of this night sky, star-wrapped scene is the relentless snoring of Molly Hook, the obnoxious nose and throat rattle of it bouncing between the canyon walls.

Greta assesses the snoring girl and rolls her eyes. Molly lasted thirty minutes by the fire before she was dead to the world and now she sleeps, deep and loud, turned on her side on the flat rock, knees pulled to her chest for warmth, arms over her shins. It's cool and getting cooler in the bottom of the canyon.

Greta turns back to the pilot. He's still stuffing his face with soggy canned beef, licking his fingers. No helmet and goggles on his head now. His hair is black and militarily cut, short and neat. The pistol rests on the flat rock by his right knee.

Yukio notices Greta staring at him. He stops eating. He offers her the open can of beef. 'You?'

Greta shakes her head, looks away, repulsion in that head shake.

Yukio turns to Molly. The brown-haired girl who likes to talk is finally speechless, yet she makes noise even in her sleep. He smiles. He sees that she is shivering in her sleep. He places his near-empty can of beef down by his side and stands and walks softly over to her.

'What are you doing?' Greta asks, protectively. 'Get away from her.'

Yukio does not stop. He unbuttons his flight jacket. It's rust-coloured, made of a cotton and silk blend, thick and heavy. A blue chrysanthemum has been stitched into the jacket sleeve, the sacred mark of the Japanese naval aviator. He wears only a plain white T-shirt now, tucked tight into a thick brown military belt and pants. The shirt hugs his body and his body is all bone and muscle. A body of pure military means: lean, fit and useful. He kneels down and gently lays the flight jacket over the gravedigger girl. He walks back to his place at the fire, picks up his soft leather helmet – fur-lined and insulating – then he walks back to Molly and, carefully lifting her head up briefly from the slab of hard sandstone, gently slips it onto her head. Molly gives a loud snort, turns over onto her other side, instinctively pulls the welcoming jacket tight around her body, and nestles into the flight helmet.

Yukio nods. He offers a half-smile as he turns back to Greta. 'I musume,' he says. Greta stares at him, puzzled.

He looks back down at Molly. The brown-haired girl has a good heart. He points at her. '"I musume,' he says again, tapping his own heart.

Greta nods with a vague sense of understanding.

Yukio nods.

He sits back down by the fire opposite Greta and warms his hands. A long silence between the man and the woman, no sound but the cicadas and the crackle of burning eucalypt logs.

Yukio taps his chest. 'Yukio,' he says. He taps his chest again. 'Yukio.'

Greta nods. She taps her chest reluctantly with her forefinger. 'Greta,' she says.

Yukio repeats the name. 'Greta.' He nods and taps his chest again. 'Yukio Miki,' he says.

Greta takes a pained inhale. She nods, tapping her chest. 'Greta Maze,' she says.

'Greta . . . Maze,' Yukio repeats.

He taps his chest again. 'Yukio Miki . . . kara . . . Sakai . . . Japan.'

Greta nods. 'Greta Maze . . . Sydney . . . Australia.'

Yukio nods, smiling. 'Sid . . . inny,' he says.

Greta nods. She slides her backside closer to the fire, lies down on her side, rests the side of her face on her cupped hands. She still feels the bruising around her eye but the aching in her head is easing.

She stares into the fire and the fire plays the flickering film reel of her life and how she left Sydney on a train as a young woman with a bag of clothes and then the train of her life ran off the tracks and careened into the arms of Aubrey Hook, and those arms of Aubrey Hook are whaling her now. Fists against the bones in her head. And she closes her eyes to sleep because sleep is the only thing that will stop those fists from flailing. But when she closes her eyes she sees something worse. A sterile white hospital room and a baby in her arms and the baby wailing. 'Ssshhhhh,' Greta whispers. 'Ssssshhhh.' But the baby's wailing only grows louder. And Greta cries now, too. Greta Baumgarten in her mind and Greta Maze on a cold hard bed of sandstone. Both those women crying.

'Tori no hoshi,' Yukio says softly into the night air. Greta opens her eyes to see Yukio with his right arm pointing to the night sky. 'Tori no hoshi,' he says. And he smiles.

The bird star story. The story of the brightest star he sees shining up there far beyond the canyon walls. That's a good story to tell by a fire like this one. The nighthawk star story. The ugly nighthawk who felt ugly on the inside because all the other birds in the forest said he was ugly on the outside. They said his feathers had no colour, only the reddish-brown colours of dirt and clay. The crimson finch he saw today. That bird reminded Yukio of the nighthawk. The other birds said the nighthawk's beak was flat and useless and pointed out that his mouth was so wide it stretched from one ear to the other. And the nighthawk was so saddened by his ugliness he decided to leave the forest, but when he left he was still sad and he thought the only thing that could take his sadness away was to leave the earth altogether, and so he flew high into the blue sky, so high that his beak bumped into the sun. And the nighthawk told the sun he was fixing to die. And the bird asked, 'Sun, will you take me with you when you fall into the night? I'll be glad to die in your fire. And my ugly body will give out one single flash of light as it burns and that light will be beautiful.'

'I cannot take you with me,' the sun said. 'I belong to the day, my friend, and you belong to the night. You need to fly on, nighthawk, fly on to the stars, who belong to the night like you.'

And the bird flew on, flapping its tiring wings, up, up, up into the night sky until it ran into three young night stars who were talking among themselves.

'Excuse me,' said the bird. 'I'm wondering if you could take me with you when you leave before daylight.' But the three young stars laughed at the bird and said they would never welcome such an ugly colourless creature into their star sky. The nighthawk wept but it flew on, higher into the night sky, so high that it was soon soaring above every star.

The nighthawk looked down upon the stars now instead of looking up at them, and it felt proud to have soared so high – surely higher than any other forest bird had ever flown. But then the nighthawk's wings stopped flapping because it was exhausted by its journey from the forest to the stars, and its eyes closed and the bird fell asleep, just as its tired wings made their final flaps. The bird died in that moment, but it did not fall from the sky for it was then reborn. Transformed.

That night back on earth and deep in the forest, the pretty birds who had laughed and joked about the ugly nighthawk were stunned to see a new star in the night sky. It sat higher and burned more brightly than any other star and inside it twinkled every colour of the spectrum. It was the prettiest thing the forest birds had ever seen.

'Tori no hoshi,' Yukio says to the night sky.

'The stars?' Greta nods.

'Tori no hoshi,' the pilot says, nodding.

Greta watches the pilot lie flat on his back, his eyes fixed on the stars in the night sky. The pinholes of light are losing the war between the stardust and the darkness, but the stardust won't give up the fight.

'The stars,' Yukio whispers. And his heavy eyes close to darkness.

*

Molly wakes with a hand on her face.

'Sssshhhh,' whispers Greta. The actress stands silently, a fore-finger to her lips.

Molly rubs her eyes. Embers in the fading fire. She can see her duffel bag hanging over Greta's shoulder.

Molly stands silently. Greta takes several light-footed steps in her saddle shoes across the flat rock to where Yukio sleeps on his side, close to the edge of the fire, arms across his chest, hugging his body tight. The handgun rests behind his back on the rock. His family sword rests by the handgun.

Then the pilot shifts his position, turns hard to his other side, back to the handgun, and then his head shakes rapidly in his sleep.

Greta stands still, watching him.

Molly freezes.

'Ssshhh,' Greta whispers again, her eyes fixed on the pilot who appears to be struggling with the dreams inside his head.

Then a sharp and aching 'Ugghh' emerges from his lips and seems to hurt him. He jolts in his sleep. He shudders in his sleep. Then he turns back to the fire, eyes shut. 'Ugggghhh,' he groans again and that sound seems to come from deep within his corned-beef gut. It's a rumble, a pain rattle, the echo of a thousand sorrows, and it makes Molly move closer to the pilot. She sees that his whole body is shaking now.

'What's wrong with him?' Molly whispers.

'Ssshhh,' Greta snaps back sharply, silently stepping over Yukio's body and bending down to pick up the handgun. She shakes her head towards the dark valley running out of the canyon and deeper into the black scrub.

'C'mon,' Greta whispers.

'We can't just leave him out here in the bush like this,' Molly says.

'Ssshhh!' Greta says again. She grits her teeth, nodding furiously at the gravedigger girl then runs a finger along her neck and that finger turns into a fist and a thumb pointing up the canyon. She silently mouths her final word. *Now!*

Molly turns back to Yukio. He's sweating. There's a war going on inside him and Molly knows the strange and warm-faced pilot is losing that war like Darwin is losing a war north of here, back by the sea. Molly has seen her father shake like this. Deep shaking. Involuntary. She knew when she saw that shaking that her father had a trouble inside him that could not be soothed from the outside. All she could do was pat her father's forehead and whisper, 'Sssshhhh, Dad, sssshhhh. It's all right, Dad.' What she meant was that she knew she was only ten or eleven or twelve but everything was going to be all right as long as they had each other. Then she sees her father in her mind, limbless and bomb-torn and wedged inside the fork of a tree. She closes her eyes and when she opens them again she removes the aviator jacket and places it over Yukio. 'Sssshhhhh,' she whispers into his ear and the sound seems to still the pilot. So she whispers again: 'Ssshhhh. It's all right, it's all right.'

*

She is still wearing his flight helmet when she turns and follows Greta into the forest darkness that waits beyond the canyon, and she is still wearing it when they stumble blindly through a thick infestation of thorny mesquite trees with branches that seem to reach out to Molly and tear at her exposed skin.

The earth rebels, she tells herself. It rebels against wrongdoers, she tells herself. Sam knew this. Molly knew this. The earth in rebellion. Buffalo charging at cars. Crocodiles stalking girls in creeks. Tree branches reaching out to strangle her dead in the dark.

She's still wearing the pilot's helmet when she walks facefirst through the circular web of a golden orb spider. The web is made of golden yellow silk and its miraculous architecture is so grand that it stretches the whole way across the path they follow through moonlit monsoon vine thickets. The girl feels the web's maker, a female spider with a body three inches long, land on the back of the pilot's leather helmet and she leans forward knowing she's in the wrong here, knowing that the golden orb spider spent hours in this forest darkness constructing her grand silk insect trap only to have it destroyed by the careless head of a Darwin gravedigger girl.

She puts a light hand to the back of her head, brushing the spider off the helmet. 'I'm sorry,' she says, as much to the spider as to the Japanese pilot they left back in the canyon. The foreigner in as foreign a land as he could ever fall into from the sky. If the earth can rebel, she tells herself, then the sky can, too. A sky gift rejected. A sky gift left behind. A sky gift abandoned in a canyon.

'We shouldn't have left him back there,' Molly says.

Greta holds Bert the shovel in her hands, waves it at the darkness before her, batting down branches and vines.

'He's been droppin' bombs on folks across the world,' Greta

says. 'Stop sparing thoughts for the bastards who just blew half your house to Adelaide.'

'The sky wanted us to meet him,' Molly says.

'Is that right?' Greta replies. She stops and turns to Molly, agitated, tired. 'And I guess the sky wanted your father blown to bits?'

Molly stops now, too. She wonders who, indeed, wanted that to happen to her father. Her father, Horace, the good and the bad one, blown across the yard and lodged in the fork of a tree. Blood dripping from his thigh where the rest of his leg used to be. Who did ask for that? She'd asked for another gift from the sky. Then the sky had rained Japanese bombs. Who did ask for that?

*

They beat a loose path through a fringe of red ash trees that meets a rocky incline where a solitary pandanus tree stands, its wedge-shaped, bright-red fruits looking like the kinds of jewels Aubrey and Horace Hook would rob from Hollow Wood's dead. When their improvised course takes them higher across sandstone ranges and rises, the moon throws enough light down for the actress and the gravedigger girl to see the land that unfolds before them. Then they follow a clearer path through the trees and the sandstone gullies and outcrops. Sam Greenway might have walked this way once, Molly tells herself. His people have walked this path for millennia and so have the short-eared rock wallabies and the black-footed tree rats and the short-beaked echidnas and the golden bandicoots. And now the gravedigger girl and the actress.

The moon is silver and the stars surrounding it dutifully assemble into shapes for Molly. An arrow. An elephant. A warrior's shield. A gravestone.

Her mother, Violet, made her promise she would make her life beautiful and grand and poetic and she promised her mother that she would write her own epitaph, that she would live a life that could be written about with ease on an upright slab of limestone.

Now the night sky whispers to her, 'What would it say, Molly? And be honest. I'm not like that fool the day sky. I will know if you are lying.'

'I know exactly what it will say,' Molly whispers.

HERE LIES BRAVE ORPHAN MOLLY HOOK WHO LOST HER MOTHER AND FATHER BEFORE THE AGE OF 13 AND SET OFF INTO THE NORTHERN AUSTRALIAN WILDERNESS IN SEARCH OF A SORCERER NAMED LONGCOAT BOB BUT WHAT SHE WAS REALLY SEARCHING FOR WERE ANSWERS TO QUESTIONS SHE COULD NOT BRING HERSELF TO ASK. IN A PITIFUL ACT OF BLIND VENGEANCE, MOLLY BLUDGEONED LONGCOAT BOB TO DEATH WITH A BLOOD–COLOURED ROCK SHE BELIEVED WAS HER MOTHER'S TRUE HEART TURNED TO STONE. MOLLY DIED MANY YEARS LATER, RIDING HER BICYCLE OFF A KATHERINE GORGE CLIFF FACE, AGED 122. SHE IS SURVIVED BY HER HUSBAND, SAM, AND THEIR HANDSOME AND RICH TWIN SONS, TYRONE AND GARY.

Molly stops and reaches into her duffel bag to check the blood-coloured stone is still inside, but really she doesn't need to check because she knows she carries her mother's heart inside her duffel bag as much as she carries it inside her chest. Greta moves on ahead in the dark.

'Is that really your plan, Molly?' asks the night sky.

'Maybe,' Molly says. 'If he doesn't cooperate.'

Molly closes the bag and walks on again.

'You're going to crack that rock over Longcoat Bob's skull?'

'Yep,' Molly says. 'If I have to.'

'You don't have to do anything you don't want to do, Molly.'

'Really?' she says. 'Really? You could have fooled me. My whole life I've been doing things I don't want to do.'

Greta emerges from the darkness.

'Who you talkin' to?' she asks.

'I'm talking to the sky,' Molly says.

'Oh, good,' Greta says, straight-faced. 'I thought you'd lost your marbles for a second there, but you were only talking to the sky.'

*

They negotiate a series of sandstone outcrops and step slowly through a blind natural alley between two rock walls. They come to a clearing of quartzite the size of half a football field and the silver moon reflects in pools of water collected in eroded holes the size of wagon wheels. The clearing blends into a scree slope that runs down to a thick patch of floppy billygoat plum trees and little gooseberry trees, through which they have to battle hard, with Bert in full swing.

Brute wandering. Always Molly breaking the silences. High on another outcrop, she sees a dark, black-brown bird in the sky. 'Wedge-tailed eagle!' Molly rejoices.

The glorious bird circling in the thermal updraughts of its own shimmering sky. That heavenly wingspan looks as wide to Molly as some cars. It's not even flapping its wings, Molly tells herself. It's floating. It's levitating. The bird is magic up there in its sky territory, where it circles now beneath a cloud shaped like a domed castle, and there it is home and there it is queen.

'She's the queen,' Molly says. 'Her majesty!' she calls to the sky, waving in the same way she might wave at a royal from the mother country. She breathes deep and beams.

'She's just like us, Greta,' Molly says. 'She's free.' Molly nods. 'Yep, this is full life livin', Greta. This is how we're supposed to be livin'.'

'I can think of several other ways I'd prefer to be livin',' Greta says. 'And I'm holding a glass in every one of 'em.'

'I mean this is what we're supposed to be doing with our lives, isn't it?' Molly replies. 'We're supposed to find ourselves things to etch on our gravestones. And now we're writing our own epitaphs, Greta. You're writin' yours. I'm writin' mine.'

Greta can see her grave now. '"She was the next Greta Garbo,"' she says, '"but she died prematurely from prolonged exposure to the sun and girls who talk to the sky. The Palmerston Players closed their theatre two days later out of respect, and also due to the fact that its troupe numbers were cut by a third upon Miss Maze's untimely demise."'

'I'll always remember this long walk with you, Greta,' Molly says.

'That's good, Molly,' Greta says. 'Because if we don't find your grandfather's silver road this may be the last walk you'll have to remember.'

A spring-fed forest of monsoon palms thins out briefly to reveal a wide bed of sandstone rising to a wave-shaped over-hang that is blocking the wind and prompts Greta to stop and suggest they sleep before they set off on a day of sunlit wandering. She sits down between a large boulder and the overhang, drops her head to her knees. But Molly still stands because she is struck by the outline of an unusual rock forma-tion on top of the overhang: a red sandstone block that has been weathered into the rough and jagged shape of a human face, albeit one with square-shaped eyebrows and a diamond-shaped nose and a dusty crease for a half-smile. A face, the hard face of a man, worked by water and wind and ancient friction and the rising and falling of seas and the landmass that holds Australia's greatest mystery – the time trapped inside all that is moving and all that is still. And this face is alive to Molly in the moonglow, as if it might turn and look down at her and tell her that it is bad manners to stare so hard at your elders.

'I'll be back soon,' Molly says. She rushes around the base of the rock.

'Where are you going?' Greta shouts after her, confused.

Molly doesn't even hear the question because she's focussing on her footing in the dark as she clambers over boulders and scree and lifts herself up onto shelves and ledges.

Greta stands, concerned now, and tries to follow Molly's footsteps with her eyes, but the girl has disappeared into the dark, scampering quickly around the corner of a sloping stone shoulder that rises to the top of the wave-shaped overhang that supports the formation that contains the face of a man.

'Molly!' Greta calls. But the gravedigger girl is too quick. And now the gravedigger girl is gone.

*

Small scree rocks sliding beneath her boots. At this hour, so close to dawn, everything is a shimmering blue in Molly's eyes. She approaches the overhang from a sharp rubble slope that runs down its back like a spine. It's so sheer that she has to fall to her hands and knees and crawl up it, her fingers tingling with flurries of fright whenever she loses her grip on the shifting stones.

The flat top of the overhang is small in comparison to the plateaus she's seen so far today in the deep country, but it's still big enough to drop a small house on or Dottie Drake's hair salon or Bert Green's lolly shop. The lolly shop. What she wouldn't give for a tall glass of sarsaparilla. What she wouldn't give for a green and red apple-flavoured all-day sucker.

She approaches the strange rock formation from behind and then she shivers in the blue moonlight when she realises the carved face is performing a miraculous balancing act, somehow leaning forward with all its weight on a single, small slab of ancient rock. A full human face of rock resting on only one-third of a neck. The formation should, by the natural rules of gravity, have plummeted off the overhang a thousand years ago, but it stays in place, leaning forward to say to Molly that it's trying to look at something, that it's trying so hard to see something, but sandstone eyes can't see, so the face will stay right here in this precarious place until those eyes turn to the colour of the sky and they can see for miles like Molly Hook.

She runs her hand over the diamond-shaped nose and the remarkable crease that looks like the valley where an upper and bottom lip meet, and she runs her hands over the eyes that cannot see and she sees someone she knows, someone she longs to see.

'Dad,' she whispers. And Walt Whitman reminds her of the deathless death. '"I know I am deathless."'

'"Missing me one place, search another,"' she says. '"I stop somewhere waiting for you."'

And she sees her father's deep eyes. The overhang of his sorrow. The rubble of his past. The jagged edges of his weaknesses. The dusty lips of his regret. Her father sits with Ol' Man Rock now, she tells herself. Horace Hook and the maker of mountains, she tells herself, trying to make sense of what happened here on earth. Trying to understand the making of men like Aubrey Hook.

Sam says he can ask Ol' Man Rock anything and he always receives a correct answer.

'Where is the silver road?' Molly whispers.

And she finds her answer in those deep sandstone eyes. She follows the gaze of the rock face and she walks to the edge of the overhang, so close that she could fall to her death with a careless misstep. And she leans her head down like the rock face does and she can see what the rock face cannot see. A still freshwater lake lit by the moon, and from the edge of this lake runs a twisting path that shimmers like it's made of stardust. A crystal glass snake winding through darkened monsoon forest. And as she stands there, the sun wakes up and the first rising slice of its light meets the glowing of the moon and the silver road sparkles like a luminous diamond necklace, unfastened and endless, dropped in the deep country, bending and curving and cutting through the forest. A magic road for those with the kind of eyes that can see it, twisting and turning towards the silver horizon, towards the gold, towards the treasure, towards Longcoat Bob.

'Greta!' Molly shouts, and the name echoes across the deep country.

The Admiral's Frock

An olive-coloured Model A Ford pulls over to the side of a thin red dirt road lined with orange-flowered honeysuckle trees. Aubrey Hook yanks hard on the Ford's handbrake and the action makes the wound in his left shoulder howl with blinding pain. He slowly unbuttons his work shirt. The dried yellow-white pus of the bite wound has stuck hard to the fabric of his shirt. He pulls on his sleeve, tearing away the pus-rimmed scabbing that has built up around the edge. Only hate could have caused such a wound, he tells himself. Only hate could turn a man into a dingo like that, turn his younger brother, Horace, into a wild dog who could bite the flesh from his own brother's shoulder.

He gets out of the car and assesses the damage to his shoulder in the car's side mirror. An infected mess of pus and blood – his brother's teeth were rotting like his own. There are white-bellied mangrove snakes sliding along the mudlined creeks beyond those honeysuckle trees and they spend their days eating dead mud crabs and poison-bellied toads and they still have fangs less infectious than Horace Hook's pearly blacks. He looks at the wound and all he sees in the side mirror is the gravedigger girl and her miserable story and the series of miserable events that placed his brother beneath that Japanese bomb that removed his body so inconveniently from his left leg. Not a Hook at all, he tells himself. The girl is a Berry through and through.

He buttons his shirt and walks along the dirt road. On the right side of the road he drops his head to follow two parallel wheel tracks that run down an incline to his own red utility truck, which sits abandoned with its front bonnet crumpled hard against a cluster of stringybark trees. The truck's windows are wide open and, on the driver's side, it appears that something smashed into the vehicle. Aubrey retraces his steps and paces back along the road, past his parked automobile, to a series of skid marks bending and curving across the damp dirt road. Then, back further along the road, a series of animal footprints running from one side of the road to the other. He turns to the roadside trees and scrublands that wall a fertile woodland stretching to the sea in the far distance. Not the prints of horses. These hoofprints are too widely spaced for cows. These animals had agility. Buffalo, he tells himself. And he ponders the grave misfortune of the actress and the grave-digger girl. Imagine living with that kind of luck, he tells himself. To be cursed with such black fortune that your vehicle is run off the road by a panicked herd of Northern Territory water buffalo. That's a Tom Berry kind of luck, he thinks. That's a Berry family kind of misfortune.

*

'What are the chances?' Tom Berry rejoiced, spilling his beer on the unvarnished wooden floors of the Hotel Darwin's public bar. 'There I was, thinking I was the unluckiest son-of-a-bitch to ever hold a pickaxe, and then I look up and see this bare-foot blackfeller dressed like feckin' Napoleon!'

Aubrey restarts the Ford on the side of the dirt road and motors on at a pace not much quicker than he could walk if his body wasn't so broken. He remembers the smile on Tom's face. The sheer wonder of it all. The sheer good fortune.

There must have been twenty or so local goldminers in the bar that afternoon and Aubrey Hook was one of the youngest. The men were celebrating the miraculous return of Tom Berry, who had gone missing three months earlier while prospecting alone in the rocky tablelands far beyond the Clyde River. Tom bought three rounds of whisky for every man present and then, to a chorus of rowdy hoots and hollers, he told the extraordinary and seemingly implausible story of the three months he was missing in the deep country.

For several days, he recounted, he'd made progress on a quartzite seam, in a location he was careful not to disclose. There he lived on beans and whisky, and he spoke of the seam's potential only to his packhorse of twelve long years, Samson. Tom told his horse how he would be returning home a rich man and that his beloved wife, Bonnie Berry, and his beloved children, then-teenaged Violet and Peter Berry, would be waiting for him and he would tell them to pack up their things quick smart because they were moving to Sydney because Tom was getting out of the gold-digging business and getting into the caviar-scooping business because their ship had just come in on waves of raw gold. He told Samson how he would then march on down to Smith Street, Darwin, and find every last smug goldminer in every last dark corner of every last pub in town; every last man who had ever laughed about his gold-digging abilities; every man who'd ever said he had more book sense than gold sense; every man who'd ever said there was more twinkle in Tom Berry's eyes than there ever was in his pan. And he would gather these men together and he would glow like gold itself when he told them of his riches.

Then, hacking away at the quartzite seam, Tom noticed a rash across the underside of his left forearm and that rash began to spread across his whole left side. He worked on with his axe and rock hammer, but soon he began to cough uncontrollably and his chest began to wheeze and he could not suck enough air into his lungs. In a fevered sweat, he wisely chose to pack his tools and provisions, and he climbed onto Samson and steered the faithful horse towards Darwin, where Tom Berry would see a doctor for what he was convinced was a deadly case of influenza.

But soon his limbs grew so weak he could not stay upright on his horse and he rode for three miles on his belly with his dead arms hugging Samson's side. With little instruction, the horse walked aimlessly through the deep-country scrub, then took a path high into the plateau lands. It chewed on grasses by the sides of paths and when it came to a choice of routes it simply based its choice on the quality of grass each one had to offer.

The horse clopped along for ten miles through treacherous mountain country until it came to a wild, fast-flowing river that led to a thunderous waterfall down below that Tom was only just lucid enough to register in his ears.

Samson stopped at a bridge crossing the rapids. 'But it was no bridge made of nail and hardwood,' Tom Berry whispered to his transfixed audience in the public bar. 'It was a bridge made by the blackfellers, ya see, a few thin logs that felt like twigs to a packhorse. Samson refused to go any further.'

Tom Berry slid from the horse and landed in a mess of

arms and legs on the dirt and stone edge of the rapids. He could no longer walk, as his legs were paralysed. Half his face was paralysed, too – the whole left side was numb and sagging so much that he felt it was going to drop clean off his head. With his face pressed against the earth and his dry tongue licking dust, he tried to drag himself towards the bridge and he moved a couple of yards, but he was spent altogether when he got within an arm's reach of the bridge.

He closed his eyes and he slowed his breathing and he regretted the fact he lacked the strength to throw himself into the rapids, where he could die quickly, smashing his head against a rock or being sucked down into the waterfall and sprayed off a clifftop and then drowned soon enough in pounding whitewash. Instead he would die slowly of thirst in the dirt beneath the baking northern Australian sun. He thought in that moment of how there was a time in his life when he'd intended to put his brain to better use than swinging a sharp axe at rock faces he was always too proud to admit were barren. He had planned to be a schoolteacher. A local priest, Duncan Hall, in Palmerston had been starting up a small Catholic school, largely for the children of mining families, and he'd asked Tom if he would teach the kids grammar and rhetoric, given he was such a keen and well-spoken advocate for the wonders of literature. But Tom had turned the priest down because he carried a weakness inside him and that weakness glowed between cracks of grey rock like a fire and that fire lit his soul. He then thought of his wife, Bonnie, and his son, Peter, who was a quiet and good boy, and his daughter, Violet, and how it made sense that such a fine woman as Bonnie would raise such a fine young woman as Violet. A voracious reader of books like her father. She'd been eating up his poetry books. She'd recite lines to her father over breakfast and her oats would go cold because she was so lost in the worlds of Byron and Wordsworth and Whitman. But the glow of the gold blinded him to all that. The glow saw him work too much on rock faces, and then it saw him drink too much because the drink kept lethargy away from the rock face, kept him working too much.

Now the miner turned over and stared into a different golden glow, and that was the full sun, and he willed it to set him alight, to burn his gold-lusting soul to ash.

'But then I heard Samson holler out with a neigh like he was startled by somethin',' Tom Berry told the wide-mouthed whisky drinkers at the bar. 'And I felt footsteps coming towards me in the dirt and I could not even move my head, gentlemen, because I was so weak. But I could move my eyes and I turned my eyes to the footsteps in the dirt and then a figure stood over me.' Tom Berry paused for effect in the telling of his great tale and he lowered his voice. 'The figure of a man, and this man blocked out the sun and all I could see was his coat. His long . . . black . . . feckin' coat! A French admiral's frock coat.'

Calls of 'balderdash' and 'bunkum' and 'bullshit' echoed across the beer-stained pub floor, but Tom Berry stood adamantly by his story. Longcoat Bob was old and tall. He was shirtless under the coat, but his long thin legs wore brown riding pants. There was scarring across his chest like the staff lines on the piano music sheets Bonnie Berry played from after dinner. He had a mess of curled silver hair and he had creases so deep in his long, thin face that the creases looked like battle scars. He wore the French admiral's frock coat as naturally as a white man wears a vest. It was made of military-grade navy blue wool, with gold buttons and elaborate gold embroidery on the lapels and cuffs. The collar was so high and stiff it brushed against Bob's earlobes. But the coat was no museum piece; it looked like the old man had worn it for decades, as it was torn at the elbows and covered in dust.

'It was the real thing, too,' Tom said, and men laughed and spat beer from their lips as they slapped their thighs.

'I speak the truth,' Tom gasped. 'That coat had made its way from them Napoleonic Wars all the way to that bloke Bob up in those mountains.'

Tom's audience was sceptical. 'You went mad up there in those mountains, Berry,' called Albert Strudwick, a seasoned digger from South Australia. 'Tell me how a blackfeller all the way out there comes by a coat sewn by the French Empire?'

Tom knocked back a small glass of whisky and followed it with a swig of beer.

'Well, there's something you need to know about this feller Longcoat Bob,' Tom said. 'He's not like other blackfellers.'

Tom then recounted how he dropped out of consciousness at Longcoat Bob's feet because the vision of the strange Aboriginal had felt like a dream and there was little else he could do with his life at that point except slip away into that dream. He woke two days later inside a small hut with supports made of tree branches and walls made of rusting corrugated iron. The hut smelled of eucalyptus oil. His neck was throbbing, but he was no longer suffering the flu symptoms that had left him near dead by the rapids crossing. He ran his fingers across the back of his neck and felt a hole in the soft flesh behind his right ear. The hole was filled with a paste that smelled like piss and old grass.

Then an Aboriginal woman entered the hut. She said her name was Little Des, daughter of an older woman named Big Desree, and she wore an old grey linen shirt and she spoke in her people's native tongue as well as English and told the lost goldminer just how fortunate he was to have been found by the extraordinary man they called Longcoat Bob, who had brought Tom Berry back to his camp and identified the paralysis tick the size of a pepper corn that had burrowed into the back of his skull and was digging a tunnel out of feasted human flesh that was about to break through the soft and juicy wall of his brain. At the same time as it was gorging itself on his insides, the tick was filling Tom Berry's head with poison. Longcoat Bob had drowned the tick in wet tobacco ashes then dug it out with a burnt knife tip. He'd filled the hole it had left with a healing paste he made out of emu bush, tea tree oil, mashed moth larvae and one more secret ingredient that Little Des said he refused to disclose to tribe members, in order to maintain his superior air of medicinal mystery.

'What are you doin' wanderin' about out here?' Little Des asked. And Tom told Little Des about his shameful lust for gold and how he had found a promising quartzite seam maybe twenty miles from Longcoat Bob's camp and he had hoped he would return to Darwin a wealthy man who could provide for his beloved family.

Stepping out of the hut later, Tom smiled wide at what was a small tribal camp of huts and firepits spread across a clearing fringed by stringybark trees and lush cycad bushes with ten-foot-tall stems. A trio of shy young women approached him with paperbark plates filled with boiled goose eggs and freshly cooked fish and freshwater eel. He found Samson in a shaded corner of the camp, joyfully slurping from a bucket of water next to a mountain of collected grass and bush apples.

Longcoat Bob subsequently ordered Tom to eat fourteen billygoat plums each day for a week to fight off infection. And soon Tom's strength was restored, but he did not rush to climb onto Samson and clip-clop his long way back to

Darwin. He had developed a fondness for Longcoat Bob's people and they had developed a fondness for him.

Longcoat Bob enjoyed sitting by the fire at night telling the wayward traveller stories of how the land around him came to be, and in thanks for those stories Tom Berry recited descriptions of landscapes penned by famous English poets. Then Tom Berry told Longcoat Bob the story of his life. He told him of his love of the written word, from which he had been distracted by the glowing of gold. He spoke of how hard he had toiled for nothing, and the terrible cost of that fruitless toil to his wife and children, and how every gold-empty rock and cave and dugout he ever climbed down into was another reason to feel bitter and angry at the spinning earth. But, alas, he had felt like a changed man sitting by the fire with Longcoat Bob. He'd come to the deep country to dig up a gold lease, he said, but he'd dug up a new lease on his own life. Were he to strike a gold run of any significance now, he told Longcoat Bob, he would return the grace shown to him by God and Longcoat Bob in those recent days by creating a school where Darwin's children of all colours and creeds and religions could study both the wonders of the written word and the wonders of Longcoat Bob's creation stories. And Longcoat Bob stared at the goldminer across the fire and he stood and he moved closer to Tom Berry and he reached a long arm out and pointed at Tom's chest. 'Good heart, Tom Berry,' he said, tapping Tom's chest twice. 'Good heart.' Then Longcoat Bob turned towards the forest. 'I must talk to the stars for a moment,' he said. And he disappeared into the night.

The next evening, before sunset, Longcoat Bob met Tom at his hut. 'Sunrise tomorrow, Tom Berry and Bob go for a long walk,' Longcoat Bob said.

'And that surely was a long walk, my friends,' Tom Berry

said to his audience. 'We walked for six days. The land was Longcoat Bob's kitchen. He turned grubs into fire-cooked delicacies. He reached his hands into rivers and long-necked turtles seemed to come to him willingly. And that land he showed me, my friends, was like no land I had ever seen. He led me through the most treacherous and deep country. He took me through ancient galleries and across crocodile-infested waterholes and through cave systems that felt like portals into different dimensions in time and space. I saw things in that country, gentlemen, that I'd never dreamed existed. There were tests, I tell you. I had to show my courage. I had to show my faith in Longcoat Bob, and faith in things beyond my under-standing, and I believe he was testing me. The more worth I showed, the closer he took me to his secret place.'

'And where exactly was this secret place?' shouted Albert Strudwick.

'Well, I'm sure you'd like to know, Albert,' Tom said. 'But Longcoat Bob's secrets will remain safe with me. Though, make no mistake, dear friends, I am, at heart, a scholar, and a good scholar always takes notes.'

Tom Berry laughed and tapped his temple and he did not speak then of how the closest thing he'd had to a pencil on the long walk was a pocket knife and the closest thing he'd had to notepaper was the back of a goldminer's pan. But then he did speak of how Longcoat Bob's long walk ended at a miracle. A place of pure impossibility.

'It was a vault,' Tom Berry said. 'A vault of gold in the heart of the deep country. A vault built by the earth. A safe room beyond my wildest imagination, housing more raw gold than I could have carried home on the backs of ten horses.'

'Step inside,' Longcoat Bob said at the entrance. And Tom Berry stepped cautiously into the vault and his dark brown eyes were lit up by a blaze of raw gold. Too many fat and raw gold nuggets to count. Gold nuggets the size of apples. Finds the size of oranges. Nuggets shaped like tree stumps as long as Tom's hand. Triangular nuggets. One nugget as big as an eggplant and so heavy that Tom needed two hands to hold it.

'These are all yours?' Tom asked Longcoat Bob.

Longcoat Bob shook his head. 'Not mine,' he said. He told Tom the gold belonged to the land. He said his people had been finding gold nuggets like the ones in that vault for centuries. But in all his years, he said, he was yet to come across a single gold nugget that brought any real happiness to the person who held it. Longcoat Bob said his family had found one large nugget long ago – centuries back – that resembled a human hand and it became so coveted by members of his family that it caused fights between brother and sister, sister and mother, father and son. During one dispute, an old woman struck her nephew over the head with the gold hand. The nephew was struck dumb and his mental capacity was like a waterhole that could never be more than half full after that, and the old woman was so ashamed by her actions that she begged Longcoat Bob's grandfather, the oldest living member of the family, to hide the gold away in a place where no one else could find it. And any other gold nuggets that were found from that moment on, Longcoat Bob's grandfather reasoned, were best hidden away with it too.

'And you wouldn't believe what he said then,' Tom Berry whispered to his enraptured audience. 'He said he and his family saw no value whatsoever in all that gold. He said real treasure was a freshwater spring. He said the real jewels of the earth were gooseberries that grow on trees. He said a good dig in his world is when you stick your fist down a bubble in the mud and find a long-necked turtle to grab hold of. He said true wealth isn't havin' your pockets filled with coin but your belly filled with white turtle flesh cooked in its juices, shell down, on a bed of coals. He said the only use for gold was to glitter, and he said the glitter of gold was like the glittering smiles of us white men he'd seen in town dressed in expensive clothes. He said that gold can't be trusted. He said we all got the gold disease and it rots our hearts. It poisons us. He said it changes who we are, how we behave.'

'Too right it does!' said a liquored prospector also from Halls Creek, raising his beer glass. And the other gold diggers raised their glasses in agreement.

'He said the long-necked turtle didn't do that,' Tom Berry said. 'He said the turtle was a gift from the earth that kept on giving. He said he rubbed turtle fat on the chests of sick infants to make them strong again. He said the oil and meat from a single turtle could keep a dying elder alive to see an extra month of sunrises. And then he asked me if I thought a month of sunrises was worth more or less than the box of gold that rested in the hole below us. I said it depended on how you spent the gold and how you spent the month of sunrises.

'And Longcoat Bob smiled at that and he pointed again at Tom Berry's chest and said, 'Good heart, Tom Berry. You speak of good things that can come from gold.'

Then he gestured towards the gold vault. 'You may take what you can carry in your hands, Tom Berry,' he said.

And in the public bar of the Hotel Darwin, young Aubrey Hook felt as envious as he did sceptical as he watched Tom Berry finish his tall tale of gold lust and gold rewards.

'But then Longcoat Bob placed a hand on my arm,' Tom Berry said. 'And he told me something I will never forget for all my years because it sent a shiver down my weary spine.

He said, "Carry all you own, Tom Berry But own all you carry."

And the men across the public bar sipped their drinks in silence and confusion.

*

On the red dirt track far south of Darwin, Aubrey Hook brings the Model A to a stop once more. By the side of the road he can see two sets of shoe prints. One set bigger than the other. Further on he can see the snaking track left by something that was dragged carelessly behind the smaller set of footprints. A large stick, perhaps. Or a tool of some kind, he considers. A shovel.

He kneels down by the shoeprints. He traces his forefinger along the shovel's line. The gravedigger girl, he tells himself. The miserable legacy of Tom Berry's long walk into the wilderness.

He remembers the looks on the faces of every man in that bar that day when Tom Berry told his fabulous story of Longcoat Bob and the mystical vault of gold. Disbelief. Disregard. And just the slightest glow of gold envy.

'So how much did you take?' asked Albert Strudwick, eyes alight.

'I'm not gonna tell you lot,' he said. 'But rest assured it's enough to buy you all another round.' And he raised his whisky and triumphantly downed another shot.

'Go on Berry,' Strudwick urged with a treacherous gleam in his eye. 'Tell us how much you took!' The greatest supply in the prospector's kit is reliable information and Albert Strudwick wanted more of it. 'We know you want to tell us, Berry!' Strudwick urged. 'Go on. Tell us how rich the most hapless prospector in Australia has become!'

Tom had promised himself he would not reveal the weight of what he'd carried from that natural vault that day, but he felt the pride of his glittering achievement welling up inside him, and he was going to burst if he held it inside any longer, the molten-lava eruption of his good fortune. There was something that always trumped wisdom in any conversation among gold prospectors and that was luck. The brightest, shrewdest prospectors – and Albert Strudwick was one of them – knew well that all the planning and information and hard graft in the world were nothing against the all-conquering force of a stroke of good luck.

'We're about the same build, Albert,' Tom Berry said. Both men were short and thin. 'How much can you lift in pounds?'

'I once carried two seventy-pound bags of flour in my arms,' he said. 'Reckon I could carry more on me shoulders.'

Tom nodded, sipped a newly arrived whisky shot. 'Reckon you could carry a couple pounds more, too, if you knew you was carrying pay dirt.'

The men in the bar were silent then. Some scratched their heads. Some slapped their knees in awe, some shook their heads in disbelief. Aubrey Hook was only young, but his father, the late Arthur Hook, had taught him how to find a hole in any surface. And he knew the surface of that grand and miraculous story of Tom Berry's was like the surface of any gold country – full of holes.

*

On the dirt track, Aubrey Hook follows the two sets of footprints and he eventually comes to a short bridge crossing Candlelight Creek. He and Horace walked up Candlelight Creek when they were boys. Horace was so scared by the darkness that they were forced to turn back after half an hour of walking inside its twisting tunnel foliage. Darkness and light, Aubrey tells himself. There are some who can walk further into the darkness and there are some who always run back to the light. A world of absolutes. Rich and poor. Cursed and blessed. Good and bad. Truth and lies.

'But I am a man of my word,' Tom Berry announced in the public bar on that revelatory afternoon. 'I told Longcoat Bob I would do good with that gold and I fully intend to do just that.'

At the same time as the newly wealthy Tom Berry was building his wife, Bonnie, and his children, Violet and Peter, a new and grand house on the Darwin waterfront that overlooked the Timor Sea, he set about drafting plans for a new school, one street back from the waterfront at Mindil Beach. Aubrey and Horace Hook attended the very town hall meeting at which Tom Berry stood on stage in a new black suit and vest and tie and proclaimed proudly to the gathered residents of Darwin that Mindil Beach Primary School would be a place of learning for children of all colours and creeds, all races and religions. 'From the grandsons of our Afghani cameleers to the descendants of our Aboriginal elders who are the children of what they call "the Dreaming",' he read from a page of inspired pencil notes. 'The Mindil Beach Primary School will open its doors to all who are willing to learn. And what learning they will enjoy, from the poems of Edgar Allan Poe to the theories of Pythagoras and, yes, to the traditional campfire histories of this very rich and promising shared territory passed down by its original inhabitants over the course of millennia.'

But then the doors of the town hall swung open loudly and some four hundred seated attendees turned their heads to the voice of an Aboriginal woman standing at the entrance of the town hall, calling, 'Thief!'

It was Little Des and she had come from the deep country to tell the residents of Darwin that Tom Berry's tale of good fortune and long walk redemption was a charade, an elaborate work of fiction masking the fact he had stolen from Little Des's family.

'We took care of you,' Little Des shouted boldly across the town hall as the heads of suited guests reeled in shock and dismay, 'and you stole that gold right out from under us.'

Tom Berry snapped back at Little Des from the stage. 'Longcoat Bob told me it didn't belong to your family,' he shouted. 'He told me it belonged to no one. I had every right to take it.'

Then a tall figure in a long black coat emerged behind Little Des. Some of the town hall guests questioned their eyesight because they struggled to comprehend the vision before them: an ageing Aboriginal man, thin and lanky but taller than any man in the room, walking silently down the central aisle of the hall, dressed improbably in an old black and gold French admiral's frock coat. The Aboriginal man raised his right hand and exactly what he carried in this hand would be debated for all the years that followed in the pubs and general stores and hair salons of Darwin. Some said it was a stick shaped like a knitting needle with brown emu hairs tied to the end of it. Some said it was just the man's extended forefinger but the finger was so long it looked like a sorcerer's wand. Some said it was the bone of a sinful human covered in ochre and resin and maybe even the sinner's blood. The man pointed at the newly rich prospector on stage. 'Tom Berry,' the old Aboriginal man said loudly. 'A heart of stone.' And that was all Longcoat Bob had to say.

*

At the side of the bridge crossing Candlelight Creek, Aubrey Hook kneels down and stares up the black tunnel of foliage that encloses the thin freshwater creek he walked up as a boy.

The longer I stand, the shorter I grow, he tells himself. He remembers the gravedigger girl writing those words in the scrub. She would write them everywhere. On the back of the Hollow Wood water tank, on the side of the thunderbox. She carved those words on trees, she wrote those words with letters made of broken twigs. The ramblings of a grandfather who ran into madness to escape the shame of his lies. To escape the curse of his past.

Resting beside Aubrey Hook's left boot on the side of the bridge is a find that he might have once linked to luck back when he was foolish enough to believe in it. An empty round fruit can, its tin lid peeled back so coarsely that he wonders if its owner cut herself when she opened it, leaving drops of blood on her fingers and clothes, stains she would struggle to wash away.

The Devil's Heartbeat

The silver road glitters brighter than gold in the daytime. For almost two hours Molly's been walking along the winding track that shimmers with silver light and still she stops to look at what presents to her eyes as flakes of clear cut-crystal glass beneath her dig boots. Each flake bouncing light and turning that light, up close, to flashes of pink and purple and aqua. Millions of clear flakes piled upon each other over time, which, seen as a whole, form a gleaming road of silver that Molly feels like she could mould together to form the shining armour of a Camelot knight. Or she could turn all the flakes into building bricks and she could make a glass castle that she and Greta could escape to after all this searching and questing is over.

She sweeps her hands over the silver road flakes and she cups them in her palm and they feel like fish scales but their colour is more magnificent, like they are the scales of silver mermaids from deep down in the kinds of seas sailed by Odysseus.

'It's ground mica,' Molly says. 'Rock crumbs left behind by time.'

Flakes as thin as the film stock they load into the projectors

242

at the Star, but clear enough and twinkling enough to form the fake night sky that hangs above the picture house marquee. In some places the clear mica sheets have joined together in layers to create silver book-like structures that Molly can grip between her fingers and whose pages Molly can count, with one eye closed for clarity.

'Isn't it beautiful,' Molly says. 'Sam told me about the silver road. He called it the glass river. He reckoned a Dreamtime serpent snaked through this whole deep forest here and that serpent was made of stars and it was slithering through here for so long it kept shedding its skin. The serpent meant to leave the star skin behind because it knew the silver road would help people find their way through the forest at night.'

The silver road winds through a valley of cycads lining a narrow creek where Molly and Greta stop to rest and eat. They share a can of tinned corn from Molly's duffel bag and Greta asks the gravedigger girl for an update on their food stocks. Six cans left in the bag, half a tube of condensed milk. Two cans of baked beans, one of oxtail soup, one of ham, one of corned beef and a can of peaches, which Molly keeps resisting the urge to open.

'What else you got in that bag?' Greta asks. 'Looks like more than six tins of food in there.'

Molly's fingers run over the blood-red rock she took from her mother's chest.

Then she pulls out a book.

'*The Complete Works of William Shakespeare*,' she says. 'Well, if we have to lie down and die somewhere out here,' Greta says, 'at least we'll have the Bard to send us off to sleep.'

Greta rests by the creek, Yukio's pistol in her hands. She thinks of the curious soldier who fell from the sky. She pictures him dead by a bedrock, a full day's walk behind them. In her mind he's long lost and given up, slumped over in a successful act of ritual self-sacrifice, the ornamental sword he seemed to cherish so much having disembowelled his flat stomach.

'You ever fired one of those?' Molly asks.

'A couple of wood ones on stage,' Greta replies.

'Maybe you should get some practice,' Molly says.

'I don't need any practice,' Greta says. She stares down the length of the gun barrel with one eye closed. 'Not much to it. Point and shoot and phone a lawyer.'

Molly pours the last mouthfuls of corn down her wide-open throat and rushes to a large black rock leaning over the creek like a warthog bending down for a drink. 'You don't necessarily have to shoot someone,' she says. 'You just have to be able to show them you could shoot them if you wanted to. That's how Gary Cooper does it. He'll shoot a can three times and make it bounce in the air so all them bad guys soil their pants and drop their guns.'

She rests the empty corn can on top of the rock. 'See if you can hit that,' she says.

Greta rolls her eyes, reluctantly plants her feet in a shooter's stance and aims the handgun at the corn can. She fires a shot and the bullet chops the head off a young rock fig growing out of a rock wall across the creek, some ten feet above the level of the corn can.

Molly laughs. 'Point and shoot and phone an eye doctor.'

Greta feigns anger. 'I'll point it at you if you're not careful.'

'Have another try,' Molly says.

Greta inhales deeply and aims again, her left eye closed tight and her right eye zeroed in on the can with its aluminium top peeled back like an open hatch on a submarine. Her tongue licks her bottom lip and she stops breathing as she pulls the trigger.

And no bullets explode from the barrel.

She looks at the gun in confusion and she pulls the trigger once more. Nothing but the click of the trigger. She pulls it again. Nothing. And again. Nothing.

'There's no more bullets,' Greta says.

'What?' Molly replies.

'Who flies into battle with a gun with only one bullet?' Greta asks.

Molly holds the gun now. She feels the weight of it. 'He only needed one, for himself,' Molly whispers.

Greta shakes her head.

'Just put it in the bag, will ya?'

They walk on.

*

Five miles along the silver road. Six miles. Seven. In the afternoon, Molly rests against a bronze quartzite boulder being colonised by red shells of wild ruby dock weed. She sips from her water bag, reading her Shakespeare.

'Which one are you up to?' Greta asks.

'*The Tragedy of Hamlet, Prince of Denmark,*' Molly says.

Greta lights a smoke. She has six left.

'You can just call it *Hamlet,*' Greta says.

'Yeah, I know,' Molly says. 'But I like to use the full title.'

'Where are you up to in *The Tragedy of Hamlet, Prince of Denmark*, by William Shakespeare, Bard of Avon?' Greta asks.

Molly places the open book in her lap. 'I just passed the bit where the gravediggers are wondering if Ophelia should be allowed a Christian burial if she took her own life,' Molly says.

Greta nods, drags on her smoke.

'Do you think Ophelia killed herself?' Molly asks.

245

Greta exhales a long cloud of smoke. 'Course she did,' Greta says.

'He doesn't write it like she definitely did,' Molly says. 'He says a branch might have broke and she fell in that pond.'

'She didn't struggle too much in the drink, though, did she?' Greta replies, stretching out beside the creek edge, resting her head on her propped arm. 'Ol' Bill's bein' all cagey because it's hard for blokes to admit a woman might choose death over putting up with more of their bullshit.'

Molly nods, thinks for a moment. 'Do you think Ophelia deserved a Christian burial if she took her own life?'

Greta shrugs. 'Poor girl wasn't thinkin' straight,' she says. 'That's what men can do to ya, Molly. Drive a girl bonkers; make her wanna go sleep forever in the nearest brook.' Greta looks into the clear creek water.

Then she turns to Molly, realises the girl has invested more in this question than humour could return for her. 'God would take Ophelia in, don't you worry,' Greta says, nodding. 'I reckon He'd know she deserved a proper burial and the only thing she didn't deserve was some of those fellers in her life.'

Molly smiles weakly.

'You think there's more good fellers in the world than bad fellers?' Molly asks.

'Oh, there's plenty of good fellers in this world,' Greta says.

'Like who?'

'Romeo Montague,' Greta smiles.

Molly smiles, too. 'I like him,' she says. Then she looks up to the blue sky. 'I reckon my mum didn't deserve some of the fellers in her life.' She looks over at Greta now.

'Yeah, I reckon you'd be right there, Mol',' Greta says.

'One of Ophelia's gravediggers was saying this thing about

whether or not she went into that water or if that water came to her,' Molly says. 'I wonder about that with my mum. Did she go to that grave in Hollow Wood or did life bring the grave to her?'

'Life's always bringin' the grave to us, kid.'

'Yeah, but why bring it so early to some and so late to others?'

'I'm afraid Hamlet's mum was right about all that, Mol',' Greta says.

'I forgot what she said about it.'

'She said all that lives must die,' Greta says. 'And she said we all know that shit's common.'

'That shit's comin'?' Molly ponders.

'Common,' Greta clarifies. 'That shit's all too common.' Greta drags on her smoke, rests her head back on a rock. 'But I guess it's always comin', too.'

*

The silver road bends through a forested gully and then a brief canyon lined with hanging five-fingered ferns that look to Molly like a thousand little green hands reaching out of the rock face. She tests the echo of her voice and it bounces through the canyon.

'Marlene Sky,' she hollers between two hands.

Birds fly out of the canyon, startled by the noise. Rainbow bee-eaters, hooded parrots, bustards and two northern rosellas with black, white and blue-violet wings.

Molly and Greta can feel and smell the humidity of the north. Everything sweats. Everything is damp. The walls of the canyon are smooth and stained black by water run-off. Greta's saddle shoes slip on wet, slimy rocks and she fights to fill her lungs in the thick air and she doesn't feel like smoking so much in these strange places.

The silver road meanders on through great green palms shaped like wood screws stuck in the earth and passes a great sandstone outcrop that Molly sees as a giant wombat, except the wombat wears a jagged battle helmet on its head with shards of sandstone jutting abruptly from the top in case the wombat's unlikely battle foes – echidnas dressed in chainmail, possums wearing platemail – choose to leap atop its head.

Molly pauses to stare at a majestic green emperor dragonfly caught and tangling itself further in the sticky web of a St Andrew's Cross spider. The dragonfly looks to Molly like something flown by the Wright brothers, with a torso made of what seems to be some rare kind of soft velvet pea beaded on a black string, and a scorpion's tail and vast wings that are clear but somehow shimmer with purple light as the dragonfly flaps in fear of being so close to the web's master builder.

'The dragonfly's still alive,' she calls to Greta, who has stopped to scratch the back of her calves with a stick. 'The spider's comin' to get him now,' Molly says. 'I'm gonna pull the drag-onfly out.'

'You can't do that!' Greta says. 'That spider probably hasn't eaten a meal in days and it's gone to all that trouble to build a web to catch some lunch.'

'Does it have to eat something so pretty?' Molly asks.

'Don't think spiders give a damn about pretty, Molly,' Greta says.

'They just haven't seen a Carole Lombard film yet,' Molly says. 'I'm gonna pull the dragonfly out.'

'How could you be so cruel?' Greta responds. 'I reckon a dragonfly would be better than rump steak to the average spider, and you're gonna come along and rip that poor spider's lunch away just as it's tucking its serviette down its shirt front. What sort of monster are you, Molly Hook?'

*

At a small freshwater spring Molly and Greta stop to share a can of corned beef and refill the water bag. Molly scoops her half of the corned beef onto a plate fashioned from a strip of smooth paperbark and sits on a flat rock by the spring.

Greta complains of a throbbing pain in her lower back. She slips off her emerald dress, turns her back to Molly and asks her to inspect her lower spine. Molly places her paperbark plate of corned beef on the flat rock, walks over to Greta and immediately spots two fat leeches sucking their way along the top lining of the actress's underpants. There's another leech crawling up the back of her left thigh.

'Leeches,' Molly says.

'What?' Greta gasps. 'How many?'

'Three,' Molly says.

Greta executes a strange shuffle that makes her look like she's barn dancing. 'How big are they?' she asks, panicked.

'Well, judging by their size I'd say they've had main course and they're progressing to dessert.'

'Get them off!' Greta howls.

'Nah,' Molly says.

'What are you talking about, "Naaahh"?' Greta exclaims. 'Get the bloody bloodsuckers off me, Molly!'

'You're best to just let them have a feed and then they'll drop off all by themselves,' Molly says.

'That's ridiculous!'

'It's not. They keep all this filth inside their stomachs, and if I was to go ripping them off halfway through a meal, there's a chance some of that filth could get stuck inside your open suck wounds.'

'Suck wounds?' Greta repeats.

'Oh dear,' Molly whispers.

'What?'

'One just crawled on to your backside.'

'Get that thing off me!'

'Just relax and let them finish up,' Molly says. 'Besides, just think of all the trouble they went to crawling up those long pins of yours. They probably haven't eaten for days and now you want to just rip them away from their grub. What sort of monster are you, Greta Maze?'

'Molly, get them off me, dammit!' Greta screams.

'All right, all right,' says Molly, who has already found the paring knife in her duffel bag. 'Don't chuck a willy.' She scrapes the paring knife gently and carefully beneath the narrow head of each fat-bodied leech, flicking them in turn from Greta's pale skin.

'You'd better move away,' Molly says. 'I think those leeches have got a taste for German rump.'

Greta rushes across the flat rock, slipping her dress back over her shoulders, zipping it up at the back. But then she freezes because she hears something moving in the wall of scrub fringing the freshwater spring.

'You hear that?' Greta asks.

'Hear what?' Molly replies, finding the place in the scrub where Greta's eyes have been drawn.

Stillness now. A bird whistle. A trickle of spring water. And the actress and the gravedigger girl staring at a wall of palms and cycads and banksias.

More a feeling than anything else. No evidence for it. Just a chill down Greta's spine.

'You think he's following us?' Molly asks.

'Who?'

'Yukio.'

'You guys on a first-name basis?'

Molly shrugs. 'I'm just saying his name.'

'I think we'd be dead by now if he was following us,' Greta says.

Molly turns back to the rock beside the spring just in time to see something she has to look at twice to be sure it's not an illusion, not deep-country magic: the wide, black-brown wings of a wedge-tailed eagle plummeting downwards.

Greta spots the bird now, too. 'Ahhhh!' she screams.

Molly is frozen by the silent predator and keeps watching as it swoops down to her flat rock and, without ever touching ground, claws two large clumps of her corned beef in its large talons and then arcs back up and out of the clearing as gracefully as it entered it. It's an act so bold it could only be the work of a queen. Close up, Molly could see how beautiful she is, how regal, how strong. If she'd wanted to, Molly tells herself, she could have lifted the whole duffel bag in those deadly talons – food cans and rock heart included – taken it high into the sky and back to her family to inspect her plunder from Horace Hook's pantry.

Molly can push only one word out of her voice box. 'Wait!' she calls to the eagle.

'Jesus Christ!' Greta says. 'What the bloody hell was that?'

'She was beautiful,' Molly says. 'Have you ever seen anything so pretty?'

'Scared the shit out of me,' Greta says. 'Cheeky bitch stole your lunch.'

'She needs it more than me,' Molly says and shrugs. She thinks to herself for a moment. 'Imagine being that brave, Greta. Only mums are that brave. Mums with kids to feed.'

Then a thumping sound from beyond the spring. It sounds like it's coming from deep beneath the forest floor. A thunderous drumming in hell. *Thump. Thump. Thump.*

'What is that?' Greta asks.

Thump. Thump. Thump. Something heavy pounding into earth.

Molly has no answer for Greta. She reaches for her friend, the shovel she calls Bert because Molly and Bert *are* on a first-name basis.

*

The gravedigger girl follows the thumping sound along the silver road that runs through an avenue of blue cycad trees with leaves the colour of the moon. *Thump. Thump. Thump.* Louder now. A thin walking trail branches off the road of shimmering mica and Molly and Greta branch off with it, Molly leading the way, gripping Bert's handle ever tighter as the thumping grows ever louder.

Thump. Thump. Thump. Something being crushed. Something breaking into pieces. Rock.

Then a noise so loud it hurts Molly's ears and makes her shoulders jump. An explosion inside a cave.

'Gelignite,' Greta says.

Molly quickens her step, follows that sound along the thin trail, which breaks through a screen of ferns and hanging vines into a clearing where Molly stops before what she can now see is a small mine built deep in the heart of the deep country. *Thump. Thump. Thump.* Molly and Greta kneel behind the cover of a thick fern bush to assess the scene. There is a rudimentary crushing plant housed beneath a triangular shed of rusting corrugated-iron sheets leaning on poles made of the blue cypress pines Molly and Greta have been passing since the Clyde River. A tin mine most likely, Molly tells herself, built against a sloping wall of dark grey rock crawling with weeds and vines.

Two men in blue singlets and wide-brimmed hats are overseeing the crushing of hulking chunks of white quartz. The rocks are being placed under a motorised crusher made out of three heavy, rusting steel-block stamps that are being raised and dropped by a series of rusting camshafts.

Thump. The steel stamps pound so hard upon a quartz boulder that the rock breaks into four pieces. The miners then feed the pieces into a rattling jaw crusher that mashes the stone into a gravel that will be transferred to a sluicebox, which Molly figures must be somewhere close to this mine, beside a natural waterway. Cut along the upper side of the rock slope is a small rail line about fifty yards in length that extends from the crushing plant to the mine entrance, a hole blasted into the side of the rock face, just like the ones Molly remembers her father showing her on Top End bush camping trips not so long ago when Horace Hook still walked in light moods. Horace told her most of those blown-out mine shafts were only useful now to the ghost bats who call them home during the daylight hours. 'But there's fellers still finding their riches all across this country,' Horace said. 'And they guard those treasure holes the way a magpie guards its nest. Every bastard is a threat.'

The mine entrance is not much wider than the door to a two-man tent and a man emerges from it now, hunching down and pushing a cart of mined ore. He wears a singlet and pants and a brown stockman's hat. His brown beard is full and billowing down to his chest.

'His skin,' Greta whispers.

Molly looks closer. There are small lumps across the man's arms and shoulders. Ulcers and scarring. His right cheekbone is abnormally enlarged and the skin on his forehead is swollen and so dry it's started to crack like the clay in Hollow Wood Cemetery during a drought. The man lifts heavy rocks from the mine cart into a hopper connected to the crushing plant and Molly can see now that three of the fingers on his right hand have been severed at the middle knuckle. On his left hand he's missing his thumb and forefinger.

'Let's keep going,' Greta says, standing and turning to go back the way they have come but she stops because she is confronted by a large man resting a pickaxe on his shoulder, filling the width of the trail back to the silver road. Greta inhales sharply, reels back at the sight of him. His face, too, is dry, and so swollen that it looks distorted, like it's been moulded out of shape. There are patches of scarring and discolouration across his neck and arms. Welts and small growths. But Greta is drawn mostly to his eyes. He has no eyebrows nor any eyelashes, and he only has one eye he can see out of, his left one. Where his right eyeball once was, there is an empty socket containing a thin pool of blood. His nose is distorted and big. Molly can't remember when she last saw a man built like this. He's a giant to her. Big broad shoulders. Big biceps. Big legs. Big fingers and thumbs. Big brown hair on his head, in natural and careless curls.

'I'm sorry,' he says, softly. A thick Irish accent. His face is so stiff his speech feels like old air being forced through a crack in a mountain. 'Not so easy on the eye am I?' He chuckles to himself. 'We've been up here so long we almost forgot what we must look like to pretty girls like you.'

Greta gives him a halfhearted smile. She studies the man's face.

'You two lost or something?' he asks.

Molly jumps on the question. 'We're going to find Longcoat—'

'My feller and this one's dad are camped back along the plateau,' the actress interjects, with a natural ease. 'We were out looking at the birds and butterflies when we heard that rock crusher thumping away and we thought we'd come and have a look at what was scaring all the birds off.'

The man with the pickaxe nods. He looks at Molly and she nods too.

Then the large man smiles. 'Well, let me fix you a warm brew before you go.'

The crusher hammers into another chunk of quartz. *Thump. Thump. Thump.* Twigs and dry leaves break beneath boots behind them. Greta looks over her left shoulder to see the two miners from the crushing plant now standing behind her.

'Thanks for the offer, but we'd best be pushing on,' Greta says, moving forward. But the large man steps sideways to block her.

The beating of Greta Maze's heart. *Thump. Thump. Thump.*

'Please,' the large man says, dropping the pickaxe to his waist. 'I'm afraid I must insist.'

*

Two thick logs for seats and a stump for a table. A black billy simmers on an iron heat rack stretched across a fire set inside a circle of broken rocks. The large man with one eye holds an enamel cup filled with tea in his left hand. He sips and he appreciates the warmth of the brew.

Molly holds her tea in two hands, her elbows resting on her knees. She's staring at the swelling and crusty ulcers across the one-eyed man's face. She sees his fingers more clearly now, sees how he still holds the teacup comfortably by its handle despite having lost the little finger of his left hand.

Greta sips her tea and the large man watches her do so and so do the four miners standing behind and to the sides of the improvised tea setting. Each one has his own unique range of visible swellings and lesions across his face and limbs. One of the miners is a red-haired boy, who can't be much older than Molly. His left cheek and left upper lip are so swollen that it looks like they might swallow up his mouth, which has retreated into his chin.

'Thank you,' the one-eyed man says.

'For what?' Greta asks.

'For drinking from my cup.'

'The cup was clean,' Greta says.

'They always are,' the one-eyed man says. 'But few are willing to drink from them.'

He sips again.

'My name is George Kane,' he says.

'Greta Maze.' Greta turns to Molly, the girl's cue to say her name.

But Molly isn't following the conversation. She is too transfixed by the red pool in the well of George Kane's right eye. He winks his left eye and the action snaps Molly out of her staring. She drops her head to focus on her tea.

'And what's your name, young lady?' Kane asks.

'Molly,' she says. 'Molly Hook.'

'Go ahead and ask me,' Kane says.

'Ask you what?' Molly replies.

'That question on the tip of your tongue.'

'What question?' Molly asks.

'I know,' Kane says, smiling. 'How do I keep my hair so

clean all the way out here in the scrub?' He runs his hand through his thick brown mop. 'Vinegar!' he laughs. 'I wash my hair in vinegar!'

Molly smiles. 'I'm sorry I was starin',' she says.

Kane shakes his head. 'There's a lot to look at, unfortunately.'

'You boys come over from Channel Island?' Greta asks.

'You know Channel Island?'

She nods. 'I act a bit,' Greta says. 'Me and some friends, we were asked by the church to go over and perform for the kids.' One of the toughest performances of Greta Maze's fledgling career. Crossing Darwin Harbour and disembarking at the Channel Island Leprosarium. Good money. Bad memories. Singing popular showtunes for a group of children — mostly Aboriginal — living with leprosy and forcibly removed from their families in Darwin and sent to Channel Island. Minimal access to doctors and medicine. Scarce food and running water, even for the visiting theatre troupe. Armies of mosquitoes and flies and an island of dead bodies in shallow graves.

'I didn't know quite what that place was,' Kane says. 'I thought it was a prison at first, but then I realised it was a cemetery. They sent us there to rot. We should have burned that place to the ground."

He stands and addresses the men around him. 'But now we're here safe in the scrub.' He smiles. 'While Australia burns.'

And the men around him smile and nod their heads and Greta Maze wonders exactly what kind of place they have walked into.

'What do you mean "Australia burns"?' Greta asks.

'Haven't you heard?'

'Heard what?' Molly asks.

'We're done for,' Kane says.

'Who's done for?' Greta asks.

'Australia,' he says. 'It's done. It's no more. All those selfish, proud men in red coats that turned into black suits. The ones who came here from across the sea. They thought they could turn this place into a new England. They chased everyone who didn't look like them out of the cities. And now the Japs have burned all them city princes and princesses to dust.'

He drops his voice to a whisper. 'They hit Brisbane with twice the force they hit Darwin,' he says. 'Boom. Boom. Boom.'

Stalking around the campsite now, charged by the electricity of his own visions. 'Then they moved on to Sydney and all those fat men in all those tall buildings didn't see the fire coming. They could only stare at it through their office windows. And they watched the heat blister their skin. They watched the fire distort their faces.'

Seated on the log, Greta slips a hand around Molly's arm, squeezes it, discreetly shakes her head.

The girl knows her now. She knows her looks, she trusts them, and this one says this can't be true, he's not a good one, Molly.

'And in the reflections of their office windows,' Kane says. 'The last thing they ever saw was the monsters they had become.'

Then Greta sees George Kane whispering to a younger, thinner man with lesions across his bald head. Kane has his back turned to Greta and Molly, and Greta can't figure out what he's saying to the bald man, only that he's saying something he doesn't want her to hear.

Greta whispers to Molly. 'Give me the bag,' she says.

Molly unslings the duffel bag and slides it to Greta with her foot.

Kane turns back around and resumes what Greta notes is rapidly becoming a sermon. 'And now the meek shall inherit the earth,' he proclaims. And the men around him nod because they are as easily impressed as they are led.

Kane finds his seat again on the log in front of Greta and Molly. 'All of us exiles and outcasts,' he says. 'We'll start all over again. And we'll be happy and a century from now the people of this land will celebrate the day the bombs of the Imperial Japanese Navy blew greed and avarice into the wind.'

He takes another sip of tea then throws what's left into the fire. He turns to speak to Greta, who now has her hands inside the duffel bag. No welcome and no warmth in his voice anymore. Only suspicion. 'What's in the bag?' he asks.

'Just a few tins of food,' Greta says. 'Water. Stuff from home.'

Kane looks deep into her two eyes with his one eye. A long, painful silence.

'There's no one waiting for you back by that plateau, is there?' Kane asks.

Greta is silent. Then she smiles and says, 'Thank you for your hospitality.' She taps Molly's shoulder. Gets up. 'We'll leave you fellers to it.'

Molly stands, gripping Bert the shovel. 'Thanks for the tea,' she says.

George Kane nods at Molly, remaining seated. He nonchalantly waves a finger at the men behind him. They immediately close in around the actress and the gravedigger girl.

Greta turns to face the men and swiftly pulls the Japanese handgun from the duffel bag. She points it confidently, sweeping her arm across the men.

'Get back,' she snaps. 'Back!'

And George Kane laughs. 'The gun has no bullets,' he says. He gets up from the log, struggling to haul his large limbs into motion, then he points to the red-haired boy. 'Shane over there was quite taken by you girls back by the creek.'

Shane gives two short snorts that constitute his laughter. Another large man in a hunting jacket turns to Shane and makes fun of his snorting by snorting loudly three times and this makes all the men laugh and they're laughing now like deranged clowns and their bodies close in on the girls and Greta steps back from them.

'Get back!' she says, feebly.

But the bodies come closer and the deranged laughter makes Molly Hook think of her Uncle Aubrey and she finds the eyes of the bald man with lesions across his face and his scalp and his mouth is wide and his laughter sounds like a car horn and his hands are reaching for her and all she has in this strange world is her best friend after the sky, Bert the shovel, and she swings him hard at the bald man's nose and blood rushes from his nostrils as he falls to his knees.

Greta steps back further from the men, who rush at her now, and she falls into the arms of George Kane, who bear hugs her with all his strength, the crusty welts and scabs across his arms rubbing against her shoulders. The actress stomps her feet on his boots, kicks her heels against his shins.

Molly turns her head in time to find the red-haired boy charging wildly at her. But the gravedigger girl is wilder and she swings her gravedigger shovel and the root cutting teeth of Bert's blade meet the red-haired boy's left ear and the top half of that ear pops away from his head and soars momentarily through the air to land a foot from the crackling campfire. Stunned, the red-haired boy falls to the ground clutching his severed ear, his fingers running through dirt and gravel in search of the rest of it.

'Run, Molly, run!' Greta shouts, twisting her body in the grip of the heavyset Kane.

Molly sprints through a gap in the group left by the stunned and bleeding boy.

And the day sky talks to her now. 'Run, Molly, run,' it says. And she listens. She listens so well. She bashes through ferns and figs and palms and her shoulders and legs are scratched by the thorns of weeds. 'Don't look back, Molly, don't look back,' the day sky says.

'Greta!' Molly screams, as she turns into the detouring path that took her away from the silver road and down to the bad ones.

'Don't look back, Molly,' the day sky says.

She runs and she runs and she runs.

'Greta!' she calls to the sky.

'Don't look back, Molly,' the day sky says.

And Molly sprints on through the scrub and she bursts through a fringe of palms back to the side of the creek where she leaned happily against a rock reading the works of William Shakespeare.

'Greta,' Molly says.

'Don't look back,' the day sky says. 'Run, Molly, run.'

But she stops. She turns around, sucking air into her lungs, and she knows now why the sky asked her not to look back. The bald man with the bloodied nose is bursting through a natural fern wall and charging at her. She turns to run again but he's too fast, too filled with rage, and his right hand grips her shoulder and the momentum of his running is enough to drag Molly along the creek bedrock, the skin on her kneecaps and shins tearing away against the sandstone surface, and he drags her to the creek and he dumps her head, face-first, into the water and her world exists only underwater now.

Clear water. Bubbles from her mouth. Pebbles on the sandy creek floor. The bald man holds her head down and the shock of these actions unfolding within a second causes Molly to suck a belly full of water and that water has nowhere else to go but to circle around her good heart that has been turning, turning, turning to stone.

*

George Kane dragging Greta along the ground by her right arm. The man in the hunting jacket dragging her by her left arm. Greta kicks uselessly at the earth.

'Let me go!' she screams. 'Fucking animals. Animals! Let me go!'

There is spit coming from Kane's mouth. Sweat across his face. He turns to a man in a black stockman's cap with a red work shirt and braces.

'Kenny,' Kane says. 'Go help Hoss with the girl.'

Kenny runs off towards the thin path Molly ran down moments ago. Kane points at Shane, the red-haired boy, now with a rag pushed hard against his left ear, still stunned by the actions of the gravedigger girl.

'Crank the plant up!' Kane barks.

'She chopped my ear off!' the boy says, sounding as hurt by this event as he is confused.

'Just get the fuckin' crusher started!' Kane hollers.

And Greta hears the spitting of oil inside a rusting generator and then she hears the movement of cranks and pulley systems coming to life again and she's being dragged along on her back and she can see flashes of cloud and blue sky and she leans her head back hard to her left to see where she's being taken.

Greta screams, a primal howl. Deep terror in it. But rage in it, too. Fight. She thrashes along the ground and an arm slips free and she punches at her captors. The man in the hunting jacket kicks her hard in the stomach and the blow winds her and she sucks deep for breaths that don't fill her lungs.

'Lemme go,' she says, but the words barely come out.

George Kane stands over her now as she lies flat on the ground, his face – his disfigured and crusted face – close to hers. His right hand is big enough to grip both of her cheeks and squish her lips together.

'Don't you see?' he sneers. 'Don't you see, pretty girl? We cannot let you go, pretty one. You will run back to what's left of your home and you will tell the survivors of that airborne apocalypse that you have found a paradise deep in the scrub and they will come for us and they will bring all their fear and prejudice with them and they will turn our new sanctuary into the same hell they just watched burn to dust.'

Then the thumping. Greta turns her head and sees the three rusted steel-block stamps piled on top of each other thumping into flattened earth. *Thump. Thump. Thump.*

Kane grips Greta by the neck and pulls her. Closer, closer, closer to the thumping stamps of the crushing plant, which feels alive to Greta, a living thing of metal and oil, monstrous and hungry, with rotating arms and jaws and a need to crush her skull like a block of mineral-rich quartzite.

Kane shouts at the red-haired boy. 'Rope!'

*

Molly drowning. Molly with nothing left. The bald man's right arm forcing her head into the still creek water. She is Ophelia now in the grip of the brook. She will not have her Christian burial. Maybe she doesn't deserve one, anyway. She thinks of her father in the fork of the tree in Hollow Wood Cemetery. She should have buried him properly. She counted at least six holes the Japs had dug deep enough with their sky bombs. She could have pulled Horace from that tree and placed him in one of those holes and sent him back to the earth that made him.

But she had to walk away. She had to find Longcoat Bob before it was too late. She had to find the sorcerer before her heart turned to stone like her father's did so close to the end. A stone heart like his brother's, like her uncle's. Uncle Aubrey. The bald man's face, she remembers. It was disfigured. But beneath the bald man's swellings and lesions was a face that reminded her of her uncle's face. Could that be possible? A dark magic, perhaps. The work of Longcoat Bob? She left her uncle to squirm and rot in the Darwin sun back there in Hollow Wood Cemetery. But maybe Longcoat Bob resurrected Aubrey Hook's soul, or the earth did, and placed it in the body of the deranged bald man whose arm seems so filled with strength and hate as he holds her down, down, down inside her water death.

Sam said the earth would rebel. Sam said the earth would not want her here. But who said Molly Hook was not allowed to rebel too? Dig, Molly, dig. Dig for your courage. Dig for your rage.

And the gravedigger girl thrashes her head in the water and pushes her head back against the hand that holds her down. Her legs kick and kick and thrash against the rocks on the surface and then, as if the earth is responding to her will, relenting to it, the hand holding her hair and her head falls away, the pressure eases. And the clear water surrounding her turns red.

Her head is still underwater when she sees the body of the bald man fall in and down into his own water death, the eyes open on his disfigured face, looking back at Molly. Such surprise on that face, such confusion. Then Molly's underwater eyes find the source of his puzzlement: a hole in his stomach, leaking blood into the water in the languid way the smoke from Bogart's cigarette can fill an office. Blood folding in the water like cirrus clouds in a blue sky.

Molly lifts her head out of the water and sucks air into her lungs and turns to find the Japanese pilot standing above her, his sword fixed in his right hand, its short blade red with the blood of the man who now floats face down in the creek.

'Yukio,' Molly whispers. She breathes again, hard and fast, her backside flat on the rocky creek bank. Soaking wet.

'Yukio Miki,' she says, pointing at the pilot, between further sharp inhalations. 'The good one.' Gathering her breath, but needing to acknowledge this. 'I knew it, Yukio, I knew it.'

The wonder of all this. She points at him again. 'The good one who fell from the sky.'

*

Thump. The steel block stamps meet the ground and the brief shockwaves of that meeting reverberate beneath Greta's flat back. *Thump.*

'Who told you about us?' Kane barks.

'Nobody!' Greta says. Her arms are outstretched and her hands are bound by rope that tears at the skin on her wrists. Circles of blood around her ankles where her feet have been roped together too tight.

'Who else knows you're here?' Kane blasts.

'Nobody does,' Greta says. 'Please. Please. Nobody knows we're here. We came looking for someone.'

Thump. Thump. Thump. Steel blocks smashing against the earth.

'Who are you looking for?'

'The girl,' Greta says – there are tears in her eyes now – 'the girl believes she's had some sort of curse put on her. She wants to find the blackfeller who can take the curse away before her heart turns to stone.'

She shakes her head. It sounds foolish saying it out loud. She breathes hard. 'That's the truth,' she says. 'You let us walk out of here and we won't tell a soul about this place. I swear that to you.'

Greta pants. Panicked. Primal. Kane studies the actress's eyes.

'Throw me that bag,' Kane says to the red-haired boy, who immediately slings Molly's duffel bag to his boss. Kane kneels, dumps the bag's contents at his feet. He inspects a couple of food tins. Flips through the Shakespeare. Scans the gold pan briefly and tosses it aside. Then he holds the blood-red rock up to Greta's eyes.

'What's she carrying a rock for?' Kane asks.

Greta shakes her head, confused. 'I don't know,' she says. 'I've never seen that rock before.'

Kane drops the rock and finds Molly's paring knife. 'The girl is not cursed,' he says. 'How could she be cursed when she has just lucked upon the new world.'

The steel stamps thump into the ground. Kane leans over Greta's face. His body so large. The smell of toil. Yellow pus inside the open lesions on his neck. He runs the point of the knife along the bruising on her eye.

'Someone tried to disfigure you,' he says. 'Who did this to you?'

Greta is silent.

'Answer me,' Kane says.

'Just someone I knew back in Darwin,' she says, quietly.

'Someone you loved?' Kane asks, softly.

Greta nods. Kane turns to the red-haired boy. 'Go to the house, Shane.'

The boy stomps like a petulant child. 'But you said I'd have my time.'

'Your time will be with the girl,' Kane says. 'But all in good time, Shane.'

Shane runs off along a path that fringes the mine entrance and disappears into the scrub.

Greta reels in horror, bringing her knees to her chest. 'Get away from me, you fucking animal,' she screams. She pushes herself across the ground with the heels of her tied feet.

'Sssshhh,' Kane says. 'Please understand that if you move again I will be forced to keep your head extremely still beneath those steel blocks. Please tell me you understand?'

Thump. Thump. Thump.

'It's a new world, Greta,' Kane says. 'There are no rules in this new world of ours. There are no laws.'

Greta shaking. She nods. She weeps.

Kane's thumb wipes away a tear. 'He tried to make you ugly,' he whispers. He runs his thumb now across her face. 'He failed.' He smiles. 'Who would do this to something so beautiful?'

Greta shivers.

'I will never do this to you,' Kane says. 'We will treasure you. We will always know what you are.'

Greta shivers, moves her head away from Kane's fingers.

'What am I?'

'You are the beginning,' Kane says. And his eyes move down her body to the hemline of her emerald dress and the skin of her thighs beneath it.

'You are Eve,' he says.

*

The man in the red shirt with the black stockman's cap runs along the path to the creek to help his friend, Hoss, bring back the strange girl who could handle herself with a shovel. His name is Kenneth Spencer and he's thirty-six years old. He has always believed in the things George Kane told him, but he believes them more than ever now. George told his men the old world was done for. He told them about the Kraut with the funny moustache who was putting an end to England. He told them about the Italians and the Japanese who would help destroy the old world. He promised his men there would be women for the new world when the old world ended, and Kenny Spencer knew every one of those words to be true the second he saw the gravedigger girl and the actress wander into their bustling tin-mine utopia.

Kenny Spencer bounds through a thick wall of palms and ferns and finds himself at the flat rock by the mine's well-frequented creek, where he sees the girl who steeled his beliefs. She's sitting by the creek edge on her backside. He runs to her but then he stops. The girl hugs her knees to her chest looking into the water at something that has made her frightened. It's a man floating face down. A tall bald man. It's his friend, Hoss.

The girl turns to Kenny Spencer. 'Please don't hurt me,' she says.

And Kenny Spencer realises there is more to this girl than George led him to believe, and if there's more to the girl then there might be less to George, and that makes him uneasy about the new world. And this is the last thought he has, staring into the eyes of the girl by the creek, before a cold blade slices across his Adam's apple.

Molly watches the man in the red work shirt and braces collapse onto the rock floor, blood streaming from his neck like a burst water bag, leaving only the figure of Yukio Miki, of the day sky, standing, with his pilot boots two feet apart, braced for any further attack from beyond the forest walls.

Molly nods her approval, then she stands and hurriedly dusts the dirt and rock debris from her hands. 'Greta,' she says, rushing past the man with the bloody sword.

She leads the way back to the tin mine through the avenue of blue cycads the colour of the moon. The loud thumping of the rock-crushing stamps rumbles beneath their feet and Molly treads lightly as she approaches the mine entrance.

She turns back to Yukio and puts a finger to her mouth. 'Sssshhh.'

*

The metal arms and jaws and legs of the crushing plant. Cranks turning, shafts spinning. The steel block stamps, still thumping into the earth. The loudness of it all. The machinery of it. The man in the hunting jacket standing at a distance from the drop of the crusher stamps. He watches his boss, George Kane, who has his back turned to him, leaning over the actress, cutting the last threads of rope that bind her ankles. The colour and shape of the actress's legs have excited the man in the hunting jacket and he thinks about running his hands over those legs and spreading those legs apart and he thinks about pounding the actress's insides with the force of the crushing stamps that pound so loudly behind her and this thought is the last he has before a cold, sharp sword blade runs silently across his throat. The man in the hunting jacket falls to the ground, but Kane does not hear his friend's death unfolding over the sound of the turning and thumping machinery.

Yukio Miki now silently approaches George Kane's turned

back. The heavyset miner cuts the last link in Greta's ankle ropes and gently shifts her legs apart. Yukio raises his sword, two hands on the hilt held high, the blade pointing downwards like a fighter plane set to fly into the target of the stranger's large back. He says a word in Japanese: 'Yamero.' But he's not heard in the sound of the machinery. *Thump. Thump. Thump.*

He says it louder: 'Yamero!' And Kane turns and his face turns white when he sees the vision of a Japanese soldier with the sun behind his back, body glowing, light shimmering off the blade of a raised sword.

Yukio's eyes fix on the stranger's blood-red eye and then fix on the paring knife he holds in his right hand, and the pilot hacks instantly at Kane's right wrist, but the hallowed Miki blade severs limbs in a single swing only in the family stories that Miki men have passed down through generations. Yukio hacks again at the wrist and Kane is left stunned by the sight of his right hand hanging loosely by a thin bridge of flesh.

Eventually he gathers his thoughts and, in turn, finds his rage and he charges at the Japanese sword carrier, who changes the thrust of his elbows and instantly braces himself to drive the blade deep into the giant one-eyed man's round belly. But the rage-filled miner keeps moving forward along the blade until the hilt guard is pressing against his skin and the blade tip has pushed through to his spine.

Kane's big left hand reaches for and grips Yukio's throat, and the bloody nub of his severed right wrist pushes deep into the underside flesh of the pilot's jaw. Kane drives with his legs and Yukio, two hands still grasping the sword hilt, is lifted up and carried for several yards before Kane drives the pilot's back hard into the ground as he falls forward on top of him. Then the giant with the sword through his gut presses all of his weight on Yukio and invests every last ounce of his strength into choking the Japanese pilot to death.

Five seconds. Eight seconds. Yukio gasping for air. Up this close to Kane, Yukio Miki wonders for a moment in this brief hell if he has found himself before an *oni*, one of the supernatural demons his grandfather Saburo told him about as a boy, those giant disfigured monsters who passed across the demon gate from the world of darkness. They had a third eye mashed into their foreheads and they had extra fingers and toes and strength enough to walk with blades pierced through their stomachs.

Ten seconds. Twelve seconds. Yukio out of breath, feeling like he's swallowing his own Adam's apple. The hand and the nub of a monster. I'm coming Nara, he tells her. I don't know how it came to end like this, dear Nara, but I am coming.

Then a large red rock shaped like a heart smashes into Kane's right temple. Then it smashes again and again and Greta Maze howls with fury as the blood-red rock that Molly took from inside the bone pillow of her mother's chest meets the bones of George Kane's face. Still the monster squeezes the pilot's throat and still the actress smashes the rock against the side of Kane's face.

'Animals!' she screams, and she is rage and blood and fear and she is past and she is present and when she screams that word again – 'Animals!' – she is including herself in the gallery of monsters in her mind.

The falling steel stamps of the crushing plant. *Thump, thump, thump.* The rock hitting the side of the giant's head, his blood splattering onto the face of the Japanese pilot, until, at last, George Kane slumps still and dead on top of Yukio Miki. Greta pushes hard at Kane's side and Molly is there now to help her, and the actress and the gravedigger girl heave the miner off Yukio and onto his back with the hilt of the blade still lodged in his belly.

Greta stands over the Japanese swordsman. Her hands and body are covered in blood. Yukio sucks air back into his lungs as he watches the actress go and wipe her hands on the pants of the dead miner and then he watches her walk back to him and stand over him once more, breathing, breathing, breathing and studying his face, staring into his eyes, examining the splatters of blood across his skin. And then she extends her right arm. She offers the pilot her hand, her shaking right hand. And he raises his right hand up to hers and the two hands meet in the middle of the silent space between them.

Greta Maze pulls Yukio Miki to his feet.

Delirium Tremens

The questing shadow man. He does not stop to vomit. He spews three mouthfuls of blood and bile as he walks, and the vile stomach slurry showers the spear grass of the floodplain far beyond Candlelight Creek. The sun is high and hot but his body is cold and shaking. He drinks from floodplain waterholes but what his body needs more than water is gin, vodka, whisky. Turpentine. His hands shaking, his knees shaking, but he walks on because the hate inside him is the only thing he has to keep him warm and moving. Only animal now. Only hate.

Head aching. Clammy skin. The bite wound in his shoulder blade still weeping and full of vivid yellow pus. Dizzy. He passes purple and pink flowers and he turns back to these kneehigh flowers on occasion because he could swear the flowers have eyes for petals and these eyes are following him, but every time he turns back to catch them staring they look away. Weak muscles moving so slow but a heart beating so fast. He walks through a small city of meridional termite mounds and he believes for a moment he is walking back into Hollow Wood.

In one straight row of termite mounds he sees the names

of Tom Berry's kin because all he sees is hate. He sees their names on their gravestones and he sees their reasons for being buried in the ground. The most profound and rotten season of bad luck to ever befall a single family in all of Darwin history. Some four members of Tom Berry's kin, all of whom perished within three months of the night the black sorcerer named Longcoat Bob pointed his finger at Tom Berry from the doorway of the Darwin town hall.

Aubrey looks deep into the face of a large termite mound. He sees a name in bold letters written across a gravestone. 'Theodore Berry, 1866–1916'. Tom Berry received the news in a telegram only five days after Longcoat Bob made his announcement in the town hall. His brother, Theo, the eldest of the three Berry brothers, had been working alone as he often did during the slower seasons on his wheat farm in Clermont, central Queensland. When production was halted by a blockage in his grain silo, he tied a safety rope to his waist, as he had done numerous times, and lowered himself into the silo to unclog it. When the safety rope snapped, Theo found himself immersed to his shoulders at the centre of a cone-shaped depression of wheat grains. When he tried to dig himself out, the mounded grains began to slowly slide down the cone-shaped slopes and engulf him. He called to his wife, Marg, who could not hear his desperate pleas for help because she was weeding the front garden of the couple's farm cottage, some sixty yards from the grain silo. Remaining perfectly still, Theo Berry managed to slow the gradual slide of the suffocating grains, which was pressing down hard on his chest and eventually his throat, long enough for Marg to realise her husband wasn't coming to the house for his usual afternoon tea. Theo heard Marg's calls beyond the silo walls just as his mouth and nostrils were filling with seed.

'Theo!' Marg called. 'Theo!'

Theo used his last gasp of air to holler, 'I love ya Marg and I always will'. Then his head was drowned by the grains.

Aubrey chuckles. Then his eyes find another epitaph in the termite mound city. 'Esme Berry, 1843–1916'. Tom Berry's aunt died three weeks after Theo from a gastrointestinal infection.

'Clara Berry, 1845–1916'. Tom Berry's beloved mother, Clara. A month after her sister-in-law died, Clara's right leg fell clean through a rotting wooden board on the thin rear deck of her small home in Batchelor, south of Darwin. Her leg was gouged sickeningly through the rear calf when it landed on the large rusted tooth of an old manual crop cultivator which was being stored in the space beneath the deck. The tooth went so deep that the town surgeon said the leg would have to be amputated above the knee, but the surgery was poorly carried out, the leg became infected, gangrene set in and Clara Berry died a painful death some two months after the death of her sister-in-law.

Aubrey's eyes move to another mound. 'Charles Berry, 1909–1916'. It was at Clara Berry's wake that Esme Berry's seven-year-old grandson, Charles, was challenged by two older boys to eat a peculiar slug they had found crawling in the backyard tool shed of the man who was hosting the wake, Darwin councilman Henry Pegg.

That afternoon in Pegg's living room, with his fingers sticky from the scone he was eating with jam and cream, Charles Berry fell to the floor and began frothing at the mouth and shaking with convulsions. He died on the right shoulder of Henry Pegg, who was then running towards the Darwin emergency hospital.

And Aubrey Hook smiles. He laughs at the wild misfortune

of it all. Then he howls, his deranged and deep guffaws echoing across the still floodplain.

It was after the death of young Charles Berry that the *Darwin Examiner* made the first public press reference to a rumour that had been swirling across town: Longcoat Bob had put a curse on Tom Berry for the sin of his greed, and the curse was proving to be real. The newspaper ran a quote from an anonymous source who claimed to have been in the Darwin town hall the night Longcoat Bob placed his so-called curse on Tom Berry. 'The sorcerer had a bone in his hand,' the anonymous witness said. 'He pointed it at Mr Berry and he said in a loud and commanding voice, "I curse you and your kin, Tom Berry. Your hearts will turn to stone." That's what he said. And look at all the bad fortune that's come over that family. That blackfeller was talking black magic and the rest of us was lucky he didn't decide to talk to us.'

Tom Berry tossed the newspaper into his living room fire when he read it. 'There's a difference between a curse and piss-poor luck,' he screamed, so loud it made his wife, Bonnie, jump in her armchair beside his. 'Did any one of those people die of a stone heart?' Tom Berry barked, uncapping a bottle of whisky and reaching for a glass. 'Has my heart turned to stone! Has your heart turned to stone, Bonnie? Have mercy!'

Bonnie Berry sat in silence, looking into the warm fire and wondering if her husband's statements were entirely true. She'd seen something change inside her husband since his return from his strange and fruitful odyssey through the deep country, and despite his newfound wealth, a cloud seemed to follow him wherever he went. He was irritable and, although now more generous, less kind. And how was Bonnie to explain the heaviness of her own heart, were it not itself undergoing some slow transformation? How was she to explain how low she had felt in recent months? She had tried to express to friends the feeling of unwillingness she had carried for so long, a dread of living that made her belly sick. Unwilling to rise in the morning. Unwilling to cook. Unwilling to clean. Unwilling to love. Anyone and anything. She read so many poetry books that sang of the workings of the human heart, its mystic machinery, of the fountain inside of us all that gives and receives love in the endless and glorious thud of a chest beat. She placed her palm on her chest by the fire and she could feel the beat of her heart, but she could not feel the love she had once kept inside it for her husband. A heart that can no longer love, she told herself, might as well be made of stone.

'Tom,' Bonnie said by the fire.

'Yes, my love.'

'I think you should put the gold back where you found it.'

*

Aubrey Hook stares into the floodplain sun and his fever vision splits the sun into two, like a double-yolk egg frying on a skillet. He dumps his head into a waterhole, slaps his face hard. Then he marches on across the floodplain, his hatred giving him pace.

His mouth is dry and desperate for spirits. He wonders about explorers who came through here on horseback and on foot. He wonders if they ever tossed their whisky bottles from their horses. Buried them in dirt to save for return journeys. Buried spirit treasure. He curses the blacks who walked these isolated lands for millennia and never once took the time to construct a saloon among the forests and plains, a glowing two-storey pub with piano music and song echoing through its windows, high up on the range he can see in the distance.

He walks along a woodland avenue of fern-leafed grevilleas and milky plum trees with yellow fruits that he rips from the branches in desperate grabs and shovels into his mouth like they were pub bar peanuts. 'The damned,' he tells himself, his mouth full of fruit, juice streams spilling down his chin. 'The daaaammned!' he laughs. He knows whose footsteps he's following. The footsteps of damned Tom Berry, the accursed goldminer who made his intentions clear for all to read when he placed an announcement in the *Darwin Examiner*.

PUBLIC NOTICE

I, Tom Berry, hereby proclaim my solemn vow to return all the gold I recently acquired to the godforsaken hole in which I found it. It is with great displeasure that I must publicly acknowledge the growing hysteria and muddy rumour that has swirled in recent months around the Berry family. I do not believe in blackfeller magic. I do, however, believe in plain bad luck. And ever since I brought this gold back to Darwin, it's the only kind of luck my family has seen. I swear, under God, Longcoat Bob told me that gold did not belong to anyone. But, I am man enough to admit, at no time did he say that gold should belong to me. I have been found guilty of my own pride and my own greed. I do not believe in curses. But I believe a man should admit when he's wrong and, where possible, he should endeavour to right his wrongs. I will travel back into the deep country as soon as I am able and I will put that gold back where I found it. And, should Longcoat Bob's finger indeed wield a dark and inexplicable power and should he still be pointing that finger at my family, I expect him to promptly stick that finger someplace else.

Aubrey Hook howls again and his laughter fills the space between two walls of a jagged sandstone canyon. The double sun falls in the sky. He stops by a swamp to feast at a gooseberry shrub that has dropped an entire season's worth of green tomato-like wild fruits, some twenty-six of which Aubrey shovels down his throat the way he used to shovel grave dirt into buckets.

'Berries!' he howls to the sky. 'Tom's berries!'

He drops his strides immediately after feasting on the gooseberries and he squats and releases a diarrhoea torrent onto a patch of grey sand. After cleaning up as best he can, he fills his right pants pocket with more gooseberries and he fills his left pants pocket with a handful of eucalyptus leaves that he rips from a young stringybark. Further along his frenzied journey, he finds a rusting billy can in a natural rock dish in a sandstone outcrop and he lights a night fire from gathered sticks and paperbark that he ignites with one of his lit cigarette papers. He boils the eucalyptus leaves in the billy can and drinks from the can then splashes the boiling water over the festering bite wound in his shoulder.

He lies by the fire with his arms gripping his pounding chest, his body shaking. He stares into the fire and he repeats the words of Walt Whitman. "'I laugh at what you call dissolution.'"

And inside the fever and inside the flames he sees a memory of himself. A young man, tall and handsome. That young man kept his promise. He survived the rockfall that killed his hate-filled father, Arthur Hook, and he held true to his private pact. He had only love in his heart that Sunday afternoon when he rode his horse to Violet Berry's home on the Darwin waterfront. He roped his ride out of view of the house's windows to lengthen the odds that Tom Berry might see a son of Arthur Hook approaching his yard. He walked to the front door unseen and was about to knock when he heard Violet's laughter echoing from the backyard. Aubrey trod lightly down the side of the house and, half-hidden by the curve of a rusting water tank, he spied Violet beneath a sprawling backyard milkwood tree. And he saw the awful reason for her laughter: the hands of the young man who lay beside her, squeezing her ribs. And then he saw the awful owner of Violet Berry's heart. That soft young man beside her. That vibrant and joyful and weak young man beside her. That second son of Arthur Hook. His own beloved brother, Horace.

Aubrey Hook went riding alone along the waterfront that Sunday afternoon. He took his horse to the highest point he could find along the Dripstone Cliffs overlooking the beach stretching beyond the Rapid Creek inlet. He gave the horse a fifty-yard run-up and he heeled it hard in its belly and it galloped towards a blind clifftop horizon. They were but ten yards from the edge when something inside Aubrey's heart caused him to pull hard on the reins and circle away from the void. This certain something inside him would prove in the decades to come to be a light in all of his endless dark hours. Nothing else would prove so sustaining. Not love. Not work. Not liquor. The only thing that ever saved Aubrey Hook was hate.

"'I laugh at what you call dissolution'" he mumbles at the fire. "'I laugh at what you call dissolution.'"

Repeat. Repeat. Repeat. And if he says these words long enough, then she might return to him.

"'I laugh at what you call dissolution,'" he says. "'And I know the amplitude of time.'"

Repeat. Repeat. Repeat.

"'I laugh at what you call dissolution and I know the amplitude of time.'"

Repeat. Repeat. Repeat.

"'Failing to fetch me at first keep encouraged. Missing me one place, search another. I stop somewhere waiting for you.'"

And he sees the face of Molly Hook's mother.

"'I laugh at what you call dissolution,'" he mumbles. "'And I know the amplitude of time'" . . . "'Failing to fetch me at first keep encouraged. Missing me one place, search another. I stop somewhere waiting for you.'"

And he sees the face of Violet. Repeat. Repeat. Repeat.

THE THIRD
SKY GIFT

Ophelia

She is drawn to the rapids. She is sixteen years old and walking barefoot along a plateau buried in blue sky. Her infant son is four months old and curled comfortably inside a sling carrier made of bush string, paperbark and cane strips. From terraces high above, a river plummets into a deep, craggy, sandstone gorge and the force of the great and relentless water rush against the rocks sprays a fine mist onto her face even as she stands some twenty-five yards back from the lip of the gorge.

She climbs up the side of the clearwater rapids and stops at a deep pool where the current moves more slowly. She lays her baby down inside the sling on a flat rock and the boy's eyes find points of colour and movement and light and settle on his mother's eyes staring back at his. But then the mother's eyes start weeping and then the mother's eyes turn to the pool. And she walks away from her baby. Reaching the water's edge, she plants a hand on a large water-worn boulder for balance, finds her footing among the loose black rocks on the surface of the deep emerald pool. She dives under the water and propels herself only with her legs, mermaid-like, emerges with a deep breath, then breast-strokes in a circle before turning to float on her back with her arms and legs outstretched and her eyes filled with all of the blue in all of the sky. Just one fluffy fat cloud and she tells herself it looks like a big white witchetty grub without its yellow head. She can hear herself breathe and she can hear the rush of the rapids downstream. And she lets the water push her.

The witchetty grub starts to crawl across the blue roof, but that's just an illusion. The cloud isn't moving. She is. The slow, gentle push of the current. Push, push, push, and the girl drifts slowly along the surface of the water towards the gorge.

And to the sky she makes a wish. She wishes to be water. Because water has no feeling. Water feels no pain. Water is never afraid. Water feels no sorrow. And she thinks about the life she could have had if she'd known how to move through this complex earth the way water always knows how to move through it.

The Sky Buried Treasure

The stone country. Three wanderers of the silver road that turns and twists – just like a python turns and twists as it slides along the base of a nearby ironwood tree, its movement and its size drawing applause from a foreign spectator named Yukio Miki.

Single file. Greta Maze walks in front and Molly Hook pads along in the middle, turning her head back regularly to find the strange pilot stopped before another natural northern Australian point of wonder. He bends down to a frill-necked lizard resting on a burnt log, and the lizard fans its red frills in defiance of the smiling man's inspection. He passes a euca-lypt tree with a hole in its trunk the diameter of his own head. Molly watches Yukio insert his right arm into the hole, pull his arm out and study his right fist, now crawling with orange and white termites.

Yukio watches Molly reach into a nest of stingless black bees wedged between two branches of a stringybark tree and pull out a handful of deep red sugarbag honey, which looks to Yukio like melting wax. She drops a dollop of the honey in Yukio's hands and she eats a dollop herself. Greta finds

287

another nest nearby and grabs a handful of the dark, strong-flavoured gloop too. Yukio tentatively licks the honey in his palm. Liking the taste, he slips it all into his mouth and his eyes light up like his smile. 'Migoto!' he says.

'Very, *very* . . . migoto,' Molly says, licking her hands.

At a slow-moving freshwater stream that cuts across the silver road, Greta relieves herself behind a thick wall of shrubs with red pendulous flowers whose small pink fruits sprout tentacle-like fibres that make the fruits look like they've been snap-frozen in a state of self-combustion.

Yukio follows Molly to the stream. He stands above her as she kneels down.

She points two fingers to her own eyes and then she points to the stream.

'You,' she says. 'Watch for crocs.'

Yukio is blank.

'You be on the lookout,' Molly says, pointing to her eyes again and then pointing to the water. 'Crocodiles,' she says, forming her hands into a snapping crocodilian mouth. 'They'll drag you down underwater. Wedge you under a rock and let you tenderise for a month.'

Yukio nods, casting a keen and immediate eye across the stream.

Molly places Bert the shovel on the muddy ground beside her boots and reaches into the duffel bag. She pulls out the blood-red rock that she found inside her dead mother's chest. It's stained now. Covered in splatters of blood from the smashed head of the one-eyed tin-miner monster. Molly places the rock in the clearwater stream and rubs the monster's blood away. "Out damn spot. Out, I say," she says to herself.

Yukio studies the girl's actions, curious.

Molly feels him looking over her shoulder. 'It's my mum's

heart,' she says. 'It's what happens at the end of the turning, Yukio. It's what Longcoat Bob done.'

Molly looks up at Yukio. The weight of the story across her face. 'He said our hearts would turn to stone and my mum's heart slowly did. And now I can feel my heart going that way, too. It's getting heavier, Yukio. I feel it inside me. I've stopped caring about people.'

She looks at the sword hanging from his belt. 'I watched you cut the throats of those men back there and I felt nuthin' for it,' she says. 'Do you follow me, Yukio?' she asks, but she doesn't care if he doesn't. It feels good to say it out loud and maybe even better saying it to someone who can't understand. 'I wasn't scared,' she says. 'I wasn't sorry. If anything, I was glad you did it to 'em.'

She studies Yukio's face. Blank but for his eyes, which say he's listening hard to the gravedigger girl.

'Can you understand anything I'm saying to you?'

Yukio is silent. He smiles uncertainly. 'You,' he says, enigmatically, repeating the last word he heard.

'You can't understand a word, can you?' Molly asks.

'You,' he says again.

Molly nods, smiling. She turns back to the water, stares at the red rock in her hand. 'That's how it starts,' she says. 'You go numb. You stop caring about people. You start to hate things. You only care about yourself and all the things swimming around in your own head.'

She grips the rock, squeezes it hard like she wants to break it in two, but it has no give in it. 'Then you wake up one day and your heart has finally turned all the way to rock and you feel nothing whatsoever, so it makes no difference if you're here or if you're not. This rock can't feel nuthin', Yukio. No matter how much I could feel for it, it can't feel nuthin' for me. Why am I even carrying it, Yukio? It can't feel nuthin'. It can't give nuthin' back. I should just let it go. I should just drop it right here and let it sink to the bottom of the creek and it can sit there feelin' nuthin' for a million years.'

Yukio notices a cloud of colour mixing with the water. A thin layer of red-brown clay or dirt pulling away from the rock, like it's losing a layer of skin. It looks to Molly like the blood of the bald man she saw rising like smoke in the creek water.

'It's bleeding,' Molly says.

She watches it bleed, bleed its colour into the water and she watches the folds and waves of that colour disappear into the slow current. And at first she doesn't realise that Yukio is kneeling beside her now. Then he's gently lifting her arm up out of the water and he's reaching for the blood-red rock and holding it in his cupped hands. He dries the rock with the inside of his flight jacket and he places it gently in the duffel bag. Then he hands the bag by its strap to Molly.

'You,' he says, and Molly hears something instructive in the word. Something encouraging. Something with care in it.

*

Purple sky with streaks of pink and red, streaks of fire. Three wanderers moving under and over sandstone ledges, around freestanding rock outcrops. A shifting landscape, stone country turning to brief rainbow-coloured clusters of orchids and banksias and woollybutt trees, then turning back again to stone country filled with runs of misshapen boulders that the grave-digger girl and the actress and the pilot who fell from the sky must clamber over for two, three, four miles.

Yukio tells himself to stop sneaking glances at the actress, but his eyes have a will of their own and thcy keep finding new small wonders in the things the blonde woman does. The way she helps Molly over two slippery moss-covered rocks. The way she tucks a clump of that wild hair behind her right ear. The way she pretends not to see the way he looks at her and then the way she decides to stare straight back at him, looking so deeply that he doesn't speak a word inside his mind in case she hears it. And then he must look away from her because he feels she could turn him into a scared boy with a single glance, and then he must look to the sky for his manhood. And he looks at the purple and pink afternoon sky, he talks to it because when he talks to the sky he is talking to Nara. 'Can you see me, Nara? I was coming to you. I am coming to you, Nara. I promise. Will you wait for me?'

*

At a muddy billabong, Greta spots a thick-bodied, light-brown snake with a small head shaped like a bulldog's head. The snake burrows itself down into a sloshy bed of mud to hide, but Molly spots the black and scaly tiger prints of its skin before it disappears. 'File snake,' she says, digging Bert deep into the mud. She heaves a mud load from the ground and the file snake is pulled up with it, wriggling and fretting on the shovel blade and then leaping off it towards Yukio's military boots. He steps back with a brief yelp and only has a moment to see the snake's head before it's chopped off by the side of Bert's blade. Molly picks up the file snake's still wriggling but headless body and hands it to Yukio.

'Hold this for me, will ya?' she asks.

*

Yukio builds a tepee-shaped campfire out of dry branches and paperbark and when the fire has turned to hot coals Molly drops the file snake on top of them, whole and unskinned. While she waits for the snake to cook she reads *Romeo and Juliet* aloud to Yukio. She acts out Romeo's passages in her best Tyrone Power voice, fair Verona by way of Universal Pictures, Los Angeles, California. '"If I profane with my unworthiest hand this holy shrine, the gentle sin is this, my lips, two blushing pilgrims, ready stand, to smooth that rough touch with a tender kiss."' Molly's eyes light up with the matinee-idol thrill of Romeo Montague's boldness.

When she acts out the words of Juliet she channels a love-sick and exasperated Vivien Leigh in *Gone with the Wind*. '"Come, gentle night,"' she gasps, '"come, loving, black-browed night; give me my Romeo; and, when I shall die, take him and cut him out in little stars, and he will make the face of heaven so fine, that all the world will be in love with night."'

And the night comes and Molly cuts up the file snake by flamelight with Yukio's *wakizashi*, slicing its fat and juicy but stringy flesh into segments the size of sausages, which Yukio and Greta chew and suck and swallow down with deep gratitude. In the flickering flamelight Molly takes a long moment to admire Yukio's shortsword. She runs a light finger across the cutting edge and that finger finds the engraving of a butterfly above the sword's hilt.

'Why a butterfly?' Molly asks, holding the image up to Yukio.

Yukio nods.

'Butterfly?' Molly repeats.

Yukio nods.

'Butterfly,' Yukio says.

'Yes, it's a butterfly,' Molly says. 'But why do you have a butterfly engraved on your sword?'

Yukio is silent for a long moment. He smiles. 'Butterfly,' he repeats without confidence.

Molly tears a mouthful of snake flesh from its crispy skin and turns to Greta. 'He can't understand a thing we're sayin'.' she says, her words muffled by the snake meat.

'I can't understand a thing you're sayin' when you talk with half a snake in your gob,' Greta replies. She looks at Yukio and Yukio looks back at her. Greta smiles back at him. 'I reckon he understands enough,' she says.

'I'm gonna test him,' Molly says.

'How about you quit ramblin' and just eat your mud snake before it goes cold?'

But Molly doesn't take to that suggestion. She lifts her head to the stars in the sky, but the words that come from her mouth are not related to the stars.

'I think he's handsome,' she says.

'Molly!' Greta shrieks, short and flustered.

Molly continues to talk to the stars and Yukio's eyes follow Molly's to the heavens. 'He has a smile like Clark Gable,' she says, staring deep into the night sky.

'Stop it, Molly,' Greta says gently.

'I think he's smitten with you,' Molly says, head up still. 'He's been staring at you all day. And I saw you staring at him once, too!' She chuckles to herself.

'Molly, that's enough!' Greta says, louder than she had intended.

Yukio whips his head around to Greta and she is forced to ease his curiosity with a smile and a shake of her head. 'She does love those stars,' Greta says, pointing upwards.

Yukio nods, smiles.

*

Three wanderers flat on their backs around a campfire, staring up at the stars. Molly's fingers turn into a pair of scissors. "Cut him out in little stars", she says to herself, and when she cuts out the face of Romeo from the star-filled night sky it's the face of Sam Greenway she sees. Sam Greenway, hunter of buffalo, star-crossed thief of hearts.

Greta's eyes are closed but she does not sleep. She still hears the thump of the rock stamp from the tin mine worked by the monsters. The fear of it lingers and that fear reminds her of hopelessness and pressure and those things remind her of the hospital room and the baby in her arms so she opens her eyes to fill her mind instead with a cinema screen of pulsing stars.

Still night. No wind this deep in the country. The sound of cicadas and the sound of wood popping and crackling in the fire, the skin layers of a dry ironwood log the size of a full Christmas ham being eaten away by flame. Nothing more but the night.

And then Yukio Miki speaks.

'Yukio . . . had wife,' he says. 'Nara.' He thinks on his words. He thinks on his English, a hundred or so words that he might be able to drag up from his tired mind to answer the girl's question. 'Died,' he says. 'Sick . . . very sick.'

Greta turns her head to see the pilot talking to the sky on the other side of the fire. She looks at Molly and her puzzled face says the same thing Greta's does. He can speak English.

'Yukio held . . . held . . . arms . . .' he says. He's crying now. He holds his own chest. 'Yukio . . . speak . . . Nara. No . . . afraid. No afraid. Yukio . . . promise . . . promise. Nara . . . change. Nara . . . fly away. Nara . . . still beautiful.'

Molly and Greta prop themselves up on their elbows, waiting for the pilot to say something else. He turns his back to them and lies on his side, closes his eyes. Only one more line to say before he sleeps and it comes out slowly and clearly.

'Nara . . . is . . . butterfly.'

*

In the dawn light, they pass three large spherical boulders left balancing and exposed by erosion on a ridgeline that lights up in the rising sun.

'Look, that's us,' Molly says. 'Greta, that's you up front, the bigger boulder. That's me in the middle, the little one. And that's Yukio up the back. See it, Greta, see?'

'I see it, Molly,' Greta says, rubbing sleep from her eyes as she hauls her body over several jagged sandstone rocks.

Molly stops abruptly and Yukio and Greta stop with her.

'What is it?' Greta asks, concerned.

Molly swings her head around. She breathes the morning air in deep through her nose. She looks up at the sky, shimmering with pinks and reds slowly transforming to blues. She breathes in the trees, the rocks, the insects beneath the rocks, the lizards beneath the dirt, the worms beneath the lizards, the dirt beneath her fingernails, the blood beneath her skin.

'What if we're the treasure?' she asks. She looks back up at the sky. 'I'd try to hide us, too. That sky is the lid of a treasure chest. That sky is a blanket. Or a cloak.'

Molly turns to Yukio, who struggles to understand the girl.

'We are treasure buried by the sky,' Molly says.

A brown and emerald-green bird in the sky makes a *kak-kak-kak* sound and spreads its wings wide to show two white coin-shaped dots on their undersides.

'Dollarbird,' Molly says. And she talks back to it. 'Kak-kak-kak.'

Yukio joins in from behind. 'Kak-kak-kak,' he says, laughing. 'He . . . say . . . "Good morning . . . Molly . . . Hook."'

Molly smiles. The bird makes another call. *Kak-kak-kak.*

Molly turns back to Yukio.

'He just asked us around to his place for breakfast,' she says. 'He's got fresh coffee and he's fried a bunch of eggs and some bacon steaks as thick as my head.'

Molly responds to the bird's kind invitation. 'Sorry, mate, can't stop. We've got to find Longcoat Bob. You know where he is, Mr Dollarbird?'

'Bob,' Yukio says. 'Long . . . coat . . . Bob.'

'Yeah, Longcoat Bob,' Molly says. 'Didn't realise you spoke such good English, Yukio Miki?'

Yukio raises his forefinger and thumb, leaves a small gap between both. 'Little . . . little,' he says. 'English . . . come . . . Sakai . . . Molly . . . speak . . . English . . . good,' he says.

'You bet your arse I do, Yukio Miki,' Molly says. 'I'm poetic. Poetic and graceful.'

She spots a large army of green ants building a nest between two thin twig branches of a flimsy tree with floppy green leaves. 'Look at this, Yukio,' Molly whispers, leaning in to the tree where a line of ants with amber bodies and glowing jade-coloured abdomens are carrying a white grub along a designated worker road on a branch. 'They make their homes out of leaves. Some of the ants are the tough ones who will work together to hold the leaves up and some of the ants are the clever ones who will weave the leaves together and some of them are gluers who use that white stuff they're carrying to stick all the leaves in place.'

Yukio releases a brief sigh of awe. 'Mmmm.'

'See the bridge?' Molly asks. The ants have built a bridge out of their own connected bodies to create a shortcut for the gluers wanting to access a branch below them.

'I wish that feller Adolf Hitler could see this,' Molly whispers.

'Hitler?' Yukio echoes, confused.

'Yeah,' Molly says. 'We could get Hitler and what's his name, Mussalino . . .

'Mussolini,' Yukio says.

'Yeah, Mussolini,' Molly says. 'We get Hitler, Mussolini and Winston Churchill all together and they could come and look at this ant bridge for a while. Calm themselves down a bit. Just watching some green ants working for an hour or two.'

Yukio turns to the girl for a moment, puzzled by her words.

'Sam says he once saw a group of these fellers combining their strength to drag a dead honeyeater bird back to their nest,' Molly says. 'That's like you and me carryin' a brewery home for afterdinner drinks. These fellers will build this home for themselves and they'll take care of the other insects on the branch as well. They'll protect the little caterpillars and aphids around them who thank them for the protection by shooting honeydew from their arses.' Molly nods her head in reverence. 'Yep, gotta bow down to the aphids, Yukio, even their shit tastes like sugar. These ants drink honeydew like my old man drinks plonk.'

Drank, Molly tells herself. Drank. Her old man doesn't drink anymore because she asked for the sky gifts.

'Plonk?' Yukio repeats.

'Yeah, plonk,' Molly says. 'Grog. Slops. Piss. Plonk.'

Yukio then watches Molly grab a green ant by its head and bite its backside clean off. 'They're tasty, too,' Molly says.

She eats another. 'Try one,' she says, nodding to the ants. 'But just bite the arse, not the head.'

'Arse,' Yukio says. 'Not head.'

The Japanese fighter pilot eats the arse of a green ant. 'Ooohhh!' he says.

Molly nods. 'Tastes like mint,' Molly says.

'Mint,' Yukio nods.

'Good for a sore throat.'

Molly grips her duffel bag strap and takes one last look at the ant nest.

'Yep, them ants, they're the ant's pants,' she says.

She continues along the path and Yukio walks with her.

'Ant's . . . pants,' he says.

'Yeah,' Molly says, 'that's Australian for "the bee's knees".'

Yukio doesn't follow.

Greta watches these interactions unfold, shaking her head.

'Look, Yukio,' says Molly, 'you're probably gonna be spending a bit of time here in Australia, so I guess you should learn how to speak like one of us.'

Yukio struggles to understand but nods his head anyway. Molly strolls on, using Bert the shovel like a walking stick.

'If you walk into a pub here, let's say, I don't think it would be good for you to be speaking all that Japanese,' Molly says. 'People talk different in those pubs. They've got their own language and it's not Japanese, but it's not English either.'

'Not . . . English?' Yukio asks.

'"This crow eater had a fair dinkum blue with the trouble and strife,"' Molly says. 'That's Australian for "The man from South Australia had a genuine disagreement with his wife."'

Greta, who is walking five yards ahead, turns to smile at Molly.

'If you want a meat pie, you ask for "a dog's eye",' Molly says. 'If you don't know where some place is then you can say it's in "Woop Woop".'

'Woop . . . Woop,' Yukio repeats.

'If you're out of money, you say you haven't got a brass

razoo.' Molly adopts her thickest outback Australian drawl. 'Haven't got a brass razoo, so I'm gonna shoot through.'

'Shoot . . . through,' Yukio says.

'Yeah, you've gotta go,' Molly says. 'You've gotta leave. Shoot through.'

'Shoot . . . through,' Yukio repeats.

'Yeah, that's it,' Molly says. 'But slow it down and stretch it out: "Shyuuuut theruuuuuu".'

Yukio ponders her words and responds. 'Shyuuuuut theruuuuuu.'

'That's it, Yukio,' she says. 'Now here's what you say if you need a shit . . .'

*

The silver road lost its lustre long ago, the peppering of shimmering mica flakes slowly giving way to rocks and pebbles and thin stretches of dirt covered in rock wallaby prints and the tail-drag marks of black wallaroos.

They pass a group of brilliant green and yellow figbirds fussing about in the upper strata of a cluster of tall fig trees. The pilot and the actress walking side by side in silence now. Mica flakes beneath their shoes. Bird whistles. Molly has skipped ahead.

'Thank you,' Greta says. Yukio turns to Greta, confused.

'Thank you for saving me,' she says. 'You saved me from those men.'

Yukio nods. They walk on in silence for another minute, a long one.

'I've never killed anyone before,' Greta says.

Yukio thinks on this for a moment.

'Greta Maze . . . no kill . . .' he says, shaking his head,

pointing back over his shoulder to the tin mine, to the recent past. 'Yukio kill . . . man.'

Greta takes a breath. 'That's nice of you to say, but I think I might have helped a bit,' she says.

Another long pause.

'War,' Yukio says, shaking his head.

Greta can only assume what that means and she takes it to mean that Yukio believes one-eyed giants of the woods act differently amid the pressures of war.

'Guess you might have killed someone before?' she asks.

Yukio looks at Molly. He nods only once. He watches the girl as her eyes follow the soaring flight path of a gold and green pigeon with a rose-pink crown.

'I thought it was beautiful what you said last night,' Greta says.

Yukio stiffens.

'What you said about your wife,' she says.

Yukio nods.

'Where were you going?' Greta asks.

Yukio is confused.

'In your plane,' Greta says. 'When we saw you come down? Where were you going?'

Yukio looks at Greta. Her face, her green eyes the colour of her dress. Her hair when it moves in the light like that. He looks away from her and he's saved from the moment – saved from feelings he does not understand – by Molly running back to him.

'Yukio!' she hollers. 'Yukio!'

Her hands are cupped, holding something inside them.

'I've got a gift for you,' she says. She uncups her hands and a butterfly with flapping wings the colours of a tiger launches itself haphazardly into the sky.

'Butterfly,' Molly rejoices.

'Butter . . . fly.' Yukio smiles.

Greta walks on ahead by herself. Molly and Yukio watch the tiger butterfly disappear into the thick vine scrub lining the path.

'I've been thinking about what you said last night,' Molly says. 'You said your wife didn't just die.' She stops and thinks harder on what she's trying to say. 'Well, ummm, she didn't just go into the ground.'

Yukio turns to the girl, expressionless. Molly continues.

'You said she turned into a butterfly,' she says. 'What a beautiful thing to turn into.'

Yukio nods, silently.

'I lost my mum when I was seven years old,' Molly says.

Yukio nods, silently. Molly tells Yukio Miki again about the curse of Longcoat Bob. She tells him about her home at Hollow Wood Cemetery. A place where she helped her father and her uncle bury people in dirt. She hoped for so long that there was more to death than dirt. 'Then you come along and say there's butterflies,' she says.

They walk along silently for a stretch, passing a rocky vine thicket studded with pale grey trees with shiny dark green leaves and bright orange berries.

'Them Japanese bombs blew Hollow Wood up,' Molly says. 'Them Japanese bombs blew my dad to bits.'

'I sorry,' Yukio says.

'Nah, I know it wasn't you, Yukio,' Molly says. 'I didn't see no place for bombs on your little plane.'

She kicks a rock the size of a tennis ball with her right boot. It rolls along for ten feet or so and she kicks it off the path with another solid boot.

'But maybe my mum and dad transformed, too?' she says.

'Maybe they're butterflies now. Or maybe they're the grass like Walt Whitman says, or maybe they're the sky.'

Molly looks up to the blue sky. Thin day sky clouds like flour dusting a bread loaf. 'The day sky and the night sky,' Molly says.

'Day sky.' Yukio nods. 'Night sky.'

'Night skies tell no lies,' Molly says.

'Night skies tell no lies,' Yukio repeats, smiling.

The three of them stop to drink from a thin freshwater creek. Molly shows Yukio her grandfather's gold pan. She runs her fingers along the line on the flat underside.

'This was the first gift from the sky,' Molly says. 'It's leading us to Longcoat Bob.'

She looks to the blue sky again. It's now filled with high puffs of small round clouds that look to Molly like the scales on a black bream. 'Then I asked the sky to drop them bombs on Hollow Wood,' Molly says. 'But I didn't want those bombs to blow my dad to bits.' She puts the pan back in the duffel bag and they all walk on.

'You were the next gift, Yukio,' Molly says. 'You fell from the sky. You came to help us.' She looks further along the dirt track at Greta who is marching ahead through a mess of strangler figs inside another pocket of vine forest.

'Or maybe you came to help Greta,' Molly says.

'Greta,' Yukio repeats. He watches her walking when he says her name.

'She's sad, Yukio,' Molly says. 'There's something inside her that makes her low. My friend, Sam, he's a blackfeller who knows all there is to know about this deep country and he said the land gives you all you need if you know the right way to ask for it. I reckon the sky is like that, too. You saved us back there, Yukio. You fell from the sky because you knew you had to save us. You had to save me. And you had to save Greta. The sky knew she needed you.'

The vine forest clears and the thin track disappears into a giant sandstone rock formation shaped like an igloo, split by a thin crack down its middle with enough space for a body to walk through sideways. Greta turns to her side and puts her arms out as she squeezes through the narrow space, eyes raised to the line of sky running across the dome. Molly and Bert the shovel follow Greta and Yukio follows Molly.

Yukio's eyes light up when he emerges from the crack to find he's standing inside a kind of natural gallery space enclosed by high walls of sandstone and a wide rock overhang. On the other side of this space are three openings, like exits, one leading to the east, one to the north and one west. The floor of the space is dotted with smooth, eroded grinding holes. On the wall beside each opening is a vivid and ancient rock painting. The eastern wall features a painting in reds and browns and whites and yellows of three tall, thin figures wearing dresses, which seem to Molly to be women but are also strange-looking and not of this world. They have no eyes or noses or mouths but seem to be staring at her and she is unsettled by these stares. On their heads are what appear to be headdresses shaped like quartered lemon pieces. The figures seem important, like they have all the answers to all of Molly's questions.

'Where am I going?' she asks them. 'Why have I come this far?' Then the whole truth of the gravedigger girl in a single conundrum: 'Why did she go?'

On the northern wall is a painting of a white kangaroo standing tall on the tips of its back legs and looking down on something and on closer inspection that something is a tall ship at full sail. Yukio runs his fingers over the ship's faint white sails and the ship seems like a ghost ship to him, sailing across a mystic sea of ancient red rock, sailing away from the giant kangaroo, who looks to Yukio, when compared to the tiny tall ship, like one of the giant sea monsters his grandfather spoke of when Yukio was a boy, creatures that rose from the seas to drag mariners to their death. His grandfather said some of those monsters were so big that it took Japanese mariners three days to sail past one. And young Yukio pictured a monster watching the mariners as they passed by, the creature pondering when it should strike, the men wondering when they might die. His grandfather said some mariners could not stand the wait, the terrible suspense, and threw themselves overboard in preference to being swallowed up and sucked into the slimy innards of the sea monster. Yukio, aged eight, told his grandfather he would wait it out. 'What if the monster let them sail by?' the boy asked. 'What if things got better for them?'

'Yes,' his grandfather said. 'But what if those three days sailing past that monster were the most terrifying and hellish three days any human could ever be subjected to? Looking into the eyes of those creatures was a hell beyond anything our books could conjure.'

'I'd just close my eyes,' Yukio said. 'When I opened my eyes, I'd be alive and the three days would be over. If I didn't open my eyes, I'd be dead and I wouldn't have to open my eyes at all.'

His grandfather smiled. 'Aaaah, dear grandson,' he said. 'You always seem to open my eyes a little wider every day.'

Yukio smiles now. He follows Molly to the western wall where Greta is captivated by the image of a creature that looks like a cross between a man and a bug and a fish. Thin human arms and legs spread wide, but the torso is made of what looks like a fish skeleton, with the tail placed where a man might normally find his backside. Molly sees that the painted creature-man has a head like a cartoon beetle's head with big circles for eyes, no mouth or nose, and two upright antennae. From the sides of its head, what look like two bamboo sticks curve down to its feet. Two rods, thinks Molly.

'The Lightning Man,' she says. 'Sam told me about the Lightning Man.' She traces the rods running from his head. 'Lightning shoots out from his ears and he bends it down to us, all of us down here on earth, because he wants to show us that everything we need in life is coming soon.'

Molly places a palm against the rock. 'My grandfather was here,' she says. She pulls the gold pan from her duffel bag. She runs her fingertip along a sentence etched into the pan.

'"West where the yellow fork man leads",' Molly says. 'My grandfather was poetic. He didn't see the Lightning Man. He saw a yellow fork man.' And Molly whispers now, 'The Lightning is a Yellow Fork.'

'Come again?' Greta asks.

'Emily Dickinson,' Molly says. 'She wrote about the sky. She must have seen the most incredible lightning in the sky. Forked lightning. She saw things in the sky like I see things. She looked up there and wondered where that gift of the lightning came from. She wondered who was up there dropping things from that house in the clouds.'

Molly slings the duffel bag back over her shoulder.

'It's coming,' Molly says to Greta, eyes alight. 'Let's go. It's coming.'

And Molly rushes through the western archway, which opens onto a thin brown dirt path bordered by tall trees.

'What's coming, Molly?' Greta calls.

Molly turns and talks as she marches backwards.

'Everything we need, Greta,' she says. 'Everything we need.'

The Ten Second Sky

The red-haired boy, Shane, has knotted a lengthy rag around his head to staunch the blood that wants to spill from his severed left ear, and now he swigs from a bottle of moonshine, hoping all that hut-brewed white spirit will give him spirit enough to join his friends in the afterlife. He has dragged the bodies of his dead tin-mining colleagues together beside the campfire. He had thought that laying the men down in a uniformed row would give his dead friends the respect they deserve. There was something right about the effort it took to do that under God's watchful eye. Fishing Hoss with the stab wound through his belly from a crimson-coloured corner of the creek. Dragging Kenny Spencer with his sliced throat back through the scrub to the mine site to lie beside McDougall, the man in the hunting jacket, also with a sliced throat. George Kane was the toughest to pull into the uniformed line, not just because of his dead weight, but because the one-eyed Kane was the man who raised the red-haired boy. Shane looked upon George as father and mother, two parents inside one giant man, making up for the mother and father who had left him on the doorstep of the Darwin police station fourteen years earlier.

Shane lined the bodies in a row, flat on their backs, their faces to the sky, then staggered back down the bush path leading to the stone, wood and tin hut where the workers had their swags. In the kitchen he cut himself a thick slice of cured kangaroo meat and wet his dry throat with a long guzzle of tank water. Then he went to George Kane's raised stretcher bed and found the bottle of moonshine by a pair of old boots and then he reached under his pillow to find the loaded six-shot Enfield No. 2 revolver that he now picks up in two sweaty hands and holds between his knees as he sits on the thick log in front of the dying campfire. He takes a deep breath and he nods and walks to the four bodies lined up on the grass and he lies flat on his back beside George Kane with the caved-in skull and he looks up to the blue sky. There are two clouds up there, one fat and shaped like a wagon and the other thin and stretched like a crocodile.

The red-haired boy with half a left ear cocks the hammer on the revolver and breathes deep as he brings the barrel to his temple. He closes his eyes and his right forefinger slips cautiously over the trigger. He weeps, and the tears squeeze through his closed eyelids. His mouth is closed and he screams through gritted teeth. A guttural howl, a lunatic wail, death-frenzied, life-crazed. But confused, mostly.

The finger on the trigger. Pull it, he tells himself. Be brave like George, he tells himself. He breathes deep again but he can't pull the trigger and he opens his eyes and is met by the face of a man looking down at him.

'Almost there,' the man says.

The boy screams in fear and raises the gun. 'Get away,' he spits. 'I'll do you in, I will. I'll shoot your face right in.'

The man nods casually and steps away and the boy watches him move to the campfire as he aims at his back.

'I mean you no harm,' the man says.

The man is tall and lean. A bushy black moustache over his lips. A white shirt covered in dirt and blood. Black pants and boots and a large black hat with a wide brim that shadows his face.

'Who are you?' Shane spits.

'I'm the gravedigger,' the man says, smelling the tea inside a cup he's found by the campfire logs. He slurps that tea down like it was made for him.

'Have you come to bury the bodies?' the boy asks, because his mind moves slow, and the man with the tea knows this already.

'No, I'm not here for these bodies,' he says, now sipping the tea. 'But bodies are what I'm looking for.'

'Are you one of them?' the boy asks.

'Who's them?'

'Them what done all this?' the boy replies, casting his eyes over his dead friends in the human line. The man turns his eyes to the bodies.

'What happened here, boy?'

The boy speaks through tears. 'There was two girls, one younger and one older,' he says. 'I saw them by the creek and I ran back here and told my boss, George, about them and then they came on through and we gave 'em some tea and . . . and . . .'

The boy weeps.

'And?' the man prompts, running his fingers across his left shoulder where a bloodstain has seeped through his shirt.

'And the boys were gonna have their way with the blonde woman, and my boss, George, he sent me down to the hut but I didn't go all the way down. I hid behind them shrubs because I wanted to see them have their way and . . . and . . . then he came out of the forest.'

'Who came out of the forest, boy?'

'The ghost,' the boy says. 'He moved like a ghost and crept up behind McDougall and cut his throat open before I had a chance to say a word of warnin' and I froze a bit but my pecker didn't because it pissed in my pants and I looked down and saw my wet pants and when I looked up again that ghost had stuck a sword inside George.'

'A sword?' echoes the man, intrigued.

The boy cries hard now, the events rising together in a great wave of chilling reality.

'What did this ghost man look like?'

'He was a Japanese,' the boy says.

The man with the moustache shakes his head. 'Extraordinary,' he says.

He nods at the boy's left ear, where blood is pooling in the worn rag dressing.

'What happened to your ear?'

'The younger girl was carrying a shovel and she swung it at me and cut my ear fair in half,' the boy says.

The man smiles beneath his moustache. 'And why would she do a thing like that?'

The boy shakes his head. 'I was trying to grab hold of her.'

'Why were you grabbing hold of her?'

'We were gonna keep her here,' the boy says.

The man nods. Then his eyes turn to the log by the camp-fire and find the bottle of moonshine the boy was just swigging from. The man's eyes light up as he throws his teacup in the fire. He picks up the bottle of moonshine and the very touch of it makes him exhale with relief. The bottle has humbled him somehow.

The boy watches the man sit on the large fireside log closest to him and remove his hat with what looks like exaltation.

The man smiles and holds the bottle up to the boy. 'You mind if I have a splash?'

'Go ahead, mister.'

The boy could only sip that moonshine because it burned like liquid fire inside him, but the man puts that bottle to his dry and blistered lips and glugs down half of it in a single blast, his cheeks puffing like a bullfrog, his throat working hard like he's sucking on a water hose after a day's work in a wheat field.

The man brings the bottle down and closes his eyes, breathing slow and deep. 'What's your name, boy?'

'Shane.'

He opens his eyes again, turns to the boy. 'What were you gonna do to the girl, Shane?'

The boy shakes his head. 'No, no, I'm not gonna tell you that.'

'You can tell me,' the man says. 'Go ahead, Shane. I promise you no analysis and I promise you no harm.'

'*Anala* . . . what?'

'Analysis, Shane,' the man says. 'Thinking on an event then considering the meaning and the making of it.'

The boy thinks on this for a moment. He turns to George beside him. Then he speaks softly. 'George said she was gonna be my first.'

The man nods. 'You were gonna have your way with the girl?'

The boy drops his eyes, nodding.

The man swigs from the bottle again. 'Tell me, Shane, what stopped you from pulling the trigger just now when you had that gun at the side of your head?'

Shane rests the gun in his lap now, sits up with his legs crossed.

'I couldn't do it,' he says. 'I kept thinkin' God was up there in the sky looking down on me and he was gonna send me to hell for doin' it.'

'Why did you wanna do it in the first place?'

'My friends have all gone,' he says. 'And the world has ended and all that, and what do I have to stick around for now?'

'Who told you the world has ended?'

'George,' the boy says, nodding at Kane. 'He said that Hitler feller's runnin' the north of the world now and the Japs are runnin' the south and I knew that was true when I saw that Jap come out of the forest like that.'

The man nods, rubbing his moustache with his forefinger and thumb. He is silent for a long moment.

'It is true, Shane,' the man says. 'Firestorms have engulfed every major city of the world. There are no vehicles moving through streets anymore because the streets are filled with skinless bodies. Gravediggers across the world are naming their price for their highly valued services. Ash rains across the east coast of Australia. The Thames runs red with blood. German soldiers march through Times Square.'

The boy shakes his head, dismayed. But confused, mostly. 'George was going to start a new world here,' he says.

Shane lies back down beside George and weeps.

The man looks to the sky and raises his bottle to it, like a toast. Then he swigs again and turns to the boy. 'Would you like to know the truth, Shane?'

'Yes,' says the boy.

'The truth is, Shane,' the man says, 'God is not watching you. God has never bothered Himself with the business of death. He only focusses on His successes and never bothers with His failures. He's always too concerned with the wonder of birth and the business of life. He lets death unravel down

311

here with all the purpose and predictability of a father of four children tripping down a lighthouse stairwell. He cares for death about as much as the bullets in your gun care for bone. He makes no analysis of it, Shane. He has no interest in the meaning of it, nor the making. God knows nothing about death.'

He drinks again and points the bottle at the boy. 'But the gravedigger, Shane! The gravedigger knows everything there is to know about death.'

And Aubrey Hook whispers now. 'Let me tell you the story of a man who once passed through this way,' he says. 'Let me tell you the story of Tom Berry. It's a story about death.'

*

And here in this godforsaken and blood-strewn tin-mine campsite Aubrey Hook's long story meanders haphazardly to a recollection the gravedigger has of the look upon Tom Berry's face when he stood in the workshed at Hollow Wood Cemetery reciting from a notepad the words he would like chiselled into his gravestone. Less an epitaph than a warning. An act of anger. An act of love.

Tom Berry took Longcoat Bob's gold by horseback deep into the deep country from whence it had come. Then he put that gold back in the hole in the earth he had left behind. But the fortunes of the Berry family were not miraculously reversed.

Tom Berry returned to Darwin from his fortnight-long journey to and from the deep country to find an inexplicable and unsettling melancholy spreading through his home. The hearts of the people he loved most, it seemed, were already turning cold in his presence, as if they were, indeed, already turning to stone. His wife seemed uninterested in his trip. In the ensuing months, she barely smiled at his humour, barely heard his comments on the weather and work and the welfare of his children. His son, Peter, had grown insular and detached and uncaring. His wife said early on that it was just the lingering sadness over the rash of impossible deaths that had struck the wider Berry family throughout the year. She wondered out loud one evening as she knitted a winter blanket if sadness was a contagion, as hazardous to heart and soul as smallpox was to mind and body.

But then Bonnie Berry revealed her deeper feelings in the fireside heat of a living room row between husband and wife. She said the truth was that she resented her husband for putting Longcoat Bob's gold before their marriage. She hated him for his gold lust that had long ago overwhelmed his simple love of words and sentences. She resented him for being away so long in the deep country on that first fruitful and fateful trip. She said she had assumed he had died and she had steeled her heart for the worst kind of news and when she saw him alive she was dismayed to discover her heart did not soften back again.

'I have no love for you, Tom,' she bellowed across the living room. She held her chest and she spoke like a devotee of Dickinson. 'There is nothing in here for you.'

And Tom Berry drove his fist through his living room window and a curving line of blood dripped down his forearm like the line he had etched on the back of his gold prospector's pan, the secret map of the route to Longcoat Bob's treasure, annotated with cryptic and clever words from a man who'd once prided himself on his way with them. That long walk through that strange and deep country recollected in a crooked line; the start and finish of all his failures.

Then he realised that map he'd etched on his prospecting pan was not just a reminder of how to find his lost gold, should he ever wish to return to it, but also a way to hunt down Longboat Bob. 'I'll kill that Longcoat Bob!' Tom Berry screamed now, his own rage and regret and shame finally convincing him of the veracity of Longcoat Bob's command over black magic. And no matter how many times Bonnie Berry told her husband that her once warm heart had grown cold towards him long before any suggestion of a black man's curse upon their family, Tom Berry kept his shadow gaze on the sorcerer.

And when he was told by his daughter, Violet, that she had fallen in love with and was surely going to marry Horace Hook, youngest son of Arthur Hook, it was Longcoat Bob he saw through the red mist of rage. When an outraged and immovable Tom Berry instructed his daughter to end the union, Violet left the family home and vowed never to return until her father accepted her love for Horace.

Anyone but a Hook, Tom Berry pleaded to the night sky. Anyone but a son of Arthur Hook, his former best friend and goldmining partner who had long despised Tom and he had long despised in return – a man whose untimely death to cave-in he had toasted in a solitary moment with a raised glass of Irish whisky. When Tom Berry considered the implausibility of the union, the divine and impossible insult of it all – the union of all that he loved with all that he despised – he was convinced, in heart and soul and mind and body, that the curse of Longcoat Bob was real. And inside the cyclone's eye of their endless and bitter arguments over the estrangement of their daughter, Tom and Bonnie Berry failed to see the heart of their beloved son, Peter, growing as cold and hard and incapable of feeling as the hearts they carried inside themselves.

At 6.55 a.m. on New Year's Day 1917, Bonnie Berry looked out her kitchen window to find her son hanging from a branch of the milkwood tree Peter and Violet would lie beneath as children, looking up at the sky.

'You are the curse!' Bonnie screamed at her husband as she collapsed on the grass beneath the milkwood tree, a stretch of cut rope by her side and her son in her arms. 'You are the curse, Tom Berry.'

*

A large green caterpillar with red spots across its back walks in a body-looping fashion across Aubrey Hook's black right boot. He puts his arm down and allows the creature to roll its belly on to his hand and looper-walk along his knuckles.

The red-haired boy, Shane, looks up at the blue sky that is turning, turning, turning with shifting cloud.

'Was he really cursed?' the boy asks.

'That depends what you mean by the word, Shane.'

'What happened to his wife?'

'He found her six months later hanging from that same milkwood tree,' Aubrey says. 'Violet had her buried in Hollow Wood Cemetery alongside one whole sorry row of Berrys. My brother and I buried her.'

'What happened to Tom?'

'He became a recluse when his wife went,' Aubrey Hook says, assessing how much drink is left inside the bottle. 'He quarantined himself in his house. He didn't want to get close to anyone in case Longcoat Bob's curse rubbed off on them. He'd chase people from the front gate, screaming like a madman, "Don't come any closer! Don't come any closer! Don't you know this place is damned!"'

The red-haired boy shakes his head in disbelief.

Months before he died, Tom Berry knocked on the front door of the cemetery keeper's house at Hollow Wood. He told his long-estranged daughter, Violet, that he was dying. His lungs were shot from breathing in all that rock dust in his dig days. It was with great reluctance that Tom Berry asked the sons of Arthur Hook to give him a proper burial beside the grave of his wife, but he endured the conversation as a means to an eternal end beside the only woman he had ever truly loved.

'And what would you like as your epitaph?' Aubrey Hook asked Tom Berry in the Hollow Wood Cemetery workshed, the men seated by a standing stack of grey headstones.

'No epitaph,' Tom Berry said. 'Just a message.'

*

'How could one man be so unlucky?' asks the red-haired boy.

'That's not the question you need to ask yourself, Shane,' Aubrey Hook says. 'The question is how could God allow such misery to fall on one man?'

Aubrey Hook caps the moonshine bottle and places it by his feet. He turns to the boy.

'I know why you struggled to pull the trigger, Shane,' he says. 'It is a question not of God in the sky, but of value in your heart. No matter how miserable your life is, Shane, even to the point at which you have a loaded revolver placed against your temple, you have still found, deep within your heart, some inexplicable value in your existence. Usually, of course, the rippled complexity of your particular choice of ending is compounded by the phenomenon that there are others in this world who have also placed inexplicable value upon your life:

parents, siblings, lovers. But in your case, boy, it appears the only people who placed any value whatsoever on your life are now lying in the dirt beside you. So, in turn, one can safely say that you are, to every living creature on this planet outside of yourself, completely and profoundly worthless. Therefore, I say to you, boy, if you have a lingering attachment to the earth and its people that is prohibiting you from pulling that trigger, you would be well advised to discard it. Which then leaves you to challenge only one remaining notion: that you inexplicably consider yourself, deep down in your heart, to be of some value.'

Aubrey holds the caterpillar on his hand out to the boy whose wide eyes study the looping caterpillar searching for a safe exit off the human platform.

'Do you think God placed any more value upon you, Shane, than He did upon this caterpillar?'

The red-haired boy rubs his eyes, ponders a response.

'This caterpillar will transform soon into a glorious butterfly that will float high over rivers and flower beds, and if you saw it in flight you might say to yourself that it was the prettiest sight your sore eyes had ever seen,' Aubrey says. 'But does that mean the caterpillar's life has more value than yours, Shane?'

Shane shakes his head slowly.

'No, it does not, because we know, deep down in our hearts, that all of God's creatures – you, me and my furry friend here – are of perfectly equal value. And by that I mean, Shane, we are all perfectly and profoundly worthless.'

The boy watches the caterpillar and then he watches Aubrey casually lob it into the campfire, the creature roasting to a black ball within seconds.

'Would you like me to help you?' Aubrey asks, soft and tender.

The boy holds the gun in his hands. He considers the offer for a long moment. He hands the pistol to the man.

'Thank you,' the boy says. He lies back down beside the man he loved most in this turning world, the one-eyed giant named George Kane.

'You just look on up to the sky, young Shane,' Aubrey says. 'I will count backwards from ten and if you want me to stop at any time, you just go ahead and sit up.'

The boy settles into place and nods his head, arms straight and flat by his side.

'Ten . . . nine . . . eight . . . seven,' Aubrey says, his right arm out and the pistol pointed at the boy's head. 'Six . . . five . . . four.'

The boy closing his eyes.

'Three.'

The gun's barrel the length of a hand away from the boy's temple.

'Two.'

The boy opening his eyes again to the blue sky.

'One.'

'Wait,' says the boy.

And the gunshot echoes across the deep country.

Dreams of Love

Prove it, Nara, Yukio Miki says silently to the sky. Prove to me that this is not your Plain of High Heaven that I have parachuted into. For all I see is your paradise. There are things in this world down here so beautiful that they must have been made by you.

The pilot runs his hand through a bed of vivid purple flowers and then to a thick grey eucalypt covered in so many hanging red and green figs they could form a dress for the tree. Or a silk kimono. There are birds in the trees with orange breasts that glow like the setting sun and azure shoulders that shine like a blue moon. There are birds on the ground making homes for their lovers and the homes are made only of curved twigs but the homes have great archways and the birds gather bright-coloured shells and flakes and stones and they lay them at the entry to their houses in the hope that a lover might care to drop by.

He finds a climbing vine with soft, round green leaves covered in fur and from these leaves sprout lilac and white sepals, and from the purple base of those sepals rises a fountain of green and yellow petals and from those petals emerges the fine and fragile shape of a woman dancing – the flower's style and stigma and anther. The woman's leg is raised and her elbows are high and her head is tilted, lost in the music that makes her move. And Yukio can see Nara in this high heaven flower. Prove it to me, Nara, Yukio Miki asks the sky. Prove it.

'Looks like a music box ballerina,' Greta says, appearing at Yukio's side. 'It's beautiful.'

Yukio nods. He looks into Greta's eyes and nothing he sees in her emerald iris galaxies serves to weaken his theory that he may have fallen into his own Takamanohara. 'Beautiful,' he says.

And Greta feels something strange and unsettling and tender passing from the pilot's eyes in that moment, so she turns away and they walk together down a thin path that leads through tall trees and past thick walls of scrub.

Molly walks three paces behind them, thinking about a story Yukio told her over breakfast. He spoke of it in broken English but his flailing arms and finger gestures were enough to communicate its essentials to a girl so ready to hear it. The story of the assassin known as the White Tiger, who came to Yukio's village all those years ago to meet the maker of a blade designed to cut the beating heart out of the very man who forged it. He spoke of the cemetery keeper who spent his life polishing the grave of his one true love. Molly wasn't sure if she got the story right, but she thinks the old man died and when he died he turned into a white butterfly and flew on up to heaven to be with his one true love who was now the most beautiful butterfly in a sky full of butterflies. Molly knew that when he told this story Yukio was thinking of his wife, Nara. That's why people tell stories, she thinks. They remind us why we love things. They remind us why we love other people.

Molly is struck by a notion she wants to share with Yukio, so she rushes forward and wedges herself between her travelling companions.

'I reckon that old man did turn into a butterfly, Yukio,' Molly says.

Yukio nods. He chuckles to himself. 'Butterfly . . . in . . . sky,' he says.

'It was like magic,' Molly says. 'And I was thinkin', Yukio, that what Longcoat Bob did to my grandfather was a kind of magic, too. But it was bad magic. And if there's bad magic then there's gotta be good magic, too.'

'Good . . . magic,' Yukio nods. He likes the thought of it.

'Good magic like turning the people we care about into butterflies when they die,' Molly says. 'But there's somethin' I don't understand about the story, Yukio?'

Yukio slows. He turns his head down to Molly. 'Molly . . . no . . . understand?'

'Yeah,' Molly says. 'I don't understand why he turned into a butterfly. Why turn him into something that's only going to die a few days later?'

Yukio stops on the spot and the travelling party stops with him. He kneels down before Molly. 'Nooooooo, Molly Hook,' he says with a knowingly theatrical hint of the mystic. 'Butterfly . . . short life. But butterfly . . . see . . . all world. Butterfly . . . love . . . all world. Butterfly . . . short time . . . no lose time.'

He raises his arms to the trees around him and the insects in those trees and the sun over their heads. He beams as he turns his head across all of the life he sees before him. 'Butterfly knows way,' he says. 'Butterfly see everything. Tree. Sky.'

He points at the sun. 'San,' he says in his native tongue. He points at a log by the side of the path. 'Uddo,' he says.

Greta watches him closely. She sees the way he speaks, like every thought was formed in his soul and every word was ink-pressed in blood from his heart.

He points at two birds circling each other in the sky. 'Bird,' he says. 'Water. Air. Light.' He points at Molly. 'Butterfly see you, Molly Hook.' Molly smiles. 'Butterfly short life,' Yukio says. 'But butterfly live forever . . .' – he raises a single forefinger – 'in one day.'

Molly nods appreciatively, eyes wide and awed. The trio press on.

Silence for two full minutes. Then Molly breaks the silence. Molly always breaks the silence.

'That's like you and Nara,' she says, looking straight ahead, speaking words as they come to her. 'You only had a short time. But she could give you everything . . .' – she knows now that the words she is saying are for herself – 'in one day.' This is why people tell stories, she thinks.

Yukio nods. His head turns to the ground and Greta can see the pain inside him and she wants to move three steps to the side and wrap her arms around that strange pilot's shoulders, but that's a move for different worlds, softer worlds than this one.

'Molly Hook understand,' Yukio says, softly.

*

Hot air and humidity. Greta rubs the sweat from the back of her neck and uses it to wash dirt from her hands and face. Molly is still pressing on quick and hard, walking alone some thirty yards ahead of them. Yukio quickens his walking pace to catch up to Greta's left shoulder.

'Bob,' Yukio says.

'Yeah,' Greta says, shaking her head as she plods along. 'Longcoat Bob, the magic man.'

'Magic,' Yukio says. 'You . . . be . . . ahhh . . . believe?'

Greta gives a half-smile, shrugs her shoulders. 'Not really,' she says.

'Why you come?' Yukio asks. 'Why . . . come . . . far?'

'I don't really know,' Greta says. She nods at Molly, ahead of them, just at the moment she mistimes her step over a fallen branch. She trips, but plants a steadying foot to stop herself from falling flat on her face. 'Someone had to keep her out of trouble.'

'You . . . want . . . gold?' Yukio ponders.

'Well, I wouldn't say no to it.'

They walk in silence.

'Aisuru,' Yukio says.

'Huh?'

'Aisuru,' Yukio repeats. He nods at Molly. 'You . . . Molly.' And he puts his hand on his heart and pats it four times like it's beating. 'Aisuru.'

'Love?' Greta suggests.

The first word of English his father did not learn. 'Love,' he smiles. 'You . . . love . . . Molly.'

Greta smiles. Considers that notion.

'Like . . . child,' Yukio adds.

Greta is taken aback by the comment, but she shrugs it off with a nervous chuckle. Her eyes return to Molly ahead, off the path now, inspecting something she's seen beneath a broadleaved paperbark tree.

'Well, yeah, I care about the kid, but I'm not about to stick her photograph in my purse,' Greta says.

'Girl . . . want . . . mother,' Yukio says. 'Girl . . . love . . . Greta.'

Greta speaks more sharply this time. 'I don't think for a second she's my child, if that's what you're saying,' she says. 'The girl's got a mother. It's just a shame she's six foot under.'

Yukio is bright enough to tune to the frequency of anger in her voice, despite his inability to understand all of her words.

'Hey, Yukio,' hollers Molly, running back to her fellow wanderers, one hand holding Bert and the other holding a black rhinoceros beetle in her hand. 'You have these in Japan?'

She holds the beetle up to Yukio's eyes and this armoured tank of an insect hisses with the roughhouse handling.

'Ohhhh,' Yukio says, leaning back with a show of great respect to the insect. 'We have . . . Japan . . . but . . . but . . .' Then he brings his hand to his face and makes the shape of a long horn extending from his nose. 'Like,' he says and he puts his lips together and he blows hard with his puffed cheeks and his fingers play a brass instrument as his feet dance on an imaginary stage.

'Trumpet!' Molly says. 'They have trumpets on their heads in Japan?'

Yukio nods.

'How about that!' Molly says, chuffed by the knowledge. 'You have trumpets in Japan?'

'Haaaaa!' Yukio smiles, jumping into a rousing trumpet number played through his thumb.

'You have good music in Japan?' Molly asks. 'You have songs?'

He nods enthusiastically. 'Song!' he says, and he starts to sing as he skips down the path.

'Getsu, getsu, ka, sui, moku, kin, kin,' he sings and he makes the song sound so joyous despite the song's content – and title – speaking of the restless drudgery that comes with being a member of the Imperial Japanese Navy: 'Monday, Monday, Tuesday, Wednesday, Thursday, Friday, Friday'.

Molly joins in the singing and they link arms as they spin around Greta, who rolls her eyes.

'Hey, Greta Maze,' Molly beams, stomping her legs in the path's dirt. 'Sing Yukio a song.'

Molly turns to Yukio. 'She's some canary when she gets goin', Yukio. Wait till you hear her voice. Go on, Greta.'

Molly spins on Yukio's arm now and her head flies back and her eyes go to the sky.

'Sing him a song about the sky, Greta,' Molly laughs.

It never takes much for Greta Maze to see a spotlight turned on her. And Yukio watches her make her transformation from sweaty wanderer to one-show-only Carnegie Hall sell-out torch singer lit up by the lights. And Greta hits a perfect high note, a voice that is pure Cotton Club. Pure Harlem, 1933. Pure jazz and blues and pure martini. It's not a song about the sky. It's a song about the weather. It's a song about the rain, and Molly and Yukio stop spinning and they start marvelling, lost in the corridors of Greta Maze. A weepy torch song about hearts breaking and storms comin', and Yukio can't understand a word of what she's singing but he follows every beat of her big heart.

Greta smiles as she spins under the spotlight, waves to her audience, to some folks deep in the back row. She winks at Molly and Molly waves back. She raises her palm to the stage lights. She sings about the darkness in them all, in men and women, in lovers, but all Yukio Miki sees around her is light. And the actress knows he sees that. She stares at him now when she sings because she's never had an audience like this. A face in the crowd so spellbound. A face so full of devotion. Protection. Loyalty. And maybe something else.

She sings of wild black storms, but all Yukio Miki sees is sunshine. And she saves her last word and her last look from the stage for the pilot who fell from the sky. And he understands that last word of her song, he can translate it, and that word is drawn from the end point in the maze of Greta Maze, and what's waiting at the end of that maze is that last word and that word is 'together'.

Molly claps loudly. 'Bravo! Bravo!' And Greta Maze bows to her imaginary audience and Yukio Miki wants to open his mouth but he's frozen stiff and what use has he for a mouth, anyway, when no kind of mouth, not Japanese or English or French or Woop Woop, could ever convey his desire to hear her sing an encore or how good it feels to know what high heaven sounds like?

*

Silence now in a bush cathedral of trees where little light gets in. Molly walks ahead, Greta behind her, then Yukio. Darkness in the deep country and a narrow dirt track running deeper still into dense wilderness.

'Do you hear that?' Greta asks, stopping.

Molly and Yukio stop with her.

'Hear what?' asks Molly.

The sound of cicadas. A bird whistle.

'Never mind,' Greta says.

They walk on through ferns and rambling monsoon forest climbers.

Greta stops again. 'You hear that?'

'Hear what?' Molly asks.

'Piano keys,' Greta says.

But Molly doesn't register what Greta says because she has

spotted a fork in the path ahead and she runs to it because she can see something flashing among a stand of trees where the path splits in two, one path turning west around the trees and the other turning east. The forest is dark, but dappled light shimmers through it when the wind blows and then shadows move across the strange cluster of seven grey-brown trees standing almost sixty feet high.

Molly walks over to the trunk of the largest of these trees and caresses its majestic torso with skin like a tessellated mosaic of thick bark fragments that took some reclusive and fine forest artisan a decade to create. Her fingers find wounds in the tree and she notices that these wounds – like bullet holes or puncture wounds from thrown spears – are on all the trees at this strange junction, and from these wounds run thin rivers of blood. She runs her forefinger along one river of blood and realises it has hardened to a waxy substance, like something her father would have used to seal an envelope.

The tree blood has stained the trunks of the towering natives. "'Out damned spot, out I say,'" Molly recites to herself. She digs out her gold pan, studies her grandfather's secret words, Tom Berry's etched notes to self. Then she calls to Greta and Yukio, "'West where the yellow fork man leads, east in the dark when the wood bleeds''!'

She looks down the eastern path, a thin animal track winding through thick forest. She looks down the western path, a thin animal track winding through thick forest.

'We go this way,' Molly says, excitedly peering down the eastern path.

Yukio nods but Greta seems preoccupied. She's looking up at the forest ceiling, a dense roof of palms like ship sails and branches that stretch and probe through all that green the way a jellyfish's tentacles stretch through oceans.

'Can you hear that?' she asks. 'It's faint.' She looks down the western path. 'It's music.' But the faces of Molly and Yukio say they can't hear it and Greta wonders if she's hearing things because she's tired and her stomach has been empty for the past six hours and her mind has been ravaged by war and monsters.

But there it is again. Music. The faintest sound of music. Piano. She wants to say a word out loud but she holds that word in. A word from her childhood. A German word her father said. *Liebesträume.*

'Greta,' Molly says. 'This way, come on!'

And Molly skips down the thin path heading east and the pilot and the actress follow. But then she stops on the spot. 'Wait, I hear something too,' she says. 'But it's not music.' She listens harder to the forest, her right ear up to the sprawling green canopy. 'It's a waterfall.'

*

Molly in the sky-blue satin dress, dirt-stained and creased, clomping along the dirt path in her dig boots. Bert the shovel helping to prop her up as she walks. The sound of a thunderous waterfall growing louder as the forest thins out. She feels it in the air, its spray fuelling a mist that seems to be permanently watering the giant ferns and grey-green cycads she passes.

And then the waterfall comes into full view and it opens up to Molly Hook like a new world. An immense natural hall with a sky roof and mighty walls made of deep red sandstone, walls so dramatic Molly has to believe they were chiselled by Norse gods or the Lightning Man or just Father Time. A waterfall that Molly finds as deafening and spectacular as would be a thousand white horses charging over that same 250-foot cliff face. A rapid torrent rush so forceful she has to shout to have her voice heard by her fellow travellers. 'Is this a dream, Greta?' she screams and Greta smiles and shakes her head, her face wet with spray.

Molly looks across the scene. A black and purple and white spider in a vast web in a tree beside her, the web fluttering in the draught from the waterfall. Vibrant native plants fringing the plunge pool. Large black boulders resting on the water's edge like polite children being read to by a schoolteacher.

What the plants, the birds, the rocks, the insects in the trees and the creatures below the pool have all come to see and hear today is the waterfall. Like Molly, they all made it this far through the deep country. The rocks rolled here, the birds flew, the plants crept, the insects crawled.

Molly looks up to the sky-blue roof above it all. The day sky. She walks alone around the pool to a corner of the natural hall, and she talks to the day sky in a soft voice, letting the sound of the waterfall hide her thoughts from her companions.

'I didn't think I'd make it so far in,' she murmurs, elated by the waterfall's power and finding something more than gravity in it.

'You've always been able to make it as far as you wanted to go, Molly,' the day sky says to the gravedigger girl. 'Why wouldn't you make it this far?'

'I've always wanted to stop at some point,' Molly says. 'I always reached a point where I was too afraid to go any further.'

'What were you afraid of?'

'Everything,' she says.

'Everything,' the day sky says. 'And only one thing.'

'What?' Molly asks.

'Not what, Molly, who?'

'My uncle.'

'Aubrey Hook,' the day sky says.

'But I don't have to worry about him no more.'

'He died back in Hollow Wood,' the day sky says.

'Yes, he did, didn't he?' Molly replies.

'Yes, he did.'

'You wouldn't lie to me, would you?'

'No, Molly.'

'But all you are is one big lie,' Molly says. 'You're a trick.'

'I guess you'll just have to trust me,' the day sky says.

'I guess so.'

'Like you trust the pilot.'

'He's a good man.'

'We'll see.'

'What does that mean?'

'It means we'll have to wait and see what comes.'

'What do you think is coming?'

'Danger, Molly,' the day sky says. 'Pain. But wonder, too, and gratitude and joy. But you'd better keep an eye on that Yukio.'

Molly looks across the plunge pool and sees Yukio drop his head and drink from its edge.

'Careful Yukio,' Molly calls. 'Crocodiles.' She snaps her arms in a chomping motion. Yukio nods, moves back from the pool edge.

They rest for an hour by the crashing waterfall. Greta washes her face and underarms. Yukio studies the plants and insects in the fringing forest. Molly sits apart by a large black boulder with a chalky rock in her hand. She scrawls a new poem on the black rock.

Yukio watches her writing. She can sense him over her shoulder. She turns and smiles at him. He sits by her side.

'Poem,' he smiles.

Molly nods.

'It's about us,' she says.

Yukio points at a word on the rock.

'Treasure,' Molly says.

'Treasure,' Yukio repeats, smiling.

Molly points at Yukio's chest and then she points at Greta who is now on the other side of the plunge pool, cupping water onto her hair.

'Both treasure,' Molly says. 'Both gold.'

'Goooolldd!' Yukio whispers, his eyes fixed on the actress who is standing now, a thick beam of sunshine backlighting her emerald dress, which is wet and sticking to her body. Molly sees the way he looks at her and, soon enough, Greta catches the pilot looking at her, too, and she returns his gaze.

'What?' she asks.

Yukio points a finger at her.

'Greta Maze is treasure,' he says, nodding his head in earnest. And he stands now as though he needs to speak this truth to the whole of the forest. 'Greta Maze is gold,' he says.

Greta freezes in confusion, then she blushes.

And Molly stands now, too, and elbows the pilot, playfully. 'Slow down, Romeo,' she says.

Yukio whips his head back to Molly. 'Romeo!' he rejoices in his broken but improving English. 'Where . . . for . . . art . . . *you* . . . Romeo!'

Molly waves him in close. She offers her wisdom with a series of backhand pats on his belly, like she's a pub bookie giving priceless horse tips to a penniless mug.

'Don't go climbin' up the balcony so quick, ya know what I mean?' she whispers.

Yukio's eyes say he's not following.

'Don't run yer race before the gun's gone off, ya follow?'

'Race . . . gun,' Yukio says.

She pats his belly again. 'Ya gotta keep yer cards close, Yukio,' she whispers. 'Then lay down that king of hearts when she least expects it. Don't go layin' down all yer joker cards. You gotta show her yer heart without spillin' yer beans.'

Yukio concentrates on her words while Molly turns to the edge of the waterfall and skims the rock she used to write her poem along the rippling pool. She counts the number of times it skips across the water. 'Five,' she says, proudly.

And from the other side of the pool Greta watches Yukio skipping stones into the water and laughing along with the gravedigger girl. And for a moment Greta wants this time in this place to slow – slow down so much the three of them could stay like this for a month, for a year, for a lifetime.

That man saved her life. He came back for her. He fought a giant for her and he nearly died in the process. And she saw his face when his neck was being strangled by the giant's hand. His face was so serene. His eyes were sailboats on calm seas and he was sailing off to some place she knows as well as him.

It wouldn't be so bad, she thinks. It wouldn't be so bad if there's nothing left. Not so bad if it's all blown up back there, beyond the beginning of the deep country. Only three people left on earth to walk it. And it wouldn't be so bad if one of them was him.

She's still staring at him when he turns to find her gaze across the pool. She's still staring at him when he gives her a kind of half-smile that tells her in the best kind of language – the noiseless kind – that he knows it makes no sense to be here. He knows it makes no sense to feel so alive when she was just so close to death. Then in the tunnel of this view between them he stops smiling because attraction is a serious phenomenon and Greta knows in this moment that heart curses are just fantasies for twelve-year-old girls to believe because nothing could still her heart when it's beating as fast as this.

*

At lunchtime Molly looks into the duffel bag for something to eat. One can left in the bag, a tin of her father's oxtail soup. The trio sit together by the edge of the black pool. Molly makes a hole in the soup can with her paring knife and the three travellers take sips of the soup, which is lukewarm from the heat of the day. Greta nearly vomits her first taste back up, but then she squeezes three more mouthfuls down out of necessity.

As she savours her mouthful of soup, Molly looks up and is struck by a peculiar cave in the cliff face behind the water-fall. She notices a series of boulders, fallen and crumbled into place over millennia, which form a rough climbing route up to the cave entrance, and she studies the curious shape of the cave's black void.

Greta washes her hands in the plunge pool. 'So where do we go now?' she asks. 'We've run out of track.'

Molly is still looking at the cave veiled by the rushing water. 'Where were you born, Greta?'

'What's that got to do with where we're heading?'

'Just tell me where you were born?'

'Leipzig,' Greta says.

'Where's that?'

'About a hundred miles south–west of Berlin,' she says. 'My family came to Sydney when I was two years old.'

Molly gulps another mouthful of oxtail soup. She sits higher up than the others, on a smooth black boulder, while Yukio sits crossed-legged on the grass and Greta lies next to him with her head resting on a grey rock slab half-buried in dirt.

'You were born in Germany,' Molly says. She nods at Yukio. 'He was born in Japan and I was born in Darwin. But I reckon we all came from the same place.'

'What are you talking about?'

'My grandfather's directions,' she says. 'The place beyond your place of birth.'

She nods to the cave behind the waterfall. 'What does that cave look like to you?'

Greta studies the peculiar shape of the cave. Like a pumpkin seed, like an oyster, she tells herself, like the fresh mussels they sell by the waterfront on Sunday mornings. Then she sees it. 'Well, ain't that just like a bloke,' she says. 'Sitting in God's country surrounded by a thousand natural miracles and all he sees is a lady's pigeonhole.'

Yukio follows the gazes of the women but struggles to see what they see.

'Pigeon . . . hole?' he ponders.

Molly howls with laughter.

Greta smiles, points at the cave beyond the waterfall. 'The shape of the cave,' she says.

Yukio squints.

'The nick in the notch, the naughty,' Greta laughs. 'The ol' rest and be thankful.'

Molly slaps her thighs and Yukio laughs with her, still not following.

'Yer periwinkle?' Molly giggles, hands over her mouth.

Greta rattles off names now, not even laughing, just stewing on the minds of all the men she's danced with and worked around since the age of twenty-two. She adopts the voice of a drunken red-dirt cattleman. 'Yer ninepence, yer nursery, yer

Itching Jenny, yer Irish fortune,' she says, picking up small rocks from the ground beside her and tossing them into the deep black waterhole. 'Tulip, pokehole, spout, twotch, twitchet, knish, naf, naggie and feckin' nettle bed.' She pauses to think on something for a moment and she returns to her natural voice. She sees all their faces and all their fingers. 'Cunts,' she says.

Rusting wheels suddenly turn into motion in Yukio's mind. 'Ohhhhhh!' he gasps, pointing at the cave, wide-eyed and embarrassed.

And Molly howls so hard she falls backwards off her sitting rock.

Yukio's laughter then echoes across the waterfall chamber and his joy is a welcome infection for Greta, who lets her pursed, puffy lips slowly break into a smile.

Molly stands up now, collecting herself, and nods her head at the cave. 'All the stories I ever heard in town about my grandfather's long walk,' Molly says, 'he never said exactly where he went. But he spoke about what it was like. He said he went into magic places with Longcoat Bob.' She looks around her setting. 'This feels pretty magic to me, this place. He said he walked through places with Longcoat Bob and he came out the other side into places that felt like different worlds. Different dimensions, even.'

Molly takes a deep breath. 'Yep, this is the way,' she says. 'We gotta swim over to the other side of the waterhole. We gotta go through that cave up there.'

'What about the crocodiles?' Greta asks.

'I think we'll be all right,' Molly replies.

'You gonna talk to them again?' Greta says, drily. 'Ask them for permission to cross?'

Molly smiles. 'Nah, them crocs will come 'ere every now

and then but I reckon they won't want to hang around too long because of that noisy waterfall.'

'Crocodiles,' Yukio says, airing his concern.

'Yeah, but just freshies this far inland, Yukio,' Molly says.

Greta places a calming hand on Yukio's thigh. 'Don't worry, the freshies only grow to nine feet,' she says.

But Yukio doesn't hear that line because he's distracted by something moving low in the sky over Greta's shoulder.

Then Greta hears it too, something familiar, something impossible. It's the sound of a baby crying, loud enough to be heard above the noise of the waterfall. She follows Yukio's gaze and turns around to see a dark, black-brown wedge-tailed eagle cutting from east to west across the wide black pool. So big and majestic and powerful is the creature that Greta flinches when she sees it. An adult female with a wingspan that must be more than eight feet across; a flying motion of such grand design and power that as the wings cut the air they make a noise like a silk sheet being shaken in the wind. And she knows it is the queen they saw before.

The great bird has a fanned and wedged tail almost two feet across – so wide and balanced Greta could serve scones on it with mini bowls of jam and cream – and a hooked grey beak appropriately shaped like Death's scythe. But the raptor is burdened. It moves slow through the sky with laboured flaps of its wings because somewhere along its endless hunt for easy prey – a moving and pitiless ground feast of rabbits and brown hares and foxes and koalas and wombats and small wallabies – its long black talons have hooked a strange treasure more cumbersome than even this raptor's normally impressive endurance and leg strength can accommodate: a howling human infant nestled in a baby sling made of bush string, paperbark and cane strips, which now hangs from the eagle's vice-grip talons by its woven cane and paperbark carry strap. Greta hears that cry again, splitting the air and splitting her heart.

Two other, smaller birds shoot down from high above towards the eagle and its plunder. They look like brown hawks, and Greta now realises that the eagle is waging a mid-air fight to keep hold of its treasure. One brave hawk flaps a wing across the eyes of the eagle, which then slows, and this slowing of momentum seems to add to the weight of the cargo and the eagle must work hard now to start the motor of its wings again and find enough energy to make it to the top of the waterfall. Then the second hawk attacks the eagle from the side with a surprise flurry of wings and raised legs and talons, and the mighty eagle is forced to defend itself. It releases its prized and howling plunder and raises its own spent legs and talons up to the spirited hawk, driving hard with a flap of its wide wings to force the hawk back so it can fly freely out of the gorge.

Molly Hook sucks air deep into her lungs as she watches the baby sling with the baby inside it falling towards the black pool. But Greta Maze, the toast of Palmerston, is already swimming across the water as the baby lands hard.

'Greta!' Molly calls.

The actress's arms turning like windmills through the water; calves and thighs thrashing through the glassy pool, her saddle shoes still tied to her feet. Her head is down in the water and she takes no breaths because she doesn't want to lose any speed. A single word crosses her busy mind while her head is under the water: freshies. But she powers on and when she raises her head she sees the baby in the sling bobbing moment-arily on the surface, but then the water fills the sling and sucks the baby under. Greta takes a deep breath and dives deep and hard. Molly and Yukio watch her disappear.

'Greta!' Molly screams.

No movement for a long moment. Just the crashing of the waterfall.

And then she reappears, the actress, one arm stroking across the water and the baby inside the sling held up to her chest. Her usually bouncy blonde curls sopped across her ears, concentration and determination and fire across her face.

Molly breathes with relief and she knows now just how much she cares for this woman in the water. A good one, she tells herself. The real good one. She would cry for her if she could, but instead she drops the empty can of soup on the ground, picks up Bert the shovel and her duffel bag, dives into the black water and follows the actress to the other side of the falls.

Yukio, the pilot who fell from the sky, stares at these strange creatures in the water and wonders what kind of place he fell into here in this continent south of everything, a place where birds drop children from the sky and angels with blonde curls dive into crocodile-infested waters to save them. But this is not a time for thinking, he tells himself. This is a time for action. For doing – doing what the actress did.

He's not a natural swimmer. He was never the kind to dive into blind bodies of water. But this place south of everything is transformative. People can change here, he tells himself. And he feels himself turning. Turning, turning, turning by the water's edge. And he dives into the water and dog-paddles awkwardly across the pool, panting with every movement and struggling to keep his heavy war boots moving. The raging waterfall thunders down to his right and he fights to stay away from the suck of the plunging water. Near the far edge of the pool his boots find purchase on moss and mud and his arms reach for a fern that he then uses to pull himself onto a thin ledge of sandstone. He stands up out of the water, puts his hands on his kneecaps to catch his breath and then staggers over to the women.

Molly huddles against Greta's left shoulder and Yukio now stands at her right shoulder and the three wanderers catch their breath as they gaze into the eyes of the newest member of their travelling party: a baby boy in Greta's arms, his big brown eyes staring back at the woman who holds him so carefully, so naturally.

'Ssssshhhh,' Greta says. 'Ssshhhhh.'

And the boy does not cry.

THE FOURTH
SKY GIFT

Everything We Need

Cold in here. Dank and earthy and smelling of bat shit. This is the dark cave Greta spoke of. 'Close your eyes,' she said. 'You don't realise it, but you're actually standing inside a large stone cave in total darkness.' This is what Molly's cave looked like in her mind. This was the place before the sad place she saw beyond her bedroom door. Outside that bedroom in her mind was a hallway and at the end of that hallway was a bedroom where the moon lit up her mother's face and where the shadow wolf moaned in the dark. Everybody has a sad place, Molly thinks. What's waiting for me outside this stone cave? What's beyond the bedroom door?

'Can you see anything ahead, Molly?' Greta asks and her words echo through the pitch-black tunnel.

Molly walks up front, banging Bert's blade against the large boulders that clutter the passageway that has so far stretched some forty yards from the waterfall. 'I can't see nuthin'.'

Greta, walking in the middle of the trio, holds the baby boy in a firm two-arm grip against her chest. If she trips again on one of these boulders, she'll twist and shoulder the brunt of the fall. 'This feller's gonna need feeding,' she says. Hold the boy, she tells herself. Protect him from this strange country. No place for a thing so perfect, no place for the miracle boy.

'That feller needs his mum,' Molly says.

Yukio Miki walks behind the actress and the gravedigger girl, running his right palm along the cave ceiling, which is only a forearm's length higher than his head.

Molly remembers Greta's words. 'Then you see a line of fire draw a door on a wall of that cave. Up, across, down again and back across.'

A fire-traced door is what she needs. She would open the door and step out of the cave into a new world. And what would that world look like? That place? What if there was no shadow in that place? No moonlight. Only sunshine. She sees her mother, Violet, and her mother is beautiful there and she wears a smart dress that her best friend, Greta Maze, bought for her – because in this place, in this world, Greta could be the friend her mother never had, the strong and reliable friend she always needed to lean on. These two best friends now sip fresh lemonade and smoke cigarettes in sunglasses under the milkwood tree in the backyard of her grandfather Tom Berry's sprawling old house on the Darwin waterfront. And Molly runs into her mother's arms and they spin and together they lie on their backs beneath the milkwood tree looking up at the sky. 'Can you feel it, Molly?' her mother asks. 'Can you feel it? We're on top now, Mol'. We're on top.'

'Greta?' Molly calls softly through the darkness.

'Yeah, kid.'

'It wasn't the sky,' Molly says.

'What's that?'

'I know it wasn't the sky who gave me that first gift,' she says.

'It wasn't?' Greta replies in the darkness, gently, tenderly.

'It was my mum who gave it to me,' Molly says. 'I know that. I've always known that. I just liked the idea that the sky might give me gifts. No one else was giving me gifts. I thought that the sky might see me down here and it might want to make me happy or somethin'.'

Three wanderers and a baby in the darkness. A long silence.

'But why would she give me my grandfather's map like that?' Molly asks. 'Why would she say it was all coming from up there and not down here?'

'Maybe she wanted you to know there was always some place beautiful to turn to,' Greta says. 'She gave you the sky, Molly. Maybe that was the gift. Not the bloody copper pan.'

'I reckon she wanted me to find Longcoat Bob,' Molly says. 'She wanted me to find him and ask him to leave me be. She didn't want my heart to turn like hers did.'

'Molly?'

'Yeah,' Molly says.

'Your mum loved you a whole lot.'

'How do you know that?' Molly asks.

Mums just know, Greta thinks. 'I just know,' she says.

'Yeah, I reckon she did. But then her heart turned to stone and she had to go away,' Molly says, her hands reaching blindly for a boulder that her boots have struck. She lifts her legs over the boulder and says, 'Boulder comin' up.'

'Hearts don't turn to stone, Molly,' Greta says. 'But they do turn. One day your heart is filled with nothing but love and then something gets inside and mixes in with all that love and sometimes that something is black and sometimes it's cold and feels just like stone because it's heavy, and sometimes it gets so heavy you can't carry it inside you no more.'

'Sometimes I feel mine turning,' Molly says.

'Yeah, I feel it, too,' Greta says.

'You do?'

'Of course, I do,' Greta says. 'But guess what?'

'What?'

'Sometimes I feel it turning back the other way.'

'You do?'

'Of course I do.'

'When?' Molly asks.

'When I talk to you for a start,' Greta says.

Molly stops walking. She reaches a hand out for Greta in the darkness. She finds her shoulder and Greta finds the grave-digger girl's hand in the black and she briefly squeezes it, but the moment is too sweet for someone so battle-hardened so she shatters it with humour. 'And then there's the times we go on long walks through old rock vaginas . . .'

And Molly laughs, but a sound makes her turn back the way she was heading, a sound somewhere in the black, some-where towards the end of the passageway. 'Can you hear that?' she asks. 'It's music.' And she quickens her pace, tapping Bert's blade against earth and rock as she goes.

'Piano keys,' Greta says. Those perfect notes. Greta knows them. Greta remembers them. 'It's the *Liebesträume*,' Greta says, 'the *Love Dream*.' She remembers every note. 'My father played this when I was a girl. I'd go to sleep at night and he'd rest his drinks on the piano top and play me to sleep with this music. My father said that was how I should always go to sleep, with a love dream.'

Molly listens hard. Notes falling into notes, echoing through the cave. Some of the long, melancholy notes moving in the opposite direction to others that are sharp and bright. The song feels to Molly like a heart that has not turned yet, a song for a heart filled as much with joy and hope as it is with sadness and longing.

Then she sees light ahead, and she rushes towards it, the strange notes leading her on to where the passageway ends at a narrow gap she finds she can slip through easily when she turns side-on and leads with her left shoulder.

She emerges into a clearing flanked by rugged and sloping sandstone. Opposite her, a loose path of dirt and small rocks splits in two. The western fork runs to a ridge of sandstone beyond which Molly can see an expanse of stone country in the distance. A fork of silver-blue lightning splits the deep grey sky ahead.

'The Lightning Man,' she whispers. '"Follow the lightning."'

But then Molly hears the piano notes coming from down the eastern fork, which heads off through a stand of black wattles and soap trees with flat round black fruits and then down an avenue of trees with mottled cream-grey bark and stiff leaves exploding with small ripe red fruits. These tree clusters are all canopied by a dense climbing vine with orange-yellow flowers shaped like starfish, and the melancholy piano notes float through this forest like saddened spectres.

Greta and Yukio emerge from the tunnel and Greta, holding the baby boy in her arms, the baby boy who fell into her arms from the sky, instinctively follows the notes down the vine forest avenue.

'Greta, where are you going?' Molly asks.

Greta says nothing, just walks deeper into the forest.

'We need to go this way,' Molly says, pointing towards the stone country. 'We need to follow the lightning. We're almost there, I can feel it!'

But Greta walks on, her head turning left and right to study the hall of trees enveloping her, swallowing her whole. Deeper, deeper into the forest, the notes of the piano drawing her along another dirt path that veers off through a wall of crab's-eye vine with purple pea-like flowers. Beyond this natural barrier, in front of a sandstone rock wall swallowed long ago by snaking and multiplying and unstoppable vines, is a circular clearing. And Greta now sees metal gold rush relics in the foliage around her: two upright wagon wheels rusting away by the rock wall; an ore cart; a wooden ladder; a pile of chains and straps and shafts and poles.

In the centre of the clearing is a single tall bombax tree, maybe sixty feet high, with rough pale grey bark covered in conical thorns. The tree is alive with fleshy red flowers and oblong brown seed capsules, hundreds of which lie on the ground, their capsules split open like they were alien vessels whose absent owners abandoned them long ago. Beneath this tree sits a skeletal old man with long white hair, snowy eyebrows, a bushy chalk-white beard and old worn hands that are moving purposefully across the black and white keys of an old and moulding walnut-wood upright piano. He wears a cheap, cream-coloured Chinese-style flowing tunic over loose brown slacks. No shoes on his feet. He's lost in his own music, his eyes closed and his head moving along the hills and valleys of his ghost notes that spirit themselves away from the piano and into the dense forest.

And Molly can see now that the old man is playing for an audience of a kind. There are eight bodies scattered behind him across the forest floor. Eight people sleeping – at least Molly hopes they're sleeping. Chinese men and women in rag clothes. All of the sleepers are old and frail. Some rest on their backs on low stretchers and some rest their backs directly on the forest floor. Some laughing in their sleep, some turning their heads. Two of them look particularly serene: asleep in the daylight, but smiling as though the music is reaching right through to their dreams, conjuring expressions of deep contentment.

'Come, come!' the old man says, still playing with his eyes closed. 'Come closer. Do not be afraid.' He sounds European. Dutch, maybe.

Greta slowly and cautiously approaches the piano, holding the sky baby close. Molly and Yukio join her and they all stare at the man with hair so lightning-white Molly wonders for the briefest moment if they have not stumbled upon Sam's Lightning Man here in the flesh, the one who sprays bending rods of electricity from his ear holes.

Yukio rests his hand on the grip of the shortsword hanging from his military belt. His eyes scan the clearing for signs of danger and the fact he sees none does not blunt the edge of his vigilance.

Greta gazes over the sleepers in the forest. 'What are they all doing here?' Greta asks.

'What does it look like they're doing?' the old man replies, not skipping a note.

'Sleeping,' Greta says.

'Not just sleeping,' he replies. 'Dreaming.'

Piano notes bending through the forest trees. 'You play beautifully,' Greta says.

The old man does not stop his fingers to respond. 'I play nothing,' he says. 'The machine plays me. I just sit down at it.'

Notes into notes. Fingers still working across the keyboard. There is little flesh in the old man's cheeks and even less hanging off his arm bones.

'I've always liked this music,' Greta says.

'Your father played it for you,' the old man says.

'How did you know that?'

'I played this for my daughters,' the old man replies. 'Fathers should always play the *Liebesträume* for their daughters.'

When the old man talks Greta can see that his teeth are

rotting and there are faint black stains on what's left of them. There's a tar-black tinge, too, around the edges of the beard hairs closest to his mouth.

'Dad said it was from a poem,' Greta says.

Notes into notes into notes.

'"O love, as long as love you can,"' the old man recites. '"O love, as long as love you may."'

Now Greta can see that the old man's tongue is black too.

'"The time will come, the time will come,"' the old man says. '"When you will stand at the grave and mourn! Be sure that your heart burns, and holds and keeps love, as long as another heart beats warmly, with its love for you."'

The old man opens his eyes now and he finds Greta staring at him but he does not stop playing and then his eyes move to the baby boy in her arms. The man's eyes are a deep blue and the colour pops from his face because everything else about him is white. He smiles, and his smile stays wide when he turns to Molly behind Greta's shoulder and Yukio behind Molly's shoulder. He stares into Molly's eyes.

'Do you want to know the secret?' he asks the gravedigger girl.

'Yes,' Molly says.

'My human heart needs to stay warm,' he says. 'But it can only stay warm by warming your heart. That's the trick of the human heart.'

The old man now stares into Yukio's eyes. 'But the music that came from that poem is far more miraculous than any poem, don't you think?' the old man asks. Yukio's face reveals nothing when he stares back at the old man. The old man plays on. 'The music! The music reminds us that the miracle of love is that it is transcendent. That's the trick of true love. It transcends even death.'

The baby in Greta's arms cries. The old man plays on.

'That baby does not belong to you,' the old man says.

Molly steps forward to stand beside Greta. 'The boy dropped from the sky,' she says.

The man doesn't miss a note, keeps on playing. Changes in key signatures, long notes with stretched stems, a high-note cadenza, a bright run of notes that feels to Greta like the story of the song is moving now into the composer's intended dream territory.

'A baby boy just fell from the sky?' the old man ponders.

'An eagle had his hooks in him but then he dropped him in the drink,' Molly says. 'It was only because of Greta that he's still breathin'.'

The old man nods at Yukio. 'Did the eagle drop the Japanese soldier down here, too?'

The baby cries again. Greta rocks him. 'Ssshhhh,' she whispers.

'I once saw an eagle flying with its claws hooked into a dead goanna twice as long as that baby,' the old man says. 'Remarkable creatures.'

'Do you know who the baby belongs to?' Greta asks.

'No,' the old man says.

'Do you know where I might find the boy's family?'

'No,' he replies. 'Because that boy's family never stays in one place. They're like these fingers of mine, always moving. But you rest assured they'll find the boy.'

'How will they find him if I have him?'

'He's a son of this place,' the old piano player says. 'The land will tell his family you have him.'

Molly spots a small green fruit resting on top of the piano. The fruit has been split open, revealing a marble-sized black seed that seems, to Molly's eye, to be covered in bright red blood. She leans closer to inspect the strange seed.

'*Myristica insipida*,' the old man says. 'Native nutmeg.'

'Who are you?' Molly asks.

'I'm Lars,' he says. 'Who are you?'

'I'm Molly Hook from Darwin,' she says. 'I'm looking for a blackfeller named Longcoat Bob.'

The old man's fingers stop with a low note thud and he slams the fallboard down hard over the keys, making Molly jump on the spot.

'Why do you want to find Longcoat Bob?'

'You know him?'

'Everybody in this forest knows Longcoat Bob for one reason or another,' he says. 'But what's your reason for knowing Bob?'

'He put a curse on my family because my grandfather stole his gold long ago,' Molly says.

'What happened to your family?' the old man probes in a soft voice.

'Longcoat Bob turned their hearts to stone,' Molly says. 'They all started dyin'. Some died quick and some died slow and some died long before they should have.'

'Everybody dies, child,' the old man says. 'I suspect there are hundreds lying dead in your home town as we speak.' He swings round to Yukio. 'They died before they should have, too, and not at the hands of a black man's magic stick.' He turns back to Molly. 'But one should never mourn the dead, Molly Hook from Darwin, for they have embarked on a journey far more wondrous even than the one that brought you here. You stumble blindly in your boots here on earth. But the dead take flight, Molly Hook, through light and through dark and through light again.'

'I need to find Longcoat Bob,' Molly says. 'Is he anywhere in this forest? Are we even going the right way?'

'Yes,' the old man says. 'He's nearer to you than you think.'

The baby cries again.

'The boy is hungry,' the old man says, turning back to Greta.

'We've run out of food,' Greta says.

The old man smiles. He raises his arms up to the forest.

'There is food all around you,' he says. 'This forest has everything we need.'

'The boy needs milk,' Greta says.

The old man nods. He rises slowly to his feet and walks towards a thick layer of wild passionfruit vine hanging off the rock wall bordering the circular clearing. 'Come meet my friends,' he says. He pulls a thick clump of vine back as sure as he would pull a curtain on a window frame, revealing a tunnel cut into the rock. 'Come,' the old man calls, waving his arm.

Molly casts her eyes over the sleepers on their backs in the forest. 'You're just gonna leave these people 'ere?' she asks.

'Of course,' the old man says. 'Their dreams haven't ended yet.'

Molly turns to Greta at the piano. 'We need to keep going,' she whispers.

Greta assesses the old man, looks down at the boy in her arms. 'He needs milk,' she says.

'But we need to follow the lightning,' Molly says.

Greta turns back to the old man. Weighs her options.

'Come,' the old man calls. 'Don't be afraid. Come meet my friends.'

'The boy needs to eat,' Greta says to Molly. And she walks across to the old man, who smiles when Greta ducks her head into the black void of the cave.

*

His home is an underground network of old goldmine tunnels lit by lanterns and candles. Lars leads his guests through a central corridor and Molly walks behind Greta looking left and right at the corridors branching off the main walkway. There are other people in here. Many others. Down one corridor on the left, a slim Chinese woman, maybe in her mid-twenties, leans against the entrance to another branching passageway, with a young Chinese girl, five or six years old, standing by her side. Molly watches Lars say something to the young woman in Chinese and the young woman appears to acknowledge his words and she slinks away with the child, drifting into the darkness.

On the right of the main corridor now, in the entrance to another corridor, stands a young red-haired woman in a loose and dirt-stained linen dress.

'Have you seen Marielle?' Lars asks the red-haired woman.

'She's in the reading room,' she replies.

'Inform her of our guests,' Lars says. 'We have an infant here in urgent need of milk.'

Molly smiles politely at the red-haired woman as she passes, but the red-haired woman does not smile back.

'How long have you been living down here like this?' Greta asks.

'Seven years,' Lars says, nonchalantly, as if that is a perfectly reasonable amount of time to live inside a large hole in the earth.

He comes to a stretch of red matting laid down in the corridor in front of the entrance to another, more expansive cave lit up by flamelight. By the side of the natural arched opening sits a row of shoes and sandals. Lars spreads his right arm out. 'Please, after you,' he says.

Greta steps into a spacious circular chamber lit by six rows of thick white wax candles lining the walls at separate points. Six wooden workbenches are spread across the room, each one three feet wide and one foot across and poorly knocked together from found timber and nails. Atop these benches rest specimens of native plants, some in large glass jars and some in pots filled with soil and some dried out and pressed flat between sheets of paper.

'What is all this?' Greta asks.

'Test samples,' Lars says. 'Research.'

Molly puts her eyes up close to a jar of white globular fruits the size of sweet peas.

'What are they?' Molly asks.

'Magic beans,' Lars says. 'Make a paste out of those and rub them across your chickenpox, you'll be healed right quick. Just like magic.'

This room has given the old man energy. Greta sees a new oddness in him. His speech quickens. His thoughts bounce from notion to notion, idea to idea. He says he is a man of science. He says he is a man of medicine.

'What's that one?' Molly asks, looking into a jar of stalks with red fruits.

'It's an insect repellent and a contraceptive all in one,' he says.

'A what?' Molly asks.

He says he calls himself a botanist but the description speaks nothing of his life's work. He says he came to Australia with his wife, Marielle, to document and share his observations on the uses and compositions of ancient bush medicines long known to northern Australian Aboriginals.

'What's that one?' Molly asks, looking at a prickly bush.

'The cure for rheumatism,' he says proudly.

He tells them that he has found things in this wild southern world that could transform global medicine but that the world has always moved too slow for men like him.

Molly studies a jar of lemongrass.

'Earache,' Lars says.

Yukio is taken by a jar filled with a succulent bushy plant not unlike a Japanese bonsai. 'Toothache,' Lars says.

Greta holds a long green stalk with a green orb at the end opening to a crown of small green-yellow spikes.

'*Papaver somniferum!*' Lars says, with great reverence for the plant. 'Opium poppy.'

'You're making opium here?' Greta asks.

Lars scoffs. 'The extraordinary properties of the opium plant figure prominently in my research, but to say I make opium is to say Moses tended to sheep,' he says, 'or Michelangelo painted walls.'

He says he has reasons for never going back to Sydney, and the wild beauty and bounty of the northern vine forests are the only things that matter to him now.

'Yes, I have made my mistakes,' he says. 'Yes, I have sinned. But who upon this earth has not?' He turns to Greta. 'Have you not?' he asks abruptly.

Greta shakes her head.

He turns to Yukio. 'Have you never sinned?'

Yukio struggles to understand but he's always following Greta's lead lately and he follows it now, shaking his head.

'I ask you, what's the greater sin,' Lars continues, 'using my gifts to ease their pain or knowing I can ease their pain with my gifts but refusing to use them?'

'Ease whose pain?' Greta asks. Lars does not answer because he's too gripped by his own increasingly erratic thoughts. 'We have found God's medical box,' he says. 'We must open it up for all the world to see.'

Molly holds a naked and floppy segment of a tree branch up before her eyes. Shiny dark green leaves and green and white flowers and circular fruits with hard orange skin, like small two-inch-wide oranges.

'What's this one for?' she asks.

'*Nux vomica*,' Lars whispers, wide-eyed and mystical. He leans down to the gravedigger girl. 'Strychnine tree.' He pulls a fruit from the branch, holds it up with wonder and awe in his blue eyes. 'Magic fruit. Eat one of these whole, seeds and all, and you'll disappear from this earth and reappear in an instant at the pearled gates of heaven! Voilà!' He shakes his head. 'Extraordinary! This forest is filled with them!'

Lars moves to the centre of the softly lit chamber. He speaks to his guests now the way he spoke to halls of academics in Sydney and Melbourne, all those men who drove him out of academia with their lack of vision and petty jealousies and their cowardly reluctance to experiment. 'What an extraordinary continent we have found ourselves in,' he says, holding up the orange fruit. 'A place where death grows on trees.' He tosses the death fruit up in his hand and catches it. 'Is there a land in this world more in awe of oblivion? Death resides in its branches, in its rivers, in its soil. Death crawls here and death slithers. It bites and chomps and infects and infuses. Tell me of a land more determined to kill those who would dare embrace its beauty.'

Lars shakes his head, looking down again at the orange fruit in his hand. He looks back up to find his three guests staring at him with visible concern for his sanity.

'Milk?' Greta asks.

*

357

A long dark tunnel then a corridor turning left. Another young Chinese woman standing at the entrance to what Molly assumes is the woman's cave version of a bedroom. She nods at Molly but she does not smile. Molly catches up with Greta in the corridor. 'We feed the boy then we leave as soon as we can,' she whispers.

'It's getting dark out there, Molly,' Greta says. 'We need to eat and we need to rest. He's gonna let us do both, so you just remember your manners and be thankful for the kindness.'

Lit by candles and lanterns, Lars's dining hall is a cold, rectangular cave with several hardwood poles capped by broad beams acting as cave-in props. Its walls are scarred with pickaxe marks where hopeful miners chased gold along quartzite seams. Molly casts her eyes around the space and the first thing she sees is a rusted candelabra hanging from the centre of the ceiling. There is a dining table below it, long enough to seat eight people. Another upright piano rests against the wall facing her. There are lounges and armchairs and there is a daybed made of bamboo, and there are stretcher beds made of canvas and cracked wood, set out in rows. And there are people here and they are old. Ten, twelve, fourteen people. They look to Molly like they are wilting, like they are dissolving into their beds, their skin hanging loosely from their bones. Most of them are old Chinese men, their beards long and braided, and old Chinese women in loose black robes. There is one old Afghani man, and three others are European white and European wilted, laid out flat and sleeping upon the beds and lounges or upright in the armchairs and dining table chairs with their eyelids half-closed and their heads wobbling and wanting to fall into their chests. The warm yellow glow of the candles and lanterns reflects from their faces and the rock walls.

'What is this place, Greta?' Molly whispers. 'I want to leave.'

Greta hears the girl but keeps her eyes on Lars.

'Friends,' Lars announces to the room. 'We have visitors.'

Greta turns to the people in the room, smiling. Few of Lars's friends even register they are there. 'Where did they all come from?' she asks.

'Same place you came from,' Lars says. 'They came out of the birth cave. They travelled far like you, but they found us here. And here they stayed.'

A rattling wheeze echoes from a skeletal elderly Chinese man lying flat and shirtless on a stretcher. He coughs and spits saliva and blood into a bowl carried by a young Chinese woman who seems to be nursing several of the men and women.

Greta looks around the room. Bodies thin as glass. Chest bones sucked down into flesh by time and sickness. 'They're all dying,' she says.

Lars nods his head. 'And they will die without pain.' He says they are the unwanted. He says they are the ones who ran to the gold then ran further into the deep country when the government asked them to sail back home.

'What do you all live on down here?' Greta asks.

Then a voice from an entrance to her right. 'Understanding,' says a thin, slow-moving woman in her sixties or seventies with long straight hair as white as Lars's. 'Compassion. Sacrifice. And . . .' – the woman hands Greta an aged glass nursing bottle – 'kindness.' The bottle has a rubber teat fixed to its top, and is full of milk. Greta takes the bottle with gratitude then gently brings the teat to the baby's mouth and the boy's lips suck on instinct and relief spreads across his face.

The white-haired woman smiles. 'I'd say he's never had evaporated milk before,' she says. 'It's sweeter than what he gets from his mother.'

'This is my wife, Marielle,' Lars says to Greta, who shakes Marielle's hand.

'Thank you for helping us,' Greta says. 'I'm Greta. This is Molly. That's Yukio.'

Marielle casts a curious eye towards the Japanese pilot, who is standing back from the group, studying the bodies laid out across the room.

'Don't worry about him,' Greta says.

'He jumped out of his plane out past Candlelight Creek,' Molly says.

Marielle smiles at this fantastical story, examines the pilot standing in her makeshift cavern home.

'Why is he travelling with you?' Marielle asks.

'He was sent to protect us,' Molly says, sounding more defensive than she intended. 'He's our friend, that's all.'

Marielle nods.

'The baby dropped out of the sky, too, it seems,' Lars says.

Marielle is silent for a long moment, nodding to herself. She focusses on Greta. 'Like a gift from God,' she says.

'A gift from the sky,' Molly says.

'They're searching for Longcoat Bob,' Lars says to his wife.

Marielle nods slowly and gracefully. 'I see,' she says.

A young Chinese woman approaches Greta with a bowl of sliced apple and boiled bush yams. Marielle waves an arm towards the dining table. 'Please, eat with us,' she says. 'You must be so tired. You need rest.' Then she turns to Molly and smiles warmly. 'You have come so far to be with us. You have seen so much.' She puts her hand under Molly's chin, stares deep into her eyes. 'You carry so much with you,' she says. 'So much pain.'

*

They eat surrounded by the dying. Greta and Yukio spooning up mouthfuls of a hot bush onion soup that's the colour of dirty water but tastes so good slipping down their throats and filling up their bellies that they splash it across their chins in their hurry to get more down. Yukio stuffing boiled yam chunks into his mouth with his fingers. Greta sucking on the skin of a cured eel that Lars pulled from the traps he keeps in the waterfall pool back beyond what he calls the birth cave.

'The people who find us leave their old selves on the other side of that birth cave,' Lars says. 'They come to us reborn at the very moment they are ready to die.'

When he says things like this Molly turns to Greta and gives her an urgent and brief look that says they should leave, but Greta stays because she is tired and she needs to rest and she will do that tonight, even if it means sleeping among the living dead.

'I know it must seem strange to you,' Lars says. 'A hospice in a goldmine. But the fact remains that I have achieved more in the field of plant science and pain reduction in this unlikely cave than I did in a lifetime inside a laboratory.'

'These people,' Greta says, spooning up more of her soup. 'You . . . give them things?'

'Yes, of course,' Lars says. 'And they are grateful for it. That is why they stay. Where would these people go in Darwin? Who would look after them?' He turns to Molly. 'The only help they'd ever receive is a free ride on the back of a wagon to the nearest cemetery.'

Molly pecks lightly on long roasted yams that taste like sweet potato, but she reaches more frequently for a bowl of sliced wild passionfruit.

'You're not having your soup?' Lars asks Molly.

Molly shakes her head. 'I'm not hungry,' she says.

*

361

An hour passes at the dining table. They eat brown, grape-sized balls of bush-bee sugarbag honey for dessert. Marielle speaks of the couple's long journey into the forest. Amsterdam as young lovers. From Amsterdam to London as students of science. From London to Shanghai and back to Amsterdam and then down into wild Australia.

Greta watches the boy who fell from the sky sleeping inside a canvas sheet on the daybed beside the piano. A sleeping baby, she tells herself. Something so perfect and vulnerable in a world so deadly and cruel. Her vision is blurred briefly and she loses focus on the boy, so she rubs her eyes and considers how little sleep she has had since going on this foolhardy journey with the gravedigger girl. Foolhardy journey, she tells herself. Foolish journey, she tells herself. What on earth is an actress like Greta Maze doing in a cave for the dying in the middle of Australia's northern nowhere? Why on earth is a Japanese fighter pilot by her side?

She turns to Yukio and he smiles at her. There is a boy-like warmth to that smile. There is innocence.

'Greta?' Yukio begins. 'Greta . . . okay?'

And Greta dwells on those words of Yukio's because there is something strange about the way those words came out. The way they came out so slowly from his mouth. Then Yukio taps the fingers of his right hand and waves his fingers oddly in front of his eyes.

Greta turns to Lars and Marielle and she realises the room is warmer, the glow of it has brightened. Lars and Marielle speak of their strange cave hospice in the deep country; how they would travel deep into this forest on research trips from Darwin; how they decided one day to simply stay put. Why go back when the forest had everything they needed? 'Anyone we met in the course of our journey, we invited into the forest to join us,' Lars says. 'Broken down and penniless Chinese goldminers. Starved Chinese farmers who'd fled to the forest hills when the towns of the Northern Territory had no place for them. Criminals and vagrants and men with dark pasts. They all had their reasons for coming, but they all came to ease the pain. And they all found salvation here in the underground.'

A young Chinese woman brings a clay jug to the table. She places five clay mugs on the table before Lars and Marielle, who nods permission for the girl to pour drinks for the group. Molly watches a thick black liquid run into the mugs. It looks to her like syrup, but it's the colour of the sarsaparilla in Bert Green's lolly shop on Sugar Lane, that place of her dreams that belongs to a world that feels so far away now. She walked through that birth cave and she came out into a different time, a different world. Nothing makes sense in this new world.

She looks at Greta. Even Greta seems different here. She looks at Yukio. He's staring at a rock wall and his eyes seem different. There's no more life in his face. She watches Lars sip his drink like it was breakfast tea. He closes his eyes after several sips, breathes deep.

Marielle looks across the table at Greta. 'Is that why *you* have come?' she asks. 'Have you come to ease the pain?'

Greta focusses on the question. 'What?' she replies, and her mouth feels dry.

'Why have you come to us?' Marielle asks, smiling tenderly and speaking as softly as a cloud. 'Have you come to ease the pain, Greta?'

Greta has an answer to this question but she can't wrap a knot around it in her mind. She can't focus, but a name comes to her.

'Longcoat Bob,' she says.

'Greta,' Molly says.

'We're looking for Longcoat Bob,' Greta says.

'What's wrong with you, Greta?' Molly asks. She turns to Lars and points to her cup. 'What is that stuff?' she asks.

'It will help you sleep,' Lars says, sipping from his cup. 'It will help you dream.' He turns to Greta. 'You will have dreams of love,' he says. 'It will take your pain away. It will drain the pain out of you and you will sleep for fifteen hours and you will wake with a clarity of mind that you did not think possible.'

Greta studies the clay mug before her. Her fingers wrap around it.

'We need to go, Greta,' Molly says. 'We need to find Longcoat Bob.'

Marielle reaches a hand across the table and rests it on Molly's wrist. 'I'm so sorry, Molly,' Marielle says.

'What?' Molly asks.

'I'm so sorry, child,' Marielle says mournfully.

'Sorry for what?'

She rubs Molly's wrist. 'So much pain,' she whispers.

Molly pulls her wrist from her touch. 'What are you sorry for?' she asks.

'You will not find Longcoat Bob, child,' Marielle says, gently. 'Longcoat Bob has gone from us.'

Molly studies Marielle's face for a moment. The white-haired woman with the skeleton body. Her cheekbones high and the flesh on her face drawn into her mouth.

'That's not true,' Molly says, indignant. 'That's not true. Sam said he went for a walk. He's just gone walkabout.'

Greta raises the mug in her right hand.

'He's dead, Molly,' Marielle says. 'You have come all this way for nothing.'

'That's a lie!' Molly says. 'You're lying!'

Lars discreetly leaves the table, walks over to the piano, sits down at it and raises the fallboard.

'But you have found us now,' Marielle says, softly. 'You can rest now.'

Lars begins to play. The *Liebesträume*. The love dream. Gentle keys. Soft notes falling into soft notes. And Greta drinks from the mug.

'Don't drink that, Greta!' Molly calls. But Greta keeps drinking.

'You can all stay here,' Marielle says. 'You can rest. You can sleep.'

'I don't want to sleep here,' Molly says. 'I don't want to stay here.'

Molly turns to the pilot but he, too, is drinking from his mug. 'Yukio,' she says. 'We need to keep going.'

'Do not be afraid, Molly,' Marielle says. 'We will take the pain away. You carry too much. Too much pain for one little girl.'

Then a tear forms in Greta Maze's right eye and it runs down her cheek. She turns to the sleeping baby she saved from the deep black water.

'Have you come to ease the pain, Greta?' Marielle asks.

Another tear falling down the actress's face. 'Ease the pain, Greta,' Marielle urges. 'Ease the pain.'

Greta rises gently from the dining table and she walks to the sleeping baby.

'Greta, we have to go!' Molly says.

'I'm staying, Molly,' Greta says. 'I want to stop. I want to sleep.' She lies down beside the infant and weeps openly now.

'What's wrong with you, Greta?' Molly asks.

'I'm staying Molly,' Greta says. 'I can't walk with you no more.'

'But we need to find Longcoat Bob!' Molly says.

'Stop, Molly,' Greta says. 'Stop it. I should never have come with you.'

Molly stands up. 'But you got us this far!' she barks. 'It was you who got us here.'

Greta shakes her head, weeping. 'I'm not what you think I am,' Greta says. 'You don't need me, Molly. You've never needed anyone.'

'I need you, Greta,' Molly hollers. 'I need *you*.'

'You need to go home, Molly,' Greta says. 'We went too far in. You need to go home. You don't belong here.'

Molly rushes towards the bed. 'I'm getting you out of here,' she says and she reaches for Greta, pulls hard at her arm.

'Get away from me!' Greta screams, snapping. And her anger makes her cry harder and Molly can only step backwards from her friend in confusion. Greta turns her face back to the sleeping baby. 'I won't leave you,' she whispers.

Yukio rises from the table and he slowly walks over to Greta on the bed. He lies down on the other side of the boy, the child between them.

'What are you doing, Yukio?' Molly asks. 'It's that black stuff. They poisoned you, Yukio. They gave you poison. They're gonna make you sleep here.' Molly looks at the faces of all the skin-and-bone men and women, dazed and sleepy and half-dead and sinking into their stretchers and daybeds and worn and torn lounges. 'They're gonna make you sleep here forever!'

Greta won't stop weeping. 'They took my child,' she whispers through her tears. 'They took my child.'

Then tears fall from Yukio's eyes. One tear, two tears, then a flood. He speaks in Japanese through his tears and he cries harder when he finishes his sentence. And Molly watches Greta reach an arm over to Yukio and Greta leaves that tender hand on his side and he reaches an arm over across the baby and he rests his trembling hand on her side and Molly watches these two strangers – her companions, her friends, her strange longwalk family – weeping together. Weeping without her because she is the girl who cannot cry. She is the girl who was born into the curse of Longcoat Bob. She is the girl whose heart will turn to stone. Then she hears more weeping from the dining table. It is Marielle. She is staring at Greta and Yukio, tears streaming down her face. Then she begins to wail loudly. Hysterically.

'Stop it,' Molly says.

But Marielle keeps wailing.

'Stop it,' Molly says.

Lars's melancholy piano notes grow louder and then the pianist with hair like lightning begins to wail with his wife.

'Ease the pain!' Marielle howls. 'Ease the pain!'

'Eeeeeease the pain!' Lars hollers.

Lars's tears fall onto his piano keys and a crazed guttural wail echoes through the orange-glow cave chamber and this wailing seems to make the near dead rise. The patients in their stretchers sit up and weep and others roll and squirm in their beds, releasing their own stored-up tears, spreading infections of weeping through the room and triggering one crazed and primal bout of sobbing after another.

Molly screams, 'Stop it. Stop! Stop!'

But the lunatic wailings only build and they swirl around her dizzy head and she closes her eyes and blocks her ears with her palms and all she sees is her Uncle Aubrey now and all she hears is his deranged howling laughter and all she sees is his smile beneath his black moustache, his deep satisfaction rising up from the cave of his cold stone heart.

She opens her eyes again and she finds Bert — the only friend she has in this upside-down world who is not crying. He's guarding her duffel bag, which carries the rock that she pulled from the chest of her mother, where once a good and kind heart beat warmly.

She grips her shovel and grips her bag and she runs. Dig, Molly, dig. Run, Molly, run. Run from this terrible mine. Run from this terrible wailing. Run towards the night. Run towards the night sky that tells no lies. Run towards the lightning. Run, Molly, run.

The Owner of the Waterfall

He is content because the gastric mill of his digestive tract is grinding the body of an orange-footed scrubfowl swallowed whole some way back through the vine forest. And he's almost home.

The crocodile's slender, darkly speckled snout pushes through a wall of evergreen ferns whose serrated fronds barely register on his pebbled and armoured scales. He can smell the water-fall almost as well as he can hear it, and he can see it all in colour. He stops at the edge of the black pool and his heavy, shielded triple eyelids open and close as he scans his surroundings for threats and prey. He moves his nine-foot body slowly forward to the smooth black rocks that edge the pool, but then he stops because his eyes have locked onto an object across the water. It is blurred to him, too far away to be clearly visible, but he registers it as a threat and, as always, his instincts are correct. Were he to slip into the water, swim nearer and, with his two eyes just above the surface, observe the object closely, he would see that it is organic. A thing of flesh and blood with a thick moustache, wearing a black hat and sitting on a rock. A man. A shadow. In his right hand he carries a gun. In his left he holds an empty can. He's reading words roughly scribbled on a rock.

No weights of gold to measure
Only scales of truth and lies
For we are living treasure
Under all our shimmering skies

The man in the black hat looks up at the waterfall, stares through it to the cave behind its cascading freshwater veil. He is so transfixed by what he sees that he pays no heed to the crocodile, which remains frozen at the water's edge, breath slow, heart slow, then retreats quietly through the wall of ever-green ground ferns, convinced the waterfall now belongs to a new creature of the forest.

On the Plain of
High Heaven

He dreams of Darwin. His Zero fighter plane has stopped in the centre of Smith Street, the fuel gauge reading empty. He pushes open the cockpit canopy and he can see the town's destruction. Every stone building ripped apart by bombs. A silence so heavy his own breathing sounds intrusive. No wind. No movement in the town. Only desolation.

He climbs down from the cockpit and stands in the street, the only man here, the only man alive in all the world. He looks to his feet and he sees that he's standing on a silver road, a road of glittering mica. And he walks up this straight silver road and he turns left and then right and he sees that this silver road is not fringed by vine forest but by the limbless bodies of dead Australians. Piles of bodies, hundreds of bodies, their arms and legs branching into other arms and legs like the limbs of the sprawling and nightmarish forest trees that he saw with the gravedigger girl and the actress. Flesh-and-blood pavements of women and men split by a thin silver road that he must walk down. He removes his soft pilot's helmet out of respect for the dead, but he can't bring himself to look sideways anymore so he looks down at his boots, his war boots crushing the silver flakes of mica as he walks and walks and walks until his boots have no more silver road to walk on because they are blocked by a bed.

It's Nara's bed and Nara lies upon it, sleeping. And Yukio Miki wants to lie down beside his wife but his body won't move forward. His legs won't walk and his arms won't move. He wants nothing more than to fall asleep with Nara's breath on his face, but he can only call to her. 'Nara,' he says. 'Nara.' And she wakes and she coughs twice because she is sick, but she smiles for him because she is strong and she always smiled for him like that.

'Forgive me, Nara,' Yukio says.

'Forgive you for what, Yukio?' Nara replies.

'I was coming to you,' Yukio says. 'But I could not leave this world.'

'You saw the woman in the grass,'

'I thought there was no more beauty left to see,' he says. 'But then I saw it everywhere in this strange place. There was so much of it here I thought it must be Takamanohara.'

'But, don't you see, Yukio,' Nara says. 'It is. All of it. It always has been.'

'I'm coming Nara,' Yukio says.

'But what about the girl?' Nara asks.

'The woman in the grass?'

'The gravedigger girl, Yukio.'

'The gravedigger girl,' Yukio repeats, and he turns around to look at the ruins of Darwin town. Rubble and dust and waste. But there are no bodies in Smith Street now. There is no silver road. There are only butterflies, hundreds of white butterflies rising up to the blue sky.

'Wait,' Yukio calls to the butterflies. 'Wait.' But the butterflies keep rising.

*

He wakes in sweat. His flight jacket wet with it. The bed he lies on wet with it. An orange glow. Firelight. Rock walls. A dining table. Stretcher beds and daybeds and armchairs. All empty. He's the only person there. His mind is slow and his brain is heavy, trying to replay the events that placed him inside this cave.

His heart races and he stands quickly and collapses immediately, but then he stands again slowly and he moves to the dining table where he recalls spooning mouthfuls of onion soup, but little else. He stumbles groggily to an opening in the rock face and he looks down the corridor beyond it, but he can see nothing in the darkness. He moves back to the other side of the cave where another opening leads to another blind corridor. 'Greta Maze,' he calls in his best English, and his voice echoes down the corridor. 'Molly Hook,' he calls.

He finds a third opening and he rests his arm against the rock wall as he calls again. 'Greta Maze!' Only his echo is returned.

He breathes quick and deep. His mouth is bone dry. Only darkness in his vision. Then, far along the corridor, he sees someone, a woman, walking across the tunnel from left to right, from one side passage to another, holding a lantern up with her right arm. She moves quickly.

'Hello,' Yukio calls.

But the figure does not stop.

Yukio barrels down the dark corridor blindly, his right hand feeling the rock wall for the entryway the lantern carrier scurried into. With his left hand, he pats the handle of his family sword and the touch of it brings a comfort that does nothing to slow his heartbeat. His boots kick up dirt as he walks and the corridor is cold and the air is thick.

'Hello,' he calls.

His right hand finally finds a wide space. 'Greta Maze,' Yukio calls. 'Molly Hook,' he calls into the passageway.

His feet move faster as he turns into the black void and he keeps his hands on the walls to feel his way along the corridor. 'Hellllooooo!' he hollers, the sound echoing through the tunnels. He moves faster still because his heart beats faster still and he cuts his hand on a sharp rock edge sticking out of the wall and then he releases his hand from the guiding right wall and breaks into a jog.

'Greta!' he screams. 'Molly!'

And he builds to a blind run and then his face slams hard into a junction wall and he has to stop and put his hands to his nose because it feels like it's about to run with blood. He breathes hard, looks up once again, looks left, looks right, but finds only darkness. Then he looks left again and sees the woman with the lantern once more, turning right into another passage, and he runs after her. 'Wait!' he says. 'Wait.'

And he charges down the passage and his arm reaches out for the guidance of the rock wall and his palm finds air and he turns right quickly into a new passage and he sees the lantern woman moving slowly now into a doorway from which light spills into the darkened corridor. Yukio pads quickly to the glowing light and turns into the opening. 'Greta Maze!' he barks as he enters another spacious cavern that looks almost identical to the one he just woke up in, except there is only one large wooden bed with no mattress here – no tables, no chairs, no stretchers, no piano. And the bed is in the centre

374

of the space and all the people of this troubling underworld, all the sleepers, all the half-dead, have formed a circle around it. 'Ssshhhhh!' says Marielle, turning from the circle to admonish the Japanese pilot. 'They are dreaming.'

Yukio can make no sense of the scene and the confusion makes him ache and the incongruity of it all makes his head throb even more than it throbbed when he woke from his dreaming. He must catch his breath and as he does he sees that Greta Maze is lying on the large bed, lying on her side in a deep sleep and the baby who fell from the sky is sleeping there, too, nestled in the warmth of her chest. Yukio can see now that all the men and women of the cave hold wax candles aflame and they are watching Greta sleep and they are whispering in Chinese and at the head of the bed stands the piano player with the hair as white as Sakai snow in winter, scribbling his observations in a notebook with a pencil as long as his thumb.

Yukio's fast-beating heart turns to fire, and a rage inside him compels him to break through the circle of cave dwellers and crawl onto the hard bed. 'Greta Maze!' he screams. 'Wake up.' He screams again in broken English. 'Wake now. Wake now.'

Two old Chinese men with thin bones and long beards reach for Yukio. 'Noooooo!' one old man wails. 'She is dreaming. Nooooooo.' And then more of the cave dwellers reach for Yukio, tugging at his arms and shoulders and speaking in Chinese, loud and panicked.

'Wake up, Greta!' Yukio hollers, his hands shaking her now. He pushes her hard and she flops over onto her back, eyes still closed.

'She will not wake,' Lars says, matter-of-factly. 'She does not want to wake.'

'Why did you wake, Yukio?' Marielle asks. 'You were dreaming so beautifully.'

Yukio shakes Greta again. More cave dwellers crowd around him, hands reaching for him. The pilot turns and all he can do is roar because he doesn't have the words to speak to them. He pulls his shortsword from his belt and he charges at Lars, whose bulging blue eyes are so crazed and wild they can only stare in wonder at the stranger who now raises a blade to his face and drives him hard against the cavern wall.

'Back!' Yukio snarls as he tears the notebook from the old scientist's hands and throws it across the room. Yukio grits his teeth – the wild dog of his fury, the tiger of it – presses the blade tip hard against Lars's throat and lets loose a barrage of hate-filled words in his native tongue that spray against the old man's face, words about how Yukio came to this forest to escape the killing of men but every bone in his rabid body right now is willing him to resume it. He roars and raises his elbows high and drives the blade hard and straight towards Lars's eyes, adjusting his thrust late so that the sword slices the top of the botanist's right ear and stabs through the handle loop of a gas lantern that hangs from a nail against the rock wall.

Yukio lifts the lantern up with the sword blade and transfers it to his left hand before sliding his sword back into his belt. He bites on the metal lantern loop, moves to the bed, drags Greta to its edge and heaves her onto his right shoulder, adrenaline supplying the extra strength he needs to lift her dead weight. Then he reaches for a handful of the sheet that's wrapped around the baby who fell from the sky, and the baby rises with the sheet like he's sleeping in a pillow case.

'Noooooo,' wail the woozy onlookers as they circle around the pilot.

Yukio kicks at them hard, thrashes his legs around wildly, driven by primal fear and primal rage and he barges through the group and back out the cavern's entrance, back into the black corridor, the lantern providing just enough light.

'Ease the pain!' Marielle hollers after him. 'Ease the pain!'

And Yukio runs because he now knows what this place is. So far from the Plain of High Heaven. This is the nether world. This is Yomi-no-kuni. This is the World of Darkness. This is the land of the dead.

Moon Truth

She stands alone at the edge of the world. The gravedigger girl
and a high night wind behind her back pushing her floppy
brown hair, curled like her mother's, forward across her face. I
will never be afraid, she tells herself. But she is. That is the truth
of it. Night skies tell no lies. She is alone. That is the truth of
it. She is sick in the stomach because she dragged her only friends
into a hell that she made. Only her. That is the truth of it. I feel
no pain, she tells herself. But she does. Night skies tell no lies.
Night skies tell her the cold hard truth that she's on her own.

The gravedigger girl in the sky-blue dress with the shovel
and the duffel bag, standing on a sandstone plateau overlooking a valley of natural stone formations so bizarre and
intricate she wonders if they were made by the ancients.
Made by the women with the quarter-lemon heads she saw
back in the gallery chamber.

Three distant forks of electric-blue lightning strike the
moonlit horizon and the stone valley becomes a city. A city
of giants. Men and women of stone bending and bowing and
reaching for each other in the night wind. Molly tilts her head
to the night sky. Star blanket with a full moon pillow.

'"City of stone 'tween heaven and earth,"' Molly says to the night sky.

And the night sky responds. '"The place beyond your place of birth."'

Molly plants her boots into a loose scree slope of sandstone rubble and begins to slide down the edge of the plateau.

'Where are you going, Molly?' the night sky asks.

'I'm going to find Longcoat Bob,' she replies.

'But you heard the woman in the cave,' the night sky says. 'Longcoat Bob is dead.'

'Do you believe her?' Molly asks the night sky.

'No.'

'Night skies tell no lies,' Molly says. 'But why would that old woman lie to me?'

'Because she wanted you to stay there with them.'

'Why would they want me to stay?'

'Because you're a good one, Molly,' the night sky says. 'Because you're special.'

'I'm not special,' Molly says. 'I bring bad things to every single person I care about. That's why my grandfather locked himself away for all those years in that house. He didn't want the bad things to spread. He knew he had to be alone.'

Molly comes to an expanse of white rocks, a scattering of angular chalky boulders maybe one hundred yards wide and one hundred yards long. She talks to the night sky as she frog-hops between the rocks, her legs moving faster than her eyes sometimes, instinctively bouncing between the flattest landing surfaces she can see in a night turned to deep blue and silver by the moon.

'You should turn back,' the night sky says. 'You should go home.'

'Home?' Molly echoes. 'I've got no home to go to. Darwin

doesn't even exist anymore. I'm not even sure if Australia does. Why are you telling me to go home?'

'Night skies tell no lies,' the night sky says. 'You have come too far and you know it. You were so brave to make it this far, but you need to turn back now. You will die out here, Molly. That's the truth.'

'But Longcoat Bob is out here,' Molly says. 'I need to find him.'

'What if you find Longcoat Bob and you don't like what he has to tell you?' the night sky asks.

Molly hops to her left, hops to her right, zig-zagging over the rocks. At one point she props Bert the shovel in the dirt floor and pole-vaults between two high slabs of stone.

'What could he possibly tell me that could be worse than anything I've already been through?'

'He'll tell you the truth, like me,' the night sky says.

As she leaps from the last of the white rocks, she comes to two towering, human-shaped formations, maybe eighty feet tall. Each of these segmented rock structures has a pillar for legs, a fat slab of sandstone for a torso and a balanced ball of rock for a head. They seem to be looking down on her and they stand like sentinels tasked for eternity with assessing all those who would pass between them into the city of stone at their backs. And she feels that they watch her as she passes between them and enters that city, a place carved by wind and time and turned into something as big as all the street blocks that make up Molly's Darwin town.

Millions of years of erosion have fashioned freestanding sandstone blocks with shoulders and wonky heads that seem to be falling off their necks, and fat men pillars that seem to be leaning over in hysterics, and tall graceful women pillars that seem to be gathering in gossip circles, and some conjoined pillars that look like twins or triplets. Hundreds, maybe thousands, of them across the entire city, as crowded together as the punters in Gordon's Don Hotel public bar on Melbourne Cup race day. Molly was always the short girl moving between all those legs, trying to find her father at the bar because she was hungry and wanted to go home and eat something, but all those tall, high-panted legs became like walls in a maze and she would always find herself lost inside them. 'Dad!' she'd scream. 'Dad.' But he never heard her amid the din.

And that's what this place is. Less a city than a maze. A maze of stone legs separated by alleys of dirt and short clumps of dry spear grass.

'Which way will you go, Molly?' the night sky asks.

'I don't know,' she says.

'Go back home, Molly,' the night sky says.

'I'm not going back when I've come this far,' she says. 'I'll die out here if I have to.'

'I'm sure you will,' the night sky says. 'You'll get yourself lost in here and nobody will ever find you. You'll waste away at the foot of one of these pillars and the birds will peck out your eyes while you're still breathing.'

'Stop it,' Molly says. 'You're scaring me.'

'Night skies tell no lies, kid.'

Molly makes her choice. Molly makes her move. She walks into a narrow alley between two rows of pillars, some with two heads, one with a head like a dingo, one with a head shaped like an axe blade. She tells herself to follow the lightning. Move forward. If she's moving forward, she is moving towards the lightning and the lightning was striking on the other side of the stone city. If she moves forward she won't get lost in the maze of stone legs.

'No one is going to come for you, Molly,' the night sky says.

'Why are you saying that to me?'

'Greta has turned, Molly,' the night sky says. 'Yukio has turned. Your mother is dead. Your mother left you here alone, and you will be alone always.'

'Stop it.'

'Your mother abandoned you.'

'Stop it.'

'She left you for dead like a lame fawn, Molly. That's what happens to people with hearts of stone.'

'Stop it.'

'She wasn't running away from them, Molly. She was running away from you.'

'Stop it.'

And Molly darts between pillars, skirts the legs of the stone giants, moving forward in diagonals. Diagonally right, diagonally left, speeding through the maze of legs. Always towards the lightning that flashes ahead in the distance. But then she comes to a wall of eight, nine, ten sandstone pillars that are joined together at the hips. She must go hard left or hard right and she chooses hard right and she comes to a rock shaped like a tortoise and she pats it because she feels that if she pats it she will remember it if she passes it again. 'Tortoise rock,' she says.

She takes a hard left into another alley and then it splits three ways – left, straight ahead and right – and Molly takes the forward path because she needs to follow the lightning and then she can only turn hard left and then hard right into an alley that runs straight for so long that she can break into a jog and she needs to jog because she is frightened and because in the moonlight the stone figures look like creatures bending down to curse her without words.

She comes to another stone wall and she must turn hard

left and she spots a pillar that's been severed down its middle, as if by a samurai sword and she calls this pillar 'Yukio' and she pats it to remember it, and even if she passes it again and is lost she feels that Yukio will save her the way he saved her from the tin miners so far back now in the deep country.

'He's not coming for you, Molly,' the night sky says.

Molly's heart beating faster. Her mouth dry. She runs down another alley. Forward. Left. Forward. Right. Forward again. Surely she is getting closer to the city's edge?

She runs and she runs and she runs and she comes to another wall of pillars joined at the hip and she turns hard right and passes a rock she has seen before. 'Tortoise rock,' she gasps. And she panics and she runs faster because she feels the pillars are closing in on her now.

As she did before, she takes a hard left into the alley that splits three ways – left, straight ahead, right – but this time she takes the left alley which leads past a row of S-shaped pillars like snakes rising to strike. Like the whipsnakes Bert would slice up at home. Like the brown snakes that would cool themselves on the concrete floor of the laundry back home. Home, she tells herself. I want to go home.

'I want to go home,' Molly tells the night sky.

'Then go home,' the night sky says.

And Molly turns back and runs right along an alley and she takes a hard left and then a hard right and comes to another set of snake-shaped pillars, four of them this time, and she runs left and right and zigs past a pillar with a small round head the size of a coconut resting on a torso the size of a large ice chest. Then she zags right alongside a pillar with a horse head and then a pillar that curves like a crescent moon.

'You are lost, Molly,' the night sky says.

'Stop it,' Molly says.

And she runs and she runs and she runs. Left and right and right and left again and she comes to a wall and she turns and comes to a wall and turns and comes to a wall and then she stops to breathe. She rests her head against the sandstone.

She's in a box of stone legs with only one way out. And there is no lightning to be seen. No lightning to be followed.

'You are lost, Molly,' the night sky says. 'Nobody is coming for you. Nobody wants to help you because you are cursed.'

'Stop it.'

This stone city has darkened. This sprawling city has shrunk. This place has turned into a cave. This is the dark place. The sad place.

'I know why she left you, Molly.'

'Shut up.'

'She left you because she could not love you.'

'That's not true.'

'I know why you want to find Longcoat Bob.'

'Shut up!'

'Shut up!'

And Molly closes her eyes and she's standing inside her bedroom again and she's opening her bedroom door and she's walking down the hallway.

'He will not tell you what you want to hear, Molly.'

'I said "Shut up!"'

And now she's standing in the doorway to her mother's bedroom and the moonlight shines across her mother's face and Violet Hook is staring at her daughter, Molly, and Violet Hook is weeping.

'You want to find Longcoat Bob because you want him to tell you lies,' the night sky says. 'You want him to say it's not true.'

'Stop it.'

'You want him to say it's not true what he did to her.'

'Stop it!'

And the shadow wolf is moaning in the dark and the shadow wolf is clawing at her mother. And a voice from behind whispers her name. 'Molly.' It's the voice of Horace Hook, standing in the light of the kitchen.

'You want him to say he's not the wolf.'

'Stop it.'

And Molly Hook turns back to the bedroom to find the face of her mother in the moonlight, but it's not her face she finds. It's the moonlit face of the shadow wolf. It's the night sky face of Aubrey Hook.

'You want him to say he's not your father.'

'STOP IIIIIIT!' Molly screams to the night sky and she grips Bert in her hands and she swings hard at the sandstone wall and Bert's blade hits it with such force that brief firework sparks pop from its edge and Molly plants her boots in the dust and swings again and the blade smacks against the stone but the stone does not crack in two so she swings again and again and again and the stone is her past and her present and her sky and her mother and her father and the stone is Yukio Miki and Greta Maze and the stone is Aubrey Hook.

'Stop it!' she screams. 'Stop it!' *Crack.* And Bert's blade snaps clean away from his long wooden handle.

The gravedigger girl beneath the night sky holding the headless body of her only friend. She looks to the ground and finds the shovel blade in the moonlight. 'Bert,' she whispers. And she falls to the dirt and spear grass floor and she holds Bert's blade in her lap as she rests against the rock wall and she wants to cry but she can't because she's cursed.

'Your pocket, Molly,' the night sky whispers.

And Molly reaches into the pocket of her sky-blue dress and grips a small piece of fruit. She turns the fruit in her palm. Orange and round and hard-skinned. A death she carries in her hand. A death that grows on trees in the deep country.

True Love is Buried Treasure

Yukio Miki holds the winged brown seed capsule of a stink-wood tree. It is long and curved and shaped like an aeroplane propeller blade. He raises it high and drops it and watches it twirl as it falls, spinning fast like the propeller blades on the Zero fighter he watched crash into a sandstone escarpment and burn. That seems so long ago now that he feels it was a different man who parachuted from that death fighter compared to the one who rests now on a sandstone rock beside Greta Maze and the baby who fell from the sky. The new man who is worried for them both. The new man who woke from a long sleep.

Morning sun warms his head and he turns to it and he finds it rising beyond a thin gravel path that leads out of the forest into stone country that spills away to the distant plateau over which he saw electric-blue lightning flash in the dark early hours of the morning. A thin freshwater stream flows by the stinkwood tree carrying fallen seed capsules that now resemble canoes rowing gently into the forest. Yukio wears his white undershirt because he has made a kind of crib out of his flight jacket for the baby to sleep in. He knows the boy, like Greta Maze, has slept too long and he wonders what strange potion those white-haired people in the miner's cave might have given the infant and the actress to make them both sleep through the brute body-heaving forest trudging that brought them out of that strange monsoon vine land.

He has rested Greta's head upon a pillow of rolled-up paperbark he stripped from nearby trees. Her back lies flat on a patch of soft, shaded grass beneath the stinkwood tree, whose shiny silver-brown trunk rises at least fifteen metres from the ground. The wind blows and the tree's leaves shake and more propeller-blade seed capsules twirl to earth. For the third time in the past thirty minutes Yukio places his forefinger beneath the baby's nostrils and for the third time he is relieved to feel the boy's soft outbreath.

Yukio studies Greta's face. The curve of her cheekbones. Her closed lips and their gentle contours. Her chest rising and falling in the emerald dress. He looks away from her at the very moment when his heart tells him he wants to look at her forever. *Zutto.* Boundless, measureless, endless.

He shakes his head. We must keep moving, he tells himself. We must find help for the baby. But you are the enemy, he reminds himself. They will kill you. Because you killed them.

He kneels now over Greta and claps his hands, hard and loud. Once, twice, three times. 'Wake,' he screams. 'Wake . . . Greta Maze!' He pushes her left shoulder and her body moves but she does not wake. He puts his fingers on her neck to find her pulse and it throbs every second for five seconds. He's tired, so he lies down beside the sleeping actress.

His eyes find a full sky of blue and he begins to talk in Japanese. He speaks of his dream. He speaks of Nara and the weeks and the months during which he watched her disintegrate. He speaks of how he saw no beauty in the world when she left. No colour anymore in the trees and the leaves and the flowers of Sakai. No story anymore in its rivers and creeks. No joy anymore in its people. He recalls how the violent and bloody world war followed her sickness and he felt it was right that the world should burn for letting her go, so he climbed into a fighter plane and his hands that had once gripped wondrous knife blades in his family's workshop now gripped gun controls and he aimed those bullets and bombs at other men and he cursed them all for being human, for knowing love but not knowing what it feels like to lose it.

He remembers what the gravedigger girl said in the gallery chamber staring at the Lightning Man: that we are treasure buried under sky. He couldn't follow all her English words, but he could sense the timbre of her heart, the strange beat of her soul. Love is a hidden treasure, too, he thinks. You meet the one the universe forged in the fire just for you and they bury their love deep inside you but sometimes you don't even know it's inside you until it's ripped out of you, until it's dug up out of you like pure gold dug out of earth. The hole remains. The hole is never filled and your blood and your soul and your joy and your life leak out of that hole, until you are empty. Until you are a ghost.

Then he tries his English words again for Greta Maze, digs up every last one of them that he stores in his busy mind and he tries to explain something to the sleeping actress. He lies on his side and he rests his head on his right elbow and he leans in to Greta Maze's ear and he whispers, 'Greta . . . make . . . whole again . . . Yukio . . . wanted . . . to go.' He looks to the sky. 'Yukio . . . wanted . . . sky.'

The actress is sleeping but still she makes him nervous. Every broken word an act of release. An act of confession.

'I want to stay,' he whispers. Clear English. Near-perfect English.

The admission feels like a betrayal as much as it feels like the truth. And the truth of it makes him weep. 'I want to stay,' he whispers. Words between tears. 'I want to stay . . . Greta Maze . . . I want to stay.'

He wipes his eyes. Rubs them. Pulls himself away from the actress. Standing now. Ashamed. Embarrassed. He walks to the stream by the stinkwood tree and he watches the seed capsule canoes flow into the forest. Rowing away.

The pilot's back is turned to Greta, so he does not see her open her eyes. He does not see her looking to the sky through the branches of the stinkwood tree, her eyes slowly adjusting to the light. Her mind is processing the information of the moment – birdsong, running water, the smell of earth and bark, the touch of the grass on her palms by her side, the beating of her heart. And her heart is absorbing the words of Yukio Miki, his whispered broken-English confession. She woke to those whispered words. They opened her eyes, but she kept them closed. The treasure he dug from deep within his heart and soul and handed to a woman he barely knows.

She stands in silence and she treads softly on the grass beneath her saddle shoes. This might still be the long dream, she tells herself. Her cave-bound stupor. She turns and finds the pilot standing at the stream. Yukio doesn't hear her footsteps. To him she only appears, as if she has come from another dimension, from that world to this one, from the vanished to the found.

'I just had the strangest dream,' Greta says.

Yukio's head is turned to his side and his eyes are on her face and her face is staring deep into the tangled vine forest.

'I dreamed that I was dreaming,' she says. 'I didn't want to wake up from the dream. But you were beside me, Yukio. You kept waking me up. I wanted to sleep but you kept waking me up. You didn't want me to sleep. You didn't want me to go to the dream. You kept screaming a word at me. The same word over and over.'

She turns to him. 'Stay.'

She steps closer to him. Closer to the pilot who fell from the sky. Who fell for her. She raises her left hand and her fingers brush his cheek because she needs feeling, touch, to tell her this is not the long dream. And that touch makes him close his eyes because that touch is too gentle, too caring, and so warm and filled with such feeling that he wants to pull away from it. But he will stay. Stay.

'Stay,' he says.

And she moves closer still and their bodies are touching now and he can feel her breathing and he can feel her chest against his and the curls of her hair are brushing his forehead and he can smell her and that smell is earth and life and future and past and his doom and his regret for finding this stranger in this upside-down land where he is the enemy, and her cheek is brushing his cheek now and his body and the motion inside it make him a sinner. Forgive me, Nara, he tells himself. Her skin is a landmine. Her skin is a dropped bomb. Her skin is the end of this world war and it's the world exploding into pieces. Forgive me, Nara. And the movement in his neck is a betrayal and a truth and the weight he shifts to his cheek to brush back against hers is a crime and a miracle and a crime. And in the violent war inside his mind a call of retreat is made and Greta can feel the conflict in his muscles and he's about to pull away but he's held in place by a single word.

'Stay,' she whispers, and her arms wrap around him and her sweeping lips find his temple and the bone around his left eye and then his high cheekbone and she breathes deep and the motion in her body feels like meaning. And the pilot's lips touch her skin.

And then a baby cries. The infant wailing of the baby who fell from the sky, and it is the sound of the baby waking from his long sleep but also the sound of Yukio Miki and Greta Maze waking from a dream they both walked into.

Greta breathes and breaks away from the embrace. She rushes to the baby, cradled in the pilot's jacket. She picks him up and draws him to her chest. 'Sssshhhh,' she says. 'Ssshhhhh.' She rocks the baby in her arms. Then she looks up at the pilot. 'Where's Molly?' she asks.

Own All You Carry

A girl's open mouth. The girl in the sky-blue satin dress lying on her side in the sun. Half an orange strychnine fruit sitting in her open palm. Her eyes closed. Brown boots covered in dirt and dust. Duffel bag straps over her shoulder. She lies motionless at the foot of four stone pillars that look like family members standing over a crib, peering down at a newborn.

The girl's name echoes across the maze of stone pillars. 'Molly.'

She stirs. Her left boot moves. Her left leg kinks at the knee. Her name echoes again across the stone city. 'Molly!'

The girl's eyes flash open. Her view is dirt and spear grass and stone. She looks up to the sun and the sky and she finds the stone pillars of last night. They're not as threatening in the daylight. Not as monstrous. She feels the fruit in her hand and she brings it to her eyes and she throws it at the rock wall opposite her. The fruit bounces off the sandstone and lands a few feet from the other half of the fruit that she spat out last night because it was so bitter and dry and near impossible to swallow. But she remembers how willing she was to swallow it and she is ashamed of this.

She turns to the sky. 'Why did you tell me those things?' she asks.

But she gets no reply.

Then her name again, echoing across the stone city. 'Mollyyyyy.'

She knows that voice. There's projection in it. There's performance. Greta.

'Moll–yyyyy!'

She stands and runs towards the voice. She attempts to say her name but her throat is parched and she needs to swallow saliva twice before she can get a single word out. 'Greta,' she says weakly.

She runs closer to the voice. She breathes deep and summons a louder call and lets it rip across the stone city. 'Gret–aaaaaaaaa!' she hollers. She darts left and right and ducks into alleys running diagonally right, then veers into passages running diagonally left and beats her own path through the maze of stone pillars.

'Moll–yyyyy!'

'Gret–aaaa, I'm coming!' Molly screams.

Hard left, hard right. Pillar after pillar after pillar. Follow the voice, Molly tells herself. She came for you. She cares for you. Because you care for her. The heart is warmed by warming the hearts of others. You only had a stone heart to give, she thinks, but she took it anyway. Run to her, Molly. Run, Molly, run.

'Moll–yyyyy!'

'Greta!' Molly screams. 'I can hear you. I'm coming. I'm coming.' And she runs. Zigging and zagging through the maze, the voice of her friend as her compass point.

'I'm coming Greta,' Molly calls. 'Keep shouting! I can hear you! I'm coming.'

'Moll-yyyyy!' Greta calls in the distance.

And the gravedigger girl smiles as she takes a blind corner around a giant pillar that stands some fifty feet tall. She takes the blind corner so fast that her boots slide on the gravel beneath her and her legs lose their footing and she lands hard on her chest and belly, and skin rolls painfully away from her kneecaps and elbows, but she doesn't care because Greta is close and she pulls herself up with her hair in her eyes and she's still bent half over when she brushes her hair back and focusses on the impossible vision of her uncle, Aubrey Hook, standing before her. The shadow.

She tells herself it can't be him, standing within arm's reach of her, towering almost as high as the monster pillars surrounding him. She tells herself she's dreaming, still back there in the heart of the maze, back there sleeping with the orange fruit in her hand. She tells herself this can't be real, but she knows it is when his long shadow fingers reach out and smother her nose and mouth.

*

'Moll-yyyyy!' Greta calls, holding the baby to her chest. Sun and sweat across her face, she catches her breath at the foot of three pillars that look regal, like a king and queen and a younger, shorter prince sitting down at a sandstone slab that holds a palace feast. Rubble for roast chickens. Fallen stones for goblets. Yukio stands a foot behind her, studying the shapes of other rocks and pillars, committing them to memory in case they have to travel back through this godforsaken maze. He knows they are up high now. He noticed that the stone city sits on an incline rising to a high ridge and when the wind blows in certain directions he can hear water flowing in the distance ahead of them. And although they are up high, this is surely a place created in the underworld. Yomi-no-kuni, he tells himself. The World of Darkness must look like this. Mazes of stone monsters where creatures lurk behind every turn. A place that can't be trusted. A feeling in his bones. In his heart.

A voice from the north-west. Faint. 'Greta.'

'Moll-yyyyy!' Greta calls again and she runs to the sound.

'Greta . . . wait,' Yukio says.

But the actress does not stop. She only runs. Startled by the movement, the baby cries loudly and Greta tries to calm him as she moves. 'It's okay,' she says, in a soft and tender voice. 'We're going to find Molly. We're going to find Molly.'

She turns left and right and left again. 'Moll-yyyyy!' she calls.

She rushes on through the maze. Her left shoulder catches on the edge of a stone pillar, tearing a hole in the sleeve of her emerald dress that is now so worn and so journeyed that it has turned a light grey from kicked-up dust and brown from the ground dirt it collected in successive nights of rough and fitful sleeps beneath stars.

Yukio runs behind her, loyally following her crooked path. 'Greta . . . wait,' he shouts.

'Come on, Yukio,' Greta calls back without stopping or turning around. 'Come on. She's close.'

The pilot who fell from the sky watches the actress who has woken from her long sleep so renewed, so purposeful, so driven. He watches her legs moving, her shoes stepping between clumps of spear grass and stepping around jagged boulder heads that have fallen from pillars. He watches her dart left and right again and he watches her stop abruptly in a ball of dust kicked up by her skidding shoes. He hears her inhale sharply and he comes to her side and looks at her face. White. Ghost-white. Horrified. Her full lips trembling. And he follows her gaze down a straight, narrow alley and he discovers that the subject of her gaze is a tall, thin man with a black moustache in a wide-brimmed black hat. And there is time enough in this moment for Yukio to see that the tall man has his left forearm around Molly Hook's mouth and there is time enough for Yukio to see the look upon the man's face and there is time enough to know that look is one of strange satisfaction and there is time enough to see the tall man's right arm pointing a revolver straight at Greta Maze.

Molly flails her legs and pulls hard at her uncle's left arm and manages to shift it enough to squeeze two words out into the still air. 'Run, Greta!'

But Greta is frozen in this moment. She's frozen in the memory of his fists. She's frozen in the muscle memory of the journey she made to this wild land from Sydney. She's frozen in the fact she was too young to care for the baby who was taken away from her and how those midwives and those hospital doctors took away more than her baby that day. They took away value and pride and purpose and they took away the notion that anyone in this world should care about Greta Baumgarten, not even herself. And so she tried to become someone else. Maybe, she thought, someone might care for Greta Maze instead. The showgirl. The public bar temptress. The punching bag. The actress.

'Run, Greta!' Molly calls.

But, standing beside the actress in the emerald dress, Yukio knows that all the time inside the moment is up.

It's just another journey in the Top End. Much shorter from start to finish than Molly Hook's long walk into the deep country. Yukio turns and twists his body to stand in front of

Greta and the baby in her arms. A hammer drops. A firing pin strikes the primer of a bullet. Yukio staring into the actress's eyes. Primer ignites propellant. *Bang.*

Yukio's arms around the actress. The propellant pushes the bullet core so fast through the air that it can't be seen. Only the end of the journey can be seen. A bullet driving through the back of a pilot's white T-shirt.

'Nooooooooo!' Greta wails.

Inside that pilot's shirt is a man Greta barely knows. A stranger who fell from the sky. Embracing her. Shielding her. Arms wrapped so tight around the actress. His cheek against hers. And he doesn't want to pull away because he is warm here and he is home here and he wants to stay here. But pull away he does. Blood spilling from his lips. 'Run!' he says.

And the actress obeys and she grips the baby to her chest and rushes through a break in a nearby wall as a second bullet cracks the sandstone mere inches above her head.

And Yukio Miki falls hard into the dust.

*

Molly watches the sky. Keep your eyes on the sky, Molly. Keep your eyes on the sky. The sky grows darker. On earth, the mad howling laughter of Aubrey Hook echoes across the sandstone maze.

'Where are you going to run to, Greta?' he calls, dragging the dead weight of Molly beside him in a headlock.

Molly kicks hard at his shins. 'Lemme go!' she screams. And her fingernails dig into Aubrey's forearms, but it only makes him laugh louder.

That deranged howling. That terrible reminder of Hollow Wood. Molly bites his hand and Aubrey loses patience and throws the gravedigger girl with force against a sandstone pillar and she falls hard to the earth. As she sits up, he places the revolver's barrel end hard against the top of her skull. Molly closes her eyes and tucks her head into her chest.

'Please, Greta,' Aubrey calls. 'Show yourself, woman. I'm not angry at youuuuuuuu. I'm angry at young Molly here. Come out now and Molly might just make it out of this alive.'

Molly moves her head away from the gun barrel and screams as loud as she can, 'Keep runnin', Greta. Don't worry about me.' And she looks up at Aubrey looking down at her. 'I'm not scared of monsters.'

Molly sees him smile a wide look of satisfaction and over his shoulder she sees a way out of this. A fork of lightning, cutlery dropped from a mansion in the sky. A sky gift for the gravedigger girl.

*

Deep inside the maze of stone pillars, Greta scurries breathlessly along alleyways, turning and turning. The baby wails in fright and she puts a hand over his mouth. 'Ssssshhhhh,' she whispers as she runs. 'I'm sorry. I'm so sorry.' The boy continues to cry beneath her muffling hand. 'Please be quiet. Ssshhhhhh.'

Greta is crying now, too, but she keeps her weeping silent. 'Ssshhhhh,' she whispers again, as much to herself as to the baby.

The endless howling of Aubrey Hook's laughter. The confidence in his voice. The whole black shadow of his being spreading across the stone city.

'You left me for dead, Greta!' he calls across the maze. 'You left me for dead in that miserable, godforsaken cemetery.'

Stone pillars gathering around Greta. Leaning over her.

Pressing down on her. They want to take her. They want to drag her back to Aubrey Hook but she won't let them.

She's spent from the running. Spent from the crocodiles in Candlelight Creek and the monsters in the tin mine and the sleepers and the dreamers and the poison-eaters inside the vine forest. She has to stop. She leans over her knees to suck in air. The baby feels so heavy. She turns in a circle looking for a place to hide and she sees an alley running to what looks like a wall of shrubbery. And shrubbery means the edge of the forest and the edge of the forest means a way out of the maze. So she runs down the alley and she's almost at the forest edge when again she hears the voice of Aubrey Hook. Too close now. Too close for her to make a single movement.

'You'll die out here alone, Greta,' Aubrey calls. 'Show yourself.'

Greta crouches down, presses her back against a stone wall. Even the baby senses the danger in Aubrey's voice and he stays silent, though Greta does not remove her hand from his mouth.

'I won't hurt you,' Aubrey calls. 'I love you, Greta.'

Even closer now. Greta realises he must be on the other side of the very stone wall she is leaning against, with her knees up to her chest where the baby rests. She can hear Aubrey's footsteps, his boots on the gravel.

She shuffles along the stone wall towards the forest edge until she runs out of wall. She cannot move any further, can only listen to his footsteps coming closer to her. One more corner for him to turn and Greta Maze will be lost again in the shadow of Aubrey Hook.

One step. Two steps. Three steps. Greta breathes deep to hold her silence in.

'Are you there, Greta?' Aubrey calls. 'I know you're there, Greta!'

Then the voice of Molly Hook. 'Stop it,' she says, flatly.

'Let her go,' Molly says. 'Let her go and I'll take you to Longcoat Bob's gold. I know exactly where it is, Uncle Aubrey. You can have it all. You can have everything you've ever wanted. But you can't have her.'

Silence now in the city of stone. Aubrey Hook turning to face Molly.

'And how will you find Longcoat Bob's gold out here?' he asks.

'I'll follow the lightning,' Molly says.

Aubrey turns just in time to see a fork of lightning shooting down from the gathering storm clouds. He turns back to Molly, points his revolver at her heart.

'Walk,' he says.

Pressed against the sandstone wall, Greta waits for the sound of Aubrey's boots to fade. Then she scampers low to the edge of the maze, a wall of shrubs with white fruits, and she ducks down into them with the baby at her chest and she crawls and crawls to the only safety she has now – the safety of the vine forest. But she's moving so fast and so frantically that she doesn't see that the shrubs screen a sharp gully slope and as she pushes face-first through the final layer of shrubs she drops down this unseen slope and it takes every ounce of her strength to roll to one side and hug the baby to her chest as she shoulder-slides on loose leaves and dirt and grass to the gully floor, which she hits with a thud.

Her view from the gully floor is of yellow flame trees. A cluster of floral fire lit by a kind of yellow Greta once thought she would see only in her dreams. But there is still danger in this gully. Footsteps. Someone padding across the forest floor. Someone so close there is no use in moving. And she resigns herself to the shadow of Aubrey Hook. He heard her in the shrubbery, she tells herself, and he followed her down the gully. She was foolish to think she could ever escape him.

The footsteps stop. Silence in the forest. Then a man leans into her view, blocking the fire of the flame trees. An old man. Black skin. A very old man. Grey hair. And a long black military coat with gold trim the colour of the leaves on a yellow flame tree.

Carry All You Own

The blue sky over Darwin saw too much, she tells herself. It could not understand the horrors it witnessed and it ran away with the wind to think on them. The sky is grey now and the grey sky will not speak to Molly.

A gunpoint walk across sandstone rubble and earth. Her dig boots on rock. Her sky-blue dress. Her Uncle Aubrey a few paces behind her, a hand inside her duffel bag.

Follow the lightning. Yellow forks dropped from mansions in the sky. The crashing lightning but still no rain. The sky can wallop but it cannot weep. She wants to go above it now. She wants to go beyond the sky to where her mother is and where her grandfather Tom Berry could tell her the true story of the long walk and she could look into his face and see when he was lying.

She places a palm against her chest. Her fingers feel for her heart, push down on her chest. I do not fear death, she tells herself. And if she does not fear death – if there is a part of her that wants her uncle to end it all here with a bullet in the back of her head – then surely her heart has finally turned all the way to stone. The curse is complete, she tells herself.

No blue sky to tell me any different. No blue sky to tell me lies I want to hear. Only grey sky truth. She had to leave, she tells herself. She had to escape. Mum could not stay. She could not live. With. The. Grey. Sky. Truth. She could not stay. With—

'Stop there,' Aubrey Hook instructs Molly.

Him.

They stand at the edge of the maze. The lightning has led them out.

A high sandstone plateau. Tree-lined edges falling away on either side to canyons far below. Only one direction to go now. Straight ahead. They can hear water. Fast water. Rapids.

Aubrey stands alongside Molly. He holds Tom Berry's gold-miner's pan in his hands. He runs a finger along the back of the pan. The final line.

Own all you carry, carry all you own
Step inside your heart of stone

'What does that mean?' Aubrey asks.

'You wouldn't understand it,' Molly says. 'You have to be graceful to understand it. You have to be poetic.'

Aubrey places his right hand on the back of Molly's neck. He squeezes hard. 'Let me try to understand,' he whispers. He shakes her hard.

Molly says nothing.

'What does it mean?' Aubrey barks through clenched teeth. He pushes her head closer to the pan.

Molly reads the words.

Own all you carry, carry all you own
Step inside your heart of stone

'It means we must face the truth of who we are, Uncle Aubrey,' she says. 'Everything you have ever done and everything you will ever do . . . you must own it. Because you *are* those things. You carry those things with you. My grandfather knew this.

My grandfather knew the person he had become. He couldn't escape it. Wherever he went, he had to carry himself with him.'

She looks up into Aubrey's eyes. 'You must own all you carry too, Uncle Aubrey,' she says. 'Step inside your heart of stone. You must embrace it now. Step inside it. You are the heart of stone.'

'Where's the gold?' he asks, impatient.

'All you've ever wanted was treasure,' Molly says.

'Where is it?' Aubrey barks.

'My mum was treasure,' she says. 'She glowed. She was like the glowing. She made you gold sick. So sick that you had to have her.'

'Where is it?' Aubrey barks.

Molly looks across the plateau to a path that climbs to a ridgeline running across the horizon.

'It's just beyond that ridge,' Molly says.

Aubrey steps back and points the handgun at the space between Molly's eyes.

'Walk,' he says.

*

They pass boulders in piles and boulders standing alone. One shaped like a hot-air balloon. Another like a tractor wheel. The gravedigger girl and the shadow walk beneath the grey sky. Half a mile. One full mile into a high range. Angular pyramidal shapes and jagged edges that remind Molly of the thorny devil lizards she once saw with her father in the central deserts beyond Tennant Creek. The path bends around a series of broken ridges that remind Molly of the meat-tearing canine teeth of the stray dogs of Darwin town, then it curls dangerously along the right edge of an exposed plateau and Molly stops to assess the drop to the canyon below. She kicks a red-coloured rock and she leans over the edge of the plateau to watch it bounce three times down an almost-sheer rock face and disappear into a vine forest canopy maybe a hundred yards below them.

The path narrows to less than a foot wide as it skirts a granite ridge that blocks their passage to the other side of the sprawling range.

'Keep moving,' Aubrey says.

'The path's not wide enough,' Molly says, studying it. Loose rocks and yellow dirt drop away sharply. 'This is a path for rock wallabies, not gravediggers,' she says. 'We gotta turn back.'

'Walk,' Aubrey says.

Molly turns her head right and peers into the canyon below, her cold skin telling her to turn back to the rock face on her left. She turns that way and hugs the ridge wall as she steps sideways, one slow and sure foot after the other, along the narrow path, her uncle following close behind. Pressing her chest against the rock, she feels for handholds but finds only smooth grey granite. She keeps shuffling along, boot after boot after boot, and then one of those boots steps on a loose rock and Molly slips and she feels her body part from the rock face. Her arms flail, trying to find something to take hold of, but all she can grip in her fists is air and her body falls backwards towards the canyon below. Then a hand wraps around her left wrist as she falls and all the weight of the gravedigger girl is dangling from the bony left arm of Aubrey Hook, who screams in pain as the girl's weight pulls on the festering wound from his brother's rabid dog bite back in godforsaken Hollow Wood Cemetery.

Aubrey's agonised wailing echoes across the canyon and he

closes his eyes to fight the pain and when he opens them again he's staring into the eyes of Molly Hook. Own all you carry, he tells himself. Carry all you own. The eyes of Molly Hook. Lift her up, he tells himself. Let her go, he tells himself. Step inside your heart of stone, he tells himself. The girl offers nothing. The girl, he tells himself, is ready to fall.

Then Molly poses a question he has never asked himself. 'Why could you not love me?' she asks.

Such calm in the way she asks it. Such ease in the way she hangs from his hand.

Let her fall, he thinks. Lift her up, he thinks. And he howls as he lifts the gravedigger girl back up to the narrow path. As he drops her, he catches his breath and she does too, her body pressed flat against the hard granite wall.

'Walk,' he whispers.

*

They march across a tableland of red sandstone studded with clusters of ironwood and paperbark trees. The stone is cracked and layered, forming natural steps in places and wide slabs that look like theatre stages where Greta Maze could perform all five acts of *The Tragedy of Hamlet, Prince of Denmark*. Molly hopes Greta Maze made it out of the maze. She hopes she's on her way back to Darwin now. I never should have mentioned the gold pan map to her, she thinks. I never should have dragged her through the darkness of Candlelight Creek. Never dragged her through the colourful wonders of the floodplains.

Yukio, Molly says to herself. She wishes Yukio Miki had never fallen from the sky. And if she has a stone heart inside her, it's fracturing and cracking in two. It is useless to her now. Rock is not hard. Rock is brittle. Rock is weak.

'Rapids,' Molly says. She hears them first. Then she sees them.

They have come to an open expanse of rugged sandstone cut deep by two parallel rivers tumbling down from higher up the range on Molly's left, their white waters rushing through narrow gorges towards the eastern edge of the plateau. Molly steps towards the first gorge and feels the spray from the water slamming against rocks. The gorge is about fifteen yards wide and there is only one place where it can be crossed: a thin makeshift bridge made of four slender eucalypt trunks tied together with thick vine. The bridge is not fixed in place, its ends simply resting on the rock, and with the rapids roaring no more than six feet below them, the tree trunks have turned slimy and black and slippery. Molly walks to the start of the bridge and turns around to look tentatively at Aubrey.

'Walk,' he says, not feeling the need, yet, to point the handgun at Molly.

Molly steps carefully onto the bridge. She puts her arms out to balance herself and she shifts some weight onto her left leg to test the integrity of the structure, which tilts and bends even under her modest weight. But she walks on, boot after boot after boot, and the tree trunks bear her weight. Halfway across, though, she makes the mistake of looking down and she is momentarily transfixed by the rapids' power, the deadly confusion of all that pressure and all that water and all that rock in a meeting that has lasted millennia. Her legs wobble briefly, but she looks up and focusses on the end of the bridge and her balance is restored. She's so frightened and in such a hurry to get off the tree trunk platform that she shuffle-runs across the last six feet or so. Reaching solid ground, she exhales and closes her eyes before turning round to watch Aubrey make his unsteady way across.

She asks things of the water. Take him down. Take him down, down, down into the black. She watches him step awkwardly to the centre of the bridge then she looks down at her end of it. She could heave that end up and tip the whole bridge into the water and Aubrey Hook would be tossed in with it. He would be sucked over the side of the range and his shadow would never cross her light again.

'Get back,' Aubrey calls from the bridge, pointing his gun at Molly. 'Right back.'

Molly retreats as Aubrey advances to the end of the bridge. 'Walk,' he says.

*

It's a short walk across stone to the second river, where the bridge is made of just three eucalypts but the crossing is only ten yards wide. The gravedigger girl steps carefully across it. On the other side the plateau ends at a narrow sandstone promontory. It's oval and featureless. There is nothing here. There is nothing but rock and air and sheer drops on all sides. To her left she can look over the edge and see the rivers dropping down the side of the range then merging and running beneath a majestic rock arch. To her right she can see another river system being sucked into a narrow valley that, she thinks, must push the water on down the range so that it can end with a curtain-call bow at one of those spectacular waterfalls that spills into the kind of crystal pools that exist only in dreams – dreams that unfold in colour far above the grey sky.

And from that grey sky the lightning strikes again and the wild and terrifying grandeur of this strange place wraps itself around the gravedigger girl. The dream of it. A paradise for her light and for her black shadow. A city of elaborate, ancient rock architecture threaded by rivers that twist and turn and dive deep into black holes. The promontory feels like the central point of all this natural wonder and she turns in a circle to drink in the cave dwellings she can see on a distant cliff face, the rainbow-coloured and red and black velvet birds flying in circles around her. These birds call as if they are welcoming her, as if they are congratulating her for coming so far into the deep country. She breathes deep and she smells the rapids and she senses the earth shifting deep, deep, deep underground and she feels the electric air that turns like this only when it's about to storm in the north of a raw southern land. And the Lightning Man in the sky mansion bends the rods down from his ears and the forks of his magic seem to strike directly above Molly Hook's head and the wind blows her hair across her face and it blows the hemline on her sky-blue dress and the grey sky wants to weep so hard that the gravedigger girl can feel it in her cold bones. And she looks ahead across the rough surface of the narrow promontory and she can see now where she must go. So she starts walking towards the edge of the plateau, some twenty yards in front of her.

'Where the hell do we go now?' Aubrey barks behind her. But the volume of his voice has been turned down by the wind in Molly's ears.

Her eyes straight ahead. Her eyes fixed on the end of the promontory.

'What the hell are you staring at?' Aubrey calls to her.

And the wind blows so hard now against Molly that it's an effort to walk forward, and she has to push her slight frame on.

'Where on earth do you think you're going?' Aubrey shouts.

He watches the gravedigger girl walk slowly across the flat

rock. She seems transfixed by something. Mesmerised by a sight he cannot see. All he sees is the deep country below them. All he sees are the edges and Molly Hook walking towards the void. Her boots occasionally lose their footing on the uneven surface but she keeps going. Her hands gripping her chest. Her palms over her heart.

'Get back here, Molly,' Aubrey hollers through the wind.

She's following in the footsteps of her mother, he tells himself. A Berry through and through, he tells himself. He raises the gun.

'You don't get out that easy,' he shouts.

The girl keeps walking. Aubrey fires a warning shot above Molly's head.

Molly freezes. Aubrey can see she is still a yard or two from the end of the plateau. Molly turns around.

'Not until you've found my gold,' Aubrey calls, his pistol pointed at her chest.

The wind blowing the curls of her dusty brown hair across her face.

'I wrote a poem, Uncle Aubrey,' Molly says. 'It's about you. And it's about me and Mum. It's a beautiful poem, Uncle Aubrey. It's graceful.' She looks up at the grey sky. 'It's called, "We Are Treasure Buried by the Sky".'

And Aubrey Hook watches the gravedigger girl turn around again and then he watches her disappear into the rock surface. She simply vanishes. Not over the edge. But into the very rock itself. And for a moment Aubrey Hook believes in magic. For this trick must be the work of Longcoat Bob or the work of the spirits because children don't just vanish into sandstone.

He lowers his gun and, confused, dumbfounded, edges slowly forward to the place where Molly Hook disappeared, and he sees now that she was standing above a cavity, a hole in the rock that drops into blackness. Roughly ten feet wide and ten feet long. A bizarre eroded opening with the most uncommon shape.

Aubrey Hook recognises that shape immediately. It's the shape of a human heart. She did it, he thinks. She stepped inside her heart of stone.

*

She sits in a bed of dirt, nursing an ankle that twisted and almost broke when she landed. She sits inside a rock cave looking up to a ceiling as high as the ceiling in the cemetery house in Hollow Wood. She looks through the hole in this ceiling and that hole is the shape of a heart, a heart framing nothing but grey sky.

The outline is rough but plain as day, like the hearts she has seen tattooed on the arms of singlet-wearing soldiers and farmers in the pubs along Smith Street. A fiction heart. An artist's version of a heart. The kind of heart shape you draw an arrow through.

She turns her head and sees an opening where more light is shining in, a natural archway at the bottom of a short downward slope. An access point not much bigger than the door of any Darwin house that suggests there are other ways to enter the belly of this strange rock formation than from a hole in its roof.

Her hands run along the dirt floor and she finds several rocks that are cold to the touch. Then she finds more rocks sitting on top of these rocks and more on top of those. A whole pile of rocks. One or two the size of honeydew melons. Some the size of mangoes. Some the size of cricket balls.

Then a sound from the cave roof.

'Make yourself scarce,' Aubrey Hook calls.

She looks up to see him standing in the grey-sky light. He's looking down into the darkness, his eyes finding the shape of the girl below. He drops Molly's duffel bag through the hole and he uses the bag's thump to gauge the distance to the ground. He doesn't step into the hole like Molly did, but slides into it like he used to slide into the sacred graves of Hollow Wood, clinging now to as much ceiling rock as he can, leaving his legs to dangle in the black air before dropping down to the unseen floor he can only hope exists.

He falls hard on the earth and his legs collapse and his side slams into the pile of rocks that Molly just ran her hands over. The pain in his shoulder causes him to howl and the howl bounces between the walls of the cave.

Aubrey breathes deep. A wheezing in his lungs. Molly can't see him clearly. Too dark. But she can smell him. The alcohol still leaching out with his sweat. The odour of tobacco in his clothes and from his mouth. He's running his hands frantically across the rocks he tumbled onto. Now the smell of naphtha fluid, the flash of the turning flint on Aubrey's worn metal cigarette lighter. Flash and flash and flame. The small lighter flame inside the cave, and then his face lighting up. His black eyes. The flame shimmering against his black eyes and Molly sees something in those eyes. A kind of dark wonder across them. A fever.

He feels it before he sees it. The tingle of it runs from the base of his spine to its top. He swings the lighter over the pile of rocks and the rocks bounce light back to him. A gold light. A vivid and wondrous and fevered gold light from the patches of precious gold metal inside these rocks.

The lighter flame roams across the pile of rocks and Aubrey allows himself a smile. A pile of gold ore. Rough gold nuggets in hard rock casings. Flashes of their wondrous gold light demanding to be exposed to the world.

Even Molly feels the glowing. Some nuggets are so exposed and pure already that they look to Molly like large clumps of roughly torn honeycomb. Like stuff she could pull from holes in trees.

This precious gold stuff Aubrey will pull from the heart of stone and carry back to Darwin as a new man. He will be transformed by the deep country and the twinkle of his eyes and the shine of his shoes will say nothing of the blackness inside him.

Aubrey tries to count them all. Thirty gold nuggets. Forty nuggets. But he loses count. And he allows himself a giggle. And that giggle turns to a laugh and that laugh turns to a howl that echoes through the cave.

Molly has seen that look upon Uncle Aubrey's face before. It's a look of satisfaction. He turns to Molly and howls and the girl brings her knees to her chest and she wraps her arms around her legs, studying the fevered man before her. Howl. Howl. Howl. That deranged howling from deep inside his white spirit stomach. The noise that is made when the tectonic plates in the stone of his heart rub against each other. Howl. Howl. Howl.

Aubrey stands and rushes, breathless and panting, through the arched opening. His eyes adjust to the light and he sees that the cave opens onto a sandy clearing fringed by black wattle trees and native nutmeg trees and patches of vine forest. He looks back and up to find that he is now standing below the high promontory where he and Molly stood minutes earlier. To his right is another rushing waterway crossed by another makeshift bridge of eucalypt trunks, and to his left he sees a narrow path that disappears between rock walls. Two ways out of the clearing.

He rushes back into the cave, picks up Molly's duffel bag and dumps the contents in the dirt. The goldminer's pan that started all this. Shakespeare's life's work. The red rock that Molly pulled from her mother's chest, the red heart of Violet Hook that turned to stone.

Aubrey frantically fills the duffel bag with the nuggets that shine brightest in the flamelight. Less rock, more precious metal. Smaller nuggets that might weigh ten pounds, larger ones of maybe twenty pounds and even a few he's certain are heavier than thirty in his hand. He's working with such urgency that he pays no mind to Molly when she reaches her hands across the floor in search of the rock she pulled from her mum's chest. Violet's rock. But she finds something else instead. Something that cuts her forefinger when she tries to grip it in the darkness. The paring knife.

She crawls along the dirt floor with the knife and her left hand finds her mother's rock and she has all she cares about, so she crawls into a space against the cave wall and this space has a view up to the grey sky through the heart of stone. And she asks the sky for just one more gift. A fork of lightning to stab through that hole and burn Aubrey Hook to cinder. A bomb from a death plane. The same kind that tore Horace Hook in two and wedged him inside a tree. A long-lost mother with curled brown hair to come and take her away from the shadow. Take her away from him.

Aubrey slips a total of ten gold nuggets into the duffel bag and braces his legs as he tests the weight. He strains. He feels a vein in his right temple about to pop, but the gold fever gives him strength. He manages to haul the bag over his shoulder and, satisfied he can bear the weight of all this found gold, he carries it out of the cave and drops it in the centre of the sandstone clearing. He then marches hurriedly back into the cave and picks up one of the largest nuggets, a hunk of gold-heavy ore shaped like a bull's head that must weigh forty pounds or more. He drops it at Molly Hook's feet.

'I'll carry the bag,' he says. 'You'll carry this one.'

Molly holds her mother's red rock in both hands.

'No,' she says.

'Come on, child, let's go,' he says. 'Pick up the rock.'

'No.'

'You will carry that rock out of here or you won't be goin' out at all,' Aubrey says.

Aubrey stands over her now. His black hat and his black shadow face fill the heart-shaped skylight.

I don't fear death, she thinks. I have a heart of rock. Molly shakes her head. 'No,' she says.

Aubrey takes the pistol from the back of his trouser belt. Points it at Molly. Casts his eyes briefly around the dark cave.

'Then I guess this hole is the last grave you'll ever dig yourself into,' he says.

His right forefinger slips across the trigger.

Molly looks past the gun to the sky above the shadow's head.

And the frame of grey sky now fills with the frame of Yukio Miki. The sky gift pilot wobbling, groggy and spent, and living and dying. His family's sacred shortsword in his right hand. His eyes struggling to fix on the shadows moving in the darkness below him.

Aubrey Hook and his long and bony trigger finger.

Then Molly holds the red rock up with two hands. She presents it to Aubrey, presents it to the sky. There is little light flowing in through the heart-shaped frame, but all of it catches the colour of the rock. The colour of blood.

The girl holds the rock as if it is a source of power, as if it is some kind of magic shield forged inside her dead mother's chest that could somehow protect her from a bullet. Her mother's stone heart. Her mother's heart. She holds it there. She holds it there. She holds it there.

'Why couldn't you love me?' she whispers.

And Aubrey Hook is momentarily entranced by the rock's colour. He's taken with it. He's frozen by it, and a long-buried truth is briefly revealed in his voice, an honesty exposed to the light of day, a flash of gold in the broken ore of his life. 'She wouldn't let me,' he says. His eyes on the rock. His finger on the trigger. His eyes on the rock. His finger on the trigger.

Then Molly drops the red rock and grips the paring knife she holds in her hands behind it and she lunges forward and she screams as she brings her hands down hard, driving the short blade into Aubrey's right thigh. And Yukio drops blindly through the hole, the near-dead weight of his body landing heavily on Aubrey's shoulders. His sword spills from his hand on impact but he keeps a grip on Aubrey's neck, his left arm around the older man's throat and his right arm already reaching for the pistol that Aubrey instinctively tries to bring to the head of his impossible assailant.

Aubrey still has Molly's paring knife stuck in his thigh when he rushes blindly backwards and slams Yukio's back into the cave wall. There's a bullet still resting in Yukio's back and the cave wall meets its point of entry and the pilot screams in agony but he will not release his grip.

Aubrey is a wild dog now. He roars. Saliva and sweat and blood and bruising across his face. He charges sideways, driving Yukio towards the arched opening. Molly scrambles along the floor, her hands searching blindly in the darkness for the shortsword. Aubrey roars again as he builds to a run and he carries the pilot like a wheat sack and he drives himself and his assailant hard against another wall and the men bounce off this wall and stumble into a roll that spins them out of the cave, where they land hard on the rough rock of the sandstone clearing, just beside Aubrey's bag of gold.

The sound of the full river running alongside them, its whitewater spray. The pilot has fate on his side and he has Nara, and he ends the tumble with his weight on top of Aubrey Hook and he can grip the gravedigger's pistol hand well enough now to smash it three times against the bag of gold and then he watches the weapon bounce across the ground. Then Aubrey twists hard and fast and the men roll twice again across the sandstone and in the chaos of their movements they do not see that the gun has landed only a yard from two black bare feet poking out of a pair of brown slacks. Aubrey slips a hand free and reaches for the paring knife still stuck in his thigh. He pulls it from his flesh and shoves the blade into the side of Yukio Miki's stomach.

What little strength the pilot has left in his arms now abandons him. Aubrey turns him over easily and reaches again for the blade sticking out of Yukio's belly. He pulls the blade out and he breathes deep and hard and he raises the blade over Yukio's heart and the only thing that stops him from driving the short knife down into the pilot's chest are the words of a sixteen-year-old Aboriginal buffalo hunter named Sam Greenway. 'Hold up there, feller.'

Aubrey turns to his left to find a pistol pointing at his head. The young man's face is covered in faded strips of white paint. He's shirtless and barefoot and in his left hand he carries a long, carved wooden spear almost twice his height. Across his chest are more white lines that rise and bend like fountain water over his shoulders and arms.

'Sam,' says Molly, standing now at the entrance to the cave, the shortsword in her hands, momentarily dazed by the sight of him. Tyrone Power by way of Mataranka. Her cowboy carrying a spear and a gun. She wanted to say his name louder but it came out so soft. So beaten.

'You all right, Mol'?' Sam asks.

Molly has no answer to that. She can only turn silently to Aubrey sitting atop her friend who fell from the sky.

'This feller hurt you, Mol'?' Sam asks.

Molly has no answer to that one either. Too dazed. Too spent. She sees movement to her left. Four more Aboriginal men, a similar age to Sam Greenway, emerging from the path between the two rock walls on the left side of the clearing. Same faded paint across their faces and across their chests. Same spears in their hands. The young men say things to Sam in their own language. Sam says things back to them and the young men hiss. One young man taps his spear twice on the ground.

'You want me to plug this feller for you, Mol'?' Sam asks.

Molly is silent. She doesn't take her eyes off Aubrey. 'Get away from Yukio,' she says to him.

The gravedigger drops his head and smiles. He takes his time to adjust his skewed black hat then he stands confidently, shaking his head. He steps back from Yukio and Molly rushes to the bleeding pilot. His head is limply turned to the side. Blood across his belly. A line of blood running from his mouth. Molly kneels down beside him and she places her hand over the leaking knife wound.

'I'm sorry, Yukio,' she says. 'I should never have led you here.'

Sam keeps the pistol trained on Aubrey, who holds his arms out with the paring knife still in his right hand, staring down the young man with the gun.

'You even know how to work one of those, blackfeller?'

Aubrey asks. 'You ever held a white man's weapon, eh black-feller? You ever come across one of those on walkabout?' Aubrey chuckles to himself. 'You better not miss, boy.' And he firms his grip on the knife in his fist.

Then Sam points the gun at a spot on the ground about three feet to the left of Aubrey and six feet or so behind him.

'And you'd better pick up that hat,' Sam says.

Aubrey glances at the spot where Sam is pointing.

'What hat?' Aubrey asks, puzzled.

With lightning speed, Sam fires a shot that blows Aubrey's hat off his head and lands it in the very place Sam was indicating.

'That hat,' Sam says. Then he looks Aubrey in the eye as he spins the pistol around his finger like a Wild West circus act, stopping the spin twice to aim the weapon threateningly at his target's forehead before resuming the showy gunplay. Sam's barefoot friends laugh at the gravedigger's expense, but their elbow-nudging chuckles are silenced when the old Aboriginal man in the black and faded French admiral's frock coat emerges from the path between the two rock walls.

Molly gasps. 'Longcoat Bob,' she whispers. The old man's wild grey hair. So many lines across his face. The crevices in his cheeks are the cracks in all the rocks Molly saw along her journey into the deep country. Longcoat Bob's country. The scarring across his chest. Each line of it a rapid river running through this treacherous paradise. The long fingers by his sides. The fingers that pointed at her grandfather all those years ago. The fingers that called him out. Stone heart, Bob said. Stone heart.

Molly turns to Yukio and whispers in his ear. 'It's Longcoat Bob, Yukio. He's a medicine man. I'm gonna ask him to save you. He can save you, Yukio.' She grips Yukio's hand. She grips it to her chest. 'Just hold on. Don't go anywhere. Just hold on. Please. Please hold on.'

The old man pats Sam's shoulder and that's all that's required to make the young man with the gun step back respectfully.

Longcoat Bob runs his deep and watery and grey eyes over the scene. The girl nursing the foreigner on the ground. The duffel bag filled with nuggets. The tall man with the knife in his hand.

He points at the duffel bag. 'Them rocks,' he says. And he speaks softly but so clearly that all the heads in the clearing, including Molly's, turn towards him. 'No good.'

'I found those rocks myself,' Aubrey Hook says. 'I see no claims on them. They are mine to take as I please.'

Longcoat Bob studies the tall man's face. Looks deep into those black eyes. Deep into that tired shadow. 'Then you must carry all you own,' he says. And he holds an open palm towards the bridge of eucalypt trunks stretching across the raging river. 'Go.'

Aubrey Hook is temporarily stunned by the word. He said go, he tells himself. Walk out of here. Take your gold and leave. Go back to Darwin and build your mansion by the sea. Go back to Darwin and smile down on every last publican who kicked you out of a bar. Smile down on every last woman who rejected your advances. Smile down on every last bank manager and stone supplier and tool salesman who said your money was no good. Smile down on the woman who was meant to love you, but didn't. Go, he said.

Aubrey slips the paring knife into the back of his belt. He slowly moves across to his shot hat and takes his time to place it back upon his head. Then he walks over to the duffel bag filled with raw and heavy gold. He squats and braces his back and his veins pulse beneath his sweaty skin as he strains to lift the bag over his shoulder. When the bag is up, he turns on his heels and passes Molly without a single glance in her direction on his way to the bridge, the only exit from the clearing that is open to him.

At the foot of the bridge he is stopped by the voice of Longcoat Bob.

'You must carry all you own,' the old man says. 'But you must own all you carry.'

Aubrey stares into the old man's eyes. And he is cold now, even on a day as humid as this one.

Movement now behind Longcoat Bob. Sam's friends start talking in their own language to three Aboriginal women who have emerged from the path between the two rock walls. One of them is old, with hair as grey as Longcoat Bob's, and this woman carries the baby boy who fell from the sky. Then Molly Hook's eyes find another woman emerging from the pathway. A blonde who was born for moving pictures. Who wears an emerald dress. Has curls like a crashed wave falling across her ear.

'Greta!' Molly hollers because she can't help herself. There is relief in that name. There is love in it even more.

But Greta does not turn to Molly Hook because she is transfixed by the sight of Aubrey. They stare silently at each other for too long. Molly wants him to go. Just go. Stop staring at him, she thinks. He doesn't deserve anything from you, Greta. He doesn't deserve a single look from those silver screen eyes. Look away from him, Greta. Just look away and he'll go.

But she does not shift her gaze. She doesn't even blink. And the shadow man is allowed to speak, though he only says a single word. 'We . . .' he says. And then he stops. He says no more. He smiles. And he drops his head and turns to cross the bridge.

Aubrey steps gingerly onto three slender eucalypt trunks made black and slimy by the spray from the rapids below. Boot after boot after boot. The bridge bends under the weight of the gold on his shoulder and Molly watches him pause. He puts another foot forward and the bridge still bends, but it holds his weight and the gold's weight, too. Only six or seven more yards to the end of the bridge, he thinks. There are butterflies in his stomach and he can feel the glowing from the gold inside the duffel bag. The glorious glowing. The only thing he has ever needed.

Boot after boot after boot. Almost at the middle now and almost home to Darwin and almost home to that life with the gold, that life lived inside the glowing. Another step and the bridge bends alarmingly. A crack from the wood beneath him, so loud that everyone can hear it over the roar of the raging rapids. Aubrey takes a single cautious step backwards, but then the wood beneath him cracks again and the bridge drops lower and the gravedigger freezes.

He brings the duffel bag down to his chest, slowly retrieves a large nugget of gold and drops it into the water to lighten his load. He watches the glow fade in the water and his heart aches to see it disappear like that and the loss fills him with fury and the fury fills him with fearlessness and he takes another step forward across the bridge and the bridge does not crack but it cracks on his next step and it drops closer to the river, so he takes another nugget from the bag and drops it in the water and it sinks quickly to the river floor. But this does not stop the bridge from bending further and it is clearly close to its breaking point now and Aubrey is forced by instinct to turn around and run back towards the safety of the clearing's rocky ground in the direction of the heart stone cave where the gravedigger girl stands up like a stone pillar and watches his pitiful dilemma from the safety of a hard, rocky earth. But as he does so the tree emits one final, loud, merciless crack. Aubrey Hook stops and stands upright like a figure made of stone. Motionless.

And to Molly's eyes even the river turns to stone. The sky above him. The black wattle trees surrounding him. The birds in the air. Everything still. No more movement but for the black eyes of the shadow man in the black wide-brimmed hat turning in their sockets to find the girl who brought him here. The girl who put him on this breaking bridge. And Molly tries to understand the look upon his face but she cannot understand it because it is a look she has not yet read upon the face of Aubrey Hook, a white-faced look so far from satisfaction.

'Molly . . .' he pleads. And he wants to reach out for her because he wants the girl to save him. But he can't reach for anything with such a heavy bag of gold in his arms.

And the bridge gives up. It splits in half and Aubrey Hook is just two yards from its end when he falls into the rapids and his eyes are still open underwater as the river thrashes him back and forth and upside down, and the last thing he sees before the darkness is the glowing of his gold nuggets being flung from the open duffel bag that he refuses to let go of. The glowing. The glorious glowing.

*

'Yukio!' Greta calls. She rushes to the pilot, kneels by his side. She's already in tears before she sees the extent of his wounds.

Molly sees those tears and she is reminded of her own lack of them. Cry, Molly, cry. Cry from the place where it hurts. From the place where it has always hurt. But she can't even cry for a dying friend, and she knows who to blame for this and she turns to Longcoat Bob.

'This is all your fault!' she screams. 'He's dying.'

Longcoat Bob remains still, running his eyes over the Japanese pilot. No expression.

Molly runs to him. 'It's your fault we're here,' she says. And she pulls on Longcoat Bob's hand. 'You've gotta save him now. Only you can save him now.'

*

Lying flat on the sandstone rock, Yukio Miki can see the grey sky and he can see the face of Greta Maze. She's weeping.

'Stay, Yukio!' she wails. 'You hear me. You stay right here.'

She's wiping blood from his lips. She's placing her hand against his wound.

He reaches his hand to her. His trembling hand. Only strength enough for this. His fingers slide across her cheek. His fingers move across her eyelashes.

Her face moving closer to his now. The warmth of her. She is a light in the grey sky. She is sun. She is fire. Her cheek against his now. So close he can feel the tears running from her eyes.

'Stay,' she whispers.

Her lips moving across his face. Those soft lips he would stay for. Those lips he would fight death for. Yet her lips against his will be his end. Because he can die now with her kiss.

*

Molly pulling, pulling, pulling on Longcoat Bob's arm, trying to drag the sorcerer towards Yukio Miki. But the old man does not move.

425

'Use your magic, Longcoat Bob,' she bellows. 'Use your magic on him.'

Longcoat Bob stands firm. His face puzzled. His face tender. 'Ssssshhhh,' he says to the girl.

Then a word from the mouth of Yukio Miki. 'Molly.'

She turns.

'Molly . . . Hook.'

Molly runs back to the pilot, kneels by his side. 'I'm sorry, Yukio,' she says. 'I'm sorry. I couldn't change anything. I thought I could change it all. I didn't change a thing.'

Yukio grips the girl's hand. He lifts his head as high up as he can. 'Molly . . . Hook . . . change . . . everything,' he whispers. Then he lets his head fall back on the hard sandstone and his eyes are wide when he looks to the sky, when he looks to High Heaven, when he looks towards Nara.

'Yukio leave now, Molly Hook,' he says, smiling. Something wondrous in his eyes. The light in them. 'Yukio . . . shoot through.'

And his eyes do not close but they do not move either.

THE FIRST
SKY GIFT

The Actress and the Poet

They dance for the stranger from Japan. They believe her when she says he fell from the sky to save her. They believe her when she says he was good.

Sam Greenway and the other male members of his family discussed the deeds of the foreign fighter pilot who took a bullet for Greta Maze and saved the life of the gravedigger girl. Sam said the girl meant a great deal to him and Sam asked if they could dance for the stranger in a circle of earth bordered by a ring of huts made of paperbark and corrugated iron and ironwood branches, a small and improvised camp in the deep country, two miles north of the gold cave with the heart of stone and the river that swallowed up Aubrey Hook.

Sam and his family dancing for the fighter pilot who rests with his eyelids closed on a rectangular stack of branches, while four men carefully wrap his body in sheets of paperbark. A dance for the dead. A dance that lasts for hours, a farewell that lasts so long that Molly whispers to Sam on the outskirts of the ceremonial circle that Yukio Miki probably wouldn't mind if all the boys wanted to stop and have a drink of water.

'These boys can go for days, Mol',' Sam says. 'Can you feel it, Mol'?'

'Feel what?'

'Ol' mate,' Sam smiles, nodding at Yukio's body. 'He's going back.'

'Back where?'

'Back to where it all began, Mol'.' And Sam looks to the sky and Molly follows his eyes up to it. Sam's dancing friends in the ceremonial circle look to the sky too and spread their arms wide.

'He's going back to get amongst it again, Mol',' Sam says.

'To get amongst what?' Molly asks.

'Everything, Molly!' Sam says, with the confident smile of a matinee idol by way of Mataranka. 'Everything!'

*

They stay for seven days. Molly and Greta share a hut and sleep side by side on soft beds of stuffed paperbark tied up with reeds. Young women in the camp bring them bowls of plums and tomatoes and plates of fresh fish and crocodile and scrubfowl cooked so well on a coal fire that Molly says she never wants to go back to Darwin.

Molly tells Sam she needs to speak with Longcoat Bob. Sam says Longcoat Bob wants to talk to Molly, but Longcoat Bob is not around. Sam says Molly Hook must be patient. Sam says Molly Hook must slow down. Sam says she runs so fast towards all the answers that she runs right past every one of them.

Sam says Molly must think on her friend Yukio. He says she must be there now for her friend Greta, who keeps weeping for the stranger from Japan.

Molly and Greta wake in their sleep. In the darkness with

their eyes closed but their minds open, they try to make sense of their journey into the deep country.

'You awake?' Molly asks in the darkness.

'I am now.'

'I can't sleep.'

Greta says nothing.

'I keep thinking about Yukio.'

More silence from Greta.

'Keep thinking about his family. They'll never get to know how he died. Maybe I could go to Japan and tell them about what he done. I could tell them how he saved your life.'

But Greta remains silent and Molly knows she's saying nothing because she's crying.

'I'm sorry,' says Molly.

'Sorry for what?'

'I keep talkin' about him.'

'I reckon he's worth talkin' about, Mol'.'

Molly turns to her side and rests her head on her palm and a propped-up elbow.

'Why did you come with me, Greta?'

Greta thinks on this for a moment.

'I like gold as much as anyone,' she says.

'Then why didn't you take any from that cave?'

There's a long silence in the hut. Greta says nothing.

'I reckon just one of those nuggets would have set you up good,' Molly says. 'And what do you have now? Nuthin'.'

More silence.

Greta adopts her thickest Australian public bar accent. 'Not a brass raaaazzooo,' she says.

Molly chuckles. Then more silence. Then more fear. More loneliness. More confusion. More gravedigger girl. 'I sure made a mess of things, didn't I, Greta?'

Greta turns on her side to face Molly, even if she can't see her face in the darkness.

'You didn't make the mess, kid,' Greta says. 'You just dived right into it.'

'I sure did, didn't I?'

Molly allows herself another chuckle. Greta laughs with her. And their chuckles turn into belly laughs and it feels good to laugh because it all feels so much like a dream and a nightmare that they survived, and laughter might be the only thing they have left in their pockets between them.

'Don't worry about me, kid,' Greta says, turning onto her back again to return to sleep. 'I've had worse things than nuthin'.'

*

On the third day, the female elders in the camp visit the hut and they bring with them the baby who fell from the sky. They place him in Greta's arms and she weeps when she holds him. But they are good tears and the elders weep with her because they know the child for what he is. A gift. A gift they thought they had lost. Then he was found by the beautiful actress in the emerald dress, who they are sure does not belong in the deep country. The female elders have spoken at length on this conundrum and they have settled on the notion that the actress must belong in the wild because she survived it, she made it this far and she made it with a miracle in her arms. And she was so reluctant to part with that miracle, even though she knew she had to, that the female elders were left in no doubt that the woman in the emerald dress was as radiant on the inside as she was on the outside.

Sam visits the hut to say there is a sacred cave deep in the scrub where he and his friends will carry the body of Yukio Miki. Inside that sacred cave, Yukio's body will slowly disintegrate and when it does his friends will respectfully gather his bones and place them inside a large and sacred hollow log where they will be left alone out of respect by both human and animal.

But Molly asks if she can bury Yukio Miki the only way she knows how. With a shovel and a pair of boots. So Sam and a friend carry Yukio's body on a stretcher made of branches deep into the scrub and they place him down in a clearing of rich and soft chocolate-brown soil beside a sprawling and majestic banyan tree with spreading limbs that look to Molly like the snakes that wriggled out of Medusa's head in the world of stories. And she figures that's okay because that's the world that Yukio belongs to now. The world of stories.

Molly and Greta dig his grave together. Foot by foot. Resting every half hour to drink from their water bag. The sun is falling when they've finished filling the hole in. Molly stands in the orange light at the foot of the grave. She holds the pilot's family sword. 'Can I say somethin' for him?' she asks Greta.

The actress nods silently.

Molly holds the sword in both hands. 'Hi, Yukio,' she says. 'You probably won't even be able to understand everything I'm saying, but I just wanted to say thanks for saving us. I've never had many friends. Before I met you and Greta the only friend I had outside of Sam was a shovel. I guess that sounds kinda sad, but the only sad thing about that is that I didn't get to be friends with you for longer. And I just wanted to tell you that I'm gonna keep your sword, Yukio. I was gonna bury it down there with you, but I just couldn't do it. And then I remembered my old mate, Bert, and I thought if I could be friends with a shovel for so long then why can't I be friends with a sword?'

Molly turns to Greta, who is nodding with encouragement.

'Anyway,' Molly says. She leans down to her feet and picks up a burial cross she has fashioned out of two tree branches strung together with vine. 'I didn't have a chisel or any limestone blocks to carve you a proper epitaph,' she says. 'So I hope you won't mind this.' At the cross section of the branches she has hung a circle of rusted iron sheeting with a message carved into it. 'I didn't know what to write for your epitaph because I didn't hear the whole story of your life,' she says. 'I had to summarise it a bit, sorry. But I think I got it right. It's not very poetic but I hope it's graceful.'

Molly bangs the cross into the head of the grave and Greta places her arm over Molly's shoulder.

'Goodbye Yukio,' Greta says.

And the weary gravediggers head back into the scrub before they get themselves too lost in the dark, and the lemon light of the setting sun shines over Molly Hook's sharpened-stone etchings hanging from the cross.

HERE LIES YUKIO MIKI
HE FELL FROM THE SKY
HE DIED IN OUR ARMS
HE WAS MIGOTO

*

On the sixth day, the wind comes. The sky turns to grey and then to green. The lightning returns and the roofs of the huts must be tied down with old rope and vine. Then the rain comes. And the elders turn their heads to the sky and it is decided that the group will leave the camp and move to the shelter of a spacious cave less than a mile to the east.

As the rain falls hard on her hut, Molly sits alone on her paperbark bed holding the red rock she took from the cradle of her mother's chest.

Then Longcoat Bob opens the woven spear grass door. The girl freezes. Longcoat Bob enters the hut and kneels down beside the girl. He studies her in silence and then he reaches his hand out to hold the red rock that she nurses so fondly. He moves it close to his old face and he studies it for a long moment and then he looks into Molly's eyes.

'You stopped talking to the sky,' he says.

'What?' Molly replies, stunned, confused.

And for a moment she believes in magic. He is all they say about him, she thinks. Longcoat Bob the sorcerer. Longcoat Bob the witch-doctor magic man. Longcoat Bob the spinner of spells. Conjurer of curses. Reader of minds.

'Sam said you talk to the sky,' he says. 'But you've stopped.'

Molly nods, struggling to keep eye contact with the old man.

'I talk to the sky, too,' he says.

And he smiles.

'I heard her, Molly Hook,' he says.

'Who?'

He stares into her eyes. He places a hand on her shoulder. Then he turns to leave, taking the red rock with him.

'Come,' he says. 'She needs to tell you somethin'.'

And he walks out into the driving rain.

*

Rain so thick Molly can barely see Greta and Sam and Sam's family and friends as they set off east through high, thick scrub with baskets of provisions in their hands. Molly heads in the opposite direction, scampering west, barefoot because she left her boots back in the hut, through the slamming wind and rain behind Longcoat Bob, whose long black coat seems to be some kind of iron armour against the wild elements.

'Wait!' Molly calls as the old man cuts along a barely visible forest path through clusters of soap trees and a row of dense pongamia trees with pink and white flowers that shake like rattlesnake tails in the constant wind.

'Come, Molly Hook!' Bob calls, waving his arm as he disappears down an invisible path through thick, rambling forest climbers with purple berries. The lightning crashes in the sky and it makes Molly duck her head and when she looks back up again she can't see the old man through the grey wall of rain. So she runs and she runs, only on instinct, and she catches the swing of Bob's blowing coat as he darts left along a path through a wall of palms with yellow flowers and the fruits that Molly saw back in the camp, hanging from the necklaces of the female elders.

'Wait!' Molly calls.

Molly is lost now in a thick monsoon vine forest with no sign of Longcoat Bob and she turns on the spot in the suffocating wind and rain and she searches for a point to run to and guidance comes from the sky, a fork of lightning that lights up a narrow path that she sprints along for fifty yards or so before she comes to a field of sandstone boulders and among these rocks she can just make out the black of the old man's coat shifting in the heavy rain.

Then she sees the coat stop on the far edge of the boulder field and she hears the old man's voice through the rain. 'What are you waiting for, Molly Hook?' Longcoat Bob calls. 'Come!' And he disappears into the rain.

Molly scrambles over the boulders, her feet repeatedly losing grip in the rain. One rock to the next. Bounce. Bounce. Bounce. She loses her footing and her shins take the brunt of a sharp edge that cuts her and bruises her but does not stop her moving forward, forward, forward behind the sorcerer who placed the curse upon her heart.

The ground beneath her feet slopes up now. A hill of stone that rises for forty, fifty, sixty yards. And at the top of that hill she can see Longcoat Bob through the rain, powering up the slope, Molly's red rock gripped tightly in his right hand. Violet's rock.

Molly scrambles up after him. Far, far up the hill she climbs, breathless and rabid and close to something she can't put her finger on. Close to an answer. Closer to the curse.

And the lightning crashes and the rain buckets down on her brown curls and the wind wants to push her back down the hill. The wind does not want her to know what waits atop this hill. The earth rebels, Sam said. The rain rebels, she thinks. The wind rebels. But Molly keeps pushing forward. Pushing with her legs and feet and with her head and chest down so close to the sandstone beneath her that she's almost crawling up the hill.

She looks up to find the black of the old man's coat, but there is nothing to be seen now but rain and grey and rock. Run, Molly, run, she tells herself. Dig, Molly, dig. Dig for your courage. Dig for your strength. Dig for your truth.

And her hands are on her knees when she reaches the crest of the hill, panting for air in the thick rain, and she can see that she is now standing on a flat overhang and this startling formation looks out over the whole of the deep country and the girl and the sorcerer are so high up that Molly wonders if she could see the ocean given a sky that wasn't so cross with her. And she turns her gaze from the deep country to the old man in the admiral's frock who kneels before a large, eroded bowl-shaped hollow in the centre of the flat rock.

Wild hair and a wild black coat blowing in the wild wind. He seems possessed by the storm. In Molly's eyes he is the lightning and all his power comes from the electricity in his right hand, and inside his right hand is a large ball of perfectly rounded granite that he is furiously bashing against Molly's red rock, which he has placed in the centre of the bowl.

'What are you doing?' Molly screams through the rain. Her hair across her face. Her sky-blue dress soaked with rain. The old man strikes and strikes and strikes at the rock and the lightning strikes over him. Molly sees now that he's trying to crack the red rock. Molly's rock. Violet's rock.

'Stop it!' she screams. 'Stop it. You're going to break it.'

And she rushes towards him at the very moment Longcoat Bob drops the ball of granite and leans back with his right arm held out to stop Molly in her tracks.

'Watch,' he says through the rain.

And Molly can see it already. The rock is bleeding. Streams of red leaching from the heart-shaped rock, as if it is dissolving. A work of black magic by Longcoat Bob the sorcerer, a man so powerful he can melt rocks dug out of the dead, the dead who were buried only five feet beneath the earth.

But then Molly sees a glowing in the rock and she knows it for what it is. It is the metal earth. It is the stuff that builds and hardens below the surface. It is the great story the sky and the earth keep hidden underground. An eternal story of time and growth and movement, of secrets buried in the soil.

A loosened outer layer of soft rock, a hard clay at best, is being stripped away by the pelting rain and the truth of the rock's story is being exposed along with the glowing. More and more red running away, and more and more glowing. Patches of it showing and then whole sides of it showing. A precious metal breaking through hard earth. And Molly's never seen gold glowing so bright.

The rain builds a pool of water in the hollow and that water has turned red from the colours in the rock's outer shell. Longcoat Bob runs his hands around the rock and more earth and colour escape from the gold inside. Then Longcoat Bob sets the gold down on the plateau floor and he strikes it hard twice more with the ball of granite, which he wields now with two hands. Then he puts the granite aside and washes the gold again in the bowl and finally he stands up with a nugget of pure gold cupped in his hands. A nugget shaped like a human heart. A heart that's been bashed and worn down and eroded and aged and forgotten and carried far and proven to be unbreakable.

The rain, the relentless rain, hammering the old man's face, but it only makes him smile. And he hands the heart of gold to the girl in the sky-blue dress. And he laughs at the driving rain. 'You carry no curse, Molly Hook,' he says. 'You carry only treasure.'

And Molly Hook holds the heart in her hands. And she is certain in this moment that it is not rain that floods across her face.

And she realises that if there is treasure to be found anywhere under the shimmering skies, if there is true value beneath the high plain of heaven, then it will be the lips of lovers that will one day fire her soul and the fear that will always make her fight and the friends who will take her fears away and the children she will call her own and the wonders she will see on the trees and leaves and mountains and in the stone and iron and glass buildings that will touch the day and night skies across her world. It will be in the joy and sadness that will gather in the corners of her eyes, all that salty treasure leaking from all the life she will bury inside herself, from the glowing inside her. An epitaph with no end, leaking out of the grave-digger girl, precious drop after precious drop after precious drop.

Molly and the Epitaph

Sam Greenway the buffalo hunter knows the short way back home to Darwin, but Molly keeps insisting on going the long way. Sam makes the mistake of telling Molly about how good a mud whelk tastes cooked on a bed of hot coals. They are a delicacy, he says. They're known as 'long bums' in his family. He says it's a kind of snail that can grow as long as Molly's middle finger and when he says it possesses the strangest blue colouring, like a bright blue sea, Molly begs him to take a detour off their path to a faraway mangrove forest where Sam knows the long bums will be clustering together in shells shaped like ice-cream cones.

Sam walks in front and Molly walks in the middle and Greta Maze walks behind. Three travellers again in the deep country. Sam holds only his spear but Molly and Greta carry grass shoulder bags filled with fresh berries and bush tomatoes and snake meat wrapped in mulberry leaves and water, all given to them by Sam's aunties. Molly doesn't want this walk home to end because there is no fear now in the journey. She feels like she's walking inside the very moment in a Gary Cooper picture when the bad guys have gone away or been buried in the dirt and the sun is taking its time to set and everything seems to glow with hope and security. It's always been her favourite part of any picture. She always wanted to stay in the warmth of that balanced moment, dive into it, but then the canvas picture screen at the Star would turn to black and the picture credits would roll and people in the audience would clap their hands with joy, but Molly Hook would sit in silence because those picture credits rolling meant she had to go home. And that's what Darwin is to her now. Darwin is the black screen. Darwin is the credits rolling. Darwin is real life.

*

They pass two cascading waterfalls along the way to the mangrove forest. They see a tree that Sam smiles at and he tells them it has red-black staining berries and corky-textured branches that he uses to make his spear shafts. 'Good wood for music, too,' he says.

They see a cluster of bright pink ground-cover flowers that Sam eats raw and calls 'pigface'. They come to a clump of vivid blue weed that Sam picks for Molly and Greta and says they should store in their grass bags because it will be good for relieving any colds they get.

Passing a sprawling milkwood tree, Molly thinks of her mother and her mother's old house. She turns to Greta behind her. 'Do you think it's still there?' she asks.

'What?' Greta asks.

'Darwin,' Molly says.

Greta thinks on this for a moment. 'Yeah,' she says. 'That town ain't goin' anywhere.'

Greta ducks under the low-hanging branch of a litsea tree, from which Sam pulls bunches of leaves that he tells Molly and Greta to keep in their shoulder bags because the leaves will soothe the sore muscles they'll have after their long walk.

They light a fire and form a bed of cooking coals in a flat space inside the mangrove forest Sam promised to show Molly. They feast on the mud whelks, which Sam cooks straight on the coals before removing the snail meat from the hard, burnt conical shells by cracking them with a creek rock.

Molly swallows five snails and wonders about the Star Theatre.

'You reckon the Star is still standin', Sam?' Molly asks.

'Better be,' Sam says, working the coals around with his spear. 'I still ain't seen *High Sierra*.'

*

The next morning, Sam leads Molly and Greta through a vine forest thicket buzzing with mosquitoes. Sam lights a handful of bark he strips from a bush plum tree and the smoke seems to drive the insects away. Through a dark tunnel of climbing plants the trio walk another mile or so before the thicket opens onto a narrow red dirt road bordered by more vine forest.

Sam stops and looks left along the straight road. He turns to Molly. 'I gotta get back, Mol',' he says, softly.

'I thought you were coming all the way with us?'

'I was,' he says. 'But them tasty long bums ate up all me time. I gotta be back before tomorrow mornin'. Uncle Bob's takin' me for a walk.' His eyes light up with pride and Molly knows why. Sam's been chosen. Longcoat Bob wants him to learn things about the deep country that others will never be allowed to know.

'That's great, Sam,' Molly says. 'That's real great.'

Sam turns to Greta, who stands a few yards away, giving the gravedigger girl and the buffalo hunter some space to say meaningful things to each other should they manage to dig them up from the places where they have buried them.

'Walk up 'ere for four miles,' he says, pointing his spear along the dirt track. 'You'll come to a crossroads. Left is the road north to Darwin. Right is the road south to Katherine. And the road straight ahead will get you on your way to Sydney. But I'd be waving down a lift if you don't want to get all shrivelled up like one of them long bums on the coals.'

Greta smiles gratefully. 'Thanks, Sam,' she says.

Sam nods. He turns back to Molly. 'And I guess you know how to get back to me.'

Molly nods. 'Follow the lightning,' she smiles.

Sam nods. 'Follow the lightning.'

And he moves towards the girl like he wants to say something more, but he doesn't say a word. Instead he speaks in actions, bending at the waist to kiss his friend the gravedigger girl on her forehead.

'Bye, Molly Hook,' he says, turning and rushing back into the vine forest.

Molly watches him disappear into the deep country. 'Bye, Sam.'

*

Silent country. The stillness of the bush. Not even the cicadas making noise. It's too hot and humid after the rains for activity. Greta Maze padding along the centre of the red dirt track, her face red with heat and sweat. Molly Hook beside her but walking backwards with her head tilted up to a cloudless blue sky.

'You heard from the sky lately, Greta?' Molly asks, not turning her head from the wide blue roof.

'Not lately,' she says.

They keep walking in silence, Molly still moving backwards. She stumbles in a pothole.

'Careful,' Greta says, reaching an arm out to stop Molly from falling onto the red dirt road.

More walking. More of Molly looking up to the sky.

Greta glances right at her travelling companion. The grave-digger girl with the shortsword of a Japanese fighter pilot tucked between her back and the loop of her shoulder bag. The gravedigger girl with her eyes and her mouth wide open to the endless sky. She smiles at the life in the child.

'I notice you're not rambling to the sky as much as you used to,' Greta says. 'You run out of things to say?'

'I ran out of questions for it,' Molly says, eyes still to the sky. 'So lately I've just been listenin' to what she's tellin' me.'

'She?'

Molly nods.

Greta nods, too, chuckling to herself. 'What's she told you today?'

Molly stops on the spot, but Greta keeps walking because she can see the crossroads Sam spoke of. Their own dirt track meeting three more.

Greta realises Molly has stopped behind her. She turns around to see Molly staring at the ground. Deep in thought.

'Today's my birthday,' the girl says.

Something about those words makes Greta's flesh-and-blood heart hurt. She rushes back to Molly. 'I'm sorry,' she says. 'I didn't know.' She looks into her grass shoulder bag. She pats her sides where the empty pockets of her dress are. Looks around. It's no use. There's nothing in her bag or her pockets, nothing so far out in the deep-country silence to give her. I have nothing, she thinks. 'I don't have anything to give you,' she says.

Molly looks up at Greta.

'It's okay,' she says. 'I already got what I wanted.' And she looks down at her sky-blue dress. It's torn and covered in dirt and mud and berry stains and blood. 'I wanted somethin' nice to go dancin' in,' she says, a half-smile spreading across her face.

Greta smiles, too, wrapping an arm around the girl's neck. 'C'mon, kid,' she says.

They come to the crossroads and peer along each dirt track. Identical red clay roads flanked by northern Australian scrub. The actress and the gravedigger girl standing side by side. Shoulder to shoulder. Elbow to elbow.

'So which way you goin'?' Molly asks, staring ahead. She knows what the answer will be. Don't look at her, she thinks. Don't let her see how much it hurts when she says what she has to say.

Greta looks left and ahead and then right.

'Well,' she says, 'I thought I'd go wherever you're goin'.'

And Molly stares ahead in silence.

'Nuts like you and me should always mix together,' Greta says with a wink.

And Molly feels that the whole of the deep country is silent. Except for the sound she now makes as she tries and fails to hide her tears.

She rubs her eyes.

'Are you cryin'?' Greta gasps, theatrically. 'I thought you couldn't do that?'

The girl laughs and snorts through her tears and her face goes red with embarrassment. 'Turns out I can only do it when

I'm happy,' she chuckles, wiping her eyes with her birthday dress.

Greta elbows the girl. 'So which way you goin', Molly Hook?' she asks.

Molly turns her head to the sky for a moment and she nods her head at that blue ceiling as though she's heard a message from it loud and clear. And Greta watches Molly reach into her makeshift shoulder bag and retrieve a piece of raw gold bigger than her fist, which she then rests on her open palm.

'What's the quickest way to California?' the girl asks. And she turns her head to Greta Maze and she smiles because the actress glows. She glows so bright that she attracts a small and wondrous creature to her that flies from the edge of the vine forest. A small white butterfly that floats out of the deep green and flutters around the shoulders of Greta Maze before rising towards the blue sky and pausing to hover momentarily above the tilted and awed faces of the crossroads travellers. Molly Hook reaches both her arms up to the butterfly, beaming and bouncing as she waves at it.

The butterfly pushes on through the warm air and Greta smiles and her eyes follow its direction of travel. 'That way,' she says.

Acknowledgements

The traditional story that Sam Greenway refers to in his recollections of what his grandfather called 'The Lightning Man' is from the story of Namarrkon (pronounced *narm-arrgon*), who signifies the coming of the wet season in Australia's Top End. This story belongs to the traditional owners of this vast region and it is with utmost respect and thanks to elders, past, present and emerging that I refer to it briefly in this story. Deepest thanks to Alison Nawirridj and her husband, Leslie Nawirridj, a senior member of the Kunwinjku family of artists from Western Arnhem Land. Leslie's grandfather told him the story of Namarrkon and I am profoundly grateful that he helped me word the text and this acknowledgement.

Deepest thanks to Tess Atie and Greg Balding. Tess grew up in the area that was later proclaimed Litchfield National Park. She has family all the way from Mandorah on the Cox Peninsula to Peppimenarti, beyond the Daly River. Tess runs Northern Territory Indigenous Tours, a wholly Indigenous-owned tour company specialising in natural and cultural interpretation from an Aboriginal viewpoint. She and her partner, Greg, generously assisted me with passages of the text and showed me how to see the Top End with my heart and soul as much as with my head. Their deep knowledge and infectious love for their wondrous and vast backyard ripples through this book.

In January 2019, it was my honour to travel to Groote Eylandt, off the remote eastern coast of Arnhem Land, with the MJD Foundation, an extraordinary organisation that works in partnership with Aboriginal Australians, families and communities living with the genetically inherited neurodegenerative condition Machado-Joseph disease. The highest concentration of MJD in the world is on Groote Eylandt, where an estimated 186 members of the 1100-strong Indigenous population have parents or grandparents who inherited the disease, giving them a 50 per cent chance of also having MJD. It was amid the dream-like wilderness of Groote that Steve 'Bakala' Wurramara told me of the bush medicine and deep magic knowledge passed on to him by his father and grandmother, which he is using to assist Sydney scientists in finding a treatment or cure for his MJD condition. I could not have met a more inspiring individual just prior to writing this book and I have no doubt that a good deal of Bakala's charm and charisma unconsciously found its way into Molly's hero, Sam Greenway. Deepest thanks to Bakala and the MJD Foundation. Thanks to the team at Translationz for assistance with Yukio's dialogue.

The poem Greta enjoys in the story is 'The Woman at the Washtub', written in 1902 by the Australian poet Victor Daley. Molly and Aubrey quote lines from Walt Whitman's 1855 poem 'Song of Myself'.

Story and structure ripple through Catherine Milne's veins and her passion for books and words infects the blood of every last writer lucky enough to work with her. You saw where Molly was going from the start, Catherine, and it opened skies in my head. Thank you, dear friend. Alice Wood – wing woman, wonder, weapon – this book exists because of you. Everyone needs a Scott Forbes in their life. Sentence saviour. Error terrier. Hawk-eyed genius. Thank you, Scott. Thanks for the exceptional proofreads, Pamela Dunne and Nicola Young. Darren Holt, you are a miracle man to me. A gift, too. Thank you. Thanks to Jim Demetriou, Brigitta Doyle, Libby O'Donnell, Darren Kelly, Tom Wilson and the whole rattling and unstoppable HarperCollins Australia engine. Thanks to the great James Kellow for your faith, which turned into my belief. Thanks to every last Australian bookseller and book reader for everything you did for Eli Bell and his family and by that I mean my family.

Thanks to Christine Middap and the whole beloved Oz mag gang. Thanks to Christine Westwood, Michelle Gunn, Helen Trinca, Chris Dore, Nicholas Gray, Michael Miller, Campbell Reid, Justin Lees, Amy Lees, Andrew McMillen and all the glorious members, past and present, of that white-hot indie-pop-rock-journo band The Bureau. Thanks, Mark Schliebs, for the early read and the inspiration. Thanks, Stephen Romei, fellow rooster. Thank you, Sir Matthew Condon, fellow sailor. Thank you, Asher Keddie, Kristina Olsson, Richard Glover, Venero Armanno, Annabel Crabb, Clare Bowditch and Kathleen Noonan, earth angels all. Thanks for your magic, Mem Fox. Thanks to Adriana and Dan Penman, Kristi and Matthew Gooden, Rebecca and Chris Lane, dear laughing circle. Thanks, Kristine and Stefan Szylkarski, Suellen Cash and Brad Sonego, Serena Coates, Edward Louis Severson III and every last beloved friend I thanked the last time.

Thanks for all of it, Mum. Thank you, Darcy, Mara, James, Reggie, Ethan and Rosalie Dalton and your beautiful mums and dads. Thanks, dear Jesse. Thanks, Dawn and Bernie Franzmann. Thanks, Lenora, Michael, Patrick and David

O'Connor. Thanks, Tim, Kate, Jack and Ava Franzmann. Fiona, Beth and Sylvie, I would need to write a novel to thank you properly, which is why I wrote this one. I love you. And thanks for the skies, Dad. I see you. Rock on, George Toringo, one more time now.

BOY SWALLOWS UNIVERSE
TRENT DALTON

The bestselling, critically acclaimed and award-wining novel
that has taken Australia, and the world, by storm

Brisbane, 1985: A lost father, a mute brother, a junkie mum,
a heroin dealer for a stepfather and a notorious crim for a
babysitter. It's not as if Eli Bell's life isn't complicated
enough already. He's just trying to follow his heart and
understand what it means to be a good man, but fate keeps
throwing obstacles in his way – not the least of which is
Tytus Broz, legendary Brisbane drug dealer.

But now Eli's life is going to get a whole lot more serious:
he's about to meet the father he doesn't remember, break
into Boggo Road Gaol on Christmas Day to rescue his
mum, come face to face with the criminals who tore his
world apart, and fall in love with the girl of his dreams.

A story of brotherhood, true love and the most unlikely
of friendships, *Boy Swallows Universe* will be the most
heartbreaking, joyous and exhilarating novel you
will read all year.

'Without exaggeration, the best Australian novel I have read
in more than a decade' *Sydney Morning Herald*

harpercollins.co.uk/products/
boy-swallows-universe-trent-dalton